GILDED HOOFPRINTS

The Untold Story Of Edward Dudley

Brown & The Legendary Equestrians

With Comprehensive Reference Encyclopedia

By Sultan Zeshan

Salamun ala Yusuf Ibn Ya'qub

سَلَٰمٌ عَلَىٰ يُوسُفُ ابن يعقوب

12:4

GILDED HOOFPRINTS - The Untold Story Of Edward Dudley Brown And The Legendary Equestrians ©

Text copyright © 2023 by Sultan Zeshan.

Book cover and dust jacket copyright © 2023 by Sultan Zeshan

Published in the United States by Legendary Maestros LLC., with Project Equestrian X Ltd. Co. Georgia, USA.

For more information, please visit:

www.projectequestrianx.com

For permissions, contact:

Email: projectequestrianx@gmail.com

Formatting, Graphics & Typography: Inam Ul Haq & Safeer Ahmed

Library of Congress Control Number:

IDENTIFIERS: LCCN (2023915714) (print) | LCCN (2023915714) (eBook) |
ISBN (978-1-959210-16-0) (hardcover) | ISBN (978-1-959210-15-3) (paperback) |
ISBN (978-1-959210-14-6) (eBook) | ASIN (B0CFTPPYYR)
Library of Congress Control Number: 2023915714

Printed in the U.S.A.
FIRST EDITION

DEDICATION

———————○———————

With heartfelt appreciation, this book is dedicated to Dr. Stephen C. Finley, whose wisdom and mentorship have been instrumental in molding this endeavor.

This work also salutes the resilient spirit of Edward Dudley Brown and the legendary trailblazing Black equestrians. Their riveting stories, imbued with courage and resilience, breathe vibrancy and life into the pages that follow.

GILDED HOOFPRINTS ©

The Untold Story Of Edward Dudley Brown & The Legendary Equestrians

CONTENTS

PREFACE

During my time as a student at Louisiana State University, my undergraduate studies in philosophy and African American history led me on a transformative journey. It was there that I had the privilege of learning from esteemed professors such as Dr. Stephen Finley, whose guidance opened my eyes to the rich and often overlooked narratives within our nation's history. It was through Dr. Finley that I was introduced to Dr. Lori Martin, a distinguished scholar who shared her profound insights on the history of American sports, particularly horse racing, in a captivating TED Talk. Dr. Martin's book, a comprehensive exploration of African American sports history, unveiled the significant contributions made by African Americans to the early days of the horse racing industry. She skillfully highlighted the remarkable legacy of Abe Hawkins, the great sage of Louisiana, whose influence inspired a lineage of remarkable turfmen. Motivated by the knowledge imparted by Dr. Martin and driven by a desire to rectify the historical oversight, I embarked on a literary endeavor on the story of Edward Dudley Brown and the legendary Black equestrians. This work of historical fiction intends to shed light on the untold stories of trailblazers whose contributions to America's first sport, horse racing, have been unjustly overshadowed for far too long.

This work is structured into two parts, each crafted to offer a thorough exploration of the central themes. The first part is the historical fiction narrative as a novel, carefully crafted from a blend of real characters, genuine stories, and true historical events, supplemented with fictional creative liberties and interpretations to complete the narrative. The decision to utilize historical fiction as a medium was a consequence of the limited data available on these influential individuals. However, through diligent research and thoughtful inference, I have endeavored to complete their stories and personalities, turning them into a captivating journey for the reader. This novel portion, within the first part, is segmented into four chronological divisions spanning from the year 1861 to 1922.

The second part of this book morphs into a comprehensive

encyclopedia devoted to the intriguing realm of horse racing and the significant contributions of Black Americans. The biographies within this second part are factual and born from meticulous research, aimed to illuminate their exceptional accomplishments. This encyclopedia serves as a valuable supplement to the narrative, offering a quick reference for readers interested in delving deeper and broadening their understanding of this intricate and compelling history.

The narrative of this book in part one commences at the very foundation of the United States, rooted in the ideals of life, liberty, and happiness. Yet, for many, these ideals remained unattainable, as oppressive systems such as Jim Crow Laws cast a dark shadow over the nation. It is within this context that Edward Dudley Brown emerges—a figure whose unwavering determination defied the barriers imposed upon African Americans. Born into a family intimately connected to the horse industry in the late 1800s, Edward faced adversity head-on, ultimately shattering records and etching his name into the annals of the prestigious Kentucky Derby. Tragically, his career was cut short by the formidable challenges that loomed before him. Within these pages, readers will find a detailed timeline and a biography of Edward Dudley Brown, offering a deeper understanding of the man who dared to dream and defied the odds. Also, readers will learn about other Black athletes of American horse racing and baseball. This book serves as a tribute to their extraordinary achievements and seeks to elevate the wider, oftentimes overlooked contributions of African Americans to the world of horse racing.

It is important to acknowledge the limitations of the historical record, tainted by prejudiced journalism of the era. Many of these significant historical events remain sparsely documented, as the valuable contributions of African Americans were willfully omitted. Through the pages of this book, we aim to rectify this historical injustice, bringing to light the incredible legacy of the first sport in America. With a deep-seated admiration for equestrian sports and a fervent fascination with history, I strive to enthrall readers and foster a renewed appreciation for the enduring impact African Americans have had in shaping the sport of horse racing. My sincere hope is that these vibrant stories will resonate through the ages, inspiring future generations to unearth the tales of African American pioneers and fostering a more inclusive comprehension of our shared history. This book is not just a chronicle of past events, but a resounding call to action - an invitation to explore, learn, and, above all, remember. May this book serve as a catalyst, inspiring future generations to delve deeper into the narratives of African American pioneers and fostering a more inclusive understanding of our shared past. Through the unraveling narrative of Edward Dudley Brown and the legendary equestrians, may we all find inspiration, courage, and the audacity to dream. Welcome to their world. Welcome to their story.

FOREWORD

It brings me a great deal of joy to write this Foreword for Sultan Zeshan's book. It is a timely and necessary project that brings light and life to forgotten African American sports figures, nineteenth-century African Americans, who navigated the rocky terrain of American life and the social arrangements that were largely determined by race. Readers will find themselves transported in time through these lively pages through the stories of individuals who have been forgotten or intentionally erased from historical and cultural memory. I will return to more about this shortly.

Let me say something about Sultan Zeshan, who was my student at Louisiana State University. Sultan was a vibrant student, who had a strong social conscience, which can clearly be seen in this book. He was an astute learner, who took at least two of my upper-division seminars: Black Religion & Film and The Religious Thought of Martin Luther King, Jr. & Malcolm X. Though he moved on after graduating from LSU, we have maintained contact, and I am happy to say that I have continued to mentor Sultan in his professional and intellectual endeavors. Yet, I cannot take any credit for this book, its creativity, or its relevance.

In fact, Sultan Zeshan likely has many influences from his own cultural background and experience to other scholars such as my colleague, Dr. Lori Latrice Martin, a full professor and Associate Dean at LSU, whose writings on Louisiana jockey Abe Hawkins, Sultan marks as an important influence in his own work. What I will take some credit for is being a constant presence for him—a listener, counselor, and advisor. I care for Sultan as I have all my students, but he holds a place that is reserved for select students for whom I will always be their mentor.

At the same time, his work and commitment are his own. He decides what his projects will be. He has the intellect and skill to write and market them. He frames his vision for work that will inform readers and fill in gaps for adults and youth alike. As one reads this book, one will glean the spirit that moves the project. It is motivated by something deeper than scholarship, something much more democratic and egalitarian. Thus, Sultan Zeshan is not just qualified to write this book because he was my student, nor because he is college educated. He is qualified because he wants the past to live in such a way that it informs the present. He wants African American athletes of the past to be seen as people in our hearts and minds, a humanization that often escaped them in their own time. This is why this book is important. It informs readers even as it entertains them.

You can expect to learn something significant about these athletes as you move through these pages and as these pages move you. Listen for the whispers of voices from the past. See through their eyes. Try to walk in their footsteps. Feel the beauty and color of the illustrations. In this sense, reading this book will be more than the apprehension of syntax, more than words on a page meant merely to be read. Let the experience enchant you to see the world as it was as you envision a world that could be.

As Professor of African & African American Studies and the Inaugural Chair of the Department of African & African American Studies at Louisiana State University in Baton Rouge, I am grateful to meditate upon the importance of this book that is also inspired by my own work.

~ Professor Stephen C. Finley, PhD (author of *In and Out of This World: Material & Extraterrestrial Bodies in the Nation of Islam*, Duke University Press).

THE HIDDEN HISTORY OF BLACK AMERICAN SPORTS FIGURES

In the universe of global sports, horse racing is woven as one of the oldest threads, tracing back to the dawn of civilization. Archaeological proof from places like ancient Greece, Babylon, Syria, and Egypt indicates the wide-ranging practice of this exciting sport, underscoring humanity's timeless affinity for speed and competition. As the Romans adopted the sport from the Greeks, they morphed it into a spectacle of grandeur and danger known as chariot racing. This was not just a game but a display that could thrill and horrify, drawing vast crowds to the Circus Maximus in Rome.

With the fall of the Roman Empire, however, horse racing's formal structures fell into disarray and assumed a less organized form. During the Middle Ages, knights often showcased their equestrian prowess and speed in tournaments, which frequently incorporated horse races. This kept the spirit of competitive horse racing alive and laid the groundwork for its modern resurgence.

By the 17th century, the sport had regained an organized structure in England, primarily due to the establishment of Newmarket. This picturesque town emerged as a global center for thoroughbred racing, setting enduring standards that still echo through the sport's hallowed halls. Horse racing was also brought to America by British settlers, who laid out the first racetrack on Long Island in 1665. The sport took root and flourished, leading to the creation of the American Stud Book in 1868 and the founding of the American Jockey Club in 1894. This professionalization of horse racing in America culminated in the late 19th century with the establishment of the Kentucky Derby, Preakness Stakes, and Belmont Stakes, which together form the American Triple Crown.

Before the era of Jackie Robinson, there were the Walker brothers: Moses Fleetwood Walker and Weldy Walker. In 1884, these courageous individuals became the first African Americans to step onto the field of major league baseball. They encountered and surmounted racial prejudice from both spectators and colleagues. Similarly, in the realm of horse racing, figures like Abe Hawkins, Ansel Williamson, Edward Brown, William Walker, Oliver Lewis, Isaac Murphy, Anthony Hamilton, Jimmy Winkfield, Alonzo Clayton, James Soup Perkins, Willie Simms, and Shelby Pike Barnes claimed their places as some of the pioneering black American jockeys. Despite facing discrimination, these men remained resilient, crafting triumphant careers for themselves.

However, the history of American horse racing would be incomplete without the pivotal role played by enslaved African Americans, who despite systemic racism, made lasting contributions to the establishment of the sport in the US. These individuals, who were often expert horsemen, were forced to serve as jockeys and trainers, creating a legacy of achievement that endured despite adversity. Figures such as Isaac Murphy and Jimmy Winkfield emerged as icons, dominating early editions of the Kentucky Derby and securing 15 of the first 28 titles.

The advent of the Jim Crow laws saw African American jockeys and trainers systematically marginalized and excluded from the sport. Despite these challenges, the early contributions of African American jockeys laid the foundation for modern horse racing. African Americans continue to contribute to the sport today, with individuals like Marlon St. Julien, who in 2000 became the first African American jockey to ride in the Kentucky Derby in 79 years, and the Ramseys, who emerged as prominent breeders.

As horse racing's history continues to unfold, the significant contributions of African Americans are increasingly acknowledged. Several figures have been inducted into the National Museum of Racing's Hall of Fame, which recognizes their achievements. Concurrently, efforts are underway to increase diversity and inclusivity in the sport, ensuring that horse racing is as much about the people who ride, care for, and love the horses as it is about the horses themselves.

The narrative of African American athletes in sports, often overlooked, is essential to the understanding of America's diverse history. From the courageous Walker brothers in baseball to the pioneering jockeys in horse racing, these figures confronted and overcame significant obstacles, paving the way for equality and fairness in sports. By embracing these stories, we can ensure that their struggles are not forgotten, and their victories continue to inspire future generations to pursue their dreams despite adversity.

Today, the legacy of African American contributions continues as individuals like Marlon St. Julien, who broke a 79-year absence of

African American jockeys in the Kentucky Derby in 2000, and prominent breeders like the Ramseys, forge their paths in the sport.

Efforts are underway to recognize and honor the significant achievements of African Americans in horse racing, with several individuals being rightfully inducted into the National Museum of Racing's Hall of Fame. Simultaneously, there is a growing focus on embracing diversity and inclusivity within the sport. It is a reminder that horse racing is not merely about the magnificent horses but also about the passionate community of people who ride, care for, and cherish them.

Creating a racehorse is a meticulous art, encompassing breeding, training, and evaluation. Turfmen and trainers delve into bloodlines and pedigrees, carefully selecting potential champions. Jockeys, with their expertise, employ skill, strategy, and an unbreakable bond with their mounts to guide them to victory. Every race is a meticulously organized event, subject to pre-race evaluations and stringent supervision, ensuring fairness, compliance, and the utmost welfare of both horses and jockeys. And in the realm of horse racing, victory carries immense prestige, with coveted trophies and titles symbolizing honor and achievement.

At the summit stands the Triple Crown trophy, a gleaming symbol of triumph, awarded to the horse that conquers the Kentucky Derby, the Preakness Stakes, and the Belmont Stakes. Each facet of this prestigious trophy commemorates the victories of legendary jockeys such as Willie Simms, Isaac Murphy, and Jimmy Winkfield, paying homage to their extraordinary skill, dedication, and unwavering spirit.

It is our duty to ensure that their struggles are not forgotten, and their victories continue to inspire future generations. For within the history of horse racing lies a testament to the indomitable spirit of athletes, particularly African American jockeys, who raced against the odds to forge a path of equality and fairness in the realm of sports. By embracing their stories and acknowledging their immeasurable contributions, we ensure that their struggles are etched into the collective memory, and their triumphs continue to ignite the flames of dreams, transcending all barriers of adversity.

As horse racing's history unfolds, propelled by the resilience and determination of its athletes, the sport continues to evolve. It embraces diversity and inclusivity, fostering a future where every individual who shares a love for these majestic creatures can find their place within the racing community. For in the thunderous gallop of hooves, as horses and riders merge into a singular, breathtaking spectacle, barriers crumble, and a unified chorus rises—a chorus that celebrates not only the horses themselves but also the diverse community of people who ride, care for, and share an unwavering passion for the sport they love.

PROLOGUE

  Tucked away in the enchanting vistas of Kentucky's Bluegrass State, as well as other states, a mesmerizing symphony of nature unravels. Landscapes of rolling hills merge effortlessly with vast fields, their symphony amplified by the pulsating beats of galloping hooves. This captivating environment sets the stage for a compelling narrative of victory and metamorphosis, engaging those who dare to engage with it. The vivacious sphere of horse racing morphs into a striking mirror of society, reflecting its delicately intertwined ballot and dynamic rhythm. Dreams flourish and wilt, mirroring the collective ambitions and hardships of a country wrestling with racial disparity. Amidst these adversities, horse racing shines as a potent unifying element, serving as a potent bond uniting individuals from various paths of life, united by their shared love for the sport. As America navigates the rough seas of transformation, striving to sever ties from an oppressive history, a sliver of hope arises from the core of Kentucky's earth—where horse racing traditions have deeply rooted themselves, epitomizing resilience, heritage, and the indomitable spirit of human connection.

  In this historical fiction narrative, the marriage of real events and fictitious characters probes the complex nexus between sports, history, and the human condition within the scope of horse racing. The captivating story of *"Gilded Hoofprints: The Untold Story of Edward Dudley Brown and the Legendary Equestrians"* delves into the themes of ascension from humble beginnings, the strength of mentorship, triumph over adversity, and the relentless pursuit of justice. This riveting tale takes place against the backdrop of the vibrant world of horse racing, a pulsating sphere that transforms into a complex mirror of society, reflecting the intricate ballet of aspirations and challenges. This sporting spectacle serves as an echo chamber, magnifying the voices of dreams and despair that resonate in sync with the collective pulse of a nation grappling with racial disparity.

  However, amidst the thorns of racial tension, the compelling drama of horse racing emerges as a potent thread of unity, tying individuals of diverse backgrounds together. This shared passion for the sport stands as a beacon of hope, a symbol of shared humanity, as America traverses the turbulent waters of societal transformation, striving to extricate itself from the shackles of an oppressive past. As the echoes of the Civil War gradually fade, America stands on the precipice of reconstruction, a nation yearning for rebirth and redefinition. Despite the signing of the Emancipation Proclamation, racial tensions simmer beneath the surface, and the battle for equality rages on, fought on multiple fronts and across diverse spheres of life.

Amid this volatile societal landscape, institutions like the Shaw Institute and clandestine entities like the Ku Klux Klan play crucial roles in molding the societal narrative. This tumultuous period sees Black Americans navigating through a minefield of entrenched prejudices, their journey marked by persistent trials and gradual triumphs. As the sparkles of the Gilded Age and the promises of the Progressive Era kindle a veneer of optimism, the stark reality of racial disparities looms large, casting long shadows over the progress of the nation. The voices of luminaries like Booker T. Washington and W.E.B. Du Bois echo through these chapters of history, their contrasting views on race and equality painting a complex portrait of the human condition against the backdrop of horse racing.

Legal obstacles, such as the "separate but equal" doctrine and the reverberations of Plessy v. Ferguson, present formidable hurdles for Black Americans. Yet, the characters in our tale refuse to bow down, their spirits fortified by determination and resilience. In their defiance, they challenge these unjust laws, standing tall against the oppressive winds of discrimination. Against this backdrop of racial struggle, the narrative chronicles the Great Migration, a powerful movement of Black Americans determined to seek better opportunities and a brighter future. Organizations like the NAACP emerge as bastions of hope and support, their efforts counteracting the dominant prejudices of the era.

At the center of this narrative whirlwind stands Edward Dudley Brown. Born in the throes of bondage, Edward's life is a testament to human resilience and ambition. His ascension from servitude to prominence in the realm of horse racing is propelled by sheer determination, honed skills, and an indomitable spirit. He serves not only as a symbol of triumph over adversity but as a beacon of inspiration for future generations. Edward's transformative journey is shaped by influential mentors like Abe Hawkins and Ansel Williamson, towering figures in the horse racing community who defy racial stereotypes and challenge systemic barriers. Their vision and advocacy pave the way for change, fostering an environment conducive to progress and inclusivity.

However, the path to progress is seldom smooth. Characters like Farrar Kenner represent the deeply rooted racial prejudices that Edward and his allies must confront. Their struggle against these systemic barriers echoes the larger narrative of America's pursuit of a more equitable society. The journey unfolds across diverse landscapes, from Lexington's Woodburn Farm to Louisville's Churchill Downs, from the bustling energy of Saratoga in New York to the historic charm of Baltimore in Maryland, and even to far-off locales like Russia and France. Each backdrop lends a unique hue to the narrative, hosting riveting races and transformative moments that shape the destinies of our characters. "*Gilded Hoofprints: The Untold Story of Edward Dudley Brown and the Legendary Equestrians*" transcends the confines of historical fiction and sports narrative, morphing into a compelling testament to the indomitable human spirit. As each character gallops across the fields, their individual journeys become reflective of a larger narrative—the relentless pursuit of freedom, equality, and a sense of belonging.

The Legendary Equestrians and their equine partners create a timeless tableau, illuminating the annals of history with their triumphs. In the latter half of the 19th century, the grand stage of horse racing was graced by a multitude of charismatic characters, each possessing their own unique style and personality that commanded respect and admiration from spectators. Among them, Abe Hawkins, an illustrious jockey known for his flair, stood as a brilliant showman, captivating audiences with every high-stakes race. His skill in taming even the unruliest steeds earned him legendary status, as he danced with horses in a mesmerizing display that blurred the line between man and beast. Hawkins' exceptional understanding of equines, coupled with his remarkable riding style, created a balletic harmony that left spectators in awe.

Within this captivating world, Edward Dudley Brown, a talented protégé, found solace and guidance under the wing of Abe Hawkins. Alongside them stood Ansel Williamson, a seasoned horse trainer celebrated for his innovative and meticulous approach. With Williamson's patient touch and remarkable intuition, the raw and wild energies of the horses were transformed into refined power, propelling them to victory in the racing arena. Notably, Ansel's crowning achievement was the training of Aristides, a spirited horse that gained fame under the skillful control of Black jockey Oliver Lewis, securing the crown in the inaugural Kentucky Derby of 1875. The triumvirate of

Hawkins, Williamson, and Brown left an enduring legacy in the world of horse racing, each contributing their unique talents and gifts to pioneer the sport.

In their wake, a new generation of Black jockeys emerged, challenging the social norms of their time and fearlessly embracing the challenges of their chosen sport. Among them, William "Billy" Walker shone as a vibrant personality, known for his infectious enthusiasm and uncanny understanding of horse bloodlines. His extensive knowledge of the equine world made him a valued consultant within the horse racing community, while his string of victories, including the prestigious Kentucky Derby, solidified his status as one of the most celebrated jockeys of his era.

The era witnessed the rise of a constellation of talent, with luminaries such as Sir Isaac Burns Murphy and Anthony Hamilton illuminating the stage with their unmatched skills and unwavering pursuit of excellence. Murphy, widely revered as a paragon of jockeyship, claimed three Kentucky Derby titles, propelling him to international stardom. Hamilton, a steadfast ally of Murphy, showcased his flair and finesse in the saddle, forging a formidable partnership that earned them the distinguished moniker of the "Black Duo." Alongside these stalwarts, Willie Simms carved a niche for himself with a string of triumphs, establishing his position as one of the era's most celebrated jockeys. His victories, including multiple conquests at the Kentucky Derby, were a testament to his strategic acumen and extraordinary horsemanship.

As the 19th century gave way to the 20th, a new chapter unfurled with the emergence of remarkable jockeys. Jimmy Winkfield, a determined and ambitious athlete, etched his name in history with back-to-back victories in the Kentucky Derby of 1901 and 1902, solidifying his place as the final African American jockey to conquer the esteemed race for over a century. Alonzo "Lonnie" Clayton, a prodigious talent, achieved a remarkable feat by seizing the Kentucky Derby title in 1892 at the tender age of 15, becoming the youngest jockey to claim such an honor. James "Soup" Perkins, known for his exceptional stamina and mastery of long-distance races, joined the ranks of the era's accomplished jockeys. Shelby "Pike" Barnes, a formidable force in the racing circuit, amassed a series of victories, including the coveted Kentucky Derby, showcasing his dynamic style and unyielding determination. Meanwhile, the finesse and endurance of George B. "Spider" Anderson led him to numerous triumphs during the late 1800s and early 1900s, while James "Jimmy" Lee's relentless pursuit of victory etched his name among the greats of his era.

Collectively, these extraordinary jockeys and trainers played pivotal roles in shaping the landscape of horse racing in the United States during the dawn of the sport. Their indomitable spirit allowed them to triumph over adversity and shatter barriers of race and social norms, forever changing the face of the sport they held dear. Their remarkable achievements and unwavering belief in their abilities continue to inspire future generations of athletes, serving as a testament to the power of perseverance.

In the late 19th century, a group of exceptional individuals emerged as pioneers in a legendary tale that would reshape the landscape of American sports. Among them were Abe Hawkins, Ansel Williamson, and a team formed around the precocious Edward Dudley Brown. Hawkins was renowned for his distinguished riding style, while Williamson was celebrated for his extraordinary prowess as a horse trainer. Together, they not only molded Edward but also played integral roles in the success of many black jockeys, including the formidable William "Billy" Walker, whose extensive knowledge of horse bloodlines was highly valued.

Another towering figure in this historical saga was Sir Isaac Burns Murphy, a skillful jockey whose reinsmanship led him to victory in three Kentucky Derbies, making him one of the most decorated jockeys of his time and one of the highest-paid athletes worldwide. Alongside him, Anthony Hamilton galloped with equal zest for victory, forming a formidable partnership known as the "Black Duo." Willie Simms also etched his name deep into the annals of horse racing, achieving numerous triumphs and gaining immortal fame. Simms emerged victorious not once but twice on the hallowed grounds of the Kentucky Derby.

Among the titans of this era, Jimmy Winkfield, an accomplished jockey, etched his name in history as the last Black American jockey to win the Kentucky Derby, securing consecutive victories in 1901 and 1902. Not far behind was Alonzo "Lonnie" Clayton, a prodigious talent who claimed the Kentucky Derby title in 1892 at the tender age of 15, becoming the youngest jockey to achieve such a remarkable feat. James "Soup" Perkins rose to prominence for his exceptional prowess in navigating long distances, while Shelby "Pike" Barnes, George B. "Spider" Anderson, and James "Jimmy" Lee became enduring symbols of the sport's transformative power through their sheer grit and relentless pursuit of victory.

These jockeys and trainers unveiled an extraordinary saga that left an indelible mark on American sports. Their journey was not without challenges, as they confronted opposition and societal constraints, but their resilience and pursuit of excellence reshaped horse racing into a field of equality, rewriting the narrative of Black Americans in the sporting world. Beyond the racetracks and stables, their triumphs, struggles, and relentless pursuit of greatness were intertwined with the essence of the American Dream. The thunderous hoofbeats echoing across racing tracks stood as a testament to their victories over adversity and their defiance of societal norms. In America's horseracing heartland, they established more than just a legacy; they ignited a beacon of hope and inspiration that transcended generations. Regardless of skin color, they extended an invitation to everyone to join the thrill of the race. Their stories reverberate in every racehorse's thundering stride, reminding us that victory favors not always the swift, but those who persist.

The second half of the 19th century marked a period of transformation, and these legendary figures not only excelled in their sport but became sources of inspiration for future generations of athletes. Their victories over adversity and unyielding faith in their capabilities forever altered the horse racing landscape. In a novel enriched with meticulous historical research and imaginative storytelling, the untold stories and unheralded heroes of the horse racing community are revealed. Readers will experience a symphony of triumph, transformation, and resilience, captivated by the depth of emotion that resonates through each page.

The narrative is set against a backdrop of a nation grappling with the remnants of the Civil War and the dawn of a new era. The galloping rhythm of horses on the racetrack becomes a metaphorical portrayal of the tussle between racial tensions and societal change. Through the captivating odyssey of *"Gilded Hoofprints: The Untold Story of Edward Dudley Brown and the Legendary Equestrians,"* readers will witness the enduring influence of these extraordinary individuals who defied expectations and shattered barriers. The vibrant tracks of the Kentucky Derby will come alive as readers discover the sacrifices made in the pursuit of victory.

The novel is a celebration of justice, equality, and the unyielding passion that propels humanity towards greatness. It sheds light on the profound effect of a transformative era on individuals, communities, and the core of American history. As readers embark on this literary exploration, they will be guided by the indomitable spirit of these legendary equestrians, experiencing victories, transformations, and the pursuit of greatness. Revelations and deeper truths await at every turn, as the power of perseverance and the transformative legacy of these extraordinary individuals unfold through the pages.

This is more than a mere historical account; it is a narrative that transcends history and imagination, inviting readers to journey alongside remarkable characters who dare to dream, strive, and inspire. Delving deeper into their lives and achievements, readers will uncover hidden treasures within the lives of these legendary figures. With each note of triumph and struggle, the novel resonates with the universal human yearning to surpass limitations, rewrite destiny, and find solace in the inspiring beauty of nature and the resilience of the human spirit. The realm of "*Gilded Hoofprints: The Untold Story of Edward Dudley Brown and the Legendary Equestrians*" is a realm of inspiration, a testament to the transformative power of individuals who left an indelible mark on history and continue to inspire, challenge, and captivate. As readers immerse themselves in this literary journey, they will be forever transformed, enriched, and inspired by the enduring legacy of these extraordinary equestrians.

EPIGRAPH:

"Deep within the forgotten depths of America's history resides an extraordinary saga of valiant athletes—the jockeys, trainers, and stable owners of the horse racing industry. Their exceptional blend of talent, unwavering resilience, and enduring principles continue to reverberate in the realm of modern American sports. More than a century ago, these formidable individuals etched a timeless legacy, their indomitable spirit resounding through the sacred grounds of America's revered racetracks and enduring in the powerful strides of today's triumphant thoroughbreds. With unwavering determination, they steered the course of equestrian history, leaving an indelible mark still felt in the pulsating rhythm of contemporary competitors. This rich and evocative fictional narrative, based on historical events and characters, is an integral part of our nation's vibrant sporting heritage, forever immortalized in the annals of time."

CHARACTER OVERVIEW:

Edward Dudley Brown (1850 - 1906): Also known as Brown Dick, he was a prominent African-American jockey, horse trainer, and owner. After retiring from his successful jockey career, he trained horses and later owned his own stable. Among his successful horses were two American Derby winners, Volante, and The Bard.

Ansel Williamson (1810 - 1875): An African-American horse trainer, Williamson trained Aristides, the horse that won the inaugural Kentucky Derby in 1875 with jockey Oliver Lewis. Despite being born into slavery, Williamson became one of the most respected trainers in horse racing history.

Abe Hawkins (unknown - 1867): Born into slavery in Kentucky, Hawkins was recognized as one of the leading riders in the southwest region of the United States, especially Louisiana, during the late antebellum period. He rode for Farrar F. Kenner on the Ashland/Louisiana plantation and was renowned for his riding skills.

Chiron: Chiron, the revered centaur of Egyptian-Greek mythology, possessed exceptional wisdom and compassion. As a mentor, he guided numerous mythological figures, imparting knowledge in various disciplines. Despite his immortality, Chiron carried a profound wound, earning him the title of "the wounded healer." Through his suffering, he developed empathy and the ability to guide others on paths of healing and self-discovery. Chiron's teachings symbolize the transformative power of personal struggle and the importance of integrating our wounds. His depiction as black on ancient pottery holds symbolic significance, representing his wisdom and connection to life's mysteries. Chiron's legacy as a figure of wisdom and compassion endures, reminding us to embrace our wounds and find strength in helping others heal. He is represented by the constellation of Sagittarius.

Farrar Kenner: Farrar is an American politician, turfman, and slave owner, vehemently opposing the abolition of slavery for personal gain. Farrar, from a prominent Louisiana family, owns Ashland Plantation, where he innovatively cultivates sugar cane among other crops including a performance enhancing poison. His political career with the House of

Representatives further bolsters his influence. Proud and stubborn, Farrar staunchly defends the plantation system, manipulating others with charm to serve his own interests. A Master of Political maneuvering and strategic thinking, he seeks to preserve his family's social status and wealth. As the primary antagonist, Farrar's rivalry with Abe Hawkins, a legendary black jockey he owned as a slave, then his animosity transferring to Abe's protégé, Edward Brown.

Oliver Lewis (1856 - 1924): Lewis was an African-American jockey in Thoroughbred horse racing who won the first Kentucky Derby at the age of 19 on May 17, 1875, riding the horse Aristides. Lewis raced for only two years, but his place in history is cemented by his victory in that inaugural Derby.

Isaac Murphy (1861 - 1896): Murphy is one of the greatest jockeys in American history. He was the first jockey to win the Kentucky Derby three times and was the first to be inducted into the National Museum of Racing's Hall of Fame in 1955. Murphy's career winning percentage was an incredible 44%, the highest in racing history.

William "Billy" Walker (1859 - 1933): Walker was another pioneering African American jockey. He won the 1877 Kentucky Derby on Baden-Baden. After retiring as a jockey, Walker also worked as a trainer.

Alonzo Clayton (1876 - 1917): Clayton was a successful jockey who won his first race at age 10. He was the winner of the 1892 Kentucky Derby at 15, making him the youngest ever to win the event, a record that still stands today.

James "Soup" Perkins (1871 - 1911): Perkins, another African-American jockey, won the Kentucky Derby in 1895 on Halma. The nickname "Soup" is said to come from his fondness for soup.

Jimmy "Wink" Winkfield (1882 - 1974): Winkfield was a two-time Kentucky Derby winner (1901 and 1902). After facing increased racism in the U.S., he moved to Russia and continued his career, becoming a celebrated international racing star. He later lived in France and is considered one of the most successful jockeys in history.

PLEASE NOTE:

For more comprehensive bios and character profiles, please refer to Part 2 in the Encyclopedia.

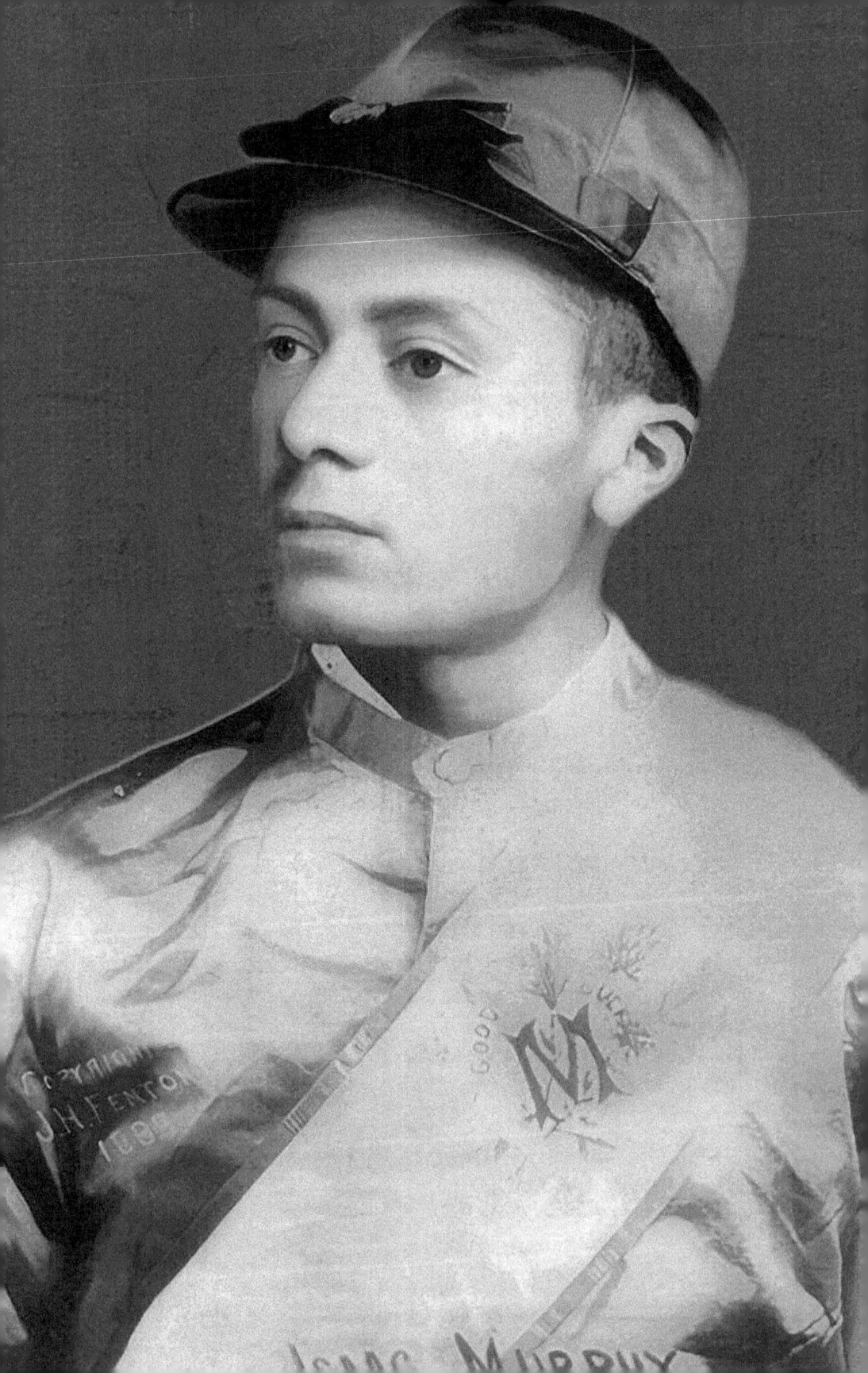

Isaac MURPHY

PART 1: THE NOVEL

I, II, III, IV SECTIONS

NOVEL PART 1

SECTION I: TIME PERIOD: 1861 – 1875

Chapter 1: The Rise and Birth of Sagittarius: The Golden Archer:

1. The Undefeated Asteroid
2. Under the Stars
3. Wisdom of the Stars
4. Interrupted Celebration
5. Witnessing the Birth
6. Three Years Later - The Race

Chapter 2: Art, War, & Freedom

1. The 13th Amendment and Emancipation Proclamation
2. Commissioning a Masterpiece
3. The Travers Stakes Announcement
4. The Guerrilla Raid
5. Pursuit of the Raiders
6. Recovering Asteroid
7. Protecting Asteroid
8. Ansel's Reward

Chapter 3: The Golden Apex: Sage's Last Echo

1. Triumph in the Travers Stakes
2. The Jerome Stakes Victory
3. Kenner's Revenge
4. Abe's Obituary and False Reports
5. Persistent Threats
6. The Black Jockey Trust
7. Abe's Wisdom and Legacy
8. Farrar Kenner's Vendetta
9. Tragic Demise of Abe Hawkins
10. Funeral and Eulogy
11. Edward's Reflection and Vision
12. Ansel's Revival and Symbolic Connection

Chapter 4: The Shadows of Courage & The Burning House:

1. Edward's Mystical Vision
2. Journey to Woodburn Farm
3. Arrival at Woodburn Farm
4. Threats and Refuge
5. The Remarkable Boys

SECTION I

Chapter 1 - The Rise and Birth of Sagittarius: The Golden Archer:

The St. Louis racetrack in Missouri thrummed with anticipation as the crowd huddled in eager anticipation. It was the year 1864, and 14-year-old Edward Dudley Brown, a young Black jockey, prepared to mount the formidable steed. The horse's ebony coat gleamed under the flickering torchlight, a testament to its undefeated record. Edward's hands trembled with a mix of excitement and nerves as he tightened his grip on the reins, ready to prove himself in the face of the unknown.

But as the race commenced, the scene shifted, transporting us back to a time fraught with danger and uncertainty. We found ourselves alongside Jockey Abe Hawkins, a man of unyielding spirit, fleeing from the clutches of his cruel slave owner, Farrar Kenner. On horseback, Abe embarked on a perilous journey, his heart aflame with the desire for freedom. Yet even in the middle of the perils of escape, he took a calculated risk, secretly sharing crucial information with Union Army generals. He revealed the whereabouts of his enslaver, Confederate General Farrar Kenner, at the infamous Ashland Plantation.

The Union Army, fueled by Abe's tip, descended upon Ashland Plantation, disrupting the lives of Farrar Kenner's family. The once-grand estate, a symbol of power and privilege, fell into disarray as Union soldiers seized possessions, tearing the fabric of their existence. Possessions were sold off at an auction in the bustling city of New Orleans, leaving the Kenner family in a state of despair and uncertainty. Fearful of capture, Farrar Kenner himself fled Ashland Plantation, his former dominion now in shambles.

But our tale twists again, taking us three years into the past, to a moment of enchantment and discovery. The year is 1861, and the moon casts its ethereal glow upon a young orphan named Edward Dudley Brown. Under the guardianship of horse trainer Ansel Williamson and renowned jockey Abe Hawkins, Edward celebrates his eleventh birthday beneath the shimmering canvas of a meteor shower. It is the Geminids meteor shower, a celestial spectacle that sets his imagination ablaze.

Edward gazes up at the sky, his eyes wide with wonder, as Abe, the sage of Louisiana, imparts his wisdom. With gentle patience, Abe answers Edward's questions about the origins of the radiant lights. He speaks of the zodiac, of constellations, and of the meteor showers that grace the heavens. In Abe's words, the mysteries of the cosmos unfold, revealing the intricate networks that connects humanity to the stars.

The young boy absorbs the knowledge like a thirsty sponge, his mind awash with the grandeur of the universe. Abe teaches Edward about the significance of meteor showers, how they symbolize birth and new beginnings. He draws a parallel to horses, creatures whose galloping strides mirror the swift motion of the shooting stars. Abe imparts his understanding of asteroids, celestial bodies that resemble stars, captivating Edward's imagination with tales of their cosmic dance.

But it is in the quiet moments, away from the splendor of the meteor shower, that Abe shares deeper insights. He speaks of the interconnectedness of all living beings, of the stardust that courses through their veins. Edward's thoughts turn to his deceased parents, lost to him at such a tender age. With a heavy heart, he wonders if they too have become stars, twinkling above him in the vast expanse of the night sky.

Ansel, the ever-watchful guardian, observes Edward's yearning gaze and exchanges a knowing glance with Abe. Ansel's voice, warm and soothing, resonates through the night air. "When a star dies in heaven, a person is born on earth. And when the person on earth dies, he or she becomes a star in heaven again." Edward's breath catches, his eyes welling with tears as Abe takes the lead, pointing towards the radiant Sirius, a beacon of brilliance in the firmament. "You see that bright, shining star over there, Edward? That is the brightest star in our visible sky, and it represents your mother, looking down upon you with boundless love. One day, you will join her up there, just as we all will ascend to the kingdom in heaven."

Abe's words hang in the air, a promise of reunion and solace. But there is more to this cosmic journey, for he introduces Edward to the wounded healer, Chiron, a figure represented by the constellation of Sagittarius. The story unfolds, tales of centaurs, mythical hybrid beings that embody both man and horse. Chiron, the wise king of the centaurs, mentor to heroes, and harbinger of healing, emerges from the stories of legends.

Curiosity fuels Edward's spirit as Abe probes deeper, asking if the young boy knows the meaning of his name. Edward's head shakes in response, his eyes fixed on Abe's face. With gentle grace, Abe reveals the hidden layers of Edward's identity. "Ead means rich, wealthy, and

Ward means guardian, protector. Your name, Edward, means a rich and wealthy guardian protector." The weight of those words settles upon Edward's young shoulders, a mantle of destiny he is destined to bear.

To commemorate this revelation, Abe reached into the folds of his weathered cloak and retrieved a necklace, its pendant glistening in the moonlight. Crafted in the likeness of a golden centaur, half man and half horse, it represented Chiron, the wounded healer and mentor. The pendant bore precious gems, meticulously arranged to mirror the constellation of Sagittarius, a celestial map of guidance and purpose. Abe presented the pendant to Ansel, who, with a gentle smile, placed it around Edward's neck.

With awe and gratitude, Edward accepts the pendant, its weight both physical and metaphorical. It symbolizes not only the guidance of the heavens but also his own capacity for strength and protection. The bond between Edward, Abe, and Ansel deepens as they exchange heartfelt wishes on this momentous occasion. The meteor shower continues to paint the sky with its luminescence as their voices mingle with the symphony of the stars.

Yet, just as the celebration reaches its crescendo, the universe intervenes, and the world of horses asserts its presence. Raleigh Colston, a black stablehands horse trainer, disrupts the revelry, calling for aid in Nebula's labor. The urgency in his voice breaks the spell, summoning Abe, Ansel, and Edward back to their duties at Woodburn farm.

Mounted on their steeds, the trio gallops through the night, their hearts propelled by compassion and purpose. They arrive at Woodburn farm, where Nebula, the expectant mare, awaits their arrival. With practiced hands and unwavering resolve, they assist in the delicate delivery of new life. Edward watches in awe as a robust male foal enters the world, its spirit already shimmering with vitality.

In the aftermath of the birth, a moment of serenity descends upon the farm. Edward approaches the foal's father, Lexington, a steed who shares his birthday and birth year. A sense of kinship tugs at Edward's heart as he comforts the majestic horse, his voice a gentle murmur from the quiet of the night.

Ansel, the ever-attentive guardian, recognizes the significance of this moment. He suggests that Edward be granted the honor of naming the foal, a gift that carries the weight of destiny. Edward's eyes wander from Lexington to the expanse of the night sky, his mind awash with the teachings of Abe, the wisdom of the stars.

Inspired by the knowledge he has acquired, Edward selects a name that encapsulates the essence of the foal, its lineage, and its celestial connection. "Asteroid," he declares with conviction. "The foal resembles my champion, Lexington, who is a star. Its mother's name is Nebula, and together, they embody the beauty of the cosmos. Asteroid, for it is a name that resembles a star and holds the power of destiny."

Abe, Ansel, and Raleigh exchange glances, their smiles a testament to the young jockey's profound understanding. "So, his name will be Asteroid," they collectively affirm, their voices resonating with admiration and curiosity. "What an interesting name choice, Edward."

Three years later, the scene shifted once more, bringing us back to the present, to the race where Edward now commanded the mighty Asteroid. The wind whipped through the horse's mane and blew against Edward's face as they thundered like shooting stars across the racetrack, hooves pounding against the earth, their spirits aflame with determination. The crowd roared with anticipation; the air thick with excitement. Edward and Asteroid surged forward, their bond unbreakable, their hearts beating as one.

In a glorious display of speed and skill, Edward and Asteroid crossed the finish line victorious, earning the thoroughbred the title of the Undefeated Asteroid. Edward, wearing the silk of blue and white colors representing Woodburn stable, basked in the triumph of this moment. It was not merely a victory on the racetrack; it was a testament to the strength of the human spirit, a testament to the power of dreams and the resilience of the soul.

CHAPTER 1 SUMMARY:

On December 20th, 1861, Abe Hawkins and Edward Dudley Brown found themselves observing the captivating Geminids meteor shower. Positioned either on a hill in Louisville, Kentucky, or atop a hill in Lexington, Kentucky, they marveled at the celestial display. The meteor shower derived its name from the constellation Gemini, as the meteors seemed to originate from that particular constellation. These meteors were, in fact, fragments of debris from an intriguing asteroid called 3200 Phaethon. When these fragments entered Earth's atmosphere, they ignited brilliantly, creating a breathtaking spectacle. Edward Dudley Brown, born in 1850, shared the same birth year as the renowned racehorse named Lexington. Lexington sired numerous exceptional winners, earning them induction into the racing hall of fame. Similarly, Edward's talents and endeavors birthed a multitude of victorious individuals who also found their place in the racing hall of fame. As Abe and Edward watched the Geminids Meteor Shower, they contemplated its occurrence. This cosmic phenomenon transpired when a meteorite collided with a stationary asteroid, resulting in a mesmerizing shower of lights in the sky. The specific year of their observation could be attributed to either 1861, 1862, or even 1864.From a spiritual perspective, the Geminids appeared in the astrological sign of Gemini, an Air sign symbolizing the power of loving partnerships. Another Air sign, Libra, with its diplomatic nature, observed the spectacle from above, seeking fairness and balance. Abe and Ed embodied a loving partnership, and Ed's connection with Lexington, being born in the same year, mirrored a bond akin to a twin. Ed fostered deep relationships with jockeys and his fellow air sign, Ansel, who happened to be a Libra, representing equality, fairness, and balance. The Centaur, a symbol of their shared birth, underscored their bond. Just like the mythical Centaur Chiron, who was half man and half horse, Ed, and Lexington, both Sagittarius zodiac signs, formed a unique connection. Ed was akin to the asteroid Chiron, while Lexington embodied the characteristics of a horse. Their intertwined destinies aligned with the mythological half-man-half-horse creature. Chiron, initially classified as an asteroid, transformed into a comet, developing a cometary coma. This dual classification prompted the name "Centaur," alluding to the mythical creature. Centaurs, like asteroids, remained stable stellar objects until they encountered a meteorite impact, transforming them into hyperactive comets. Their elliptical orbits revolve around the sun, tracing a racetrack that extends just shy of Jupiter. In recent astronomical discoveries, an object referred to as LD2, categorized as a Centaur, emerged. It bore the characteristics of an icy proto-world, akin to the mythical part-human, part-horse creatures. These objects exhibited both asteroid-like and comet-like behavior. Centaurs inhabited the space between Jupiter and Neptune, their enigmatic nature adding to their allure. In Greek mythology, Sagittarius was linked to the centaur Chiron, the wounded healer who mentored Achilles, a celebrated hero of the Trojan War, in archery.

In the captivating chapter, "The Birth of Sagittarius: The Golden Archer," we delve into the remarkable life of 14-year-old orphaned Black jockey, Edward Dudley Brown. Set against the backdrop of the American Civil War in 1864, the chapter alternates between Edward's exhilarating race aboard the undefeated Asteroid in St. Louis, Missouri, and the daring escape of renowned jockey Abe Hawkins from the clutches of his slave owner, confederate general Farrar Kenner. With the help of esteemed horse trainer Ansel Williamson, Abe flees to Kentucky, seeking freedom from the oppression of Ashland plantation's owner, Farrar Kenner. As Edward races aboard Asteroid, a magnificent and undefeated racehorse, the narrative takes us back three years before to Edward's eleventh birthday celebration under a dazzling meteor shower, where he is joined by Abe and Ansel. Amidst the awe-inspiring display of celestial brilliance, Abe imparts his wisdom about the zodiac and the profound meaning behind meteor showers, captivating Edward's imagination with the constellation of Sagittarius, named after the king of the centaurs, Chiron — the wounded healer. With this newfound knowledge, Edward becomes enchanted by the stars and their significance, finding solace and inspiration in their ethereal beauty. Witnessing the birth of a foal and choosing the name Asteroid, Edward's connection to the heavens deepens, symbolizing his own aspirations and the brilliance he seeks to achieve. The chapter seamlessly transitions back to the present, where Edward races aboard Asteroid and emerges victorious, becoming a shining star in the world of horse racing. "The Birth of Sagittarius: The Golden Archer" transports readers to a tumultuous period in history, where the convergence of bravery, determination, and the power of the stars intertwines with the struggles for freedom and personal triumph. Through Edward's journey, we explore the resilience of the human spirit, the transformative nature of chasing one's dreams, and the indelible impact that defying societal prejudices can have. As Edward races towards his destiny, he embodies hope, courage, and a profound belief in the ability to transcend adversity and leave an enduring legacy.

SECTION I

Chapter 2 - Art, War, & Freedom:

The summer sun cast a golden hue over Woodburn Farm, its rays illuminating the vibrant fields and stretching shadows of its majestic thoroughbreds. As the nation bled through the trials of war, the winds of change whispered promises of freedom, carrying hope on their wings. It was the year 1865, and the world around Abe, Ansel, and Edward crackled with the fervor of transformation. The 13th Amendment and Emancipation Proclamation had been enacted, bestowing upon them and all Black Americans the long-awaited gift of liberty. No longer bound by the shackles of slavery, they continued to work as paid employees for Robert Alexander, a man who recognized their worth beyond the color of their skin.

Edward Troye, a painter of great renown, commissioned by Robert Alexander to carry out an extraordinary task. Troye was to create a masterpiece, not just a mere painting. It was to be a chronicle of a glorious moment when a young jockey, Edward Dudley Brown, and his mentor Ansel Williamson, had bested all odds atop the Undefeated Asteroid. This was not just a victory of one race, but a testament to the unyielding spirit of two men and their glorious steed. The painter stood before his sprawling canvas; his silhouette framed by the warm light of the setting sun. Brush in hand, Troye embarked on his task with the seriousness of a historian and the sensitivity of a poet. His experienced hands danced across the canvas, layering colors and shapes with an almost reverent precision. As the hours passed, a scene of victorious triumph began to unfurl on the canvas. The young jockey, Edward, and his trusted mentor, Ansel, emerged from the flurry of colors. Their faces radiated the joy of victory, their bodies immortalized in a moment of ecstatic celebration. The Undefeated Asteroid, the equine marvel that had carried them to victory, was depicted in all its majesty, a testament to the men's skill, dedication, and their deep bond with the noble creature. As he worked, Troye seemed to breathe life into the canvas. He was not merely portraying a victorious race; he was capturing the spirit of the time, a critical juncture when these men, newly freed yet bearing the indelible scars of their past, were carving a space for themselves in a world that was still struggling to accept them. Each stroke of Troye's brush told their story - their daring spirit, their shared triumphs, and the challenges they had overcome. The painting came alive with their resilience and hope, a vibrant tableau that encapsulated their epic journey. It was more than a masterpiece; it was a tribute, a celebration of Edward, Ansel, and the Undefeated Asteroid, one that would preserve their legacy for generations to come. In the hush of the stables, amidst the warm scent of hay and the soft nickering of horses, Troye stood back to admire his creation. His painting, teeming with emotion and powerful in its storytelling, was a poignant reminder of the incredible journey these men had embarked on. This masterpiece was more than a mere painting. It was a piece of history, a testament to a time of profound change, and the unyielding spirit of those who dared to dream.

Robert Alexander, a man of vision and ambition, gathered his staff in the grand parlor of the farmhouse. A glimmer danced in his eyes as he shared news of the upcoming inauguration of The Travers Stakes, a prestigious horse race to be held on August 2nd, 1864, in Saratoga Springs, New York. The winning purse amounted to a staggering $2,500, a fortune that could change the destiny of both the horses and the men who tended to them.

However, reports of guerrilla raids throughout Kentucky by Confederate rebels soured Robert's aspirations. Fear gnawed at his resolve, for he couldn't bear to risk the safety of his beloved horses and stable. With a heavy heart, he set aside his dreams of glory, choosing the preservation of life over the pursuit of riches.

But fate had a cruel sense of humor, and on a chilling October night, the specter of war descended upon Woodburn Farm. Confederate spy Sue Mundy, a malevolent shadow disguised as a woman, orchestrated a guerrilla raid that struck at the very heart of the farm's pride and joy. Two prized horses, Asteroid and Bay Dick, were kidnapped, leaving Robert Alexander and his staff reeling in disbelief and outrage.

Driven by fury and a deep-rooted sense of loyalty, Robert and his devoted employees set forth on a relentless pursuit. They rode through the harsh wilderness, their spirits unwavering despite the formidable challenges that lay ahead. Sue Mundy, ever elusive, danced on the edge of their reach, taunting them with each fleeting glimpse.

Ten days later, on November 1, 1864, fortune smiled upon them. The weary travelers stumbled upon a hidden hideout, finding Asteroid confined within its shadowed depths. A sense of relief washed over them, and for a fleeting moment, victory tasted sweet upon their lips. Yet, even as they rejoiced, the specter of the Confederate rebels loomed, a constant reminder of the dangers that surrounded them.

Ansel and Edward, bound by a brotherhood forged through adversity, understood the gravity of the situation. In the face of relentless threats, they devised a daring plan to safeguard the Undefeated Asteroid, a horse of unparalleled skill and spirit. In the cloak of night, they employed quick thinking and resourcefulness, switching Asteroid with another horse, thus confounding the guerrillas, and leaving them none the wiser. Ansel's bravery shone through, saving Asteroid from an uncertain fate, and preserving the pride of Woodburn Farm.

But victory often came at a price, and despite their valiant efforts, the guerrillas still managed to seize two colts and two other horses, including Norwich, a promising three-year-old colt and the full brother to Norfolk, who had once electrified the tracks with his thunderous stride.

Grateful for Ansel's unwavering heroism, Robert Alexander rewarded him with a gift worthy of his courage. Entrusted with the training of a new racehorse named Merrill, Ansel felt the weight of destiny settle upon his shoulders. With Abe Hawkins, a jockey whose talents matched the speed of the wind, ready to ride, they formed an unbreakable triumvirate, driven by their shared passion and unyielding determination.

CHAPTER 2 SUMMARY:

In the year 1865, as the winds of change whispered promises of freedom, renowned painter Edward Troye was commissioned by Robert Alexander to create a masterpiece depicting the victorious race between jockey Edward Dudley Brown, mentor Ansel Williamson, and the Undefeated Asteroid. Meanwhile, Robert Alexander shares news of a prestigious horse race, The Travers Stakes, but fears of guerrilla raids by Confederate rebels deter his participation. The specter of war descends upon Woodburn Farm as Confederate spy Sue Mundy orchestrates a raid, kidnapping Asteroid and Bay Dick. Robert Alexander and his staff embark on a relentless pursuit, recovering Asteroid but losing other horses. Ansel and Edward devise a daring plan to protect Asteroid, and Robert rewards Ansel by entrusting him with a new racehorse named Merrill.

SECTION I

Chapter 3 - The Golden Apex: Sage's Last Echo:

August 1866 had marked a turning point in Abe Hawkins' vibrant career, as the gifted jockey achieved a momentous victory in the Travers Stakes. Mounted on the swift and noble Merrill, a horse owned by Robert Alexander of Woodburn Farm, Abe showcased exceptional talent and crossed the finish line in an impressive time of 3:29. Despite his modest weight of 100 pounds, his finesse and skill were unmatched. The roar of the crowd still echoed in Abe's ears as he crossed the finish line, a symbol of triumph against all odds. The triumph earned him a prize purse of $3,500, solidifying his reputation as one of the most talented jockeys of his time.

The thrill of victory was not confined to the tracks of the Travers Stakes. October saw Abe continuing his streak at the Jerome Stakes, his diminutive figure proving more than capable of maneuvering with grace and expertise. But as the news of his victory reached unexpected ears, the atmosphere turned sinister. Farrar Kenner, Abe's former slave master, learned of his success and harbored nothing but bitterness and resentment. The notion of his former slave achieving such greatness in the world of horse racing was an affront to Kenner's pride. Especially since he couldn't profit off Abe's free labor and Kenner blamed Abe for a Union army raid on Ashland Plantation, his prosperous estate. In Kenner's eyes, Abe's achievements were not worth celebrating but served as stinging reminders of a perceived betrayal.

Blinded by vengeance, Farrar Kenner sought retribution for Abe's actions. He ordered an assassination, employing the use of strychnine poison to end the jockey's life. Kenner held Abe accountable for leaking information to the Union army, which led to a raid on Ashland Plantation. Unbeknownst to him, the initial attempt on Abe's life had failed. Consumed by his twisted obsession, Kenner prematurely released an obituary, if Abe had perished.

It was a peculiar twist of fate when Abe Hawkins stumbled upon his own obituary, dated May 4, 1867. Instead of mourning his alleged passing, Abe found amusement in the false report. His hearty laughter echoed through the newsroom of the St. Louis Republican, leading to an article titled "A Race Rider Reads his Obituary and is Delighted," aptly portraying Abe's undaunted spirit. But Farrar Kenner's thirst for revenge remained unquenched. He was determined to see Abe's life extinguished and ordered a second assassination attempt using poison. Another dose of poison was readied, another plot hatched. On May 27, 1867, Abe fearlessly took to the racecourse in Cincinnati, overlooking the heightened danger that loomed over him. The race only intensified Farrar Kenner's fervor, escalating their dangerous game to new heights. Abe's every move, every race he competed in, fueled Kenner's relentless pursuit.

Faced with the imminent threat to his life, Abe knew he had to take decisive action. He established the Black Jockey Trust, recognizing the need to support and uplift promising Black equestrians. Abe passed on the reins of the trust entrusting it to his comrades Edward and Ansel, his dear brothers, with the management of the trust. This institution, later known as the Black Equestrian Trust & Co., aimed to nurture the talents of future generations, ensuring the legacy of Black jockeys would endure.

In his final days, Abe Hawkins gathered Ansel and Edward, sharing his wisdom and legacy with them. His voice trembled with emotion as he spoke, urging them to use their freedom to fight for equality and justice. He emphasized the importance of selflessness, of sharing their blessings of knowledge, wisdom, and learned techniques. Abe knew that their skills and talents were gifts, entrusted to them to shape the future of their community. The legacy of Abe, now imprinted on their hearts, molded them into visionaries committed to the progress of their community.

"We are now free men, liberated from the chains that once bound us," Abe began. "And with this precious freedom comes a profound responsibility, a sacred duty to pass on our skills and train a new generation. They will carry forward our legacy, maintaining our dominance in this sport we hold dear."

Abe's words carried the weight of experience and the fervor of a man who had fought valiantly for his freedom.

His eyes sparkled with determination as he continued, "Let us never be selfish with the blessings bestowed upon us. These gifts, like divine jewels, are entrusted to us. It is our solemn obligation to impart them, shaping the minds and talents of those who will follow in our footsteps."

Edward and Ansel listened intently, their hearts filled with a sense of purpose and determination. Abe's inspiring words instilled in them a fire that burned bright and fierce. They vowed to carry on his legacy, to fight for justice and equality, and to share the wisdom they had learned from their beloved mentor.

But tragically, Farrar Kenner's wicked plan succeeded. On June 8th, 1867, Abe Hawkins fell victim to the strychnine poison. The poison, in low doses, acted as a performance-enhancing drug, but in higher doses, it mimicked the symptoms of consumption or tuberculosis, prevalent ailments of the time.

In an attempt to cover up his malevolent deed, Farrar Kenner vehemently criticized any notion of an autopsy. He manipulated the cause of Abe's death, officially declaring it as consumption or tuberculosis, shielding himself from any potential investigation. To ensure that the truth remained concealed, Kenner defiantly refused to bury Abe in the Union soldier cemetery, where he was rightfully entitled. Instead, he chose to lay him to rest on Ashland Plantation, a location that would deter anyone from exhuming the body or uncovering the truth.

Abe's passing sent shockwaves throughout the equestrian community. It was a loss too profound to be measured, a tragedy etched in the hearts of all who knew him. His funeral took place at Ashland Plantation, a somber gathering of friends, family, and admirers. Ansel, his voice filled with a mix of sorrow and pride, delivered a heartfelt eulogy that captured Abe's character, skill, and lasting legacy, bringing the gathering to tears. He spoke of Abe Hawkins as a man of remarkable integrity, who never resorted to harsh treatment of the horses he rode. His numerous aliases, such as the wise sage, The Dark Sage of Louisiana, and The Slayer of Lexington, added to his legend.

Ansel shared that Abe's unique riding style set him apart from others, and his fierce competitive spirit earned him the respect of both white and black racing critics and enthusiasts. As he concluded his eulogy, Ansel quoted an article that aptly described Abe's passing as an "irreparable loss to the American Turf." "Good riders and strictly honest ones are rare, therefore the death of Abe Hawkins is an irreparable loss to the American Turf," he said, his voice echoing in the somber air. Tears welled in the eyes of those who had gathered to bid farewell to a true legend.

Amidst the grief so profound it threatened to shatter him and longing for Abe, Edward Brown sought solace in a secluded field near the river. He clung to the Chiron pendant necklace Abe had given him, a symbol of the bond they shared and a tangible link to the sage's wisdom. Overwhelmed by his emotions, he fell off Lexington, the horse with whom he shared a profound bond, birthday, and birth year with. In that moment of vulnerability, the unconscious Edward found himself in a trance-like vision, where stars aligned to form the Sagittarius constellation, personified by the centaur Chiron, pulling back a golden bow and arrow. Within this mystical vision, Edward transformed. His legs fused and elongated, his body taking on the form of a powerful centaur. He ran, the grass bending beneath his hooves, and soon encountered other centaurs adorned in jockey silks. Guided by the centaurs, he ascended a mountain with a golden peak resembling a fusion of Mount Rushmore and the pyramids of Giza. The centaurs recognized Edward as Chiron, their chosen leader, the king of the centaurs and offered their unwavering support.

As Edward climbed the final peak to reach the golden summit he was met by his beloved mentor, Abe Hawkins, as a centaur smiling as he helped him up. At the summit, Edward marveled at the resplendent golden apex, etching the vision into his memory. Slowly, he returned to reality, finding Ansel trying to revive him from being unconscious.

Edward's heart raced with the significance of what he had experienced, and his hand instinctively reached for his neck, only to find his cherished Chiron pendant missing. But as his eyes scanned the saddle of Lexington, a glimmer caught his attention. There, hanging from the saddle, was the pendant— symbolic of their eternal connection. And as Edward held the pendant close to his heart, a question lingered in his mind—what other mysteries and challenges awaited them on this extraordinary journey? The mysterious vision left Edward with a profound sense of purpose. He knew that he would carry on Abe's teachings, guiding and training future generations of jockeys. The legacy of Abe Hawkins, the Great Sage of Wisdom, would live on through him and Ansel. They would defy all odds, shatter barriers, and forge a new path for Black equestrians in the world of horse racing.

The answer would reveal itself in due time, beckoning them toward a future fraught with both triumphs and tribulations, a future they were ready to face head-on, in honor of the fallen sage who had lit their path with his wisdom and grace.

CHAPTER 3 SUMMARY:

With training from Ansel, Abe Hawkins won the 3rd Travers Stakes in August 1866 aboard Merrill. In this riveting chapter, Abe Hawkins' life ends tragically due to a sinister plot, resulting in a moment of profound introspection for his protégé, Edward Brown. The story unfolds during the late 1800s, spotlighting Abe Hawkins, a former slave turned victorious jockey. Despite numerous trials and tribulations, Abe's wisdom and resilience cement his legacy in horse racing. However, when Abe's past catches up with him in the form of his former slave master, Farrar Kenner, his life takes a tragic turn, prompting his fellow riders, Ansel, and Edward, to honor his legacy and continue his fight for equality. Through a mystical vision, Edward rediscovers his purpose and forges a resolute path to honor Abe's legacy.

SECTION I

Chapter 4 - The Shadows of Courage

Edward and Ansel had embarked on a long and arduous journey from Louisiana back to Kentucky, their homeland, after the funeral of a dear friend, Abe Hawkins. The weight of the recent loss hung heavy in the air as they rode on horseback towards their destination—the Woodburn Farm.

As the sun began its descent, casting a golden glow upon the sprawling fields, Edward and Ansel arrived at their destination. On their way, they passed a neighboring house where the air was thick with the scent of delicious food. Black mothers, their strength unyielding, prepared a nourishing dinner for their children, their laughter and songs creating a sanctuary of warmth and love.

The families gathered there, their husbands away in California working on the railroad, seeking solace in each other's company. The post-Civil War era had left them on edge, with the looming threat of the Confederate remnants, now rebranded as the Ku Klux Klan. Reports of lynchings spread like wildfire, and the families knew they had to remain vigilant.

America Murphy, Isaac's mother, gathers the children around her and opens a book titled "Black Beauty." As she reads, the young minds are transported to a world of compassion and resilience, their imaginations sparked by the words on the page. The young minds listened with rapt attention; their eyes filled with wonder. Among the children, four boys—Oliver Lewis, William "Billy" Walker, Isaac Burns Murphy, and George Garret Lewis—shine with their bright spirits. Their energy and curiosity set them apart.

Mother Eleanor Lewis calls everyone to supper. Oliver, the eldest among the boys, replied, "Yes, Ma'am," and they all made their way to the dinner table. As they sit around the dinner table, bowing their heads, a prayer is offered, seeking God's protection from the ever-present threat of the Confederate remnants, who have morphed into the Ku Klux Klan. Reports of widespread lynchings instill fear and anxiety in the hearts of the families.

But before the "Amen" can leave their lips, a window shatters, and glass bottles filled with oil and tar diesel crash into the house, igniting a fierce fire. Confederate attackers have taken siege of the Lewis household, throwing the family into panic and chaos. The mothers scream for their beloved sons to run and hide, but the boys refuse to leave their mothers' side, terrified and frightened.

The attackers, fueled by hatred and malice, enter the house from the back, issuing a chilling ultimatum—surrender the boys or face dire consequences. In the commotion, one mother is knocked unconscious, and another desperately tries to escape with the boys, only to be intercepted. The attackers tie the mothers up in front of the burning house, their pleas for help swallowed by the crackling flames.

Smoke fills the air as Edward and Ansel, drawn by the scent and the screams, rush to the scene. With adrenaline coursing through their veins, they navigate the chaos and untie the mothers, their hearts heavy with the weight of their pleas to rescue their boys.

Determined to bring the boys back to safety, Edward and Ansel quickly trace the hoof prints left by the attackers' horses. Their pursuit takes them to a lynch site, where the four boys are precariously tied to trees, their young lives hanging by a thread. At the top of the hill, silhouetted against the fading light, Edward, and Ansel charge on horseback towards the boys. With swift precision, they shoot the ropes, sending the boys tumbling into safety, just moments before their lives would have been cruelly extinguished.

Edward and Ansel swoop down, their horses' hooves pounding the ground, and scoop up the boys, holding them close, their faces etched with awe and gratitude. Returning the boys to their mothers, Edward and Ansel discover the charred ruins of the Lewis house. Only ashes and smoldering remnants remain, a poignant symbol of the destruction caused by hate.

Offering solace and a glimmer of hope, Edward and Ansel extend an invitation for the mothers and children to stay at Woodburn Farm until their husbands return, a sanctuary within the chaos. But peace is fleeting, as another attack ensues. Edward and Ansel, armed and determined, defend the mothers and children from the Confederate counterattack. The air fills with the sound of gunfire and the clashing of wills. In the end, they emerge victorious, yet two Confederate attackers manage to escape.

Fearful of murder charges, Edward and Ansel make the difficult decision to bury the bodies, with the grieving mothers lending their strength to the solemn task. The dead attackers find their final resting place on the land, their actions forever marked upon the scarred landscape.

United in purpose, Edward, and Ansel, alongside the mothers and children they rescued, contemplate a future where unity, justice, and love triumph over the shadows of hatred. As they stand on the grounds of Woodburn Farm, a new chapter unfolds—a chapter of resilience, determination, and unwavering hope.

SULTAN ZESHAN

CHAPTER 4 SUMMARY:

Edward and Ansel, still reeling from the loss of a dear friend, journey back to Kentucky on horseback. Their arrival at Woodburn Farm coincides with a heartwarming scene of Black mothers preparing dinner for their children. Amidst the warmth and laughter, four boys stand out, their spirits shining brightly. However, their peaceful gathering is shattered when Confederate attackers set the Lewis household ablaze and attempt to kidnap the boys. Edward and Ansel rush to the rescue, engaging in a daring pursuit and a life-or-death shootout. With the boys saved and the attackers defeated, they return to find the Lewis house reduced to ashes. Edward and Ansel extend an invitation for the mothers and children to stay at Woodburn Farm, but the threat is not yet over. Another attack ensues, leading to a fateful decision and a united vision for a better future.

SECTION I

Chapter 5 - Chiron and his students:

The sweet fragrance of the blooming honeysuckle in the Kentucky spring was replaced by the robust scent of horses, hay, and the rich earth of New York. Edward Dudley Brown and Ansel Williamson had secured the consent of the mothers of the four boys they had previously rescued, plunging them into the thrilling world of the horse racing industry. With hearts full of hope and eyes brimming with anticipation, Oliver Lewis, Isaac Murphy, George Garrett, and Billy Walker began their apprenticeship.

Although the 15th Amendment had promised the right to vote for Black American men, its echo was still faint amidst the noise of injustice. Despite the Constitutional guarantee, many southern states had devised ways to undermine this right. Yet, the boys, along with Edward and Ansel, refused to let their spirits be dampened. Their dreams took flight in the stables, on the turf, in the race.

Their journey brought them to New York for the prestigious Belmont Stakes. The city pulsed with the rhythm of life, a stark contrast to the tranquil Kentucky countryside they had left behind. Ansel's girlfriend, Ellen, accompanied them, her own heart resonating with the boys' excitement and wonder. This was her first race, their first race, and the anticipation hung in the air like a heavy, intoxicating perfume.

Saturday, June 18, 1870, was a day marked by destiny. Beneath the watchful eyes of Edward and Ansel, the boys found themselves at the Jerome Park Racetrack in the Bronx. An electric thrill ran through the grandstands as the thoroughbreds paraded in the paddock, sleek bodies glistening under the warm sun. The fourth annual Belmont Stakes had begun.

Edward and Kingfisher, his trusted steed, dominated the race. From the bleachers, the boys, Oliver, Isaac, George, and Billy, watched in awe as Edward seamlessly communicated with his horse, his words providing encouragement and motivation. "Alright, Kingfisher, let's do this. Stay steady, steady. We need to win, King. I really need this victory." His voice echoed in the hushed stillness of the racetrack, carrying with it a promise of victory.

Seven horses, seven jockeys, each more competent than the last, and the air vibrated with the tension of the impending showdown. Edward, the apprentice of Abe Hawkins, and Raleigh Colston, the black horse trainer, carved their presence amidst the white-dominated event. The boys looked on, their hearts pounding in synchrony with the hoofbeats that echoed on the turf.

Ultimately, it was Edward who emerged victorious. With a skillful blend of perseverance, endurance, and unyielding will, he guided Kingfisher across the finish line. The clock stopped at 2 minutes and 59 and a half seconds, an incredible feat that was met with roaring applause. The prize money of $3,750 marked an important triumph for Edward, but the true victory was the hope his win ignited in the hearts of the four boys.

In the throes of celebration, Ansel, seized by joy and hope, proposed to Ellen, his love and steadfast support. Surrounded by the din of cheers and jubilation, they found a moment of intimate happiness, promising each other a future intertwined with love and strength.

The sports telecaster announced Edward Dudley Brown's historic victory. The first black man to claim victory in the illustrious Belmont Stakes had etched his name in the annals of history. During an ensuing interview, when asked about his feelings, Edward shared a poignant quote from his mentor, Abe Hawkins: "A win for one of us is a win for us all." The words seeped into the hearts of the boys. Their mentor had broken barriers and etched a path for them to follow, to dream, to conquer.

As autumn unfurled its colorful palette across Kentucky, a palpable excitement coursed through the veins of Lexington. October 29, 1870, marked a day of jubilant celebration, for it was on this crisp autumnal morning that the esteemed Ansel Williamson was to wed his beloved Ellen. This was a union much anticipated, not only by the couple but by the entire community, who had embraced Ellen with warmth and affection over the past four months since the momentous Belmont Stakes.

The ceremony was arranged at the Fayette County Clerk's office, nestled near a historic church whose seasoned stones had silently borne witness to countless stories and turning points of the town. The grandeur of the occasion was palpable; a sense of joyous gravity hung in the air, brushing gently against the fluttering leaves outside.

Ansel stood in the echoing quiet of the clerk's office, his heart thundering in his chest. The excitement of the racetrack paled in comparison to the whirlwind of emotions that now threatened to overtake him. Yet, as he looked into Ellen's glowing eyes, he found a sense of tranquility and commitment far beyond any thrill a race could ever afford him.

As the vows were exchanged, each word reverberating through the chamber, a quiet stillness seemed to envelop the room. With the signing of their marriage certificate, a symbolic union of love, honor, and fidelity was forged, their names forever intertwined.

The moment they were pronounced man and wife, a wave of euphoria washed over those gathered. Among the faces beaming with joy were those of their four apprentices – Oliver Lewis, Isaac Murphy, George Garrett, and Billy Walker, accompanied by their mothers whose faces shone with pride and gratitude. Also present was Raleigh Colston, the formidable black horse trainer, his broad smile reflecting his deep appreciation for this family that had formed out of shared passion and mutual respect.

The celebration shifted to the nearby church, its towering edifice and worn pews suffused with history and countless tales of love. As the church bells rang out, their sonorous peals echoed across the verdant landscape, announcing the joyous union far and wide.

Edward Dudley Brown, raising a glass in honor of the newlyweds, found his voice echoing throughout the room, resounding with sincerity and affection. He concluded with Abe Hawkins' quote, "A win for one of us is a win for us all," eliciting a round of hearty applause, for these words held a profound resonance for this tightly-knit group.

Under the starlit canopy, the revelry unfolded. The sounds of laughter and music filled the air as Ansel and Ellen took to the floor. Lit by the soft glow of lanterns, their first dance as husband and wife was a sight to behold.

This day marked the commencement of their shared journey - a journey not just for Ansel and Ellen, but for their band of young apprentices, their mothers, and the steadfast Colston. As they all stood there, reveling in the joy of the occasion, they knew they were bound together, not just by their love for horse racing, but by their shared victories, dreams, and an enduring sense of community. As the autumn wind carried away the last notes of their celebration, they knew this was just the beginning of their shared story.

The triumph at Belmont Stakes was more than just a win in a race. It was a symbol, a beacon of hope, a testament to resilience, and an embodiment of dreams. The sun began to set, casting long shadows on the racetrack. The boys, Edward, Ansel, and Ellen, stood amidst the dissipating crowd, gazing at the horizon. There was an unspoken promise in their hearts, a determination in their eyes. This was just the beginning, the dawn of a journey that would take them to heights they had dared to dream of. Would they, too, conquer their dreams like Edward? Their hearts throbbed with the fervor of a million hopes, a silent pledge to the future. As the sun set, a new chapter awaited them, carrying the promise of tomorrow.

CHAPTER 5 SUMMARY:

Edward Dudley Brown and Ansel Williamson secure the consent of the mothers of the four boys they previously rescued - Oliver Lewis, Isaac Murphy, George Garrett, and Billy Walker - allowing them to learn about the horse racing industry. The chapter navigates their journey to New York for the prestigious Belmont Stakes, where Edward achieves a historic victory, and Ansel proposes to his girlfriend, Ellen. Set in the late 19th century, following the inspiring journey of Edward Dudley Brown and Ansel Williamson, two Black American men who rescue four boys and expose them to the world of horse racing. Amidst the backdrop of racial segregation and discrimination, the story reveals how their lives intertwine and transform, leading to a groundbreaking moment in the Belmont Stakes.

SECTION I

Chapter 6: The Birth of Churchill Downs:

The sun hung low in the afternoon sky over Louisville, Kentucky, the golden rays reflecting off the freshly painted sign that read, "Churchill Downs." Meriweather Lewis Clark Jr. stood with his hands on his hips, surveying the construction of the racetrack, his mind abuzz with anticipation and determination. This was his dream, a vision he had conceived during his inspiring trip to Liverpool, England. The prestige and grandeur of the Epsom Derby had captivated him, the spirit of horse racing had seized his heart, and he was determined to introduce it to the soil of his homeland.

The grounds sprawled over 80 acres of land that he had leased from his uncles, John, and Henry Churchill. The Louisville Jockey Club was his brainchild, his pride, and the year 1872 marked the birth of Churchill Downs. The development of the Jockey Club - destined to be known as Churchill Downs – began with Clark selling 320 memberships to raise the necessary funds. The funds he raised by selling membership subscriptions had given form to his vision: a grandstand, a clubhouse, Porter's Lodge, and six stables. The Courier Journal had announced its establishment in 1874, igniting the curiosity of Louisville's stylish residents.

Meanwhile, anticipation ran high in the stable quarters. Four young apprentices – Oliver, Isaac, George, and Billy – took in their surroundings, their hearts brimming with a blend of fear and excitement. The lads' eyes held a spark of determination, reflecting the promise of their future careers. Under the watchful eyes of Edward and Ansel, they honed their skills, each holding onto the dream of being a jockey. They had submitted their names as jockeys to race, a prospect that stirred both nervous anticipation and hope within them.

The year 1875 dawned bright, marking the year of the inaugural Kentucky Derby. The air buzzed with anticipation and the track was alive with the energetic movement of hooves, the excited chatter of the crowd, and the vibrant hues of the well-groomed Thoroughbreds. As the drum was tapped, the crowd erupted in a roar of excitement and anticipation, their cheers echoing around the track.

Fifteen starters lined up at the starting line. Among them were Oliver Lewis and William Walker, their gazes fixed ahead, their hearts pounding with adrenaline. Aristides, a beautiful blend of Arabian stallion and European mare, gleamed under the sunlight, his muscles twitching in anticipation. The signal was given, and Aristides broke ahead, the crowd's cheers loud in his ears.

The challenge was on, the race was in full swing. Aristides, under the skilled guidance of Lewis, maintained his lead despite McCreery's challenging strides. Owner McGrath, standing near the head of the stretch, urged his jockey forward, his eyes bright with a mixture of hope and anxiety. As the race continued, Aristides gradually widened his lead, his powerful strides eating up the distance.

Despite challenges from Volcano and Verdigris, Aristides was unstoppable. He crossed the finish line with a record time of two minutes and 37 seconds, leaving the crowd roaring in excitement. Oliver Lewis, only nineteen at the time, had guided Aristides to victory in front of an elated crowd of 10,000 fans.

When Ansel Williamson had brought Aristides to the post at Churchill, no one had expected the small horse to win. Aristides had been entered as a pacesetter for McGrath's other runner, Chesapeake. However, with an unexpected turn of events, Aristides emerged victorious, defying expectations, and making history.

The jubilation was palpable. Champagne was poured, and a wreath of roses was placed around the neck of the champion colt, Aristides. The crowd erupted in cheers, their applause and adulation echoing in the winner's circle. The inaugural Kentucky Derby had been a success, and Aristides, under the skilled guidance of Oliver Lewis, had become its first champion.

The following month, Ansel Williamson's trained horse, Calvin, secured first place at the Belmont Stakes, another prestigious horse racing event, with Oliver Lewis and Aristides securing a respectable second place. The triumphant outcome of these races marked the beginning of a new era in horse racing, and Churchill Downs was at its center.

The crowd began to disperse, their voices buzzing with excitement and chatter about the next race. Meriwether Lewis Clark Jr. stood by the sidelines, a proud smile on his face. His dream had come to fruition, and Churchill Downs was now the heart of Kentucky, pulsating with the thrill and energy of horse racing. His gaze fell on the jockeys, Oliver, Isaac, George, and Billy. They were the future of Churchill Downs, their careers just beginning.

CHAPTER 6 SUMMARY:

The chapter will feature the construction of Churchill Downs, the brainchild of Meriwether Lewis Clark Jr., who seeks to replicate the grandeur of England's horse racing culture in his native Louisville, Kentucky. With the foundation in place, the anticipation grows, particularly among four young apprentices – Oliver, Isaac, George, and Billy – dreaming of their debuts as jockeys. The climax of the chapter is the inaugural Kentucky Derby in 1875, where Aristides, a chestnut Thoroughbred, ridden by Oliver Lewis, seals an unexpected victory, marking the dawn of a new era in horse racing.

SECTION I

SUMMARY OF ALL CHAPTERS:

In this section we follow the journey of Edward Dudley Brown, Ansel Williamson, and their involvement in the world of horse racing. Chapter 1 introduces Edward and his mentor, Abe Hawkins, as they prepare for a race with the undefeated horse Sagittarius. Abe imparts wisdom about interconnectedness and presents Edward with a pendant symbolizing his role as a guardian protector. Chapter 2 focuses on the aftermath of the Civil War, where Edward Troye, a prominent painter, is commissioned to depict Edward and Abe's victory. The farm faces challenges during the war, including the kidnapping of prized horses in a guerrilla raid. Ansel and Edward devise a plan to save one horse, but others are lost. In Chapter 3, Abe achieves success as a jockey but faces revenge from his former slave owner, Farrar Kenner. Assassination attempts on Abe's life are ordered using poison, yet Abe survives and establishes the Black Jockey Trust. He entrusts Edward and Ansel with managing the trust and emphasizes the importance of passing on their skills and advocating for equality. Chapter 4 sees Edward and Ansel embarking on a journey after Abe's funeral. They encounter a Confederate attack and rescue four boys from a lynching attempt. In Chapter 5, the boys begin their apprenticeship with Edward and Ansel, participating in the Belmont Stakes. Edward's victory and Ansel's wedding become moments of celebration. Chapter 6 explores the establishment of Churchill Downs by Meriwether Lewis Clark Jr. The young apprentices continue to develop their skills, participating in the Kentucky Derby. Aristides, guided by Oliver, secures victory, and Ansel's horse, Calvin, wins first place at the Belmont Stakes. The story concludes with the future of Churchill Downs in the hands of the young jockeys, symbolizing the legacy of Abe Hawkins. Themes of resilience, unity, hope, and the transformative power of horse racing permeate the narrative set in the post-Civil War era.

Themes:

1. Freedom and Independence: The chapter explores the themes of freedom and independence, particularly in the context of Black Americans after the Emancipation Proclamation and the 13th Amendment. Edward and the other characters strive for freedom and pursue their dreams in the face of adversity and racial prejudices.

2. Destiny and Purpose: The concept of destiny and purpose is prevalent throughout the chapter. Edward discovers the meaning of his name, which connects him to his purpose as a jockey. The events and encounters in the chapter shape his journey and set him on a path towards leaving a lasting mark in the world of horse racing.

3. Unity and Community: The chapter highlights the importance of unity and community support. Edward, Ansel, and the other characters come together to protect each other and overcome challenges. The formation of the Black Jockey Trust and the support they provide to the young boys exemplify the power of unity within the Black American community.

4. Resilience and Overcoming Adversity: The characters in the chapter demonstrate resilience and the ability to overcome adversity. They face threats, attacks, and attempts on their lives, but they persevere and fight for their rights and dreams. Their determination and strength propel them forward in the face of challenges.

Settings:

1. Woodburn Farm: Woodburn Farm serves as a central setting in the chapter. It is where Edward, Ansel, and the other characters reside and work. It represents safety, stability, and community.

2. Ashland Plantation: Ashland Plantation is the plantation owned by Farrar Kenner, a former slave owner. It symbolizes the oppressive past and the remnants of the Confederate cause.

3. Jerome Park Racetrack: Jerome Park Racetrack in the Bronx, New York, is where the Belmont Stakes takes place. It represents the world of horse racing, competition, and achievement.

4. The Lewis House: The Lewis House, a neighboring house to Woodburn Farm, becomes a significant setting during the attack and abduction of the four boys. It symbolizes vulnerability, the threat of violence, and the strength of community bonds.

Symbols:

1. Asteroid: The horse Asteroid symbolizes victory, power, and

freedom. Edward races aboard Asteroid, and their success in the race represents Edward's journey and pursuit of freedom.

2. Chiron Pendant: The Chiron pendant, given to Edward by Abe, symbolizes guidance, protection, and the wounded healer. It serves as a reminder of Edward's connection to the stars, his destiny, and the support he receives from his mentors.

3. Woodburn Farm: Woodburn Farm symbolizes a safe haven and a community of support. It represents the possibility of a better future and the determination to overcome adversity.

Motifs:

1. Horse Racing: Horse racing serves as a recurring motif throughout the chapter. It represents competition, skill, and the pursuit of dreams. The races reflect the characters' aspirations and their journey in the world of horse racing.

2. Meteor Showers and Stars: Meteor showers and stars serve as motifs that symbolize destiny, guidance, and the connection between the celestial and earthly realms. They appear during significant moments, marking important events and illuminating the characters' paths.

Allegories:

1. Chiron: Chiron, the wounded healer, can be seen as an allegory for the characters' personal growth and the challenges they face. It represents the transformative power of overcoming adversity and the wisdom gained through difficult experiences.

2. The Undefeated Asteroid: The undefeated horse Asteroid can be seen as an allegory for Edward's resilience and determination. It represents his undefeated spirit and his ability to overcome obstacles.

Metaphors:

1. Stardust: The concept of stardust is used as a metaphor to emphasize

the interconnectedness of all humans and their connection to the universe. It symbolizes the potential for greatness and the presence of Edward's deceased parents in the stars.

2. Golden Archer: The Golden Archer is a metaphorical representation of Edward's journey and destiny. It symbolizes his pursuit of victory, freedom, and leaving a lasting mark in the world of horse racing.

Foreshadowing:

1. Confederate Guerrilla Raids: The mention of Confederate guerrilla raids and the threat they pose to the stable foreshadows future conflicts

and challenges that Edward and the other characters will face.

2. Farrar Kenner's Vendetta: The introduction of Farrar Kenner's vendetta against Abe Hawkins and his allies foreshadows the dangers and obstacles that Edward and his mentors will encounter. It creates a sense of impending conflict and sets the stage for future confrontations.

Literary Devices:

1. Flashbacks: Flashbacks are used to provide context and backstory, revealing the characters' past experiences and establishing their motivations and relationships. They add depth to the narrative and contribute to character development.

2. Imagery: Vivid imagery is employed to describe the races, settings, and pivotal moments in the chapter. It enhances the reader's sensory experience and creates a more immersive reading experience.

3. Symbolism: Symbolism is used throughout the chapter to imbue objects, events, and characters with deeper meaning. Symbols such as the Chiron pendant, the horse Asteroid, and the Woodburn Farm represent various themes and concepts in the narrative.

Willie Simms

PART 1

SECTION II: TIME PERIOD: 1876 - 1881

Chapter 1: The Shadow of Deception

1. Antagonist's Sinister Plot Unveiled

2. The Brilliant Mind of William Billy Walker

3. Tainted by Suspicion

4. The Rise of a Black Horse Trainer

Chapter 2: A Taste of Triumph and Tumult

1. The Prestige of the Kentucky Derby

2. A Threatening Ultimatum

3. The Fragile Bond of Trust

4. The Integrity of a Champion

5. The Frustration of a Sinister Mind

Chapter 3: Confrontations and Unexpected Encounters

1. The Echoes of Triumph Turn Dark

2. A Confrontation Brewing

3. The Night's Quiet Respite

4. A Meal Shared, Bonds Strengthened

5. The Eye of an Admirer

6. The Rise of a Brand Ambassador

Chapter 4: A Legacy of Resilience, Determination, and Dusty Triumphs

1. A Sinister Scheme Unfolds

2. Tragedy Strikes

3. Shattered Hearts, United Spirits

4. Embracing Joy Amidst Sorrows

5. A Final Farewell

Chapter 5: Poisoned Legacy

1. The Untimely Demise of Ansel Williamson

2. A Beacon of Hope

3. A Bittersweet Goodbye.

Weldy W. Walker

SECTION II

Chapter 1 - The Shadow of Deception

As the new year of 1876 dawned upon the racecourses of Kentucky, the anticipation and excitement in the horse racing world reached a fever pitch. The atmosphere was electric, with the racecourses teeming with energy and the air thick with the scent of ambition. The thunderous beat of hooves resonated through the hearts of spectators, setting the stage for an unforgettable year in the sport. However, amidst the exhilaration, there lurked a shadow of deception that threatened to cast a pall over the proceedings.

At the center of this unfolding drama was Farrar Kenner, an affluent owner of Ashland plantation, driven by a bitter resentment and deep-seated hatred toward the progress made by Black jockeys in the racing world. Blinded by his prejudice and desperate to halt their rise to glory, Kenner devised a nefarious plot that would send shockwaves through the entire racing community.

With calculated cunning, Kenner set his sights on exploiting the vulnerabilities and greed of white jockeys. He approached them discreetly, whispering enticing promises of untold wealth and unparalleled power into their eager ears. Manipulating their desperation and fears of being overshadowed, he skillfully persuaded them to betray their fellow riders—the Black jockeys who had already proven their remarkable worth and undeniable prowess on the tracks.

Kenner's devious plan aimed to undermine the progress of the Black jockeys, who had carved out their rightful place in the horse racing world through sheer skill, determination, and unwavering dedication. Their ascent had been marked by relentless discrimination and opposition, but their undeniable talent and indomitable spirit had propelled them to the forefront of the sport.

However, unbeknownst to Kenner, his scheme would not go unchallenged. Within the ranks of the Black jockeys existed a tight-knit community, bound together by a shared passion for their craft and a fierce determination to overcome prejudice. They formed a resilient bond that would prove unbreakable in the face of adversity.

As whispers of Kenner's treachery spread through the stables and across the racecourses, the Black jockeys refused to be intimidated. Instead, they united, their collective strength serving as a shield against the impending storm of betrayal. Drawing inspiration from the legacy of their predecessors—legendary riders who had defied the odds—they stood firm, ready to face the challenge head-on.

In the face of Kenner's orchestrated sabotage, the Black jockeys showcased an unyielding resolve, channeling their frustrations and anger into their training. Their determination burned brighter than ever, fueling their quest for victory, and proving, once again, that skill and talent transcended the boundaries of race and prejudice.

As the highly anticipated race day approached, tensions escalated, and the divide between the white and Black jockeys became more pronounced. It was a pivotal moment for the sport, a battle not only for the recognition and respect of the Black jockeys but also for the very soul of horse racing itself. The outcome would serve as a testament to the triumph of justice over deceit, talent over prejudice, and unity over division.

Amidst the tumultuous events engulfing the racing scene, William Billy Walker emerged as a remarkable figure, revered for his unparalleled knowledge of racehorse bloodlines. His expertise and understanding of the intricacies of equine genetics elevated him to the status of one of the nation's foremost experts in the field. Stable owners sought his counsel, valuing the depth of insight he brought to the table.

However, the treachery orchestrated by Farrar Kenner dealt a devastating blow to Walker's reputation. Billy was heartbroken by the events that unfolded due to Kenner's machinations, Billy found himself at the center of a storm of accusations hurled by his fellow white jockeys. Their claims of race throwing, and illicit dealings tarnished his once-pristine standing within the racing community, leaving him disillusioned and disheartened.

Nevertheless, amidst the challenges and controversies that unfolded, Walker's vast knowledge and expertise remained a beacon of unwavering brilliance. Breeders and owners, recognizing the immeasurable value he brought to the sport, continued to seek his guidance in their quest for success. Walker's enduring impact on the world of horse racing ensured that his name would forever be associated with excellence, integrity, and a profound understanding of the intricate nuances of racehorse bloodlines. His influence transcended the transient storms that sought to tarnish his legacy, leaving an indelible mark on the sport.

As the racing scene continued to evolve, another extraordinary individual took center stage. James Williams, a Black American horse trainer, had pursued his dreams of establishing a stable at the illustrious Kentucky Association Track in Lexington with unwavering determination. Dressed in his distinctive racing colors of blue with red diamonds, Williams became a symbol of hope and resilience in the face of adversity, a testament to the unyielding spirit of the Black community.

The race itself unfolded in a dazzling display of power, skill, and determination. As the field burst forth from the starting gate, the thunderous sound of hooves filled the air. Parole, guided by a skilled jockey, surged ahead, taking an early lead, and setting a blazing pace. Bullion, fueled by an unrelenting drive to assert dominance, pursued Parole with unwavering determination, engaging in a thrilling duel that captivated the crowd.

Yet, amidst the fierce competition, it was Vagrant, the dark horse of the race, that emerged as a force to be reckoned with. Executing a swift and strategic move on the outside, Vagrant gained momentum with each stride, gradually leaving its competitors behind. The gasps of astonishment from the spectators echoed throughout the racecourse as Vagrant's meteoric rise saw it surge to the front, surpassing Parole and establishing an impressive lead. The unexpected turn of events only heightened the excitement and anticipation in the air.

As the race reached its climax, Creedmore, a formidable contender, mounted a determined challenge to Vagrant's dominance. With impressive speed and agility, Creedmore closed the gap, narrowing the distance between itself and the frontrunner. The crowd held its breath, witnessing a breathtaking display of skill and determination. However, despite its valiant effort, Creedmore fell just two lengths short of securing victory at the finish line, conceding the crown to Vagrant.

Amidst the fervor and intensity of the race, tragedy struck Bullion. The treacherous clubhouse turn proved to be the site of an unfortunate collision between Bullion and another horse named Harry Hill. The impact was jarring, striking Bullion's left hind foot with a force that severed a tendon. Undeterred by the pain and adversity, Bullion displayed immense courage and determination, pushing forward to finish the race on three legs—an awe-inspiring testament to its indomitable spirit.

The events that unfolded on that fateful race day reverberated far beyond the confines of the track, leaving an indelible imprint on the fabric of horse racing history. With each stride and every strategic move, the significance of the race extended beyond the realm of competition. It became a profound symbol of the ongoing struggle for justice, equality, and the unyielding pursuit of excellence within the sport.

The race itself transcended its physical dimensions, assuming the mantle of a powerful metaphor for the broader narrative that unfolded on that day. It became a microcosm of the battle for recognition, respect, and the breaking down of systemic barriers that hindered the progress of underrepresented communities. The resounding echoes of that race served as a rallying cry, galvanizing the racing community to strive for a more inclusive future.

In the aftermath of the race, the victory of Vagrant, skillfully guided by jockey Robert Swim, took on profound symbolism. It stood as a testament to the indomitable spirit of perseverance, showcasing the triumph of talent, unwavering dedication, and the unrelenting pursuit of success. Vagrant's triumph exemplified the undeniable prowess of the Black community, which had historically encountered systemic barriers in a sport that required exceptional skill and resilience.

Yet, the significance of the race extended beyond the victor. The gallant efforts of Bullion, despite its debilitating injury, served as a poignant reminder of the unyielding spirit that permeated the racing world. Bullion's unwavering determination inspired all who witnessed its courageous performance, becoming a beacon of resilience and tenacity in the face of adversity.

The race of 1876 etched itself in the annals of horse racing history as an epochal moment. It shone as a guiding light, embodying the pursuit of justice, equality, and the triumph of skill over prejudice. The stories of William Billy Walker, James Williams, and the united front of the Black jockeys served as an everlasting source of inspiration for generations to come. Their unwavering resolve and undeniable talent left an indelible mark on the sport, transcending the boundaries of time and reminding the world that true champions know no bounds, whether they be racial, social, or any other form of limitation.

Summary Chapter 1 - The Shadow of Deception:

In 1876 Kentucky, Farrar Kenner plotted to undermine the rise of Black jockeys by manipulating white jockeys. United, the Black jockeys refuse to be intimidated, standing firm against Kenner's treachery. The race became a pivotal moment for justice and unity in horse racing.

SECTION II

Chapter 2 - A Taste of Triumph and Tumult

The atmosphere surrounding the Kentucky Derby of 1877 was charged with excitement, reaching a crescendo as the race day approached. The palpable anticipation filled the air as spectators and participants eagerly prepared for a day of thrilling competition and the chance to witness history in the making.

Among the esteemed guests in attendance was Dame Helena Modjeska, a renowned Polish actress celebrated for her captivating performances on stage. Her presence at the Derby added an extra touch of glamor and prestige to the already prestigious event. As she mingled with the crowd, the atmosphere buzzed with anticipation, racing enthusiasts and admirers eager to catch a glimpse of the esteemed actress. Dame Modjeska, known for her impeccable taste and refined demeanor, brought an air of elegance to the proceedings. She exuded poise and grace, captivating those around her with her charm and wit. Her passion for the arts extended beyond the stage, and she took a genuine interest in the world of horse racing, recognizing its cultural significance and the excitement it stirred among both high society and the common people.

As the Derby day unfolded, conversations about the upcoming race permeated the atmosphere. Dame Modjeska enthusiastically engaged in discussions with fellow attendees, sharing her insights and predictions. Her knowledge of the racing world was not mere curiosity but stemmed from her genuine passion for the sport. Immersing herself in the history and intricacies of horse racing, her opinions held great value among the gathering of racing enthusiasts and aficionados. The presence of dignitaries and notable personalities from various walks of life further heightened the anticipation and added a sense of occasion to the Kentucky Derby. Among the prominent figures in attendance were Kentucky Senator James Beck, Tennessee Secretary of State Charles Gibbs, and Massachusetts Attorney General Joseph Ewalt. Their presence emphasized the significance of the Derby as a cultural event that transcended regional boundaries, uniting people from diverse backgrounds in their shared passion for the sport.

As the race day progressed, the energy in the air reached a fever pitch. Spectators eagerly took their places, their hearts pounding with anticipation. The thundering sound of hooves resonated through the racecourse, blending with the excited murmurs of the crowd. Each stride of the horses brought them closer to glory, as they aimed to etch their names in the annals of horse racing history. The Kentucky Derby of 1877 would forever be remembered as a momentous occasion, not only for the enthralling competition it showcased but also for the convergence of distinguished guests and notable personalities. It epitomized the intersection of sport, culture, and society, leaving an enduring imprint on the collective memory of those fortunate enough to witness it.

As the sun set on that eventful day and the cheers subsided, the echoes of the Derby lingered in the hearts and minds of the attendees. The glamor, excitement, and camaraderie that defined the occasion would forever be associated with the rich silk embroidered fabric of the Kentucky Derby and its lasting legacy as a premier event in the world of horse racing.

Meanwhile, Merriweather Lewis Clark Jr., the visionary behind the Kentucky Derby, saw this as an opportunity to make a lasting impact on history. Building on the success of previous races, Clark was determined to enhance the Derby experience and solidify its status as the pinnacle of horse racing. In a moment of inspiration, he decided to introduce a special ingredient to the traditional bourbon mix enjoyed by racegoers. Churchill Downs meticulously cultivated and tended to mint leaves that would add a refreshing twist to the drink, giving birth to the iconic Mint Julep. The addition of mint proved to be a stroke of genius, as its invigorating aroma and flavor complemented the excitement and warmth of the race day.

During the festivities leading up to the Derby, Dame Helena Modjeska found herself intrigued by the concoction that had become the talk of the town. Driven by curiosity, she ventured to the Mint Julep stand, where bartenders artfully crafted the signature drink. The smooth bourbon mixed with crushed ice and a hint of sweetness, topped with sprigs of fresh mint, created a delightful libation that perfectly captured the essence of the Derby. As Dame Modjeska took her first sip, her taste buds were tantalized by the refreshing combination, and she marveled at the ingenuity behind its creation.

However, before the 1877 Kentucky Derby, rumors of race tampering began to circulate, casting a shadow over the upcoming event. Word reached Meriwether Lewis Clark Jr., who remained unwavering in his commitment to preserving the integrity of the sport. Determined to protect the race's reputation, he took immediate action. Clark sought out William Billy Walker, a prominent Black American jockey, and confronted him directly. With a stern gaze and unyielding resolve, Clark issued a chilling warning, making it unequivocally clear that any breach of trust would be met with severe consequences. The weight of Clark's admonition hung heavily in the air, serving as a somber reminder of the stakes involved.

Billy Walker, burdened with the weight of responsibility, found himself at a crossroads. Fearful for his life and unsure of his next move, he turned to his trusted mentor, Edward Dudley Brown, for guidance and protection. Brown, a seasoned veteran of the racing world, had witnessed firsthand the challenges and prejudices faced by Black jockeys. He understood the risks and the gravity of the situation, yet he also recognized Walker's talent and potential for greatness. With unwavering resolve, Brown stood by Walker's side, offering wisdom and support during this trying time.

Together, they navigated the treacherous path ahead. Walker knew that Clark and the racing community would scrutinize his every action, searching for the slightest hint of deception. Memories of his traumatic childhood and the specter of racial violence loomed large in his mind, intensifying his fear and determination to prove his innocence. Brown provided a steady presence, reminding Walker of his innate talent and the unwavering support of their community. He instilled in Walker the belief that they would overcome the obstacles before them, emerging stronger and triumphant.

As the day of the Derby dawned, tensions ran high. The atmosphere at Churchill Downs crackled with a mix of excitement and apprehension. Spectators eagerly gathered, their eyes fixed on the racetrack, waiting for the exhilarating spectacle to unfold. Among them, Dame Helena Modjeska stood in awe of the vast crowds, immersing herself in the palpable energy and anticipation.

The thunderous roar of the crowd signaled the start of the race. horses and jockeys surged forward, their determination and competitive spirit on full display. Leonard broke ahead, setting a blistering pace as the crowd erupted with anticipation. in close pursuit were Baden-Baden, King william, and Mcwhirter, their hooves pounding the track in a harmonious rhythm. trailing behind was Vera Cruz, who had a disadvantageous start but remained resilient, determined to make up for lost ground.

As the race unfolded, Leonard maintained his lead, captivating onlookers with his sheer power and speed. However, Baden-Baden started to make a move on the turn, closing the gap between him and the frontrunner. With each stride, Baden-Baden gained momentum, gradually inching closer to leonard. tension mounted as they turned into the stretch, the crowd holding its collective breath.

In a breathtaking display of skill and determination, Baden-Baden overtook Leonard just before the final stretch, his jockey expertly guiding him to the front of the pack. The burst of speed and unwavering resolve left the crowd in awe of the duo's prowess. Meanwhile, King William, who had closely trailed the leaders, made a mild rush in an attempt to challenge the frontrunners. However, as the intensity of the race wore on, King William faded, unable to sustain his momentum.

Vera Cruz, despite the disadvantageous start, showcased incredible speed and determination as the race progressed. With every stride, the colt fought to make up for lost ground, demonstrating remarkable agility and speed. The fact that Vera Cruz secured fourth place against the odds spoke volumes about its exceptional ability. As the race drew to a close, the crowd erupted into thunderous applause, celebrating the achievements of the jockeys and their magnificent steeds. The sight of Baden-Baden crossing the finish line in triumph, Leonard gallantly securing second place, and the resilient Vera Cruz claiming fourth place filled the air with a sense of awe and admiration. The extraordinary display of speed, skill, and determination left an indelible mark on the hearts and minds of all who bore witness to this remarkable race. The winner received a purse of $3,300, while the second-place finisher received $200.

The Kentucky Derby of 1877 stands as a testament to the power of perseverance and the indomitable spirit of the jockeys and horses who graced the track. It was a defining moment in horse racing history, capturing the hearts and minds of the audience and leaving an indelible mark on the sport.

In the wake of William Billy Walker's glorious triumph, another exceptional jockey, Isaac Burns Murphy, emerged as a force to be reckoned with. Murphy, celebrated for his exceptional talent and unwavering integrity, became a legend in his own right. Despite malicious rumors of bribery and relentless attempts to tarnish his reputation, Murphy remained steadfast in his commitment to upholding the principles of fairness and sportsmanship. The 1879 Travers Stakes served as a defining moment in Murphy's career as he faced formidable opponents, including the accomplished Belmont Stakes winner, Spendthrift, and the highly regarded white jockey, E. Feakes. With nerves of steel and unwavering focus, Murphy took the reins of his mount, Falsetto, embarking on a journey that would etch his name in the annals of horse racing history.

As the race unfolded, the crowd erupted into thunderous cheers, their collective energy propelling Murphy and Falsetto forward. Every stride was a testament to their unwavering determination and unyielding spirit. With expert skill and a deep bond between horse and rider, Murphy expertly maneuvered Falsetto through the competition, surging past their rivals with a resounding display of sheer willpower. In a dramatic showcase of speed, agility, and masterful horsemanship, Murphy guided Falsetto across the finish line, sealing their victory. The triumph was met with an outpouring of admiration and awe from spectators who recognized the magnitude of Murphy's achievement. He had proven himself as one of the greatest jockeys of his time, not only through his remarkable talent but also through his unwavering commitment to the principles that defined the sport.

As the cheers subsided and the confederate forces seethed with frustration, it became evident that the victories of Walker and Murphy had ignited a fire within their adversaries. The confederates, unable to impede the rise of these extraordinary jockeys through deceit and treachery, now faced the challenge of confronting their own prejudices and biases.

Summary Chapter 2 - A Taste of Triumph and Tumult:

The 1877 Kentucky Derby attracted notable guests, including actress Dame Helena Modjeska. Merriweather Lewis Clark Jr. introduces the iconic Mint Julep. Rumors of race tampering prompt Clark to confront jockey William Billy Walker. The race unfolds with tension and excitement, and BADEN-BADEN emerges victorious. Walker and Isaac Burns Murphy become legendary figures, inspiring future generations in the face of adversity.

Chapter 3 - Confrontations and Unexpected Encounters

The aftermath of Isaac Murphy's victory in the 1879 Travers Stakes gave birth to both jubilation and unexpected encounters. Ansel Williamson, the esteemed trainer of Falsetto, and Isaac Murphy himself revealed their success, celebrating their momentous achievement. The triumph had solidified Murphy's status as a legendary jockey, garnering admiration and respect from both his peers and the racing community at large.

Their joy, however, was short-lived when an encounter with a rebel Confederate survivor took an unexpected turn. This survivor, whose identity remains shrouded in the annals of history, was filled with bitterness and resentment, harboring a deep-seated anger towards the rising prominence of Black jockeys. Having been involved in the earlier attack on Black jockeys, their paths crossed in a moment fraught with tension and simmering conflict.

Ansel Williamson, Isaac Murphy, and Edward Dudley Brown found themselves face to face with the antagonist Confederate, their eyes locked in a battle of wills. Tempers flared, threatening to escalate into a physical altercation that could have dire consequences for all involved. The Confederate, fueled by his misplaced anger, spewed venomous words, seeking to undermine the accomplishments of Murphy and Williamson.

Just as the confrontation reached its boiling point, local patrolling authorities, keenly aware of the escalating tensions, intervened. Their presence served as a stark reminder of the fragile peace that governed the land, forcing a momentary pause in the hostility. The Confederate, realizing the imminent danger of punishment, and the rival jockeys, still seething with anger, reluctantly retreated, their anger simmering beneath the surface.

As the dust settled, Edward Dudley Brown, a voice of reason and wisdom, stepped forward, calling an end to the night's events. His authoritative tone and measured words resonated through the tension-filled air, compelling the protagonists to disperse. Each of them carried with them the weight of the encounter, the implications resonating deep within their souls.

Seeking solace in the comfort of a local diner, Ansel Williamson and Isaac Murphy found themselves in the midst of adoring fans. Word of their triumph had spread like wildfire, drawing racing enthusiasts from near and far. The patrons, their eyes shimmering with admiration, lined up in an orderly fashion, eager to receive an autograph from the revered jockey.

As Murphy graciously signed autographs and engaged in brief exchanges with his supporters, their genuine enthusiasm uplifted his spirits. The joyous atmosphere served as a temporary respite from the conflicts that had surrounded them. The diner hummed with excitement as conversations buzzed about the thrilling race and the remarkable talent displayed by Murphy and Williamson.

The diner's owner, a jovial and astute observer of human nature, caught wind of the excitement permeating the room. Sensing an opportunity to add a touch of whimsy to the occasion, he decided to playfully contribute to the moment. With a mischievous smile, he suggested that the dish Isaac Murphy had been seen eating be forever named "The Isaac Murphy Dish" in his honor. The suggestion elicited laughter and cheers, momentarily lifting the weight of the conflicts that still lingered in the air.

In the midst of their time at the diner, an unexpected encounter awaited Isaac and Ansel. A notable fan, the owner of a nationally distributed brand, had been observing the scene with keen interest. Recognizing the significance of Murphy and Williamson in the racing world, he couldn't resist the opportunity to meet the celebrated jockey. With admiration gleaming in his eyes, he approached Isaac, expressing his deep appreciation for his talent and accomplishments.

The initial exchange was one of mutual admiration, with the owner expressing his genuine admiration for Isaac's incredible skill and unwavering determination. However, as the conversation progressed, it quickly shifted from pleasantries to a business proposition. The owner, an astute businessman, saw an opportunity to capitalize on Isaac's popularity and reach. He proposed a paid sponsorship deal that would prominently feature Isaac's name and image on their products, promising substantial compensation and increased visibility.

The proposition hung in the air, tempting Isaac Murphy with the promise of financial security and unprecedented recognition. He couldn't help but consider the potential benefits such a sponsorship deal could bring, both for himself and for the broader cause of advancing opportunities for Black jockeys in the racing world. Yet, as he looked into the earnest eyes of Ansel Williamson, his trusted trainer and mentor, he realized that there was more at stake than personal gain.

Isaac Murphy understood the significance of his position as a trailblazing Black jockey in a predominantly white industry. He recognized that every decision he made carried the weight of representation and had the potential to shape the future for generations to come. With humility and grace, he declined the lucrative offer, explaining that his focus remained on the sport itself, on honing his craft, and on continuing to inspire others through his unwavering dedication and integrity.

The owner of the brand, taken aback by Isaac's response, was filled with admiration for the jockey's principled stance. He commended Murphy for his commitment to the sport and his refusal to compromise his values for personal gain. In a moment of profound respect, he extended his support to Isaac, promising to promote his career and amplify his impact in other ways that honored his integrity. Their encounter ended on a cordial note, with mutual respect and understanding marking the foundation of their future interactions.

As news of Isaac Murphy's decision spread, it ignited a spark of inspiration within the hearts of countless individuals who recognized the importance of staying true to one's values and convictions. Murphy became a symbol of integrity and a role model for aspiring jockeys, regardless of their race or background. The ripple effect of his principled choice would extend far beyond the realm of horse racing, influencing countless others to prioritize integrity and honor in their own pursuits.

The encounter at the diner, once filled with laughter and lightheartedness, had transformed into a pivotal moment in Isaac Murphy's journey. It reinforced his commitment to the principles that had guided him throughout his career and solidified his place as a revered figure not only within the racing community but also in the larger context of societal progress.

As the chapter drew to a close, Isaac Murphy, Ansel Williamson, and Edward Dudley Brown, the pillars of resilience and wisdom, stood united in their pursuit of excellence. The unexpected encounters and confrontations they had faced had tested their resolve and strengthened their bond, solidifying their commitment to overcoming adversity and leaving a lasting impact on the world of horse racing.

Little did they know that the next chapter in their journey would present them with new challenges and unexpected alliances, propelling them further along the path of progress and transformation. The stage was set for the continuation of their remarkable story, one that would continue to captivate the hearts and minds of all who followed their extraordinary journey.

Summary Chapter 3 - Confrontations and Unexpected Encounters:

Isaac Murphy's victory in the 1879 Travers Stakes brings jubilation and unexpected encounters. He celebrates his success with trainer Ansel Williamson. However, a bitter Confederate survivor confronts them, leading to a tense confrontation that is diffused by authorities. Later, Murphy declines a lucrative sponsorship offer, choosing integrity over personal gain.

Alonzo F. Clayton

SECTION II

Chapter 4 - A Legacy of Resilience, Determination, and Dusty Triumphs

In the year 1880, the anticipation in the racing world was palpable, and the Black horse racing community held its breath, hoping for a triumph that would defy all odds. However, tragedy struck, leaving an indelible scar on the heart of this close-knit community. The Confederate, Farrar Kenner, fueled by his relentless desire to suppress progress and maintain the status quo, devised a sinister plan. He paid rival white jockeys to unleash a brutal assault on George Garret Lewis during a critical race.

The incident cast a long shadow of injustice and discrimination, and the dust of despair seemed to hang heavy in the air. The Black riders, who had fought tooth and nail for their rightful place in the sport, now faced a stark reminder of the challenges they had yet to conquer. But even in the face of such adversity, the spirit of the Black riders refused to be suffocated.

George Garret Lewis, battered and bruised, embodied an unparalleled resilience that resonated with the crowd. With grit and determination, he mounted his horse, his eyes set on victory. The atmosphere in the stadium was electric, as the spectators waited with bated breath, eager to witness history in the making. As the starting bell rang, the horses thundered down the racetrack, their hooves pounding against the hardened earth.

Despite the physical pain and emotional turmoil, Lewis and his noble steed seemed to defy gravity itself. They maneuvered through the chaotic dust cloud that obscured the vision of both competitors and spectators alike. The thick layer of dust settled on the racetrack that day, creating an eerie silence, as if the world had momentarily held its breath. It was the dustiest of all derbies, with swirling particles reaching depths of up to five inches. The symbol of those gritty particles became an embodiment of the immense obstacles and hardships that the Black jockeys had to overcome.

As the finish line neared, Lewis's determination burned like a beacon of hope. The crowd, their voices muted by the dusty haze, erupted into a chorus of deafening cheers as Lewis crossed the finish line in first place. It was a moment that transcended the realm of horse racing, a testament to the indomitable spirit of the Black riders who had defied the odds and triumphed against all odds.

In the aftermath of the race, the victory stood as a defiant response to the forces of oppression and discrimination. It ignited a spark within the hearts of the Black horse racing community, inspiring them to push boundaries, break barriers, and strive for equality. The dust that had once clouded their path now settled as a reminder of their resilience and determination.

From that day forward, the name George Garret Lewis became a symbol of triumph over adversity, a beacon of hope for generations of Black jockeys to come. The incident served as a catalyst for change, propelling the Black riders towards a future where talent and skill would prevail over prejudice and discrimination. And so, in the annals of horse racing history, the dustiest of all derbies would forever hold a special place—a testament to the strength of the human spirit and the enduring power of the Black riders' pursuit of justice and equality.

Fonso broke in front, his hooves pounding against the hardened earth and stirring up the dusty haze that enveloped the racetrack. With every stride, he surged forward with unwavering determination, his powerful presence commanding attention. Meanwhile, Kimball, Bancroft, and Boulevard, his fierce rivals, fought tooth and nail in a battle that seemed almost mythical, their silhouettes barely visible amidst the swirling dust. The race had become a spectacle of strength, resilience, and sheer willpower.

Unfortunately, Quito, once a hopeful contender, was left at the post, starting the race far behind his competitors. It seemed as though his chances were shattered, his dreams of victory blown away like the dust that hung heavy in the air. But against all odds, Quito refused to succumb to defeat. He rallied on the backstretch, summoning a reserve of energy that pushed him forward, determination etched in every stride. With unwavering grit, he clawed his way to claim the third position, defying the expectations set against him. Yet, the relentless dust had taken its toll, leaving QUITO without enough stamina for the final drive to the wire.

At the wire, with the dust cloud settling and the finish line in sight,

Fonso prevailed. His indomitable spirit mirrored the dust-covered track, his every movement a testament to his fierce determination. Crossing the finish line, a length ahead of Kimball, he secured victory in a display of pure athleticism and unyielding resolve. The thunderous applause of the crowd mingled with the gritty whispers of the dust, as Fonso etched his name in the annals of Derby history.

While Fonso reigned supreme, it was impossible to overlook the remarkable tenacity displayed by Bancroft. Though trailing behind, he refused to yield, pushing himself to the very limits of his abilities. Finishing three lengths back from the leaders, he left an undeniable impression on all who witnessed his relentless pursuit of victory. In the dusty aftermath of the race, Bancroft stood tall as a symbol of perseverance, his journey a testament to the resilience of the human spirit.

Among the triumphs and the dust, the racing world held its breath as a claim of foul was made by the rider of Kimbal against Fonso. The air grew thick with tension as stewards carefully considered the claim, their deliberation a matter of great importance. Ultimately, after much examination and analysis, the claim was not allowed. The decision affirmed Fonso's victory, firmly establishing him as the rightful champion of the dusty Derby. The resolution of the claim marked the conclusion of a heated dispute, ensuring that the honor and legacy earned by Fonso would forever remain untarnished.

As the dust began to settle, the weighty prize of $3,800 was awarded to Fonso, a deserving reward for his unwavering determination and the treacherous path he had traversed. In contrast, second place received a modest $200, a mere fraction of the winner's purse, but a testament to the hard-fought competition and the resilience of Kimball. Beyond the monetary rewards, the true significance of their achievements went far beyond the dusty track and the prize money. It lay in the impact they had made, the barriers they had shattered, and the spirit of unity and strength they had ignited within the Black horse racing community.

In the wake of this dusty triumph, the community drew strength from their collective resolve. The dust that had enveloped the Derby became a symbol, not of defeat or setback, but of their shared struggles and their unyielding spirit. They would not allow the swirling obstacles to obscure their path.

Instead, they used the dust as a constant reminder of their ability to rise above adversity, to prove their worth on the racetrack, and to push for a better, more inclusive future.

The victory of Fonso and the remarkable accomplishments of the Black riders reverberated throughout the racing world. Their triumphs in the face of adversity became a beacon of inspiration, captivating the hearts and minds of all who witnessed their indomitable spirit. The dusty Derby of 1880 served as a stark reminder that the legacy of the Black horse racing community was built on a foundation of resilience, determination, and the unwavering pursuit of excellence.

As the dust settled and the cheers faded, the Black riders, their families, and their supporters looked to the future with renewed determination. The legacy of George Garret Lewis, the triumphs of Fonso, and the resilience of the entire community provided a guiding light, igniting the flame of progress and inspiring future generations to follow in their footsteps. They knew that the road ahead would not be easy, that challenges and barriers would continue to arise, but they were fueled by the knowledge that their predecessors had triumphed against the odds.

In the years that followed, the dusty triumphs of the Black jockeys would continue to shape the landscape of horse racing. The victories and sacrifices of those who had come before would pave the way for a more inclusive and equitable sport. The dust of the 1880 Derby would forever be ingrained in the collective memory of the Black horse racing community, a reminder of their resilience, their strength, and the enduring legacy they had created.

And so, the dusty Derby of 1880 faded into history, leaving behind a trail of dust particles that danced in the sunlight, embodying the spirit of the Black riders and their determination to rise above the obstacles that sought to confine them. Their legacy would forever be intertwined with the sport they loved, leaving an indelible mark on the racetracks, in the hearts of all who cherished the dusty triumphs of the Black horse racing community, and inspiring future generations to carry the torch of progress.

SUMMARY Chapter 4 - A Legacy of Resilience, Determination, and Dusty Triumphs:

In 1880, the Black horse racing community faced tragedy and discrimination. Despite a brutal attack, George Garret Lewis perseveres and wins the race in a dust-covered Derby. The victory symbolizes the community's resilience and determination. Their legacy inspires future generations and paves the way for a more inclusive sport.

SECTION II

Chapter 5 - Poisoned Legacy

The year was 1881, a pivotal and fateful turning point in the annals of horse racing history. In this swirling vortex of time, hope and betrayal entwined, their delicate balance hanging precariously in the air. Within the tight-knit community of Black horse racing enthusiasts, an electric anticipation crackled like static, charging the atmosphere with an almost tangible energy. The dreams of these passionate individuals soared high, fueled by an unyielding determination to etch their names into the hallowed halls of sporting greatness. Yet, unbeknownst to them, a malevolent force lurked in the shadows, biding its time, ready to unleash a web of deceit that would shatter their aspirations and cast them into the depths of despair.

As June unfolded its languid days, the racing world braced itself for a cataclysmic blow, a tempest that would cast a dark, foreboding cloud over the sun-drenched tracks. Ansel Williamson, a revered figure whose wisdom and unwavering spirit had earned him immense respect, became the unsuspecting victim of Farrar Kenner's wicked machinations. Deep within the bowels of Farrar F. Kenner's own plantation, a venomous concoction was brewed—a sinister elixir crafted with insidious intent. Cunningly disguised, this poison manifested as symptoms mirroring those of tuberculosis and heart attacks, veiling its true, deadly nature beneath a cloak of deception.

The tragic demise of Ansel reverberated through the hearts and souls of all who knew him, leaving behind an irreplaceable void that seemed to echo with the loss of his profound guidance and unwavering support. The once vibrant racetracks, which had resounded with the echoes of Ansel's encouraging words, now stood empty, devoid of the man who had ignited a flame of hope within the community. The legacy he had painstakingly built and nurtured seemed to hang precariously in the balance, teetering on the precipice of oblivion.

Yet, within the depths of grief and despair, a glimmer of determination flickered like a lone candle flame in a darkened room. Ansel's untimely death had not extinguished the fire that burned within the hearts of his disciples. Instead, it stoked the embers of their resolve, fueling their unwavering determination to uncover the truth and seek justice for their fallen mentor. They were bound by an unbreakable vow to expose the malevolence that had robbed them of their guiding light. In doing so, they would not only reclaim Ansel's legacy but also mend the fractured faith of a community shattered by the sting of betrayal.

As the curtain fell on that fateful year, the seeds of promise and treachery continued to intertwine, knitting an intricate textile of destiny. The Black horse racing community, standing at the crossroads of their collective future, faced a path fraught with danger and uncertainty. Yet, their collective spirit burned brighter than ever, their unwavering resolve serving as a guiding star. With the memory of Ansel Williamson's indomitable spirit illuminating their way, they pledged to stop at nothing in their quest to unravel the web of deceit and reclaim their rightful place in the annals of horse racing history. Little did they know that their journey for justice would unleash a chain of events that would reverberate far beyond the confines of the racetrack, forever altering the lives of those involved and shaping the course of history itself.

Kenner's initial plan, hatched in the dark recesses of his malevolent mind, proved to be even more nefarious than anyone could have imagined. His sinister intent reached far beyond the boundaries of a single life; it aimed to poison the very soul of the Black horse racing community. Ansel Williamson, a beacon of wisdom and Edward Dudley Brown, a pillar of strength and mentor to many, were the chosen targets. Kenner calculated that the simultaneous loss of these two influential figures would deliver a crippling blow, striking at the very foundation of the community and reducing it to a crumbling ruin. Chaos and despair orchestrated in a sinister symphony were his ultimate aim. However, as it often happens in the intricate fabric of existence, fate intervened, spinning its unpredictable web and unraveling Kenner's wicked plot. In an unforeseen twist of events, Edward's life was spared, and yet, the racing world was left reeling from the void left by Ansel's absence—a void that robbed them of his boundless wisdom and steadfast guidance.

The news of Ansel Williamson's untimely demise rippled through the racetracks like a resounding thunderclap, echoing with grief and outrage in the hearts of all who had borne witness to his remarkable achievements and unwavering dedication. The legacy of Ansel, once a shining beacon treachery committed against him. It was a despicable stain upon the very fabric of his existence, a stain that threatened to eclipse the brilliance of his accomplishments. Yet, even within the darkest abyss, a flicker of light emerged—a faint glimmer that ignited a rallying cry for justice and unity among the fragmented remnants of a once-united community.

From the suffocating shroud of tragedy that engulfed the Black horse racing community, a new figure stepped forth onto the stage of horse racing history. Jimmy Winkfield, born in the same year that Ansel Williamson's life was cruelly snuffed out, carried within him the untapped potential to fulfill the unfulfilled dreams of his fallen predecessor. A quiet force, concealed beneath the veil of obscurity, he possessed an innate resilience and an unyielding spirit, destined to be forged in the crucible of adversity. Unbeknownst to the world, Jimmy would become the living embodiment of hope, a testament to the indomitable spirit that pulsed through the veins of the Black horse racing community, and a shining example of triumph against all odds.

Once more, the community stood united, their collective presence a poignant testament to their unwavering resolve. As they gathered, united in their grief, their hearts heavy with loss, they found solace in the strength of their shared purpose. The battles they had fought were far from over, for the poisoned legacy left behind by Farrar Kenner lingered as a somber reminder of the injustices they had endured. However, rather than succumbing to the weight of despair, their hearts blazed with an unquenchable fire—a fire that demanded justice, a fire that fueled their determination to transform Ansel Williamson's legacy from a mere memory into a living, breathing testament of resilience, strength, and unwavering spirit.

With every beat of their hearts, the Black horse racing community vowed to carry on the torch that Ansel Williamson had passed to them, preserving its sacred flame from the relentless winds of treachery. No longer content with the mere act of remembrance, they sought to breathe life into his legacy, molding it into a radiant beacon that would illuminate the path towards triumph and justice. The pursuit of victory and the fight for justice became their rallying cry, a harmonious chorus of voices rising above the smoldering ashes of despair, their collective determination binding them together in an unbreakable bond. Their spirits, ablaze with unwavering resolve, would rewrite not only the narrative of horse racing history but also the narrative of their own lives—a tale of triumphant resilience and the unwavering pursuit of justice.

As the years rolled on, Jimmy Winkfield matured into a man burdened with the weight of Ansel Williamson's untimely departure. The loss of his predecessor had carved deep grooves within his heart, etching a profound sense of responsibility onto his very being. Jimmy recognized that he carried within him a torch, a sacred flame that must not flicker and fade. With unwavering determination, he pledged to honor the legacy of Ansel, a legacy built on resilience and unyielding spirit. Each step he took on the hallowed racetracks carried the weight of a solemn promise— an unspoken oath to bring justice to a community that had been grievously wronged.

In the depths of Jimmy's soul, the fire of justice burned brighter with each passing day. It was a fire that refused to be extinguished, fueled by the injustices inflicted upon the Black horse racing community. The poisoned legacy left behind by Farrar Kenner served as a potent catalyst for change, a stark reminder of the battles yet to be fought. It became the rallying cry for a community that would no longer tolerate the veiled specter of discrimination and bias. They yearned for equality and fairness, not only within the confines of the racetrack but in every facet of their lives.

With a renewed sense of purpose, the Black horse racing community stood shoulder to shoulder, united by their shared vision and fueled by the indomitable spirit that flowed through their veins. They understood that the road ahead would be treacherous, fraught with formidable obstacles and resistance from those who clung stubbornly to the status quo. Yet, undeterred, they faced the challenges head-on, fortified by the unwavering resolve that burned within their souls. They were determined to rewrite the narrative of horse racing history, carving a new path where justice and integrity would be the guiding principles, where talent and passion would be the sole determinants of success, and where the color of one's skin would be rendered utterly irrelevant in the grand pursuit of greatness.

And so, the stage was set for an epic clash, a battle of epic proportions between the forces of stagnation and the relentless march of progress. The Black horse racing community, propelled by the unwavering spirit of Jimmy Winkfield, embarked on a tumultuous journey that would test their mettle and redefine the very essence of their existence. They understood that they were not merely rewriting the narrative of horse racing history but also weaving a new chapter of their own lives—a journey of triumph, resilience, and the unwavering pursuit of justice.

SUMMARY Chapter 5 - Poisoned Legacy:

In 1881, Farrar Kenner plotted a sinister act to undermine the Black horse racing community. Ansel Williamson falls victim to a deadly poison, leaving a void. Jimmy Winkfield emerges as a symbol of hope. The community rallies, vowing to honor Ansel's memory and fight for justice. Their pursuit of triumph and equality becomes a unifying force.

SECTION II

SUMMARY OF ALL THE CHAPTERS:

In 1876 Kentucky, Farrar Kenner plotted to undermine the rise of Black jockeys by manipulating white jockeys. United, the Black jockeys refuse to be intimidated, standing firm against Kenner's treachery. The race became a pivotal moment for justice and unity in horse racing. The 1877 Kentucky Derby attracted notable guests, including actress Dame Helena Modjeska. Merriweather Lewis Clark Jr. introduces the iconic Mint Julep. Rumors of race tampering prompt Clark to confront jockey William Billy Walker. The race unfolds with tension and excitement, and Baden-Baden emerges victorious. Walker and Isaac Burns Murphy become legendary figures, inspiring future generations in the face of adversity. Isaac Murphy's victory in the 1879 Travers Stakes brings jubilation and unexpected encounters. He celebrates his success with trainer Ansel Williamson. However, a bitter Confederate survivor confronts them, leading to a tense confrontation that is diffused by authorities. Later, Murphy declines a lucrative sponsorship offer, choosing integrity over personal gain. In 1880, the Black horse racing community faced tragedy and discrimination. Despite a brutal attack, George Garret Lewis perseveres and wins the race in a dust-covered Derby. The victory symbolizes the community's resilience and determination. Their legacy inspires future generations and paves the way for a more inclusive sport. In 1881, Farrar Kenner plotted a sinister act to undermine the Black horse racing community. Ansel Williamson falls victim to a deadly poison, leaving a void. Jimmy Winkfield emerges as a symbol of hope. The community rallies, vowing to honor Ansel's memory and fight for justice. Their pursuit of triumph and equality becomes a unifying force.

Themes:

1. Betrayal and Deception: The theme of betrayal and deception runs throughout the chapter, as the conniving antagonist resorts to sinister plots, bribes, and rumors to undermine the black jockeys' racing careers

and tarnish their reputations.

2. Resilience and Triumph: The chapter explores the theme of resilience and triumph in the face of adversity. Characters like William Billy Walker, Isaac Murphy, and Edward Dudley Brown overcome challenges, confront suspicions, and achieve remarkable victories, showcasing their resilience and determination.

3. Integrity and Honor: The theme of integrity and honor is depicted through the characters' refusal to compromise their principles. Isaac Murphy and Billy Walker reject bribes and maintain their integrity, even in the face of false accusations and attempts to tarnish their names.

4. Community and Unity: The strength of community and unity is emphasized throughout the chapter. The black horse racing community comes together to support and protect one another, especially in times of tragedy and confrontation. Their unity becomes a source of strength and resilience.

5. Legacy and Remembrance: The importance of preserving the legacy of influential figures like George G. Lewis and Ansel Williamson is a recurring theme, highlighting the impact they had on the black horse racing community.

Settings:

1. Kentucky Derby: The prestigious Kentucky Derby serves as a prominent setting in the chapter, symbolizing the pinnacle of horse racing and the stage for triumph and tumultuous events.

2. Kentucky Association Track: The Kentucky Association Track in Lexington, Kentucky, where Raleigh Colston Sr. establishes his stable, represents the world of horse racing and the rise of black horse trainers in the face of adversity.

3. Local Diner: The local diner becomes a gathering place for characters like Ansel Williamson and Isaac Murphy, where they find solace, support, and unexpected encounters. It symbolizes the community's resilience and their ability to find moments of respite from turmoil.

Symbols:

Mint Julep: The Mint Julep, created by Merriweather Lewis Clark Jr. during the Kentucky Derby, symbolizes tradition, prestige, and the blending of cultures. It becomes associated with Dame Helena Modjeska and represents the convergence of different worlds.

The Isaac Murphy Dish: The suggestion of naming a dish after Isaac

Murphy in the diner symbolizes his status as a celebrated jockey and a source of inspiration for others. It represents his influence and impact on the horse racing community.

The Kentucky Derby: The Kentucky Derby symbolizes prestige, achievement, and the pinnacle of success in horse racing.

Mint Julep: The Mint Julep represents tradition and celebration associated with the Kentucky Derby, serving as a symbol of the event's glamor and social gatherings.

Autographs: Autographs symbolize admiration, fame, and the public's desire to connect with their idols, reflecting the impact of celebrated jockeys like Isaac Murphy.

Sponsorship and Branding: Sponsorship and branding symbolize recognition, success, and the changing dynamics of commercialization within the horse racing industry.

Motifs:

1. Bribery and Corruption: The motif of bribery and corruption recurs throughout the chapter, highlighting the challenges faced by black jockeys in an environment rife with dishonesty and deceit.

2. Confrontations and Altercations: Confrontations and altercations serve as recurring motifs, reflecting the tensions and conflicts between rival jockeys, the antagonist, and the black horse racing community.

Allegories:

1. Poisoned Legacy: The poisoning of Ansel Williamson represents the antagonist's desire to poison the legacy of black horse racing. It symbolizes the threat faced by the community and their determination to preserve their heritage.

The Rise and Fall of Characters: The narrative follows the rise and fall of characters, such as William Billy Walker and Ansel Williamson, allegorically representing the challenges and triumphs faced by black jockeys during that time period.

Struggle against Prejudice: The struggles faced by black jockeys and their pursuit of success in the face of racial prejudice allegorically reflect the broader struggle for equality and recognition.

Metaphors:

Horse Racing as a Microcosm of Society: The sport of horse racing serves as a metaphor for broader societal issues, reflecting themes of corruption, racial tension, and the pursuit of success in the face of adversity.

Racing Careers as Journeys: The careers of the jockeys symbolize personal journeys, with victories, setbacks, and character development mirroring the challenges and growth experienced in life.

Metaphors:

1. Darkness and Light: The contrast between darkness and light metaphorically represents the tragedies and challenges faced by the black horse racing community, as well as the glimmers of hope and triumph that emerge in their darkest moments.

Foreshadowing:

1. Unresolved Vengeance: The antagonist's seething frustration and unresolved vengeance foreshadow future conflicts and threats to the black horse racing community. It hints at the looming danger that the characters will face in the future.

Literary Devices:

1. Irony: The use of irony is present in the chapter, particularly in the contrast between the black jockeys' achievements and the false accusations and rumors that attempt to tarnish their reputations.

2. Symbolic Names: The names of characters like William Billy Walker, Edward Dudley Brown, and Raleigh Colston Sr. carry symbolic significance, representing their identities, roles, and impact on the narrative.

3. Parallelism: The chapter establishes parallelism between the triumphs and challenges faced by different characters, highlighting their shared experiences and the interconnectedness of their stories.

4. Imagery: Vivid descriptions, such as the dustiness of the 1880 derby, the celebration with champagne, or the mournful funeral scenes, create imagery that enhances the readers' emotional connection to the story.

END OF **SECTION II**

PART 1

SECTION III: TIME PERIOD: 1882 – 1896

Chapter 1: Proposals and Boundless Dreams

    1. The Triumph of Babe Hurd

    2. A Proposal of Love

    3. The Wedding of Isaac Burns Murphy

    4. James "Soup" Perkins's Memorable Encounter

    5. The Birth of a Nickname

    6. Embracing Mentorship and Legacy

    7. Raleigh Colston's Triumph

Chapter 2: Uniting Talents and Confronting Racism and Making History

    1. A Gathering of Prominent Figures

    2. The Meeting of Horsemen

    3. Synergy and Shared Concerns

    4. Invitation to the MLB Game

    5. Moses Fleetwood Walker's Historic Debut

    6. Confronting Caricatures at the Baseball Game

    7. Confrontation and Consequences

    8. Isaac Murphy's Triumphant Year

Chapter 3: The Black Prince And the Black Demon with Erksine, I. Lewis, and Spider.

    1. Erskine Henderson's Victory

    2. Isaac Lewis's Noteworthy Performances

SECTION III

Chapter 1 - Proposals and Boundless Dreams:

In the year 1882, the Kentucky Derby, known as the "Run for the Roses," beckoned with its aura of excitement and grandeur. Among the fourteen jockeys and horses poised for the race were some notable names. Gibbs skillfully mounted on Harry Gilmore, Kelso atop Babcock, the talented black jockey Erksine Henderson guiding Pat Mallow, L. Jones astride Robert Bruce, and Jim McLaughlin controlling the spirited Runnymede. But it was the young and determined Babe Hurd, riding the majestic Apollo, who would etch his name in history.

As the starting bell rang, the thunderous sound of hooves filled the air. The crowd erupted in anticipation as the horses burst forth from the gate. Harry Gilmore, ridden by Gibbs, surged to the front of the pack, closely followed by Babcock, Pat Mallow, and Robert Bruce. The race was on, and the jockeys maneuvered their mounts with expert precision, vying for the coveted prize.

At the mile mark, Harry Gilmore still held the lead, with Runnymede making a strong move on the outside, surging into third place. The spectators held their breath, their eyes fixed on the unfolding drama. As the horses thundered into the stretch, it seemed that Runnymede, under the skilled guidance of Jim McLaughlin, was destined for victory. The crowd roared with anticipation; their excitement palpable.

But just as Runnymede looked poised to claim the glory, Apollo, ridden by Babe Hurd, unleashed a cyclonic burst of speed. A mere eighth of a mile from the finish line, the majestic colt surged forward, his powerful strides closing the gap with every stride. The crowd watched in awe as Apollo and Runnymede engaged in a fierce duel, their hooves pounding the dirt track. And in a breathtaking finale, Apollo managed to catch Runnymede just a few jumps from the wire, securing victory by a mere half-length.

The exhilaration that permeated the crowd was matched only by the elation that flooded Babe Hurd's heart. Guided by his trainer, Green B. Morris, Babe had defied the odds and emerged triumphant. The Kentucky Derby victory bestowed upon him a purse of $4,560, a testament to his skill and unwavering determination. The feat was made even more remarkable by the fact that Apollo had not raced as a two-year-old, defying the conventional wisdom of the sport.

Babe Hurd's record-breaking win would stand unrivaled for 136 years, until 2018, when another extraordinary horse named Justify, who had also skipped racing as a two-year-old, claimed victory in the Kentucky Derby. But on that fateful day in 1882, it was Babe Hurd and Apollo who wrote their names in the annals of racing history, leaving an indelible mark on the sport.

News of Babe Hurd's momentous win spread like wildfire, capturing the attention of racing enthusiasts and the wider public. The triumph of an Black American jockey in such a prestigious event resonated deeply, offering a glimmer of hope and inspiration for a community too often marginalized. It was within this backdrop that Isaac Burns Murphy, himself a talented jockey, realized the time had come to take a significant step in his own life.

In the midst of the euphoria surrounding the Kentucky Derby, Isaac's heart yearned for Lucy Carr Osborne, a woman who had captivated his soul. Brimming with love and anticipation, Isaac approached Lucy, his voice trembling with emotion as he poured out his heartfelt proposal. The air seemed to hold its breath as Lucy, overwhelmed with joy and affection, accepted Isaac's offer, sealing their destinies together.

On a crisp winter day, January 24th, 1883, the sacred union of Sir Isaac Burns Murphy and Lucy Carr Osborne was solemnized at the esteemed St. John's African Methodist Church in Frankfort. The wedding ceremony became a grand affair, attended by a host of friends, family, and esteemed guests. Beyond the realm of love and matrimony, this union held profound significance for the world of horse racing.

On that memorable day, January 24th, 1883, Sir Isaac Burns Murphy and Lucy Carr Osborne embarked on a new chapter of their lives. As the esteemed St. John's African Methodist Church in Frankfort became adorned with an air of anticipation, Lucy, the radiant bride, took her place as the hostess of a celebration befitting their love. She appeared resplendent, draped in a flowing white silk gown adorned with delicate pearls and intricate white lace. The flicker of diamonds and the glint of gold ornaments added a touch of regality to her ensemble, an embodiment of grace and elegance.

Meanwhile, Murphy's stately residence on East Third Street transformed into a spectacle of merriment, with vibrant lights and decorations adorning the grand mansion. Every detail was meticulously arranged to create an atmosphere of joy and celebration, an ode to the momentous occasion that was about to unfold. Their abode stood as a testament to their achievements and the love that had blossomed between them.

Their union, far more than a mere union of two souls, held profound significance for the world of horse racing. The reverberations of their matrimony echoed far beyond the confines of the ceremony. The New York Times, a bastion of national news, captured the essence of their union in a report published on June 13th, 1887. The prestigious publication heralded Isaac Murphy's triumph in acquiring a splendid suburban residence in the eastern part of the city, a remarkable feat that further solidified his stature as a legendary jockey. The acquisition of this magnificent home, which bore witness to the unfolding races on the Kentucky Association track on Seventh Street from its observatory, marked another milestone in his illustrious career.

But it was not only their opulent lifestyle that left an indelible mark on history. Isaac and Lucy were prominent members of the Baptist Church, their devotion to faith weaving into the fabric of their lives. Their home, gaily lighted and adorned for their sacred union, became a testament to their unwavering commitment to each other and their shared values.

During the splendor and jubilation of their wedding, a figure stood out among the esteemed guests. James Perkins, an ambitious young man with dreams of emulating Isaac's achievements, found himself invited to witness the joyous occasion. As James indulged in a bowl of soup, Isaac's inquisitive nature led him to inquire about this peculiar choice of sustenance. James, with a warm smile, shared the meticulous regimen he followed to maintain his weight for upcoming races. Isaac's laughter reverberated through the air, cementing a bond of camaraderie between them. From that moment forward, James would forever be known as "Soup," a nickname that encapsulated their growing friendship and the shared journey they were to undertake.

Recognizing the potential within James and understanding his responsibility to nurture aspiring talent, Isaac took the young jockey under his wing. Drawing upon the invaluable lessons passed down to him by his esteemed mentors, Edward Brown and Ansel, Isaac generously imparted his wealth of knowledge and wisdom to James. Their bond deepened as Isaac selflessly shared the secrets of his success, fueling James' determination to forge his own path in the world of horse racing.

While Isaac and James Soup Perkins embarked on their journey of mentorship and friendship, the world of horse racing witnessed yet another extraordinary feat. Raleigh Colston Sr., a renowned Black horse trainer and owner of a prestigious racing stable, forever etched his name in history by triumphing in the highly acclaimed 1883 Kentucky Derby atop the majestic Leonatus. This victory served as a profound inspiration to Isaac, James, and their fellow Black horsemen, reaffirming their unwavering belief in the limitless potential that resided within their community. As the sun cast its golden rays upon Churchill Downs on May 23, 1883, anticipation reached its peak, setting the stage for a momentous race where the finest steeds and jockeys would battle for supremacy.

Atop the magnificent Leonatus, Raleigh embodied the hopes and dreams of an entire community. The track basked in a golden glow, casting long shadows that danced in rhythm with the pounding hearts of the spectators. The starting bell rang out, igniting a symphony of passion and anticipation as the thunderous cacophony of hooves reverberated through the air. Leonatus, guided by the skilled jockey William Donohue, surged forward, gaining an impressive lead after the first quarter and extending it with each stride. His sheer dominance promised victory.

Raleigh, a man whose unwavering belief in the potential of his community propelled him to this moment, felt his heart surge with pride. As Leonatus crossed the finish line, euphoria swept through the crowd like a tidal wave, recognizing the triumph of determination and resilience. Raleigh's vision had become a reality, his name forever etched among racing greats. The triumphant team revealed in the glory of their shared achievement, their unity and unwavering commitment to excellence propelling them to unprecedented heights.

The well-deserved purse awaited them, a tangible testament to their skill and dedication. But Raleigh's mind turned to the future, to the countless possibilities that lay ahead. He understood that this victory was not just his own but a beacon of hope for the entire community. Isaac, James, and others aspired to greatness, and this triumph reaffirmed their belief in the limitless potential within them. The world would now witness what they were truly capable of achieving.

The race itself was a journey of courage and resilience. Chatter and

Lord Raglan emerged as the closest pursuers, but fate intervened with an unfortunate swerve and a stroke of misfortune, clearing the path for Leonatus to surge toward glory. In a breathtaking display of strength, stamina, and unwavering determination, he crossed the finish line, his hooves thundering in triumphant harmony. The crowd erupted in exultation, their cheers echoing throughout the hallowed grounds, while Raleigh Colston Sr., the visionary behind Leonatus' success, had not only claimed victory but also kindled a flame of inspiration within the hearts of Isaac, James, and their fellow Black horsemen.

The entire team, led by William Donohue and guided by Raleigh Colston Sr., basked in the adulation of the crowd. The purse of $3,760 stood as a tangible reward for their skill, perseverance, and unyielding commitment to excellence. The celebration unfolded, epitomizing the true essence of the Kentucky Derby—a celebration of talent, unity, and the triumph of the human spirit.

During the jubilation, recognition extended to the rest of the field. Drake Carter, guided by jockey John Spellman, secured second place, their unwavering dedication and pursuit of excellence evident. The partnership between Drake Carter and esteemed stable owners, Green B. Morris, and James D. Patton, bore fruit, rewarding them with a prize of $200 for their remarkable performance.

The race had been a fabric woven with skill, determination, and unyielding spirit. Lord Raglan, ridden by the talented George Quantrell, captured third place despite a momentary swerve. Ascender, under jockey John Stoval's guidance, held firm in fourth place, showcasing unwavering resolve. Standiford Kellar, skillfully handled by Harry Blaylock, exhibited mettle, and claimed fifth place. Pike's Pride, carrying the hopes and dreams of its connections, including jockey George Evans, secured sixth place, leaving an indelible mark on the hearts of all who witnessed its determination. And even Chatter, hindered by unfortunate circumstances, exemplified the spirit of resilience by crossing the finish line in seventh place with Jockey H. Henderson in the saddle.

As the cheers subsided and the dust settled, the significance of Raleigh Colston Sr.'s victory and the collective achievements of the jockeys and horses became clear. They defied expectations, shattered barriers, and became a source of inspiration for generations. Their triumphs resonated deeply, extending far beyond the racetrack. A new era of empowerment, inclusion, and limitless possibilities dawned within the realm of horse racing. The echoes of their victories reverberated through the corridors of history, serving as a reminder that determination can overcome any obstacle and that excellence knows no bounds.

As the sun set on Churchill Downs, casting long shadows upon the track, a bright flame of hope burned in the hearts of all who had witnessed this monumental chapter in the annals of horse racing. Raleigh Colston Sr., a name synonymous with courage and inspiration, had forged a path of inclusion and empowerment. The echoes of their triumphs would forever resound through the corridors of history, reminding generations to come that the human spirit knows no bounds.

Isaac Burns Murphy, Lucy Carr Osborne, James "Soup" Perkins, and Raleigh Colston became revered figures, symbols of resilience, talent, and unyielding spirit within the world of horse racing. Their stories intertwined, each contributing to the fabric of progress and change. As the years unfolded, their collective achievements would act as a catalyst, shattering the barriers of prejudice and paving the way for greater diversity and inclusivity in the realm of racing. Their legacy, forever etched in the annals of history, would stand as a testament to the triumph of the human spirit and the indomitable power of hope.

In the midst of this vibrant journey, where dreams collided with destiny, Isaac Burns Murphy felt a fire ignite within him. He knew that the path ahead would be arduous, filled with challenges waiting to be conquered. Yet, undeterred, he placed an advertisement in the local newspaper, a proclamation of his unparalleled skills and an open invitation to those who recognized his worth. The world held its breath, eagerly anticipating the unveiling of his story, ready to bear witness to the heights he would reach and the obstacles he would conquer.

SECTION III

Chapter 2 - Uniting Talents and Confronting Racism and Making History

Under the gentle caress of golden light from the ornate chandeliers, the spacious Madison Street venue pulsed with an energy as profound as it was refined. A grand gala was underway, meticulously orchestrated by its influential hosts, Mr. and Mrs. Sadonia Wrightson, prominent members of the Black American community. The room was filled with an assemblage of the Black American elite, their laughter and chatter a vibrant symphony against the backdrop of clinking crystal glasses and the delicate notes of a distant piano. Among this distinguished gathering stood the extraordinary Isaac Murphy, revered for his unsurpassed skill as a jockey, accompanied by his wife, Lucy Carr Osborne, her radiant smile capturing the spirit of the evening. The Perry's, Abe and Margaret, who were integral figures in the Black American equestrian community, shared their joy and pride at securing Murphy's presence at this illustrious event.

Before the season's meets in 1886, many Black American horsemen knew each other and socialized together. The Perry's, Isaac Murphy, and Lucy attended events in Louisville, and on one trip, they were honored guests of Mr. and Mrs. Sadonia Wrightson, prominent members of the Louisville Black American community. The Wrightson's reputation and influence made their presence at the gala all the more significant.

As Isaac Murphy and Lucy Carr Osborne stepped into the magnificent venue on Madison Street, they were overwhelmed by the grandeur of the gala event hosted by Mr. and Mrs. Wrightson. It was an esteemed gathering, bringing together influential Black American horse owners, trainers, and notable individuals such as Sergeant Dudley Allen. Allen, a man of many accomplishments, had served as a cavalry soldier in the United States Colored Troops during the Civil War. His service as a quartermaster sergeant highlighted his responsibility and expertise in managing company wagons, property, and caring for horses and mules. After the war, Allen pursued a career in horse racing, becoming a stable owner, horse owner, trainer, and an integral part of the Black American equestrian community.

Among the notable highlights of Allen's career was his partnership with Kinzea Stone, forming Jacobin Stable. The name Jacobin, possibly a nod to the Haitian revolutionary leader, Toussaint L'Ouverture, symbolized pride and possibility for the formerly enslaved Allen. Under the Jacobin name, Allen employed notable Black American jockeys, including the legendary Isaac Murphy and Oliver Lewis, to ride in his colors of wine, yellow, and blue. Together, they achieved remarkable success, winning races with some of America's top horses and solidifying their names in Racing's Hall of Fame.

The gala event buzzed with excitement and conversations about future victories, strategic alliances, and the shared passion for equestrian pursuits. Renowned horse owners and trainers like Dudley Allen and Abraham Perry offered their insights into the world of horse racing, drawing upon their wealth of experience and knowledge. Isaac Murphy, standing among these titans, felt privileged to be part of this splendid celebration meticulously organized to honor the achievements of the Black American elite.

The guest list read like a constellation of achievement, each name representing a beacon of success in their respective fields. The iconic Madame CJ Walker graced the gathering, her groundbreaking entrepreneurship and indomitable spirit making her an emblem of Black American accomplishment. WEB DuBois, the esteemed scholar and unwavering advocate for civil rights, lent his presence, infusing the gathering with intellectual prowess and social insight. And Congressman Robert Smalls, a hero of the Union army, commanded attention, his courage and resilience serving as a beacon of hope. The attendance of these illustrious individuals underscored the burgeoning influence and affluence of the Black American community, signaling a profound reshaping of the societal fabric.

Within the walls of this illustrious gathering, Isaac found himself immersed in captivating conversations with fellow Black American horse owners and trainers. Dudley Allen, an esteemed figure in the equestrian world, impressed Isaac with his passion and dedication. As they exchanged stories and insights, Isaac admired Allen's remarkable achievements, including the historic 1891 Kentucky Derby win with Kingman, owned and trained by Allen himself. The duo of Allen and

Murphy became the last Black American owner-jockey pair to win the Derby in its history, leaving an indelible mark on the sport.

Engrossed in thought-provoking exchanges, the topic of racing for one's own people emerged, offering a fresh perspective and newfound possibilities. The attendees passionately argued that by championing the cause of his own community, Isaac could attain even greater heights of success, solidifying his position as an enduring source of inspiration and a trailblazer for generations to come. These conversations planted seeds of contemplation within Isaac's mind, igniting an unwavering fire of determination to explore new avenues and make an indelible impact within his own community.

Amidst the buzzing conversations and connections, Mr. Wrightson approached Isaac with an intriguing invitation. He spoke of the masonic lodge temple—a place where like-minded individuals gathered to cultivate wisdom, unity, and strength. Isaac's curiosity was piqued, sensing that this opportunity held the potential to transform him personally and spiritually. It was a chance to embark on a transformative journey toward becoming a master mason, guided by the teachings and rituals within the temple.

The gathering represented not only a confluence of horsemen but also a convergence of diverse fields. In the sea of faces, two brothers stood out. Moses Fleetwood Walker and his brother Weldy Walker—the pioneering Black American baseball professionals—mingled among the horsemen, entrepreneurs, and intellectuals. Their presence added another layer to the shared narratives, giving rise to discussions about the rising tide of racial caricatures targeting black athletes.

The morning sunbathed the city of Toledo in a warm golden glow, its rays casting a hopeful light on the streets that were stirring with anticipation. On May 1st, 1884, was a day that held the promise of something extraordinary - a turning point that would be etched in the annals of history. As the sun climbed higher in the sky, its radiance danced upon the dew-kissed grass of the baseball field, where the Blue Stockings diligently prepared for their upcoming game.

Yet, the energy coursing through the city was far from ordinary. It crackled with an electric anticipation, whispering of impending history and a moment that would transcend the confines of sport. The cause of this fervor was none other than Moses Fleetwood Walker, a celebrated baseball player whose presence had added a new layer of distinction to the occasion. Alongside him stood his brother, Weldy Walker, another esteemed player whose prowess on the diamond was widely acknowledged.

Their arrival at the event bridged the gap between the worlds of horse racing and baseball, intertwining the struggles and triumphs of these two sporting realms. It became evident that their collective experiences, whether on the racetrack or the baseball diamond, were deeply interconnected, representing a shared journey of resilience and determination in the face of adversity.

The spirit of unity among Black American athletes permeated the gathering, filling the air with an unwavering sense of solidarity and camaraderie. In a poignant display of their bond, the Walker brothers extended an invitation to all those in attendance, inviting them to witness a Major League Baseball game in Louisville—a city with its own rich history as a battleground for equality. Their gesture was a symbol of togetherness, a reminder of the shared experiences and challenges faced by Black American athletes across various sports.

As the news of the invitation spread, a wave of joy and gratitude swept through the gathering. The attendees rejoiced in this gesture of inclusivity, recognizing the power that resided in coming together and standing united against the injustices that sought to divide them. The Walker brothers' invitation served as a rallying point, a reminder of the strength that could be found in collective action. But as conversations expanded, the pervasive issue of racist caricatures targeting athletes of color emerged as a focal point. The offensive depictions struck at the core of their identity and dignity, casting a shadow over the progress that had been made. However, the attendees were not deterred. Instead, the offensive depictions ignited a fire within each participant—a fire fueled by a fierce determination to challenge and dismantle the systemic racism that perpetuated such harmful stereotypes.

As the gala event drew to a close, Isaac and Lucy stood side by side, their hearts brimming with a profound sense of unity and defiance. They understood that their collective efforts, alongside the Walker brothers and their peers, had laid the groundwork for a brighter future—a future where equality and justice would prevail. The echoes of their actions would reverberate through time, inspiring countless others to join the fight for a more inclusive and equitable society.

And so, as the morning sunbathed the streets of Louisville in its golden hues, another chapter in history began to unfold. The spirit of unity and resilience that had filled the air at the gala event would propel them forward, guiding their steps on the path toward progress. With hearts aflame, they set their sights on a future where the barriers that sought to divide them would crumble, replaced by a society built on the principles of equality, justice, and unwavering solidarity.

The rhythm was electric, syncopated with the restless heartbeat of one man — Moses Fleetwood Walker.

On May 1, 1884, Moses Fleetwood Walker and his team, the Toledo Blue Stockings, made their major-league debut in Louisville. Walker's reputation as an exceptional catcher had already reached Louisville, as he had previously visited the city in August 1881 as a member of the Cleveland White Sewing Machine club. However, during that visit, Walker did not get the opportunity to play against the Eclipse team due to objections from some of the Eclipse players and management. The Louisville Courier-Journal speculated that the objections were either rooted in prejudice or fear of facing Walker, who had earned a reputation as the best amateur catcher in the Union. When Walker returned to Louisville for his major-league debut, prejudice still lingered in the city, and the national press paid significant attention to his presence.

Despite facing numerous distractions, including being denied breakfast at the St. Cloud Hotel due to his race, Walker took the field as scheduled before a crowd of 3,500 at Eclipse Park. The Courier-Journal provided a detailed account of the game, describing it as a remarkably fine contest with excellent pitching and fielding. While the newspaper did mention Walker's race in its commentary, it reported no racial incidents during the game. The final score of 5-1 favored Louisville, and it was a result of strong pitching and fielding from both teams. The starting pitchers, Toledo's Tony Mullane and Louisville's Guy Hecker, were among the top pitchers of the 19th century, combining for a total of 88 wins in the 1884 season (52 for Hecker). Except for Walker, both teams played errorless ball, showcasing their defensive prowess. However, Walker faced difficulties on defense, particularly with his throwing, resulting in four or possibly five errors and a passed ball. Sporting Life reported that Toledo suffered greatly from Walker's errors, referring to them as three terrible throws.

The local press criticized Walker's performance, attributing the team's struggles to his errors. They detailed each mistake he made, including an inaccurate throw that allowed a base runner to advance and a failure to hold onto the ball in another instance. In the sixth inning, Walker dropped a caught ball and made an inaccurate throw to first base, leading to a score for the opposing team. The Toledo Evening Bee provided a less extensive account of the game under the headline "Walker Did It," mentioning that the friends of the Toledo team closely followed the game's progress in pool rooms. The article acknowledged that the fielding of both teams was generally excellent, except for Walker, who committed multiple errors and had inaccurate throws to the bases. Furthermore, Walker's participation in the game drew the ire of Cap Anson, a prominent player of that era, who initially refused to take the field if Walker was in the starting lineup. Eventually, Anson relented, but this marked the beginning of Walker's struggles as he sought to fulfill his dream of playing in the major leagues.

Despite the obstacles and hindrances, Walker would soon receive a fortunate opportunity that would alter the course of Major League Baseball history. In the 1884 season, the American Association, a newly formed professional baseball league aiming to compete with the National League, added the Toledo Blue Stockings to its list of participating franchises. Consequently, on the opening day of the 1884 season, the starting catcher for the Toledo Blue Stockings, Moses Fleetwood Walker, became the first African-American player to participate in a professional baseball game. On May 1, 1884, against the Louisville Eclipse, Walker took the field and officially broke the color barrier in Major League Baseball. Ironically, Walker had the worst game of his career on this momentous day, going hitless in four at-bats and committing four errors on defense.

During the excitement and anticipation offensive caricatures mocking Black American jockeys, trainers, and baseball players were being sold and new ones were being created. Weldy Walker, seated nearby, could not let such disrespect go unchallenged. Fueled by an unyielding determination, he confronted the publishers responsible for these disgraceful depictions, representing not only himself but the entire Black American community. Weldy's voice echoed through the room, expressing their collective displeasure and vowing to take legal action against the publishers for defamation and damaging portrayals.

The threat of a defamation lawsuit hung heavily in the air, holding the publishers accountable for their actions. The confrontation became a resolute stand against racial discrimination, showcasing the community's refusal to tolerate degrading treatment. The publishers, faced with the consequences of their actions, recoiled in shame. Their offensive content was swiftly seized and destroyed before their eyes, leaving them exposed and publicly humiliated. Escorted out of the ballpark by security, they faced the wrath of the fans, who expressed their anger and disdain by hurling objects at them. The incident became a catalyst for change, igniting a significant backlash against the publishing house. The community's solidarity and unwavering determination to combat racial discrimination became evident as people rallied behind the cause.

And as the dust settled, Moses Fleetwood Walker, still basking in the glow of his historic debut, stood tall. He had endured prejudice, faced adversity, and made mistakes on the field, but his unwavering spirit had prevailed. The breakthrough he had achieved went beyond a single game or a single season. It signified the breaking of a barrier that had held back generations of talented Black American players.

On that May day in 1884, Walker had become a symbol of hope, a symbol of the relentless pursuit of equality. His name would forever be etched in the annals of Major League Baseball, a testament to the power of resilience and the capacity to challenge and overcome injustice. The path forward was still filled with challenges, but Moses Fleetwood Walker had set a new course, inspiring future generations to continue the fight for equality on and off the baseball diamond.

In the midst of these events, Isaac Murphy continued to etch his name into the annals of horse racing history. The year 1884 proved to be a triumphant one for him—a year that solidified his status as one of the sport's greatest icons. The crowd at Churchill Downs held their breath as the horses thundered down the track, their hooves pounding the earth in a symphony of power and speed. The Kentucky Derby was underway, and the anticipation in the air was palpable. Among the contenders was a spirited colt named Buchanan, ridden by the legendary jockey Isaac Murphy.

As the flag dropped, Bob Miles shot forward, taking an early lead with a burst of speed that left the other horses trailing behind. Powhattan III, Audrain, and Admiral followed closely, their determination evident in every stride. Buchanan, however, had a rough start, fractious at the post and slow out of the gate. But Isaac Murphy, with his unparalleled skill and intimate knowledge of the horse, remained composed. Knowing that every second counted, Murphy expertly guided Buchanan along the rail, carefully maneuvering through the field. He saved ground for three-quarters of a mile, biding his time and waiting for the perfect moment to make their move. With a subtle shift, Murphy urged Buchanan to the outside, unleashing the colt's raw power.

In a breathtaking display of speed and agility, Buchanan surged ahead, leaving his competitors in his wake. He quickly established a two-length lead, his muscular frame stretching with each stride. The crowd erupted in cheers, their collective excitement building as the finish line drew near.

But the race was far from over. Loftin, a tenacious challenger, closed the gap, narrowing Buchanan's lead. Murphy, ever the master tactician, maintained a steady hand, easing Buchanan through the final eighth of a mile. The colt responded with a burst of renewed energy, refusing to yield to the mounting pressure.

Meanwhile, Admiral, once a frontrunner, faded into the background, unable to sustain his early pace. The mile pole, which had seen him in front, now seemed a distant memory. Scratched from contention, Admiral became a mere spectator to the unfolding drama. As the crowd roared, Buchanan, ridden by the incomparable Isaac Murphy, crossed the finish line in a blaze of glory. The victory was resounding, a testament to the horse's exceptional talent and Murphy's unwavering skill. Their names would forever be etched in the annals of the Kentucky Derby, their triumph a symbol of perseverance and excellence.

Amidst the jubilation, the spectators marveled at the remarkable partnership between horse and jockey. Buchanan, owned by the Jacobin Stable and trained by William Bird, had defied the odds, overcoming a challenging start to claim victory. And behind the scenes, Dudley Allen, the enigmatic figure behind Jacobin Stable, rejoiced in the triumph of his beloved colt. As an Black American owner and trainer, his success in the Kentucky Derby stood as a testament to his unwavering dedication and the collective achievements of the Black American horsemen of the time.

The crowd erupted in thunderous applause as Isaac Murphy guided Buchanan back to the winner's circle. The victory was not just theirs; it was a triumph for the entire Black American community—a shining beacon of hope and progress. The spirit of unity and resilience that permeated the occasion spoke volumes, reminding everyone present that barriers could be shattered, stereotypes defied, and dreams realized.

As the echoes of their victory reverberated through the grandstands, Isaac Murphy and Buchanan stood as a testament to the power of determination and the unwavering pursuit of greatness. Their names would forever be intertwined with the history of the Kentucky Derby, inspiring future generations to reach for the stars and believe in the extraordinary possibilities that lie within.

Jockey Sir Isaac Burns Murphy won riding Buchanan, trained by William Bird. Isaac Burns Murphy was the first jockey to win three Kentucky Derbys and was the only jockey to win the Kentucky Oaks, Kentucky Derby, and the Clark Handicap all in the same year. This amazing feat was accomplished in 1884.

With unwavering determination, Isaac guided the remarkable racehorse Buchanan to victory in the Kentucky Derby, securing his unprecedented third win in the prestigious race. The crowd erupted in jubilant celebration, recognizing Isaac's extraordinary talent and unwavering spirit. But Isaac's triumphs extended beyond the Kentucky Derby. He triumphed in the Kentucky Oaks and the Clark Handicap, further establishing himself as an iconic figure in the sport. With each victory, Isaac inspired a new generation of aspiring jockeys, leaving an indelible legacy of empowerment and progress.

The collective achievements of Isaac Murphy, Moses Fleetwood Walker, Weldy Walker, and their peers became a shining example of unity, strength of conviction, and the unwavering pursuit of equality. Their triumphs transcended horse racing and baseball, impacting all aspects of life. Their stories resonated within the hearts of individuals across generations, inspiring future athletes and activists to rise above adversity and challenge the status quo.

The journey of Isaac Murphy and his contemporaries became a testament to the resilience, determination, and unwavering spirit of the Black American community. Breaking barriers, challenging stereotypes, and leaving an indelible legacy of empowerment and progress, they forged a path toward a brighter future. Their names became synonymous with excellence, their stories serving as a guiding light for generations to come. And as the echoes of their actions reverberated through time, they continued to inspire countless others to join the fight for a more inclusive and equitable society.

SECTION III

Chapter 3 - Triumphs and Achievements

As the sun ascended above the horizon, casting its golden rays upon the hallowed grounds of Churchill Downs, the Kentucky Derby awaited the arrival of a figure destined for greatness. It was the year 1885, a time when the world of horse racing teetered on the cusp of transformation. In the heart of this pivotal moment stood Erskine Henderson, a jockey whose spirit burned brighter than the morning sun. Abraham Perry, an Black American horse trainer, had recognized the spark within Henderson from their first encounter. Together, they formed an unbreakable bond, defying the prejudices of the era. Their partnership was forged in the crucible of unwavering belief, as they dared to dream beyond the boundaries imposed upon them. On that fateful day, the grandstands teemed with eager spectators, their collective breath held in anticipation. It was a stage set for dreams to come alive, where the thundering hooves would echo through time. In the midst of the crowd, Erskine mounted the magnificent Joe Cotton, feeling the energy surge through his veins. The horse trembled beneath him, sensing the weight of their shared destiny. As the gates flung open, the thunderous symphony of galloping hooves filled the air, and the race unfolded before the watchful eyes of thousands. Keokuk, a horse known for its early speed, bolted forward, seizing the lead. But the favorite, Joe Cotton, initially lagged behind, igniting a flicker of doubt in the hearts of onlookers. Erskine, however, remained steadfast in his belief. With every stride, he communicated silently with his equine partner, encouraging Joe Cotton to find his rhythm, to unleash the untamed power that coursed through his veins. Mile after mile, they bided their time, waiting for the perfect moment to make their move. At the head of the stretch, Erskine felt the surge of adrenaline electrify his every nerve. It was now or never. With a swift maneuver, he guided Joe Cotton towards the front, their hooves pounding against the earth in perfect synchrony. Fierce competition surrounded them, as Bersan, who had maintained a strong position throughout the race, vied for the lead. Meanwhile, the fleet-footed Ten Booker threatened to steal victory from their grasp. But Erskine Henderson was a force to be reckoned with—a master of his craft. He urged Joe Cotton forward, their bodies united in purpose. In a breathtaking display of skill and determination, they gradually surged ahead, inch by inch, leaving their competitors in their wake. With each passing stride, the finish line loomed closer, victory shimmering like a mirage in the distance. As the crowd erupted in a frenzy of thunderous applause, Erskine and Joe Cotton crossed the finish line, their bond forged through blood, sweat, and tears. The margin of victory was mere inches, a testament to the fierce battle that had unfolded on the hallowed track. Ten Booker trailed closely behind Bersan, their valiant efforts etching their names in the annals of history. But this triumph was more than a personal victory for Erskine Henderson. It represented the triumph of an entire community—the Black American equestrian community that had persevered through adversity, breaking down barriers one stride at a time. In the echoes of their thunderous applause, the dreamers found hope, the marginalized found strength, and the world bore witness to the extraordinary resilience of the human spirit. In the wake of Henderson's historic victory, the equestrian world brimmed with a sense of awe and wonder. Stories of his triumph spread like wildfire, inspiring a new generation of riders to chase their dreams and defy the limitations placed upon them. Ersksine Henderson had ignited a flame that burned bright, a flame that would pave the way for future champions and shatter the confines of prejudice. His victory was merely the first brushstroke on a grand canvas.

Isaac Lewis, a name that would forever be etched in the annals of horse racing history. Born with a natural affinity for horses and an unwavering determination to excel, Isaac's journey was destined for greatness. In the year 1887, the Kentucky Derby became the stage where his talent would shine brightest, forever cementing his place in the pantheon of racing legends. As the sun rose on that momentous day, the air crackled with anticipation at Churchill Downs. The grandstands filled with eager spectators, their hearts pounding in unison, as they awaited the thundering hooves and the pursuit of victory. Among the sea of riders stood Isaac Lewis, a figure exuding a quiet confidence that belied the fire within. The starting gates swung open, releasing a cacophony of galloping hooves upon the track. Isaac, atop the magnificent Montrose, settled into his rhythm, his focus honed on the path that lay ahead. As the race unfolded, it was Jackobin who surged ahead, taking the early lead. But in the blink of an eye, Montrose, with Isaac in perfect synchrony, swiftly replaced him as the frontrunner, his powerful strides devouring the distance. With each stride, Isaac and Montrose extended their lead, their unity a symphony of grace and power. The wind whistled past their ears, the cheers of the crowd melding into a collective roar of admiration. The Kentucky Derby had become a theater of dreams, and Isaac Lewis was the protagonist, weaving his way into the hearts of all who bore witness. As they approached the three-quarter pole, a momentary tremor of doubt cast its shadow upon Isaac's spirit. Jim Gore, with a surge of strength, briefly weakened their resolve. But Isaac, a master of resilience, summoned his inner fortitude, urging Montrose to reclaim their momentum. Together, they surged forward, determination etched upon their faces. With the finish line in sight, Isaac Lewis unleashed the full might of Montrose's strength, propelling them towards a comfortable two-length lead. The crowd erupted, their thunderous applause echoing through the Kentucky sky. In that moment, Isaac knew he had etched his name in history, a name that would forever be synonymous with triumph and perseverance. But Isaac's journey did not end there. He continued to grace the tracks with his unwavering commitment to excellence. In 1888, the Kentucky Derby bore witness to his unwavering spirit as he secured a commendable 5th place finish. The following year, he demonstrated his consistency by claiming 6th place, a testament to his unwavering dedication to his craft. In 1886, a year before his momentous victory, Isaac Lewis achieved a notable 4th place finish while riding Lijero in the Kentucky Derby. Each stride, each race, was a testament to his passion and unyielding pursuit of greatness. Isaac Lewis had become a beacon of inspiration, his name whispered with reverence among equestrian enthusiasts and aspiring jockeys. Through the annals of time, Isaac's triumphs would be celebrated as milestones in the equestrian world. His victories stood not only as personal accomplishments but as symbols of hope and revelation for a community that had long been overlooked. Isaac Lewis had carved his name into the fabric of racing history, forever enshrined as a legendary figure of the track. As the sun set on the Kentucky Derby and Isaac Lewis's remarkable accomplishments, his legacy would endure, serving as a lasting inspiration for future generations. As the sun set on the Kentucky Derby and Isaac Lewis's remarkable achievements, his legacy would continue to inspire generations to come. From his momentous victory atop Montrose to his consistent excellence in subsequent races, Isaac's journey exemplified the power of talent, dedication, and unwavering belief in oneself. His victories symbolized the triumph of the human spirit and the enduring power of perseverance. Isaac Lewis, a name that would forever ignite the hearts of those who yearned to break free and gallop towards their own aspirations.

Stepping into the world of George B. "Spider" Anderson was to witness the embodiment of a jockey who defied all odds. Nicknamed "Spider" due to his small stature, George possessed a spirit that belied his physicality. His passion for horse racing burned brightly within him, driving him to conquer the tracks and prove that greatness knows no boundaries. The historic Preakness Stakes of 1889 became the battleground upon which Spider's dreams would converge with destiny. On that fateful day, the Pimlico Race Course in Baltimore, Maryland, teemed with anticipation. The air crackled with energy as the crowd gathered, their eyes fixed upon the majestic creatures that would soon thunder across the hallowed turf. Among them, George B. "Spider" Anderson prepared to mount Buddhist, a horse owned by Sam Brown and a symbol of the culmination of his dreams. As the gates swung open, releasing a torrent of galloping hooves, Spider and Buddhist surged forward with an unyielding determination. The race was a spectacle of fierce intensity, with every stride carrying the weight of history. Spider's exceptional skills were on full display as he deftly guided Buddhist through the chaos of the competition, maneuvering through the tumultuous sea of horses with a precision that captured the hearts of spectators. With each passing moment, Spider and Buddhist inched closer to the finish line, the resounding thunder of their hooves resonating in harmony with the beating hearts of those who watched in awe. The crowd's cheers reverberated through the air, mingling with the palpable sense of hope and anticipation that permeated the atmosphere. In that fleeting instance, Spider transcended the realm of ordinary mortals, his presence a testament to the indomitable spirit that resided within. As the finish line drew near, Spider and Buddhist surged forward, their collective will propelling them to an unforgettable victory. The crowd erupted in a tumultuous uproar, their jubilation a testament to the significance of Spider's monumental triumph. The echoes of their cheers resounded through the equestrian world, carrying with them the resolute belief that barriers could be shattered and dreams realized. Spider's victory in the Preakness Stakes of 1889 not only etched his name in the annals of horse racing history but further solidified his legacy within the equestrian world. His exceptional skills and unwavering determination became a source of inspiration for generations to come. Spider's triumph was not just his own; it resounded through the Black American equestrian community and beyond, a testament to the enduring power of courage and perseverance. Through the pages of time, the story of George B.

"Spider" Anderson's victory at the Preakness Stakes would endure as a triumph of the human spirit. His name would forever be whispered in reverence, his journey celebrated as a testament to the indomitable will of those who dare to dream. The echoes of his monumental victory would resonate through the equestrian world, an eternal reminder that barriers are meant to be shattered and greatness knows no bounds.

The grand stage of the Kentucky Derby of 1890 had become a beacon, calling forth the greatest jockeys and their noble steeds. It was on this hallowed ground that Isaac Burns Murphy, a figure of unparalleled skill and determination, would etch his name into the annals of history. With each stride, the thundering hooves of Riley reverberated through the air, carrying Murphy closer to his destiny. The race began in a flurry of excitement and anticipation, with Bill Letcher and Palisade surging alongside Riley, eager to assert their dominance. But Murphy's command of the reins was unwavering, guiding his noble companion with a precision that seemed almost supernatural. As they thundered around the track, their collective spirit ignited, propelling them to the forefront of the race. At the three-quarter mark, it was Riley who held the lead, his muscular frame surging forward with an indomitable strength. Robespierre and Bill Letcher, their eyes fixed on the prize, strained to close the gap. But Murphy, resolute and focused, refused to yield. With every ounce of his being, he urged Riley onward, their bond unbreakable. As the finish line loomed in the distance, a surge of adrenaline coursed through Murphy's veins. The crowd, their breath held in anticipation, watched as he and Riley propelled themselves towards victory. In a breathtaking display of power and finesse, Riley crossed the finish line, his lead insurmountable. The grandstands erupted in a cacophony of cheers, a testament to the unrivaled skill and dedication of Isaac Burns Murphy. In the moments that followed, Murphy's triumph resonated far beyond the confines of the racetrack. Thomas Fortune, a prominent figure fighting to desegregate New York hotels, sought an interview with the jockey. Murphy, known for his friendly yet straightforward demeanor, spoke with unwavering conviction. He rode to win, not just for himself but to inspire change and overcome the lingering specter of racism that plagued society. Fortune, admiring Murphy's determination and recognizing the impact individuals like him had in the battle against racism following slavery, listened intently. In Murphy's triumph, Fortune saw a glimmer of hope—a testament to the power of perseverance and the transformative nature of talent. Their conversation served as a poignant reminder that victory extended far beyond the track, spurring a movement that would forever alter the course of history. Isaac Burns

Murphy's continued success was more than just a testament to his unwavering skill and dedication. It was a triumph of the human spirit—a beacon of hope and inspiration for all who dared to dream. As his legend grew, Murphy's name became synonymous with greatness, his legacy a testament to the power of unwavering determination and the pursuit of excellence. Through his victories, he shattered the boundaries of what was thought possible, leaving an indelible mark on the world of horse racing and beyond. The echoes of Isaac Burns Murphy's triumph at the Kentucky Derby reverberated through time, resonating in the hearts of those who heard his story. His name would forever be etched in the annals of sporting greatness, a symbol of the enduring power of courage, talent, and unwavering dedication. From the track to the fight for equality, Murphy's journey embodied the spirit of a true champion—a figure who transcended the realm of sports and became a beacon of inspiration for generations to come.

In the world of horse racing, where the stakes were high and the allure of financial gain loomed large, Anthony Hamilton remained steadfast in his commitment to integrity. The corrupt forces that sought to influence race outcomes through underhanded means were met with a resolute refusal. Hamilton's moral compass guided him, unwavering in the face of temptation. As whispers of bribery and corruption permeated the air, Hamilton stood tall, his unwavering dedication a testament to the power of righteousness. While others succumbed to the allure of quick riches, he remained true to his principles, a shining example of honor and fairness in a world often clouded by deception. His refusal to be swayed by the dark undercurrents of the sport garnered admiration from his fellow jockeys, trainers, and spectators. They recognized in him a figure of unwavering commitment, a paragon of virtue amidst a landscape tainted by dishonesty. It was through Hamilton's actions that the true spirit of horse racing shone bright, reminding all who bore witness that the purity of the sport could only be preserved through unwavering integrity. In the grandstands, spectators leaned forward, their eyes fixed upon Hamilton as he guided his mount with precision and grace. With every stride, he galvanized their faith in the inherent fairness of the race, a belief that victory should be earned through talent, skill, and hard work alone. The impact of Hamilton's unwavering commitment to integrity extended far beyond the confines of the racetrack. His choices resonated deeply with a world yearning for individuals of unyielding virtue. Admirers saw in him the embodiment of a greater battle—a battle against corruption, not just in horse racing, but in society as a whole. As Hamilton took his place in the winner's circle, his fellow jockeys applauded, their respect and admiration shining in their eyes. They knew that his triumphs were not just measured by the number of races he won, but by the unwavering stand he took against the forces that sought to compromise the very essence of the sport they loved. Hamilton's legacy as a paragon of integrity would forever be etched in the annals of horse racing. His name would be spoken with reverence, a symbol of the enduring power of righteousness in the face of temptation. He had shown the world that true victory was not measured solely by the laurels won, but by the steadfastness of one's character. As the sun set on the racetrack, casting a golden glow upon the triumphs of the day, Hamilton stood as a testament to the transformative power of integrity. His unwavering commitment resonated far beyond the confines of the sport, inspiring others to hold true to their principles and strive for greatness with honor. The echoes of his choices reverberated through the hearts and minds of those who bore witness, fostering a renewed belief in the possibility of a world guided by unwavering integrity. Through his actions, Hamilton had become more than just a jockey; he had become a symbol of hope— a beacon in a world too often clouded by compromise. And so, as the curtain fell on another day at the races, Anthony Hamilton's unyielding integrity stood as a testament to the enduring power of righteousness. His legacy would forever inspire and challenge, reminding all who heard his story that greatness was not measured solely by victory, but by the unwavering commitment to principles that transcended the racetrack and touched the very core of the human spirit.

On that fateful day at the Sheepshead Bay Racetrack, Anthony Hamilton became a symbol of triumph, his victory in the Futurity Stakes echoing through the corridors of horse racing history. The grand stage was set, the air heavy with anticipation as the horses and jockeys took their positions. The Futurity Stakes, with its record-breaking purse, promised not only financial rewards but also the opportunity to etch one's name in the annals of sporting glory. Hamilton's partnership with Potomac was a bond forged in the fires of destiny. The legendary horse, a majestic creature that seemed to possess an ethereal power, was the embodiment of greatness. And as Hamilton mounted Potomac, a fusion of man and beast emerged, each relying on the other's strength and determination to conquer the challenges that lay ahead. The race began with a thunderous roar, the hooves of the horses pounding against the track like a symphony of raw power. Hamilton's command of the reins was masterful, guiding Potomac with an intimate understanding of every sinew and stride. They navigated the track, facing hurdles and adversaries with unwavering resolve, their eyes locked on the finish line that shimmered in the distance. In the crucible of competition, the race unfolded with heart-pounding intensity. Rivals surged forward, their determination matched only by Hamilton and Potomac's unyielding spirit. They pushed the boundaries of their physical prowess, their bodies straining to achieve the impossible. The cheers of the spectators blended with the thumping of their hearts, the atmosphere electrified with the promise of victory. As they rounded the final turn, the finish line in sight, Hamilton summoned every ounce of strength within him. Potomac responded, surging forward with a burst of speed that left their competitors trailing in their wake. Time seemed to slow as they crossed the finish line, the culmination of their unwavering dedication and tireless training. The deafening roar of the crowd mingled with the triumphant neigh of the horse, a chorus of celebration that echoed through the ages. In that moment, Hamilton's triumph became more than just a personal victory. It was a declaration of his exceptional talent and unwavering dedication to the sport he loved. His name would forever be etched alongside the greats, a symbol of resilience and the pursuit of excellence. As the dust settled and the euphoria began to subside, Hamilton stood tall, the embodiment of hope and inspiration. His triumph served as a reminder to all who witnessed it that dreams could be realized, that perseverance and unwavering dedication could conquer even the most formidable obstacles. The legacy of Anthony Hamilton's triumph in the Futurity Stakes reverberated far beyond the realm of horse racing. It resonated with the dreams of every aspiring athlete, every individual who dared to chase their passions against all odds. His story, a testament to the power of perseverance and the unwavering pursuit of one's dreams, became a beacon of hope in a world that often tests one's resolve. Hamilton's triumph would forever inspire generations to come, reminding them that within each of them lay the potential for greatness. His name would be spoken with reverence, his story a source of motivation for those who faced their own battles, both on and off the racetrack. As the sun set on that historic day at the Sheepshead Bay Racetrack, the echoes of Anthony Hamilton's triumph lingered in the hearts of all who bore witness. The legacy of his victory would continue to inspire, a testament to the enduring power of passion, resilience, and unwavering dedication. And as the world turned, the spirit of Hamilton's triumph would forever guide those who dared to dream, reminding them that greatness was within their reach, waiting to be seized with unyielding determination.

Chapter 3 Summary:

In the year 1885, Erskine Henderson, guided by horse trainer Abraham Perry, achieved a historic victory at the Kentucky Derby, breaking racial barriers in horse racing. Isaac Murphy emerged as an iconic figure, securing notable wins in subsequent Kentucky Derby races and becoming a symbol of talent and determination. George B. "Spider" Anderson became the first African American jockey to win the Preakness Stakes in 1889. Isaac Murphy's legacy burned the brightest, winning multiple Kentucky Derby races and solidifying his place as a legendary jockey. Anthony Hamilton stood as a paragon of integrity, refusing to succumb to bribery and upholding fair competition. The pivotal showdown between Isaac Murphy and Snapper Garrison in 1890, captured in a photo finish, forever altered the sport and immortalized both jockeys. The triumphs of these exceptional athletes reshaped horse racing, broke racial barriers, and inspired a broader struggle for equality. Their stories continue to inspire future generations, showcasing the transformative power of resilience, determination, and the pursuit of greatness.

Willie Simms

SECTION III

Chapter 4 - Legendary Races and Enduring Legacies:

The crowd erupted into thunderous applause as the photograph confirming Salvator's victory was unveiled. Cheers reverberated throughout the racetrack, the spectators recognizing the significance of this historic moment. It was a revelation that forever changed the landscape of horse racing, ushering in a new era of objectivity and accuracy in determining race outcomes.

Isaac Murphy, his face adorned with a mix of exhaustion and elation, dismounted Salvator and made his way to the winner's circle. The accolades rained down upon him, but in his eyes, there was a deep sense of humility. He recognized the gravity of the moment, not only for himself but for the sport he loved.

As the excitement gradually subsided, Isaac cast his gaze towards Snapper Garrison, his worthy adversary. The two jockeys shared a nod of mutual respect, an unspoken acknowledgment of the skill and determination they had displayed on the racetrack. Though the race had been closely contested, the spirit of sportsmanship prevailed, bridging the gap between rivals.

The impact of the photo finish was felt far beyond the confines of the racetrack. News of this groundbreaking innovation spread like wildfire, capturing the imagination of racing enthusiasts and sports fans alike. It was a revelation that inspired hope and a renewed sense of possibility. No longer would races be subject to human error or biased judgments; now, the lens of the camera would serve as the ultimate arbiter of truth.

The photo finish not only transformed the sport itself but also had far-reaching implications for society. It served as a powerful reminder that excellence knows no bounds and that the pursuit of victory can transcend the limitations imposed by race, gender, or social status. Isaac Murphy, an Black American jockey, stood as a testament to the power of skill, determination, and talent in breaking down barriers and shattering preconceived notions.

In the days and weeks that followed, the photograph circulated in newspapers and magazines across the country. It ignited conversations and debates, sparking a collective realization that the world of horse racing had entered a new era. The concept of a photo finish became the standard by which races were judged, forever etching Isaac Murphy's name in the annals of sporting history.

For Isaac, the photo finish marked a personal triumph—a validation of his years of dedication, sacrifice, and unwavering passion for the sport. It was a revelation that revealed the immense potential within him and the heights he could achieve. The image captured not only the thrilling conclusion of a race but also the indomitable spirit of a jockey who refused to be confined by societal limitations.

As Isaac stood on the winner's podium, his heart swelled with gratitude. He was acutely aware of the legacy he had forged, not just for himself but for future generations of jockeys and athletes. The photo finish had ushered in a new chapter in the story of horse racing, an era defined by fair play, transparency, and the relentless pursuit of excellence.

In the wake of this momentous event, the sport of horse racing embarked on a journey of transformation. The world looked on with eager anticipation, curious to witness the endless possibilities that lay ahead. And as the sun set on the racetrack, a sense of hope and inspiration filled the air—a revelation that greatness can be captured, frozen in time, and celebrated for generations to come.

The construction of the Twin Spires was a feat of architectural brilliance. Skilled craftsmen and engineers worked tirelessly to bring the vision to life, meticulously crafting each detail with unwavering precision. The spires soared towards the sky, their height reaching dizzying proportions. From the foundation to the pinnacle, every stone and beam was carefully selected to ensure structural integrity and aesthetic beauty. As the scaffolding was gradually removed, the true magnificence of the Twin Spires was revealed to the world.

The Twin Spires stood proudly at Churchill Downs, their resemblance to church towers not lost on the spectators. The towering structures exuded an air of reverence, as if the gods themselves had placed their stamp of approval on the racetrack. To the horse racing community, the spires became a symbol of pride—a testament to the importance of the sport and its place in the hearts of its followers. They represented the culmination of years of passion and dedication, an embodiment of the grandeur and pageantry that surrounded horse racing.

The Twin Spires were more than just architectural marvels; they were a wellspring of inspiration for racing enthusiasts. As spectators gazed upon their imposing forms, they couldn't help but feel a surge of excitement and anticipation. The spires whispered tales of triumph and resilience, their very presence stoking the flames of ambition within the hearts of those who dared to dream. They stood as a reminder that greatness was within reach, waiting to be seized by those with the courage to chase it.

Throughout history, the Twin Spires had served as a powerful promotional tool. Their image adorned countless posters, brochures, and advertisements, drawing crowds to Churchill Downs in droves. Their allure transcended words and spoke directly to the soul of the racing enthusiast. The Twin Spires promised an experience like no other, a front-row seat to the exhilaration and drama that unfolded on the hallowed grounds of the racetrack. They enticed and captivated, beckoning both seasoned fans and curious newcomers to witness the magic firsthand.

But beyond their promotional value, the Twin Spires were repositories of captivating stories and legends. Tales of legendary jockeys, awe-inspiring comebacks, and heart-stopping finishes reverberated within their stone walls. The spires had borne witness to triumph and heartache, their silent presence a constant reminder of the enduring nature of the sport. They stood as a bridge between past and present, connecting generations of racing enthusiasts through a shared reverence for the history that had unfolded beneath their watchful gaze.

The Twin Spires were not merely structures; they had become an integral part of the collective identity of Churchill Downs and the horse racing community at large. They symbolized the unity and camaraderie that bound fans and participants together, transcending barriers of age, race, and background. They represented the culmination of countless hours of hard work and dedication, a testament to the unwavering spirit that drove the sport forward.

As the sun set over Churchill Downs, casting a warm golden glow upon the racetrack, the Twin Spires stood tall and proud. They were beacons of hope, inspiration, and revelation—a tangible embodiment of the indomitable spirit that coursed through the veins of horse racing. They whispered stories of triumph and perseverance, reminding all who beheld them that greatness was not limited to the pages of history but could be found in the hearts of those who dared to dream. And as the horses thundered past the Twin Spires, their hooves echoing in unison, the crowd roared with a collective voice that reverberated through the very foundations of the racetrack. In that moment, the Twin Spires transcended their physical form, becoming a symbol of shared joy, passion, and the enduring legacy of horse racing.

In the bustling city of Lexington, Kentucky, a renowned jockey sought solace and connection within the esteemed Lincoln Lodge Masons. It was the year 1891, and Sir Isaac Burns Murphy, already established as one of the greatest jockeys of his time, felt the desire to forge deeper bonds and engage in personal growth within the community. The Lincoln Lodge Masons welcomed him with open arms, recognizing his exceptional talent and character.

Within the hallowed halls of the Masonic lodge, Isaac found a brotherhood that transcended the boundaries of horse racing. The members of the Lincoln Lodge Masons were individuals who shared his values and principles, seeking personal and communal betterment. Through their collective wisdom and support, Isaac's place within the community was further solidified, reminding him of the respect and admiration he had earned throughout his illustrious career.

Isaac's affiliation with the Lincoln Lodge Masons was a testament to his commitment to personal growth and involvement within the community. The Masonic fraternity provided him with a nurturing environment, where he could cultivate his spirit and thrive alongside like-minded individuals. The bonds formed within the lodge were forged not only through shared experiences but also through a profound understanding of the trials and triumphs that defined Isaac's journey.

The Masons recognized Isaac as a man of character and integrity, attributes that went beyond his remarkable achievements on the racetrack. In their company, he found a space where he could expand his horizons and contribute to the betterment of society. Isaac's membership in the Lincoln Lodge Masons served as a beacon of hope and inspiration, showcasing the possibilities that lay beyond the confines of horse racing.

Within the Lincoln Lodge Masons, Isaac found a sense of belonging that extended beyond the racing world. His Masonic brothers stood beside him, supporting his endeavors and celebrating his triumphs. Together, they formed a collective force that propelled Isaac forward, inspiring him to reach new heights of excellence.

As Isaac continued his journey as a jockey, his affiliation with the

Masonic fraternity reminded him of the importance of community and the power of unity. The Lincoln Lodge Masons became an integral part of his life, shaping his character and guiding his actions both on and off the racetrack. Through their shared rituals and ceremonies, Isaac learned valuable lessons of humility, perseverance, and brotherhood, which resonated deeply within him.

In joining the Lincoln Lodge Masons, Isaac Burns Murphy not only solidified his place within the community but also left a lasting legacy of personal growth and community involvement. His affiliation with the Masonic fraternity revealed his unwavering commitment to self-improvement and his desire to make a positive impact in the world. Through the bonds forged within the Lincoln Lodge Masons, Isaac found strength and inspiration that fueled his remarkable achievements as a jockey and as a man.

The Lincoln Lodge Masons became a pillar of support in Isaac's life, providing him with a sense of purpose and belonging. Their shared values and dedication to personal and communal betterment inspired him to embrace his role as a leader, not only in the world of horse racing but also within the broader community.

As Isaac embarked on each new race, he carried with him the teachings of the Masonic fraternity, allowing them to guide his every move. The Lincoln Lodge Masons had become an integral part of his identity, shaping him into a man whose legacy extended far beyond the racetrack.

In the heart of Lexington, Kentucky, the Lincoln Lodge Masons stood as a testament to the power of unity and the transformative potential of shared values. Through his affiliation with this respected Masonic fraternity, Sir Isaac Burns Murphy found a community that embraced him, celebrated his achievements, and propelled him towards greatness. Together, they forged an enduring legacy that would be remembered for generations to come.

The sun hung high in the sky as the vibrant atmosphere of the 1891 Kentucky Derby filled the air. It was a day of triumph and determination, where dreams would be realized and legacies forged. Among the throngs of spectators, Isaac Burns Murphy stood tall, ready to make history once again. His mount, Kingman, exuded strength and grace, a testament to the exceptional training and care provided by his owner and trainer, Dudley Allen.

The Kentucky Derby was the ultimate test of skill, endurance, and strategy. It was a race that brought together the finest horses, jockeys, and trainers from all corners of the country. But this year was different. This year, a wave of change rippled through the air, carried on the hooves of Kingman and the unwavering spirit of Dudley Allen.

As the race commenced, Isaac felt the familiar surge of adrenaline coursing through his veins. He and Kingman moved with the precision and grace that only comes from years of dedicated practice and unwavering trust. The crowd roared, their excitement building with every stride. They recognized the extraordinary partnership between jockey and horse, and the significance of Dudley Allen's triumph as an Black American horseman in a sport marked by prejudice and discrimination.

Isaac's connection with Kingman was a thing of beauty. Their hearts beat as one, their movements synchronized in perfect harmony. Each leap forward brought them closer to victory, each thundering hoofbeat echoing their determination to overcome the barriers that sought to hold them back. With every stride, Isaac felt the weight of history on his shoulders, knowing that their success would transcend the racetrack and inspire generations to come.

As they rounded the final turn, the crowd erupted into a frenzy of cheers and applause. Isaac could feel the energy of their support propelling him forward, driving him to give his all. Kingman's powerful strides devoured the distance, their eyes locked on the finish line. In a burst of speed and determination, they crossed the threshold, their victory etched in the annals of horse racing history.

The jubilation that filled the winner's circle was palpable. Isaac dismounted, his face flushed with a mixture of exhilaration and gratitude. Dudley Allen stood by his side, a beacon of pride and resilience. Their partnership had triumphed over prejudice and discrimination, showcasing the remarkable achievements of Black American horsemen and challenging the barriers that had long confined them.

In that moment, the significance of Dudley Allen's triumph resonated far beyond the confines of the racetrack. It was a beacon of hope, a revelation that greatness knows no bounds. The world of horse racing was forever changed, its foundations cracked open by the unwavering spirit of determination and the undeniable talent that flourished in the hearts of men like Isaac Burns Murphy and Dudley Allen.

The victory at the Kentucky Derby was not merely a personal triumph for Isaac and Dudley—it was a triumph for all who dared to dream, who refused to be defined by the color of their skin. Their legacy became an inspiration, a testament to the power of perseverance and the indomitable spirit that resided within each and every one of us.

As the celebrations subsided, and the echoes of their victory faded, Isaac and Dudley knew that their journey was far from over. They had shattered barriers, but the fight against prejudice and discrimination was ongoing. Their triumph at the Kentucky Derby had provided a platform, a platform from which they would continue to challenge the norms and pave the way for future generations of Black American horsemen.

The victory had united them, forging a bond that would withstand the test of time. Isaac and Dudley were more than jockey and trainer; they were brothers, companions on a shared journey that transcended the racetrack. Together, they would continue to defy expectations, to inspire and uplift, and to leave an enduring legacy that would forever be etched in the annals of horse racing history.

The sun dipped below the horizon, casting a warm glow over the racetrack as the crowd erupted into thunderous applause. They had witnessed a momentous occasion—a triumph that would forever be etched in the annals of horse racing history. At the center of it all stood Sir Isaac Burns Murphy, his chest heaving with exhaustion and exhilaration. He had achieved what few had before—a Triple Crown victory.

The journey to this milestone had been filled with highs and lows, victories and setbacks. Isaac had faced the challenges head-on, his unwavering spirit pushing him forward even in the darkest of times. Each race had been a test of skill, strategy, and sheer determination. And now, as he stood before the adoring crowd, he knew that every moment of doubt and every sacrifice had been worth it.

The Triple Crown was more than just a collection of wins. It was a testament to Isaac's unparalleled skill and talent, solidifying his position as one of the greatest jockeys in American history. His name would forever be spoken with reverence, his achievements celebrated and studied by aspiring jockeys and racing enthusiasts alike.

As Isaac looked out at the faces in the crowd, he saw the spark of inspiration in their eyes. They saw in him the embodiment of their own dreams and aspirations. He had become a symbol of hope, a living testament to the power of perseverance and the pursuit of excellence.

But this victory was not just for Isaac—it was for all who had supported him along the way. It was for his trainers, his fellow jockeys, and the dedicated team of grooms and stable hands who had worked tirelessly behind the scenes. It was for the fans who had cheered him on with unwavering loyalty, their voices blending into a chorus of belief and encouragement.

Isaac's legacy would endure long after the cheers subsided and the celebrations faded. His remarkable achievement in the equestrian world would serve as a beacon of inspiration for generations to come. Young jockeys would study his technique, his strategies, and his unwavering dedication. They would learn from his triumphs and failures, molding themselves in the image of greatness that he had embodied.

The Triple Crown win was not the end of Isaac's journey—it was a new beginning. He would continue to push the boundaries, to challenge himself, and to inspire others to reach for the stars. The racetrack was not just a place of competition; it was a canvas upon which dreams were painted and legacies were born.

As the cheers continued to echo in the distance, Isaac's heart swelled with gratitude. He knew that he had been blessed with a rare gift—a gift that had allowed him to leave an indelible mark on the sport he loved. And as he walked away from the winner's circle, his head held high, he carried with him the hopes and dreams of all who had witnessed his triumph.

The legacy of Sir Isaac Burns Murphy would forever be intertwined with the equestrian world. His name would be spoken with reverence, his accomplishments celebrated and honored. And in the hearts of racing enthusiasts, young and old, his story would live on—a testament to the power of the human spirit, the pursuit of excellence, and the enduring legacy of a true champion.

SECTION III

Chapter 5 - Celebrations, Loss, and New Beginnings

In the crisp winter of January 1891, the Black American equestrian community erupted in jubilation as news of Anthony Hamilton's impending marriage spread like wildfire. Hamilton, a gifted black jockey hailing from South Carolina, had found his match in the radiant Annie Messley. The anticipation and excitement swirled among friends and admirers, their hearts brimming with hope and unity. On a day bathed in sunlight, January 12, 1891, the union of Anthony and Annie was sealed in a ceremony that transcended mere vows. As they stood before their loved ones, the air thick with anticipation, a profound bond radiated between the couple. Isaac Murphy, a legend in his own right, three-time victor of the revered Kentucky Derby, stood steadfastly by Hamilton's side as the best man. Their connection, forged by shared victories and unyielding passion, was a testament to the unbreakable spirit that thrived within the Black American equestrian community. The significance of this union was not lost on the world at large, for the New York Times, ever attuned to noteworthy events, sought to amplify its importance. With their publication, the couple's story reverberated throughout the country, capturing the hearts and minds of readers from coast to coast. And as the tale unfolded, the Times also shed light on Anthony Hamilton's wealth, their words revealing that he had lavishly spent $1,000 on jewelry gifts from a local store—an extravagant gesture that only further ignited curiosity and fascination. The echoes of celebration continued to resound. Ten days after the wedding, on January 22, 1891, the Pittsburgh Daily Post chronicled the grandeur that surrounded the couple's joyous occasion. An entire upper floor of an exclusive building had been reserved for the festivities, while an esteemed caterer conjured a supper fit for royalty. The reception hall itself, lovingly transformed by the skilled hands of a florist, evoked the enchantment of a lush tropical garden. The sights and scents mingled in perfect harmony, immersing guests in a realm of pure wonderment. But the exuberance did not end there. Just three days later, on January 25, 1891, Isaac and Lucy

Murphy—though they had not been blessed with children—embodied the warmth and camaraderie that characterized their wide circle of friends. Among them stood Anthony Hamilton and his resplendent bride, Annie. In their opulent estate nestled in Lexington, the Murphys flung open their doors, inviting friends, esteemed guests, and luminaries from all corners of the country to partake in a celebration that would be etched into the annals of history. The event, fittingly named "A Colored Party," became a testament to the power of unity and shared joy, an oasis where dreams intersected and hearts were forever connected. As the night unfolded, laughter and revelry filled the air, intertwining with the melodies that emanated from musicians' nimble fingers. The Murphys' estate, a palace of opulence and warmth, provided the perfect backdrop for this extraordinary gathering. Conversations flowed, weaving a vibrant mosaic of stories and aspirations. It was a night where barriers crumbled, replaced by the unifying force of love and celebration. Those fortunate enough to be present felt the weight of history and the profound impact of this collective moment—a moment that would forever be etched in their memories as a testament to the resilience and greatness that coursed through the veins of the Black American equestrian community. And as the stars painted the night sky with their luminescent glow, a whisper of hope echoed among the attendees. In the embrace of unity, they found strength to conquer any obstacle that lay before them. For on this night, love, friendship, and the power of dreams melded into a force that would shape the course of their lives and forever alter the landscape of the sport they held dear.

The year was 1892, and within the walls of the Murphys' estate in Lexington, Kentucky, a spirit of camaraderie and support enveloped the gathering. The occasion? An engagement party that would not only honor the union of Anthony Hamilton and his beloved Annie Messley but also serve as a celebration of the deep bonds that intertwined the Black American equestrian community. As the guests arrived, an electric energy filled the air. Dressed in their finest attire, they stepped into the Murphys' abode, their presence a testament to the enduring friendships and shared dreams that had woven this community together. Old friends greeted each other with embraces, their smiles radiating warmth and familiarity, while new acquaintances forged connections, their common passion for the sport acting as a bridge between souls. The Murphys' home, a sanctuary of elegance and opulence, stood as a living testament to their unwavering commitment to the equestrian world. From the grand entrance adorned with intricate woodwork to the sprawling gardens that whispered of both serenity and vibrancy, every detail bore witness to their dedication. As the sun dipped below the horizon, casting a warm glow upon the estate, the festivities commenced. Glasses clinked in harmonious toasts, the sound reverberating through the halls like a joyous symphony. Laughter danced on the air as stories, both old and new, were shared, interwoven threads of a fabric that showcased the resilience and triumphs of those present. Each guest basked in the knowledge that they were part of a movement, a collective force that had dared to defy the constraints of prejudice and discrimination. In a world where barriers often seemed insurmountable, they had chosen to chase their dreams on the racetracks, to let the thundering hooves be their anthem of liberation. The night progressed, infused with the rhythm of melodies that swelled and surged, beckoning couples to the dance floor. As they twirled, their steps an eloquent language of grace and joy, the room pulsated with the vibrant cadence of their beating hearts. In each movement, they embodied the resilience and spirit that had brought them together, the flickering flame of hope that refused to be extinguished. The engagement party became more than a mere celebration of love and commitment. It was a testament to the unyielding determination that coursed through their veins—a collective declaration that they were the architects of their own destinies, the masters of their own narratives. And as the night drew to a close, the Murphys' estate embraced the fading echoes of revelry, as if etching them into the very fabric of its existence. The bonds forged that evening would endure, serving as pillars of strength and support in the face of adversity. For within the hearts of those who had gathered, the flames of hope burned bright, igniting a fire that would illuminate the path towards a future where dreams could flourish and barriers would crumble. As they bid each other farewell, they carried with them the warmth of shared moments, the knowledge that they were part of something extraordinary — a tapestry woven with the threads of determination, unity, and unyielding love.

In the year 1892, the world of horse racing trembled with anticipation as the Kentucky Derby loomed on the horizon—a grand spectacle that would soon witness the rise of a young prodigy. Alonzo Lonnie Clayton, a jockey whose spirit burned with a ferocious determination, stood on the precipice of history. At the tender age of fifteen, he yearned to etch his name upon the hallowed grounds of the racetrack, to defy the odds and shatter the expectations that threatened to confine his dreams. As the gates swung open, releasing a flurry of thundering hooves, the roar of the crowd reached a crescendo. Every eye was drawn to the spectacle unfolding before them, captivated by the rhythmic dance between horse and rider. Amongst the contenders emerged a formidable duo—Jockey

Tommy Britton astride the mighty Huron, surging forward with a commanding lead that stretched six lengths ahead of the chasing pack. A gasp swept through the crowd, the sheer dominance of their performance leaving spectators breathless with awe. Yet, in the heart of Alonzo Lonnie Clayton, a flicker of indomitable spirit burned. Mounted upon the back of Azra, a horse nurtured under the watchful eye of the esteemed Bashford Manor Stable and guided by the skilled hand of trainer John H. Morris, Clayton dared to believe in the impossible. With each stride, he drew upon the depths of his unwavering resolve, his hands guiding Azra with a master's touch. Step by step, they closed the gap, the thunderous applause of the crowd serving as the fuel that propelled them forward. The tension in the air was palpable as the horses thundered towards the finish line, the exhilarating rush of adrenaline coursing through their veins. It was a battle of wills, a test of skill and unwavering determination. Alonzo Lonnie Clayton, his senses heightened, could taste the sweetness of victory within his grasp. With a final burst of raw power, he urged Azra forward, their bodies moving as one, each sinewy muscle strained in pursuit of triumph. In a breathtaking finale, horse and jockey tore across the finish line, their victory decided by a mere whisper of a nose. The crowd erupted in a symphony of jubilation, their voices blending into a chorus of awe and admiration. Alonzo Lonnie Clayton had defied the constraints of age, casting aside doubt and proving that dreams were not bound by the limitations of time. As the cheers echoed through the stands, a ripple of inspiration coursed through the onlookers. A new generation of aspiring jockeys, their eyes wide with wonder, felt their own spirits ignite with possibility. Lonnie Clayton's triumph served as a beacon of hope, illuminating a path where talent and determination knew no boundaries. The world watched in awe as history was made. Alonzo Lonnie Clayton, a young jockey with fire in his veins, had etched his name in the annals of horse racing. The mantle of the youngest winner of the legendary Kentucky Derby now adorned his shoulders—a testament to his exceptional talent, unwavering courage, and the extraordinary bond forged between man and steed. In the wake of Clayton's victory, the racetracks whispered tales of his triumph. His name, like a cherished melody, danced upon the lips of racing enthusiasts far and wide. He had proven that age was but a number, that the spirit of a champion knew no limitations. And with every beat of their hearts, a new chapter in the equestrian world unfolded—a chapter where dreams blossomed, barriers crumbled, and the thunderous hooves of Azra echoed the resounding victory of a young jockey who dared to rewrite history.

The year was 1893, and in the hallowed grounds of the Kentucky

Oaks, a tale of triumph unfolded—a tale that would forever be etched in the annals of equestrian history. Edward Dudley Brown, a visionary trainer and revered horse owner, stood at the precipice of glory. His reputation had preceded him, whispers of his skill and expertise weaving through the air like a delicate breeze. Monrovia, a magnificent filly trained under Brown's watchful eye, possessed a grace that was unparalleled. Her coat gleamed in the sunlight, her spirit untamed and wild. As the jockeys mounted their noble steeds, the air crackled with electricity, a palpable energy that reverberated through the crowd. The Kentucky Oaks, a race that tested the mettle of the finest fillies, beckoned both horse and rider to reach for greatness. Jockey J. Reagan, his eyes sparkling with determination, took his position atop Monrovia. He felt the power that pulsed beneath him, a symbiotic connection between horse and human. The starting gates opened, and the thunderous symphony of hooves resounded, a chorus that echoed through the ages. Monrovia, like a shooting star streaking across the sky, surged forward with a breathtaking burst of speed. Her muscles rippled beneath the strain, her every sinewy movement a testament to her training and natural grace. Jockey and horse danced as one, their bond unbreakable. The race unfolded with a crescendo of drama. Fierce competitors vied for dominance, their hooves pounding the earth in a battle of wills. Monrovia, guided by Reagan's expert hand, navigated the twists and turns with an elegant finesse. The distance of 1+1/4 miles stretched before them, a daunting challenge that demanded unwavering focus and unwavering courage. With each stride, Monrovia gained ground, her determination burning like a flame that refused to be extinguished. The crowd held its breath, their hearts pounding in unison. The finish line beckoned, a beacon of triumph that called to Monrovia's indomitable spirit. In a final burst of raw power, Monrovia crossed the finish line, her victory resonating through the very core of the racetrack. The crowd erupted in a thunderous ovation, their cheers a testament to the greatness they had just witnessed. Edward Dudley Brown, a man of vision and unwavering commitment, stood on the sidelines, his heart soaring with pride. He had nurtured this champion, sculpting her into a force to be reckoned with. Monrovia's time of 2:16.00 became etched in the records, a testament to her speed and endurance. The triumphant pair had emerged victorious, their journey to greatness complete. Edward Dudley Brown's name would forever be synonymous with excellence in the equestrian world, his victory in the Kentucky Oaks a testament to his unparalleled skill and dedication. As the sun dipped below the horizon, painting the sky in hues of gold and crimson, the celebration began. Edward Dudley

Brown stood among a sea of admirers, the weight of their congratulations and awe washing over him. Monrovia, resplendent in her victory, basked in the adoration of all who beheld her. In that moment, a new chapter began—a chapter where dreams were realized, where talent was celebrated, and where the spirit of the racetrack beat with an unyielding hope. Edward Dudley Brown's Kentucky Oaks success had become more than a mere victory; it had become a symbol of possibility, a testament to the power of perseverance and unwavering belief. As the night unfolded, laughter and joy filled the air, mingling with the stories of past triumphs and the dreams of future glory. The Kentucky Oaks had witnessed history, and the echoes of that historic day reverberated through the ages, inspiring a new generation of horsemen and women to reach for the stars. The legacy of Edward Dudley Brown and Monrovia would forever be intertwined—a tale of triumph, of an unbreakable bond between horse and rider, and of the extraordinary heights that can be reached when dreams are fueled by passion and nurtured by unwavering dedication.

The year was 1893, a decade since Isaac Murphy and Lucy had embarked on their remarkable journey of love. Their bond, tested by the winds of change and adversity, had stood strong, a beacon of hope and resilience in a world that sought to confine them. Now, on the occasion of their tenth wedding anniversary, they chose to reaffirm their commitment, to celebrate the unbreakable thread that bound their souls. Their Lexington home, adorned with flowers and illuminated by the soft glow of candles, served as the sacred ground for this extraordinary gathering. Esteemed guests, both friends and luminaries from across the nation, arrived, their presence a testament to the profound impact Isaac and Lucy had made on the equestrian community and beyond. The air hummed with anticipation, each guest carrying their own memories and stories, woven together by a shared love for the Murphys. As the sun dipped below the horizon, casting a golden hue upon the scene, Isaac and Lucy stood before their loved ones, their eyes filled with a radiant warmth. Their vows, spoken with a depth of emotion that words could scarcely contain, echoed through the hearts of all who bore witness. The words were not mere repetition, but a reaffirmation of their journey, a testament to the unwavering love that had guided them through trials and triumphs alike. Amidst a symphony of applause and teary-eyed smiles, the couple renewed their commitment to one another, their voices carrying the weight of a decade's worth of shared memories. The room shimmered with love, a palpable energy that wrapped around each guest like a comforting embrace. The power of their love was felt by all, transcending the confines of time and space. Laughter danced through the halls, intertwining with stories of shared victories, of races won and dreams fulfilled. The evening unfurled like an intricately woven masterpiece, adorned with threads of delight and appreciation. The celebration was not just a commemoration of Isaac and Lucy's love, but a tribute to the unity and camaraderie that had flourished within the Black American equestrian community. As the night wore on, toasts were raised to honor the Murphys' enduring love and the indelible mark they had left on the sport they held dear. Esteemed figures from all corners of America, including the top black jockeys of their time, stood shoulder to shoulder, united in admiration and appreciation. The echoes of their celebration would linger in the hearts of those who attended, a reminder that love, when nurtured with care and fueled by unwavering devotion, had the power to transcend the barriers imposed by society. Isaac and Lucy's love story was not just their own; it was a testament to the resilience of the human spirit, an inspiration to all who dared to dream and forge their own path. As the night drew to a close, the air was infused with a bittersweet longing. The guests departed, carrying with them the warmth and magic of the evening. Isaac and Lucy stood in their Lexington home, hand in hand, their hearts full. The journey they had embarked upon a decade ago continued, brimming with hope and endless possibilities. For Isaac and Lucy Murphy, their renewed vows marked not just a celebration of their past, but a declaration of their unwavering commitment to the future. Together, they would navigate the twists and turns that lay ahead, their love serving as a guiding light in a world that too often sought to dim its glow.

The year was 1895, and the racing world braced itself for an extraordinary display of talent. James "Soup" Perkins, a young jockey who had honed his skills under the watchful guidance of Isaac Murphy, was about to embark on a journey that would etch his name in the annals of horse racing history. The Kentucky Derby, a stage that had witnessed countless dreams and shattered hopes, stood as the ultimate test for both horse and rider. Perkins, adorned in his vibrant racing silks, radiated confidence as he mounted Halma, a horse owned by the visionary Black American horse owner Byron McClelland. Together, they formed a formidable duo, united in their pursuit of greatness. The crowd buzzed with anticipation, their collective heartbeat echoing through the grandstands. They knew they were about to witness something special, an indomitable spirit that defied age and convention. As the starting gates swung open, Perkins and Halma burst forward, their hearts beating as one. The thunderous sound of hooves reverberated through the track, a testament to the sheer power and grace that coursed through their veins. Perkins, with a touch that seemed almost ethereal, guided Halma through the tumultuous field, maneuvering with the precision of a maestro conducting a symphony. The race unfolded like a whirlwind, each stride a battle against the wind, against the doubts that whispered in the recesses of their minds. Perkins, his eyes locked on the finish line, felt the weight of history on his shoulders. He knew he had the talent, the courage, and the unwavering determination to conquer this hallowed ground. As the race neared its climax, the tension in the air became palpable. Perkins and Halma surged forward, their muscles straining with each powerful stride. The other jockeys, their faces etched with both determination and desperation, fought to maintain their positions. But Perkins, his connection with Halma transcending the physical, urged his mount to give her all. And then it happened. In a breathtaking display of skill and sheer willpower, Perkins and Halma crossed the finish line, their victory resounding through the grandstands. The crowd erupted in a cacophony of cheers, their jubilation a testament to the awe-inspiring feat they had just witnessed. Perkins had done it. He had conquered the Kentucky Derby, forever etching his name alongside the legends of the sport. In that moment, Perkins stood as a symbol of hope and inspiration. His victory was not just his own; it was a victory for every dreamer who had been told their ambitions were beyond reach. It was a triumph for every soul who had dared to challenge the limitations imposed by society. Perkins proved that greatness knows no age, no color, no boundaries. As he basked in the adulation of the crowd, Perkins felt a surge of gratitude for those who had supported him, for the mentors like Isaac Murphy who had nurtured his talent, and for the horse owners like Byron McClelland who had believed in his potential. Their collective efforts had culminated in this historic moment, forever changing the landscape of horse racing. James "Soup" Perkins had arrived, his name forever etched in the annals of horse racing history. And in the hearts of aspiring jockeys, in the dreams of young boys and girls who dared to imagine the impossible, his legacy would live on. James Perkins effectively conveyed the profound insight that dreams should not be confined solely to the realm of fantasy. Instead, he passionately emphasized the essential importance of actively pursuing one's dreams with unwavering zeal and unwavering resolve, surpassing the constraints of imagination. Perkins's impactful message deeply resonated, inspiring individuals to wholeheartedly embrace their aspirations and persevere diligently, continuously pushing the boundaries of what they believed to be achievable. His words ignited a spark of motivation, urging them to overcome challenges and setbacks with the knowledge that their dreams were deserving of every ounce of effort and unwavering dedication. Perkins's teachings served as a constant reminder that dreams, when pursued with unrelenting enthusiasm and an indomitable spirit, possess the power to transcend the limitations of the mind, transforming mere fantasies into tangible, attainable realities.

The year was 1894, and Alonzo Lonnie Clayton stood at the precipice of greatness. Following his historic victory in the Kentucky Derby, he embarked on a remarkable journey that would further solidify his status as a legendary jockey. In the years that followed, Clayton etched his name in the annals of horse racing history, achieving triumph after triumph. In 1894, Clayton found himself in the winner's circle not once, but twice, as he guided Selika to victory in the Kentucky Oaks. The race, a testament to grace and strength, became a canvas for Clayton to showcase the depth of his skill. With each stride, he mesmerized the crowd, his connection with Selika transcending the physical. They moved as one, their hearts beating in perfect harmony. But Clayton's ascent to greatness was far from over. In 1895, he returned to the Kentucky Oaks, this time riding Voladora. Once again, he defied expectations and emerged victorious. The thunderous applause that echoed through the grandstands was a testament to the awe-inspiring talent that resided within him. Yet Clayton's triumphs were not confined to the borders of his homeland. In 1895, he embarked on a daring adventure across the Atlantic, venturing to England—a land steeped in horse racing tradition. With an American horse beneath him, Clayton galloped across the hallowed grounds of English racecourses, leaving an indelible mark on the international racing scene. The race itself was a clash of cultures, a testament to the universal language of sport. As the horses thundered towards the finish line, Clayton's unwavering determination and unwavering connection with his mount propelled them to victory. The cheers of the English crowd mingled with the whispers of admiration that traveled across the ocean, a resounding tribute to Clayton's triumph. His name became synonymous with success, his journey a beacon of inspiration for aspiring jockeys around the world. He had shattered boundaries, proving that talent knew no borders. Clayton's continued success spoke to the enduring power of dreams and the relentless pursuit of greatness. His victories were not just his own; they were a triumph for every underdog, every individual who had ever been told their dreams were out of reach. As the world celebrated his accomplishments, they celebrated the triumph of the human spirit itself. Alonzo Lonnie Clayton had etched his name in the annals of horse racing history, forever a legend in the hearts of those who dared to dream. And as he galloped towards new horizons, he carried with him the hopes and aspirations of a new generation, inspiring them to chase their own wildest dreams.

SECTION III

Chapter 6 - Challenges and Enduring Resilience

The year was 1896, and across the United States, racial discrimination ran rampant, fueled by the ominous shadow of the U.S. Supreme Court's ruling in Plessy v. Ferguson. This infamous decision, with its insidious "separate but equal" doctrine, infected every corner of society, leaving no realm untouched by its divisive grasp. From schools to restaurants, and even racetracks, the poison of segregation thrived, igniting racial tensions and deepening the disparities that plagued the nation.

Within the world of horse racing, a sport that had once promised unity and thrilling competition, the echoes of discrimination grew louder with each passing day. Black American jockeys and trainers, who had long showcased their extraordinary talents on the tracks, found themselves pushed to the margins of a sport they had helped shape. The exhilaration and triumph they once savored gave way to a bitter reality—a reality where their opportunities dwindled and their dreams were stifled by an unjust system. Yet, from the darkness, a glimmer of hope emerged—a beacon of unwavering resilience that refused to be extinguished. This chapter in the history of American horse racing was etched with the stories of extraordinary individuals who faced discrimination head-on, unyielding in their pursuit of justice and equality. Their tales would become legends, whispered from one generation to the next, fueling the flames of determination and inspiring the hearts of all who dared to dream.

As the curtain of 1896 lifted, tragedy struck the equestrian community with a force that would reverberate through time. Sir Isaac Burns Murphy, a jockey whose skill and grace knew no bounds, met a sudden and suspicious end. Whispers of foul play filled the air, as allegations of poisoning hung heavy over the racing world. Murphy, a symbol of hope and resilience, had been extinguished, leaving a void that seemed impossible to fill. The news of Murphy's tragic demise rippled through the Black American community, leaving hearts heavy with grief and questions unanswered. His wife, Lucy, clung to the memories of their love, finding solace in the outpouring of support from those who revered him. The funeral that followed was a solemn affair, attended by more than five hundred mourners, each paying their respects to a fallen champion. Jockey Willie Simms, who had idolized Murphy, stood before the crowd, his voice steady with determination as he made a vow to carry on the legacy of his beloved friend.

Isaac Murphy's funeral was a testament to the profound impact he had made on the racing community. The somber Sunday morning was bathed in a gray pallor as mourners gathered at his residence on East Third Street. The air was heavy with sorrow, yet the weight of his absence was offset by the collective love and admiration that permeated the atmosphere. The grand procession that followed was unlike anything Lexington had ever seen, stretching for miles, as prominent figures from the racing community across the nation paid their respects. The cortege wound its way through the city streets, a poignant reminder of the indelible mark Murphy had left on the sport he loved. The colored cemetery on Seventh Street became the final resting place for the great Isaac Murphy. His grave, adorned with an abundance of vibrant floral arrangements from various locations, stood as a testament to the profound impact he had made in his too-short life. Isaac had once imagined an epitaph for himself, capturing the essence of his spirit and achievements—a belief that his life would be remembered as a success, an honor to be counted among America's greatest jockeys.

Yet, in the face of immense loss, the horse racing community refused to succumb to despair. United in their grief and fueled by an unwavering determination, they came together to confront the discriminatory system that threatened to snuff out their dreams. A council meeting was convened—a gathering of Black American individuals deeply involved in the equestrian industry, all seeking solace, strength, and strategies to navigate the troubled times that lay ahead. The discussions were passionate and purposeful, fueled by a shared desire to dismantle the barriers of discrimination and reclaim their rightful place in the sport they loved. They were acutely aware that the road ahead would be arduous, but their spirits remained unbroken. From that meeting, alliances were forged, strategies devised, and a collective resolve formed, a beacon of hope that would shine brightly in the darkest of days.

However, as the Black American community rallied against the chains of discrimination, another soul faced personal trials and tribulations. Anthony Hamilton, a talented jockey, had been burdened by a devastating loss—a newborn daughter who slipped away from his grasp, leaving a void that seemed impossible to fill. The weight of grief was further compounded by the loss of his dear friend, Isaac Murphy, plunging Hamilton into a tempest of emotions that threatened to consume him. The once-solid foundation of Hamilton's marriage to Annie Messley cracked under the strain, their shared sorrow becoming a chasm that seemed insurmountable. In the face of such turmoil, Hamilton turned to his mentor, Edward D. Brown, seeking guidance and solace in a world that seemed intent on breaking him. As he confided in Brown about his plans to continue his racing career in Europe, he expressed his deep-seated fears of financial hardship during the transition. In this moment of vulnerability, Brown, the epitome of unwavering support, offered Hamilton a lifeline—an opportunity to pursue his dreams without the burden of financial strife, courtesy of the Hawkins Brown & Co Equestrian Trust.

With his belongings meticulously packed and emotions swirling within his heart, Anthony Hamilton boarded a steamer bound for France—a vessel that carried not just the weight of his aspirations, but also the collective hopes and dreams of an entire community. The rolling waves mirrored the tumultuous journey that lay ahead, but within Hamilton's spirit, a fire burned bright, unyielding in its resolve. As he set foot on European soil, Anthony Hamilton's gaze was fixed on the horizon, where new challenges and opportunities awaited him. The legacy of Isaac Murphy, his friend and guiding light, fueled his every step. His story intertwined with those of countless others who had fought against adversity and discrimination, their triumphs and indomitable spirit etched in the annals of history.

In the face of racial discrimination, tragic loss, and personal turmoil, the equestrian community stood tall, their hearts aflame with an unwavering determination to confront the injustices that sought to confine them. Their journey was far from over, but with every stride, they revealed the true power of resilience, the strength that lies within the human spirit to endure and overcome. And so, the pages of history turned, carrying with them the tales of these extraordinary individuals. Their stories served as beacons of hope, inspiring future generations to challenge the status quo and forge a path towards a more just and inclusive future. The legacy of Black American jockeys and their unwavering contributions to the world of horse racing lived on, their impact felt in the hearts of those who dared to dream, creating a journey filled with determination, resilience, and the enduring pursuit of equality.

Tragedy loomed over the equestrian community in 1896, casting a shadow of sorrow and uncertainty. It was a year etched in sorrow and disbelief, for it was the year that the beloved jockey, Sir Isaac Burns Murphy, met his untimely demise under mysterious circumstances. The news spread like wildfire, whispering tales of poison and treachery that sent shockwaves through the hearts of all who revered him. Isaac Murphy, a beacon of hope for Black American jockeys and a symbol of indomitable spirit, had become the target of a malicious plot. Allegations swirled that a rival, their face hidden in the shadows, had infiltrated the ranks of white jockeys, seeking to extinguish the light that Isaac cast upon the racetracks. The poison that coursed through his veins was not the result of an unfortunate accident, but a deliberate act meant to silence a hero and tarnish his legacy.

Officially, Isaac's death was attributed to a heart attack resulting from an alcohol overdose, a conclusion that sent shockwaves of disbelief and anger rippling through the Black American community. They knew deep in their hearts that this ruling was a mere facade, a thin veil covering the truth that lay beneath. Their hero had been taken from them, and suspicions of foul play lingered like a bitter taste on their tongues. As the waves of grief crashed upon the shores of their collective spirit, the Black American community mourned the loss of Isaac Murphy. His impact, both on and off the racetrack, was immeasurable, and his absence left an indelible void that seemed impossible to fill. But even in death, Isaac's spirit reverberated through the very fabric of their souls, inspiring a profound sense of unity and resilience.

The funeral procession that followed was a testament to the profound love and respect Isaac had garnered throughout his illustrious career. Hundreds of mourners gathered, their hearts heavy with grief, yet their souls burning with a fervent desire to pay tribute to their fallen hero. The streets of Lexington swelled with a sea of black, a solemn symphony of mourning and remembrance. It was a sight that etched itself into the memories of all who bore witness—a testament to the enduring legacy of a man who had risen above the shackles of prejudice to conquer the racetracks. The funeral service, held on a somber Sunday, was a poignant farewell to a legend. The New York Times captured the solemnity and significance of the moment, ensuring that Isaac's story would reach far beyond the borders of Lexington. At his residence on East Third Street, where he had once lived and breathed, friends, family, and esteemed members of the racing community gathered to bid their final farewells. Among them were members of Bethany Commandery, Knights of

Templars, and other Masonic lodges—honoring Isaac with their presence, a testament to the admiration and respect he commanded.

The procession that followed was a testament to the extraordinary impact Isaac had made on the racing world. It stretched for miles, winding through the streets of Lexington like a river of sorrow, as prominent figures from across the nation paid homage to a fallen champion. The equestrian community had come together, transcending the boundaries of race, to honor a man who had left an indelible mark on their hearts. Finally, Isaac Murphy found his resting place in the colored cemetery on Seventh Street, surrounded by the tender embrace of nature's beauty. The gravesite became a sanctuary of memories, adorned with an abundance of floral tributes from various locations—a tapestry of vibrant colors and scents that spoke of the love and reverence that Isaac had inspired.

As the last echoes of the funeral bells faded into the horizon, the Black American community stood united, their hearts heavy but their spirits unbroken. They had lost their hero, their guiding light, but within the depths of their grief, a newfound determination emerged. Isaac's legacy would not be overshadowed by the darkness that had enveloped his final days. Instead, his memory would fuel their collective fire, driving them to confront the discrimination and prejudice that had threatened to extinguish their dreams. And so, as the sun set on that mournful day, a new resolve took root within the hearts of Isaac's brethren. They would honor his memory by fighting for their rightful place in the world of horse racing—a place free from the chains of discrimination, where talent and skill would prevail over the color of one's skin. The journey ahead would be arduous, fraught with challenges and obstacles, but the resilience of the human spirit would prevail. For within the depths of tragedy, seeds of enduring resilience were sown, ready to sprout into a future where the legacy of Sir Isaac Burns Murphy would forever inspire generations to come.

. The news of Sir Isaac Burns Murphy's tragic demise spread like wildfire, engulfing the equestrian community in a shroud of grief. In the wake of his untimely death, the world seemed to stand still, holding its breath as the stage was set for a funeral fit for a legend. The somber Sunday arrived, its air heavy with sorrow, as the largest funeral ever witnessed for a person of color began to unfold. The news of the funeral had reached even the prestigious columns of The New York Times, their extensive coverage a testament to the profound impact Isaac had made on the hearts and minds of those who knew him, as well as those who had only glimpsed his greatness from afar. Journalists, writers, and readers alike turned their attention to the solemn proceedings that would honor the life of a man who had defied the odds and risen to the pinnacle of the racing world.

The service took place at Isaac's residence on East Third Street, where he had once dreamed of victory and carved his path to greatness. The humble abode now stood as a sacred space, a sanctuary of memories that welcomed the mourners who had come to pay their respects. Among them were members of Bethany Commandery, Knights of Templars, and other Masonic lodges, their presence a testament to the brotherhood and camaraderie that Isaac had fostered throughout his illustrious career. As the mourners gathered, whispers of awe and reverence filled the air. Prominent figures from the racing community, both black and white, arrived to bid farewell to a man who had transcended the boundaries of race and challenged the limits of what was believed to be possible. It was a gathering of hearts burdened by loss but united by a shared love for the sport and the man who had embodied its spirit.

The procession that followed was a sight to behold—a silent symphony of grief and respect that stretched the limits of Lexington's history. A sea of mourners lined the streets, their solemn faces a poignant reflection of the profound impact Isaac had made on their lives. The procession wound its way through the city, a river of sorrow flowing towards the final resting place of a legend. Isaac Murphy was laid to rest in the colored cemetery on Seventh Street, the ground beneath his feet forever holding his indomitable spirit. The finality of the moment was softened by the abundance of floral tributes adorning his grave—a kaleidoscope of colors that whispered of love, admiration, and the enduring presence of a man who had left an indelible mark on the world.

Isaac's words echoed in the minds of those who stood in solemn vigil, their hearts heavy but their spirits uplifted by the legacy he had left behind. For he had once imagined an epitaph for himself, a declaration of the pride he took in his profession and his accomplishments. Though his fame had been earned in the stables and in the saddle, he knew that his life would be remembered as a success—a testament to the heights one could reach, regardless of the barriers placed before them. As the final petals fell, the mourners lingered, their hands reaching out to touch the sacred ground that cradled their hero. Their sorrow mingled with an unyielding determination, a vow to carry forth the torch of Isaac's legacy. The funeral had been a poignant tribute, a chapter in history that would forever bear witness to the resilience and triumph of the human spirit.

In the aftermath of grief, a resolve began to take root—a resolve to honor Isaac's memory by continuing the fight for equality and justice within the world of horse racing. The challenges ahead seemed insurmountable, but the fire within their hearts burned bright, ignited by the spirit of a man who had defied all odds. And so, as the sun set on that solemn Sunday, the equestrian community stood united, their souls intertwined with the memory of Isaac Murphy. They carried his legacy within them, emboldened by the realization that they were not alone in their struggles. In the face of adversity, they would rise, fueled by the hope that one day, the words of Isaac Murphy would ring true—a hope that their lives, too, would be remembered as successes, etched in the annals of history alongside America's greatest jockeys.

In the wake of Sir Isaac Burns Murphy's tragic and suspicious demise, the equestrian community found itself at a crossroads—a pivotal moment that demanded unity and collective action. Aware of the deeply entrenched discrimination and racism that permeated every facet of their lives, the Black American community, with a particular focus on those involved in the equestrian industry, gathered for a council meeting. It was a crucial gathering, a beacon of hope amid the turbulent sea of challenges that lay ahead. The air crackled with tension as they assembled, their faces etched with determination and resolve. They were acutely aware of the implications of the "separate but equal" doctrine enshrined by the Plessy v. Ferguson ruling—a ruling that had become a veil for inequality, casting long shadows of oppression over their dreams. But they refused to be silenced. They refused to let their spirits be crushed under the weight of discrimination.

The council meeting became a microcosm of their collective strength—a space where their concerns were voiced, their frustrations shared, and their hopes ignited. With passionate pleas and fierce determination, they laid bare the challenges they faced, acknowledging the uphill battle that lay before them. Their voices rose, an anthem of resilience, demanding justice, equality, and the right to pursue their dreams without the shackles of prejudice. The room became a crucible of ideas and strategies—a melting pot of ingenuity and unwavering spirit. Each member brought forth their perspectives, their experiences, and their wisdom, weaving a fabric of resilience and determination. They were determined to carve out a path that would transcend the boundaries imposed upon them, a path that would allow their talent and skill to shine undimmed by the color of their skin.

Conflict emerged, as it often does in moments of passionate discourse.

Differences in opinion clashed, but during the heated debates, a shared goal emerged—a vision of a future where the racetracks would be a sanctuary of equality and where their talents would be recognized, irrespective of the barriers society had imposed. The conflict that arose served as a catalyst for growth, pushing them to confront their own biases, to listen to the perspectives of others, and to forge a path forward with unity and compassion. Resolutions were formed, like pillars of hope rising from the fertile ground of determination. They vowed to band together, to support one another, and to fight for their rightful place in the world of horse racing. Strategies were devised to challenge the discriminatory practices that had long plagued their industry. They would leverage their collective strength, their unwavering passion, and their shared experiences to create change, brick by brick.

As the council meeting drew to a close, a newfound sense of purpose permeated the room. They left, their hearts aflame with the conviction that they could make a difference. The challenges that lay ahead were vast, but their resilience knew no bounds. They would face adversity head-on, armed with the power of unity and the unwavering belief in the righteousness of their cause. In the days and weeks that followed, the echoes of that council meeting reverberated through the equestrian community. Seeds of change had been planted, and the community's resolve had been hardened. They were bound by a common purpose, a shared dream of a future where the color of one's skin held no sway over their destiny. The council meeting had marked a turning point—an indelible chapter in their history. From that moment forward, they would navigate the troubled times ahead with unwavering resilience, drawing strength from their collective spirit. For within the crucible of challenges, they had discovered the power of their voices, the strength of their unity, and the hope that emerged when a community stands shoulder to shoulder, ready to face the world with unwavering resolve.

The winter winds whispered through the grief-stricken streets, carrying with them the weight of loss and heartbreak. In the cold embrace of December 1891, tragedy struck the lives of Anthony Hamilton and his wife, Annie Messley, like a thunderbolt from a remorseless sky. Their joy turned to sorrow, their dreams shattered, as they bid farewell to their newborn daughter, taken from them before she could even take her first breath. The pain of their loss cut deep, leaving an indelible scar upon their souls. As if fate revealed in the torment of their hearts, the year that followed brought another blow—an anguish that seeped into the very fabric of their beings. Isaac Murphy, Anthony's closest friend and confidant, the one who had shared his triumphs and consoled him in moments of despair, was ripped away by the merciless hands of death. The weight of this dual loss proved too much for their marriage to bear.

In the shadows of their personal grief, Anthony and Annie found themselves adrift, their bond strained under the weight of their sorrow. The pain they carried within them became an insurmountable barrier, closing the doors that once connected their hearts. Inevitably, they made the difficult decision to part ways, seeking solace and healing along separate paths. It was in this dark chapter of Anthony's life that he turned to his mentor, Edward D. Brown, his unwavering rock amidst the tempestuous sea of emotions. Anthony yearned for a fresh start, a chance to rebuild his shattered dreams and find solace in the realm of horse racing. But the specter of financial hardship loomed large, threatening to extinguish the flickering flame of his ambitions.

Ever the supportive friend, Edward offered a lifeline—a glimmer of hope amidst the storm. Through the Hawkins Brown & Co Equestrian Trust, Anthony would find the means to pursue his dreams without the burden of financial struggles. Edward's act of generosity bridged the chasm of uncertainty, paving the way for Anthony's journey to Europe, where new horizons awaited him. With his heart heavy and his belongings packed, Anthony embarked on a voyage to a land unknown. The ocean breeze caressed his face, carrying the whispers of possibilities and the echoes of his cherished memories. It was a bittersweet departure, leaving behind the familiar comforts of home and the ghosts of his past. But within his core, a fire burned—a yearning for redemption, for a chance to rise from the ashes of his personal losses and reclaim his destiny.

In the vibrant story of European horse racing, Anthony sought solace and redemption. He immersed himself in the competitive world of the tracks, where renowned jockeys battled for glory atop magnificent steeds. With each race, he found himself drawn deeper into the current of passion and exhilaration, leaving the weight of his grief behind. The support of his fellow riders and the cheers of the crowd breathed new life into Anthony's spirit. He discovered a resilience within him, forged by the trials he had endured. The losses he had suffered had transformed him, shaping him into a jockey of unwavering determination and unyielding spirit. With each stride of his mount, he left behind the shadows of his past, embracing the radiant dawn of his newfound purpose.

In Europe, Anthony found a community that embraced him—a

fraternity of kindred souls who recognized his talent and shared his dreams. Their camaraderie became a salve for his wounded heart, nurturing his resilience and fanning the flames of his aspirations. They became his second family, bound by their collective pursuit of greatness and the unyielding belief that barriers could be shattered. With every race, Anthony Hamilton etched his name upon the annals of equestrian history. His skills as a jockey, honed through years of dedication and fueled by his unwavering spirit, captivated the crowds and inspired the imaginations of young and old alike. He became a beacon of hope, a symbol of endurance in the face of personal loss.

Through the chapters of triumph and tribulation, Anthony Hamilton's story continued to unfold—a testament to the human spirit's ability to rise above adversity, to forge a path of resilience and grace. His journey across continents echoed with the footsteps of countless others who refused to be defined by their past but instead embraced the infinite possibilities of their future. And as Anthony rode across the finish line, his heart ablaze with a renewed sense of purpose, he carried within him the echoes of his daughter's name, the memory of Isaac Murphy's unwavering belief in him, and the knowledge that, even in the darkest of times, the indomitable human spirit could prevail.

In the wake of personal turmoil and with a heart heavy with both sorrow and determination, Anthony Hamilton sought solace and guidance from his trusted mentor, Edward D. Brown. The weight of his losses threatened to suffocate his dreams, casting doubts upon his ability to forge a future in the sport he loved. But within the depths of his despair, a glimmer of hope emerged—a lifeline extended by Edward in the form of the Hawkins Brown & Co Equestrian Trust. Anthony's concerns about the financial hardships that awaited him in his transition to the European racing scene found solace in the generosity of his mentor. Edward, ever the pillar of support, ensured that Anthony would embark on this new chapter without the specter of hardship haunting his every stride. The financial assistance provided by the trust served as a beacon, illuminating the path that lay ahead—a path filled with opportunity, challenges, and the promise of redemption.

With his belongings meticulously packed and emotions swirling within him like a tempest, Anthony embarked on a journey that would take him far from the shores of his homeland. Boarding a steamer bound for France, he left behind the familiar sights and sounds, bidding farewell to the echoes of his past. It was a moment pregnant with both trepidation and anticipation—an embrace of the unknown, a step into the uncharted territory of the European racing scene. As the steamer cut through the vast expanse of the ocean, the sea breeze whispered tales of distant lands and new beginnings. Anthony stood on the deck, his gaze fixed on the horizon, where the sun kissed the water in a breathtaking display of colors. The weight of his losses, the memories of his personal journey, and the legacy of Isaac Murphy were etched upon his soul, fueling his determination to carve a name for himself in the annals of European horse racing.

With each passing day, the steamer carried Anthony closer to his destination—the land of dreams and endless possibilities. Thoughts of the tracks he would grace, the crowds that would cheer his name, and the challenges that awaited him stirred a fire within him, igniting his spirit with an unyielding resolve. The thumping of his heart echoed the rhythm of the waves, pulsating with a mixture of anxiety and excitement. Arriving in France, Anthony Hamilton stepped onto foreign soil, his eyes alight with the glow of a new beginning. The sights, sounds, and scents of this unfamiliar land enveloped him, fueling his senses with a vibrant energy. The French language danced upon his ears, a melody he longed to understand and master. It was a kaleidoscope of new experiences, a fabric woven with the threads of anticipation and uncertainty.

But amidst the vastness of this foreign land, Anthony carried with him the legacy of Isaac Murphy—the spirit of resilience and determination that had defined their friendship. He knew that within him resided the essence of a champion, ready to rise above any obstacle that crossed his path. And with the unwavering support of his community, their collective hopes and dreams intertwined with his own, he possessed an inner strength that would carry him through the trials that lay ahead. Anthony Hamilton walked the cobbled streets of France, a man on a mission, driven by the echoes of his past and the promise of a brighter future. The road to success would not be without its bumps and hurdles, but he was prepared to face them head-on. He had traversed the depths of despair, tasted the bitterness of loss, and emerged with a steely resolve that would propel him forward.

As the sun cast its golden rays upon the path that stretched before him, Anthony Hamilton took his first steps into the European racing scene— a realm where legends were born and destinies were realized. With every stride, he left behind the shadows of his personal losses, embracing the light that illuminated his way. It was a new chapter, a fresh canvas upon which he would paint the masterpiece of his racing career. The story of Anthony Hamilton, intertwined with the spirit of Isaac Murphy and the unwavering support of his community, was set to unfold upon the European tracks. The world would bear witness to his unyielding resilience, his undying passion, and his unwavering pursuit of greatness. And as he embarked on this journey of triumph and tribulation, the echoes of their names would reverberate through the corridors of history, forever entwined in the tapestry of equestrian excellence.

SECTION III SUMMARY OF ALL CHAPTERS

During the period from 1882 to 1896, the novel chronicles the significant events and achievements of Black American jockeys in the world of horse racing. Chapter by chapter, the story unfolds, capturing the triumphs, challenges, and enduring legacies of these remarkable individuals. In Chapter 1, the focus is on the personal lives of the characters. Sir Isaac Burns Murphy proposes to Lucy Carr Osborne, marking the beginning of their journey together. The rise of jockey Babe Hurd also takes center stage, with his victory in the 1882 Kentucky Derby propelling him to success. Chapter 2 delves into the unity and resilience of the Black American equestrian community. At a gathering of influential figures, they confront racist caricatures and stereotypes, taking a stand against discrimination. This chapter highlights the determination of individuals like Isaac Murphy to race for their own community. Chapter 3 showcases the remarkable achievements of Black American jockeys. Isaac Murphy's continued success in winning the Kentucky Derby multiple times is a testament to his skill and dedication. Other jockeys such as Erskine Henderson and George B. "Spider" Anderson achieved significant victories, inspiring hope and admiration. In Chapter 4, the spotlight shifts to notable landmarks and personal affiliations. The construction of the Twin Spires at Churchill Downs symbolizes the grandeur of horse racing, while Isaac Murphy's involvement with the Lincoln Lodge Masons demonstrates his commitment to personal growth and community engagement. Chapter 5 brings both joy and sorrow to the characters. Celebrations of marriage, such as the Murphys' lavish reception and the engagement party for Anthony Hamilton and Annie Messley, are contrasted with personal losses. Tragedy strikes with the loss of Hamilton's newborn daughter, and the challenges faced by Hamilton and Murphy's death test the resilience of the community. The final chapter, Chapter 6, explores the enduring spirit of the Black American horsemen in the face of racial discrimination and adversity. The impact of the Supreme Court ruling in Plessy v. Ferguson is felt, and the mysterious poisoning and death of Isaac Murphy brings grief and challenges to the community. However, their resilience shines through as they continue to fight against discrimination and pursue their dreams. As the period concludes, the legacy of Isaac Murphy and other Black American jockeys lives on, inspiring future generations to challenge prejudice and strive for greatness. The novel captures their remarkable achievements, unwavering spirit, and enduring camaraderie, ensuring that the contributions of Black American jockeys in horse racing will never be forgotten.

Themes:

Triumph and Achievement: The narrative explores the triumphs and achievements of Black American jockeys and trainers during a time of racial discrimination, showcasing their exceptional talent and dedication to the sport.

Unity and Community: The story highlights the power of unity and community support, as Black American equestrians come together to navigate challenges, confront racism, and celebrate each other's successes.

Resilience and Perseverance: The characters demonstrate remarkable resilience in the face of adversity, pushing forward to overcome obstacles, pursue their dreams, and leave lasting legacies.

Love and Relationships: Love and relationships play a significant role, with weddings, engagements, and celebrations emphasizing the bonds formed between characters and the importance of support and companionship.

Racism and Discrimination: The pervasive themes of racism and discrimination shed light on the challenges faced by Black American horsemen and horsewomen during a time of segregation and inequality.

Settings:

Kentucky Derby: The iconic Kentucky Derby serves as a recurring backdrop for key events in the narrative, symbolizing achievement, prestige, and the pinnacle of horse racing.

Galleries and Estates: Lavish estates and grand gatherings represent opulence, celebration, and the coming together of influential figures within the Black American equestrian community.

Masonic Lodges: Masonic lodges symbolize unity, brotherhood, and personal growth, providing a sense of belonging and community for the characters.

Currier & Ives: The publishing house serves as a symbol of racial caricatures and prejudice, highlighting the need for racial equality and the characters' fight against racism.

Symbols:

Twin Spires: The iconic twin spires at Churchill Downs symbolize the grandeur and passion of horse racing, representing a sense of identity and place.

The Photograph: The photograph capturing the "photo finish" at a race signifies progress and innovation, revolutionizing the way race outcomes are determined.

The Colored Party: The extravagant "A Colored Party" reception hosted by the Murphys represents celebration, unity, and the breaking of societal barriers.

Motifs:

Victories and Races: The recurring motif of victories and races represents the pursuit of excellence, determination, and the thrill of competition within the equestrian world.

Mentorship and Legacy: The theme of mentorship and passing down knowledge signifies the strength of bonds between experienced and aspiring horsemen, ensuring the legacy and future success of Black American equestrians.

Foreshadowing:

James "Soup" Perkins: Perkins' encounters with Isaac Murphy and his commitment to learning from his mentor foreshadow his future success as a jockey.

Isaac Burns Murphy's Legacy: The mention of Murphy's desire for a notable epitaph foreshadows the lasting impact he will leave on the sport and the hearts of those who admired him.

Literary Devices:

Allegory: The representation of Black American jockeys, trainers, and horsemen confronting racism and discrimination serves as an allegory for the broader struggle for racial equality during that time period.

Metaphor: The Twin Spires as "church towers" metaphorically connect the devotion and passion of horse racing to a religious-like reverence.

Foreshadowing: The mention of Anthony Hamilton's plans to continue his racing career overseas foreshadows his journey and the new opportunities that await him in Europe.

END OF **SECTION III.**

PART 1

SECTION IV: TIME PERIOD: 1897 - 1906

Chapter 1: The Legacy of Isaac Murphy through Willie Simms.

    1. Sir Isaac Burns Murphy's Funeral and Willie Sims' Reflections

    2. A Controversy Surrounding the Crouching Posture Technique

    3. Edward Dudley Brown Sets the Record Straight

    4. A Test of Integrity: The Bribe Offer

    5. Triumph at the Kentucky Derby

    6. Continued Success: The Kentucky Derby and the Preakness Stakes

    7. Triple Crown Status: Willie Sims Joins the Elite

Chapter 2: Murder & Downfall

    1. A Tragic Loss: Frank Perkins' Murder

    2. The Downfall of Alonzo Lonnie Clayton

Chapter 3: Adversities

    1. The Struggle for Jimmy Winkfield

    2. A Tragic Encounter with Meriwether Lewis Clark Jr.

    3. Jimmy Winkfield's Personal Struggles and Dr. Allen's Support

    4. Edward Dudley Brown's Advocacy for Jimmy Winkfield

Chapter 4: Opportunity and the colorline:

    1. Jimmy Winkfield's Continued Success at the Kentucky Derby

    2. Back-to-Back Victories: Jimmy Winkfield's Consecutive Kentucky Derby Wins

SECTION IV

Chapter 1 - The Legacy of Isaac Murphy through Willie Simms

The somber atmosphere enveloped the attendees as they bid farewell to the legendary jockey, Sir Isaac Burns Murphy, at his funeral. The air was heavy with grief as tears streamed down the faces of those who had witnessed his greatness. It was a day of mourning, a day to honor the man who had left an indelible mark on the sport of horse racing. Amidst the sea of sorrow, Jockey Willie Sims found himself standing amidst the crowd, his mind drifting back to his own triumphs and the lessons he had learned from the great Sir Isaac.

Willie's thoughts traveled back to the Belmont Stakes, where he had tasted victory in 1893 and 1894 astride the magnificent Comanche and Henry of Navarre, respectively. Those moments of glory had been guided by the sage advice imparted to him by both Edward Dudley Brown and Sir Isaac himself. It was their wisdom that had shaped him into the jockey he was today. Yet, even in the midst of his reminiscence, a cloud of controversy loomed over the legacy of the crouching posture technique used by jockeys. Tod Sloan, a rival jockey, had shamelessly claimed credit for inventing the technique, causing a stir in the racing community. Outraged by the false claim, Willie Sims could not let the audacious lie go unchallenged.

With the fire of conviction burning within him, Willie engaged in a public debate with Sloan, his voice resounding through the crowd as he vehemently defended the true origin of the technique. He highlighted the inappropriate nature of Sloan's assertion, laying bare the fallacy of his words. The racing world listened intently, captivated by the passion and righteousness in Willie's voice. Standing beside him, Edward Dudley Brown, a respected figure in the equestrian world, lent his support to Willie's cause. He shared the true history of the crouching posture technique, revealing that it was Abe Hawkins, the great slayer of

Lexington, who had first developed it. Abe had sought to protect the horses from the cruel whipping and abuse they endured during races. Brown's words carried weight and silenced the false narrative perpetuated by Sloan. The truth had prevailed.

But the test of Willie's integrity did not end with the exposure of Sloan's falsehood. As his star continued to rise, so did the attempts to tarnish his name. A bribe was offered to him, an insidious attempt to corrupt his spirit and undermine the purity of the sport. In his moment of uncertainty, Willie turned to his wise mentor, Edward Dudley Brown, seeking guidance. Edward's eyes, filled with wisdom gained through years of experience, met Willie's. He spoke with a firmness that left no room for doubt. "A man's true wealth lies in his integrity," he said, his voice a soothing balm to Willie's troubled soul. "Accepting a bribe will bring you nothing but regret. Stay true to yourself, my boy, and the path to victory will open before you."

Resolute in his principles, Willie rejected the bribe, his resolve shining like a beacon in the face of temptation. With a newfound determination, he prepared himself for the race, knowing that his integrity would be his most potent weapon. In 1896, the Kentucky Derby witnessed the triumph of Willie Sims as he rode Ben Brush to victory. The thunderous roar of the crowd mingled with the pounding of hooves, creating an intoxicating symphony of jubilation. In that moment, the weight of history was palpable, as if the spirits of all the great Black American jockeys who had come before him were rejoicing in his triumph. But Willie's hunger for success did not wane. The following year, in 1898, he once again tasted victory at the Kentucky Derby, this time atop the gallant Plaudit. The cheers of the crowd washed over him, their applause a testament to his remarkable skill and unwavering determination. Just a few weeks later, he added another triumph to his growing list of achievements by winning the Preakness Stakes on the back of the swift and cunning Sly Fox.

With these victories, Willie Sims etched his name alongside the legendary Sir Isaac Burns Murphy, achieving Triple Crown status and cementing his place in the annals of horse racing history. His journey, rife with challenges and trials, had led him to this moment of glory. The road ahead would undoubtedly hold more obstacles, but with the lessons of integrity and perseverance guiding him, Willie was prepared to face whatever lay ahead. As the sun set on the racetrack, casting long shadows across the hallowed ground, Willie Sims stood tall, his heart brimming with hope and a determination to continue defying the odds. The legacy of the Black American jockeys burned brightly in his soul, their stories entwined with his own. And as he gazed into the horizon, he knew that the world of horse racing would never be the same again.

For Willie Sims had become more than a jockey; he had become a beacon of inspiration, a symbol of triumph over adversity. His story would inspire generations to come, reminding them that no dream was too audacious, no hurdle too high. And in that moment, surrounded by the echoes of his predecessors, he knew that his journey had only just begun.

SECTION IV

Chapter 2 - Murder & Downfall

In the year 1900, tragedy befell James "Soup" Perkins, plunging his world into darkness and sorrow. The devastating news of his beloved brother, Frank Perkins, being shot dead on his own doorstep shattered Soup's heart. It was a senseless and abrupt loss that left Soup and his loved ones reeling from the cruelty of fate.

Amidst the overwhelming grief threatening to consume him, Soup's thoughts turned to seeking justice for his brother's untimely demise. He made a solemn vow to uncover the truth behind this senseless act and bring the perpetrators to account, regardless of the personal cost.

The investigation into Frank's murder proved to be a challenging and arduous journey. The leads initially appeared promising but soon grew cold, leaving Soup grappling with frustration. However, his determination remained unyielding. He reached out to his vast network of contacts, both within and outside the racing community, in a relentless pursuit of any information that could shed light on the identity of the assailant.

Day after day, Soup delved deeper into the underbelly of the criminal world, following threads of suspicion and whispers of secrets. His unwavering quest for justice brought him face to face with dangerous individuals and thrust him into perilous situations. Yet, he stood resolute, driven by the memory of his brother and fueled by an unwavering desire to bring closure to the tragedy that had befallen his family.

As Soup's investigation progressed, a tangled web of deception and betrayal began to unravel before his eyes. He discovered that Frank had become entangled in a treacherous feud between rival factions within the horse racing community. This murder was not an act of random violence, but rather a targeted strike, intended to silence Frank and his knowledge of illicit activities that threatened the integrity of the sport.

Armed with newfound determination, Soup meticulously gathered evidence and sought the assistance of law enforcement. Teaming up with a dedicated detective, they painstakingly pieced together the puzzle, connecting dots that ultimately led to the unmasking of the culprits responsible for his brother's murder. The wheels of justice began to turn, gradually inching closer to the day when those responsible would face the consequences of their heinous act.

As the court proceedings unfolded, Soup found solace in the knowledge that his brother's death had not been in vain. The truth had been revealed, and those who had sought to conceal their tracks and evade responsibility were now held accountable. It was a bittersweet victory, one that could never fully mend the wound left by Frank's absence but provided a semblance of closure.

Soup's journey through grief and his relentless pursuit of justice had transformed him. The loss of his brother had ignited an unquenchable fire within him, inspiring a newfound purpose to fight against corruption and safeguard the integrity of the sport they both cherished. Frank's memory lived on, not just in Soup's heart, but in the legacy of a man who had championed honesty and fairness.

SECTION IV

Chapter 3 - Adversities

The year 1898 tested the resolve of the young jockey, Jimmy Winkfield, like never before. His dreams of becoming a celebrated rider were shattered in a devastating accident that caused a pileup of jockeys and horses. Chaos on the track led to a conspiracy, fueled by prejudice, aimed at pushing Black Americans out of the beloved sport. Jimmy found himself unjustly suspended, his dreams hanging in the balance. But Jimmy refused to be defeated. He clung to a glimmer of hope, seeking the guidance and support of Edward Dudley Brown, a man who had dedicated his life to justice and equality in the equestrian world.

Recognizing the injustice, Brown pledged to fight for Jimmy's reinstatement, urging the racing administration to lift the ban. Together, they embarked on a mission, fueled by passion and a burning desire to rectify the prejudices that plagued the sport they loved. As they delved into the corridors of power, they encountered a figure from the past— Meriweather Lewis Clark Jr., the man who had once barred Black American jockeys from the Kentucky Derby. However, the tides of fortune had turned, and Clark had fallen on hard times. No longer the prominent figure he once was, he found himself working as a waiter.

A heartfelt conversation unfolded between William Billy Walker, Edward Dudley Brown, and Clark. Clark expressed remorse for his past actions, genuinely apologizing for the pain he had caused. Touched by Clark's plight, Walker offered an act of compassion, tipping him a generous sum. The weight of their shared history hung in the air. But Clark's turmoil overwhelmed him, and he abruptly rushed out of the restaurant, leaving Walker in shock. Driven by concern, Walker pursued him through the streets, determined to provide solace. It was a race against time until he finally discovered Clark in a hidden safe house. Inside, the broken spirit of Meriweather Lewis Clark Jr. was laid bare. Despair gnawed at his soul, and he held a gun to his head, seeking redemption. Walker pleaded with Clark, urging him to reconsider, to find another path towards healing and redemption. But tragically, his pleas fell on deaf ears. In the blink of an eye, Meriweather Lewis Clark Jr. took his own life, leaving Walker shattered and haunted by the echoes of his own near-lynching. The weight of history bore down upon him, a burden too heavy to bear alone. The funeral that followed served as a poignant reminder of the profound impact their shared history had on both men's lives.

While Walker grappled with his own grief and the ghosts of the past, Jimmy Winkfield's personal life took an unexpected turn. In 1900, he entered into a clandestine marriage with Edna Lee, defying the odds stacked against them. The challenges faced by Black American doctors like Dr. Allen in a resource-scarce state provided a backdrop to their union—a union forged in the fires of love and hope. Amidst turmoil and shadows, there was a glimmer of hope. Edward Dudley Brown's relentless efforts finally bore fruit. In 1900, the racing administration relented under his persuasion, granting Jimmy Winkfield permission to return to the tracks. It was a moment of triumph, not just for Jimmy, but for all Black American jockeys who had faced discrimination. The resilience of the young jockey had prevailed, tearing down barriers. With each stride, he raced towards a future of endless possibilities. As Jimmy Winkfield prepared to mount his horse once again, a sense of purpose burned within him. He knew that his triumph would be a victory for all marginalized and silenced. The winds of change whispered through the stables, carrying with them the hopes and dreams of a community denied its rightful place in horse racing history.

And with each thundering hoofbeat, the spirit of the Black Maestro soared, illuminating the path for others to follow. Jimmy Winkfield had become a symbol of resilience, an embodiment of the indomitable human spirit that refuses to be broken by adversity. The journey ahead would be fraught with challenges and obstacles, but Jimmy embraced them with hope and an unyielding spirit. The legacy of Black American jockeys burned brightly within him, a flame that would guide him through the trials yet to come. And as he looked toward the horizon, he knew that his race had only just begun.

Along their journey, they encountered a figure from the past— Meriweather Lewis Clark Jr., the man who had once barred Black American jockeys from participating in the Kentucky Derby. However, the tables had turned, and Clark had fallen from grace. Reduced to working as a humble waiter in a modest restaurant, he crossed paths with William Billy Walker, Edward Dudley Brown, and Jimmy Winkfield in a heartfelt conversation.

In this moment of revelation, Clark expressed genuine remorse for his past actions, extending a heartfelt apology to Walker for the pain he had caused. Touched by Clark's plight, Walker offered an act of compassion, generously tipping him $100. In that instant, the weight of their shared history, marked by discrimination and struggle, hung heavily in the air. Overwhelmed by emotional turmoil, Clark abruptly fled the restaurant, leaving Walker in a state of shock. Driven by concern for Clark's well-being, Walker pursued him through the labyrinthine streets of the city, determined to offer solace and understanding. It became a race against time as Walker followed Clark's trail until finally discovering his refuge—a hidden safe house.

Inside the sanctuary, Walker witnessed the broken spirit of Meriwether Lewis Clark Jr. Despair gnawed at his soul, and he held a gun to his head, seeking redemption for his past misdeeds. In a heart-wrenching plea, Clark begged for forgiveness. Walker's voice trembled with urgency and empathy as he implored Clark to reconsider, to seek another path—one of healing and redemption. Tragically, his pleas fell upon deaf ears. In the blink of an eye, Meriweather Lewis Clark Jr. took his own life, leaving Walker shattered and haunted by the echoes of his own near-lynching at the hands of Confederates. The weight of history pressed heavily upon him, a burden too immense to bear alone. The ensuing funeral served as a poignant reminder of the profound impact their shared history had upon both men's lives.

While Walker grappled with his grief and the haunting specters of the past, Jimmy Winkfield's personal life took an unexpected turn. In the year 1900, he entered into a secret marriage with a woman named Edna Lee. The challenges faced by Black American doctors, exemplified by the struggles of Dr. Allen in a resource-scarce state, provided a backdrop to their union—a union forged in the fires of love and hope, defying the odds stacked against them. Yet, amidst the turmoil and the shadows of tragedy, a glimmer of hope persisted. Edward Dudley Brown's unwavering efforts finally yielded results. In the year 1900, due to his relentless persuasion, the racing administration, turf association, and Jockey Club relented, granting Jimmy Winkfield permission to return to the tracks and resume his horse racing career.

This moment marked a triumph not only for Jimmy but for all Black American jockeys who had endured discrimination and adversity. The unwavering resilience of the young jockey had shattered the confines that sought to restrict him. With each stride of his steed, he raced towards a future filled with limitless possibilities. As Jimmy Winkfield prepared to mount his horse once again, a profound sense of purpose burned within him. He understood that his victory would not be solely his own but a triumph for all those who had been marginalized, silenced, and oppressed. The winds of change whispered through the stables, carrying with them the hopes and dreams of a community that had been unjustly denied their rightful place in the annals of horse racing history.

And with each thundering hoofbeat, the spirit of the Black Maestro soared, illuminating the path for others to follow. Jimmy Winkfield had transcended the role of a mere jockey—he had become a symbol of resilience, an embodiment of the indomitable human spirit that refuses to yield to adversity. The journey ahead would be fraught with challenges and obstacles, but Jimmy embraced them with a heart brimming with hope and a spirit that could not be extinguished. The legacy of Black American jockeys burned brightly within him, a flame that would guide him through the trials yet to come. And as he looked toward the horizon, he knew that his race had only just begun.

SECTION IV

Chapter 4 - Opportunity & the Colorline.

In the year 1900, Jimmy Winkfield's life took a pivotal turn, solidifying his status as a beacon of hope and inspiration in the world of horse racing. His journey had been one of extraordinary triumphs and relentless adversities, a testament to his unwavering spirit and indomitable determination. After defying the odds with a remarkable third-place finish at the Kentucky Derby, Jimmy left an indelible mark on the hallowed grounds of Churchill Downs. The thunderous applause of the crowd and the resounding hooves of the horses merged into a symphony of validation, fueling his belief in the greatness that resided within him. Undeterred by setbacks, Jimmy's determination soared to new heights. In 1901, he achieved an extraordinary feat that surpassed all expectations. With unparalleled skill and unwavering focus, he surged ahead, leaving his rivals in the dust and crossing the finish line as the victorious champion of the Kentucky Derby. The thunderous cheers of the crowd echoed through his very being, celebrating the rise of a new legend in the realm of racing.

However, April 1901 brought scandal and upheaval to the racing world, as one of its brightest stars, Alonzo Lonnie Clayton, faced arrest on charges of race-fixing. The once-prominent jockey, who had captivated racing enthusiasts with his prowess, now found himself at the center of a storm that threatened to shatter his career and tarnish his reputation. The allegations against Alonzo Clayton reverberated throughout the racing community, casting doubt on his integrity and calling into question the legitimacy of his previous victories. Speculations ran rampant, fueled by whispers of secret dealings and underhanded tactics. The tarnishing of Clayton's name cast a dark cloud of uncertainty over his once-illustrious career.

As legal proceedings unfolded, Alonzo Clayton vehemently protested his innocence, asserting that he had been unfairly targeted and framed. The ensuing trial became a spectacle, captivating the public's attention as the media dissected every detail of the case. Supporters rallied behind Clayton, steadfast in their conviction of his integrity and determined to prove his innocence. In a dramatic turn of events, evidence emerged that bolstered Alonzo Clayton's claims of being framed. Witnesses stepped forward, offering testimonies that cast doubt on the credibility of the accusations. The truth began to unravel, revealing a complex web of deceit and manipulation orchestrated by individuals seeking to besmirch Clayton's name and dismantle his career.

Ultimately, Clayton was acquitted of all charges, his name cleared, and a semblance of dignity restored. However, the damage had been done. The arduous ordeal had taken its toll on Alonzo Clayton's psyche, eroding his confidence and leaving him struggling to reclaim his former level of success. The racing world, scarred by the scandal, was hesitant to embrace him once again, thwarting his hopes of a triumphant comeback. Yet, Alonzo Clayton refused to let circumstances define him. Amidst the challenging aftermath, he found solace in the unwavering support of a few loyal friends and admirers who stood by his side during the darkest moments of his life. With their encouragement, he redirected his focus towards mentoring young jockeys, sharing his wisdom and experiences to shape the next generation of riders.

The downfall of Alonzo Lonnie Clayton served as a powerful lesson in resilience and the enduring spirit of a man determined to rise above adversity. Though his career had been marred by scandal, Clayton's impact on the sport extended beyond mere victories and losses. His legacy lived on through the lives he touched and the lessons he imparted, serving as a constant reminder of the importance of integrity and perseverance. Meanwhile, as Alonzo Clayton navigated the aftermath of the scandal, Jimmy Winkfield continued to soar to new heights. In 1902, he achieved yet another remarkable triumph, standing atop the podium at the Kentucky Derby for the second consecutive year. The deafening roar of the crowd blended with the pounding of his heart, infusing his spirit with an overwhelming sense of accomplishment. In that moment, he solidified his position among the greatest jockeys of his time, bearing the weight of history and the legacy of Black American riders with grace and unwavering determination. But even in the face of success, Jimmy encountered formidable obstacles that threatened to cast a shadow over his achievements.

In 1903, Jimmy secured a hard-fought second-place finish at the Kentucky Derby, a testament to his unwavering commitment and resilience. Though denied the top spot, he etched his name once again in the annals of history, becoming the third Black American jockey to achieve the coveted Triple Crown—an honor that could never be diminished. While Jimmy basked in the glow of his accomplishments, his revered mentor, Edward Dudley Brown, recognized the challenges that lay ahead. The era of Jim Crow laws, characterized by racial segregation, cast a dark and oppressive shadow over the South. White jockeys drew a color line, effectively excluding Black Americans from the sport they had helped shape with their exceptional talents. This bitter reality threatened to undermine the progress made by these exceptional athletes, challenging the principles of equality and fairness. Compounding matters, Jimmy found himself caught in a controversy surrounding his choice of trainer. Initially aligned with John E. Madden, circumstances led him to switch to a rival trainer. Madden, nursing a bruised ego, launched a vindictive smear campaign, intent on blacklisting Jimmy from the racing scene. The onslaught of accusations and defamation enveloped him in a cloud of uncertainty, leaving him standing at a precipice, uncertain of his next move.

Amidst the possibility of abandonment and disillusionment, Jimmy turned to his trusted mentor, Edward Dudley Brown, seeking guidance and reassurance. In moments of quiet reflection, Brown reminded him of the legacy they carried—the legacy of the Black American jockeys who had come before them, the legacy of triumph over adversity, and the responsibility to challenge the status quo. During Isaac Murphy's funeral, a fellow rider and friend, Anthony "Tony" Hamilton, revealed his plans to participate in European races. These words resonated deeply with Brown, offering a glimmer of solace. The torch had been passed, and it was now Jimmy Winkfield's turn to carry it forward, to defy boundaries and prove that talent and skill transcended color and prejudice. With the echoes of farewell still ringing in his ears, Jimmy bid farewell to his mentor and the familiar shores of America. The journey across the vast expanse of the Atlantic Ocean commenced, the ship slicing through the rolling waves towards a land brimming with potential and uncertainty. As he stood at the bow, gazing out into the boundless horizon, his heart surged with hope and determination. The Old World awaited him, with its ornate racing establishments and discerning audience. Unbeknownst to him, this voyage would become a chapter of triumphs and adversities, a testament to his unyielding spirit and unwavering commitment. The legacy of Black American jockeys would resonate on foreign soil, challenging the barriers that sought to confine them and paving the way for a future where talent and character reigned supreme.

As the ship sailed onwards, leaving behind the familiar shores of

America, Jimmy Winkfield embraced the unknown with open arms. He prepared to face a new world—one that would test his mettle, redefine his place in history, and leave an indelible mark on the hearts and minds of those who witnessed his relentless pursuit of glory. The stage was set, and the crowd eagerly awaited his arrival, their anticipation a symphony of hope and boundless possibility. In that moment, as the wind whispered through the billowing sails, Jimmy knew that his journey was far from over. The races yet to be run held the promise of new challenges and triumphs as he blazed a trail that would inspire generations to come. With each stride of his steed, he would carry the hopes and dreams of those who believed in him, defying boundaries and leaving an enduring legacy that would stand as a testament to the resilience and power of the human spirit.

SECTION IV

Chapter 5 - Farewells & Flights

In the historic year of 1903, the racing world watched with a heavy heart as the health of one of its most cherished figures, Edward Dudley Brown, began to falter. A respected icon of the sport, Edward was faced with the reality of his impending demise. As he stood on the precipice of his final moments, the aura of wisdom and strength that surrounded him remained undimmed. Recognizing the inevitable, Edward understood that the time had come to entrust his legacy to his protege, Jimmy Winkfield. With the weight of this responsibility etched in his heart, he held a private meeting with Jimmy. In this intimate setting, he imparted his last words of wisdom and inspiration to his young apprentice, emphasizing the importance of carrying their shared legacy forward.

In a moment rich with significance, Edward extended a tender hand to Jimmy and presented him with the Chiron pendant necklace. This cherished ornament had been a gift from their shared mentor, Abe Hawkins, symbolizing a passing of the baton from one generation to another. The necklace radiated a blend of strength, wisdom, and an unyielding pursuit of knowledge, representing the foundational principles that defined their joint legacy. Edward, despite his weakening physical state, communicated his heartfelt aspirations for Jimmy. He expressed his deepest hopes, envisioning Jimmy continuing their journey in the foreign lands of Russia. In his dream, Jimmy was not merely participating in races, but leaving an indelible mark of accomplishments that would illuminate the path for many others to follow.

As Edward's legacy was handed over, his breath began to falter, marking the final moments of a remarkable life. Those who had been fortunate enough to know him, to have felt the impact of his inspiring character, bid him a tearful farewell. The entire racing community mourned the loss of a true legend, someone who had served as a father figure to many within the sport. In death, Edward joined his mentor, Abe Hawkins, in the realm of eternal greatness. The funeral was held at the

Midway Pilgrim Baptist Church in Woodford County, a place that reflected the humble and principled man that Edward had been. It was a solemn yet powerful gathering, where heartfelt tributes were paid and stories shared, all of which underlined the deep impact Edward had made throughout his lifetime.

However, Edward's legacy extended beyond his triumphs and accolades on the racetrack. He was one of the wealthiest men in Kentucky, yet his wealth never overshadowed his boundless generosity. He was known for his unwavering commitment to his community, and his contributions left a lasting imprint on the lives of those he interacted with. Edward's philanthropy was both purposeful and profound. He devoted his time and resources to nurturing aspiring jockeys, sharing his wisdom, and guiding them on their path. Additionally, he was also known for his significant contributions to various charitable causes, demonstrating a genuine care for others that was unparalleled. As the racing world paid their tributes to Edward, it became clear that his memory would forever hold a special place in the heart of the sport. His mentorship, wisdom, and unwavering passion for racing were elements of his persona that would continue to inspire, motivate, and guide future generations.

The legacy of Edward Dudley Brown would not just survive, but thrive, serving as a beacon of light and guidance for those who aspired to follow in his footsteps. His life was a testament to the profound impact one individual can have, not only on a sport but on the lives of countless individuals within a community.

SECTION IV

Chapter 6 - Jimmy Visions - Echoes of the Starlit Track

In the early twilight of the year 1904, the world whispered tales of the American jockey who had embraced an unfamiliar land, France, as his own. Jimmy Winkfield, the embodiment of a horse-racing legend, sought to reconvene his life after a tumultuous departure from Russia's tumultuous clutches. As the French moonlight danced on his weary face, he relived the grandeur of his past, a life painted with victories and glory, especially the one that played out under the watchful gaze of Czar Nicholas II. In the silence of the night, his dreams were not mere flights of fancy but transformative experiences. He, a mortal man, morphed into a centaur, an intriguing blend of human and horse, with Edward Dudley Brown's spirit illuminating his path.

His dreamscape, both mystical and profound, was where he encountered an arachnid, gracefully spinning intricate webs at the entrance of a majestic mountain cavern. The celestial aura that enveloped the scene stirred within Jimmy a sense of wonder and discovery, intertwining his destiny with Edward's indelible wisdom. Upon emerging from this extraordinary dream, a significant revelation awaited him - Edward's gift, the Chiron pendant, lay nestled in a buttonhole of his old racing silks. The pendant, bearing the image of a figure wielding a bow and arrow, encapsulated the ethos of Chiron—strength, sagacity, and the relentless quest for knowledge.

This realization resonated deep within him, invigorating his spirit and renewing his faith in the bond that bound the mentor and protégé across the chasms of time and space. Seizing the sign of renewed vigor, Jimmy resurrected his dormant career, staging a triumphant return to the racing tracks of France in 1922. His father-in-law's generous gift, a grand three-story chateau christened 'Maison Lafitte,' complete with private stables, rekindled his love for horse racing and reawakened his latent potential.

The chateau, a magnificent sanctuary nestled within lush greenery, was Jimmy's personal Eden where his passion for horses could flourish unbridled, propelling him towards his relentless pursuit of equestrian excellence. Embarking on this extraordinary quest, Jimmy galloped through the annals of French horse-racing history, each victory a testament to his resilience and prowess. His triumphs transcended personal gratification and echoed the tenacity and talent of Black American jockeys who dared to defy societal norms and shatter racial barriers.

As the curtains began to close on his saga, Jimmy Winkfield dedicated his days to the care of his beloved stables at Maison Lafitte, his heart cradling the memories of his victories and Edward's invaluable mentorship. The cosmic magic that had once graced his dreams remained etched in his soul, reinforcing the profound correlation between mentorship, curiosity, and the relentless pursuit of knowledge. His unwavering dedication and love for the sport he worshiped served as a beacon, illuminating the lasting legacies left behind by the Black American jockeys who braved the odds and forever altered the course of equestrian history.

On March 23, 1974, as the French landscape came alive with the hues of spring, Jimmy Winkfield's journey reached its final milestone. Though his physical presence dissolved into the ether, his indomitable spirit and the legacies of the Black American trailblazers continued to reverberate across racetracks worldwide, inspiring a legion of horse racing enthusiasts.

The narrative of Jimmy Winkfield, a legendary jockey whose life was touched by celestial encounters, stands as an enduring testament to the transformative power of mentorship, the enchantment of the cosmos, and the endless pursuit of knowledge. It inspires each individual to seek guidance, marvel at the universe's boundless mysteries, and harness their inner potential to attain greatness. Jimmy's story continues to inspire, beckoning us all to reach for the stars, chase our dreams, and leave an enduring legacy that transcends the fleeting nature of time.

As the golden hues of the setting sun melted into the tranquility of the evening, Jimmy stood amidst the lush pastures of his French estate, the Chiron pendant glinting in his hand. The pendant, a symbol of mentorship and perseverance, brought back memories of Edward, Abe Hawkins, Isaac Burns Murphy, and others whose spirits were intricately woven into the narrative of his life.

From the clamorous racetracks of Kentucky to Russia's opulent arenas and France's picturesque countryside, Jimmy's life had been a testament to resilience and unyielding passion for horse racing, resonating with the tenacity of the legendary black equestrians. He looked at his stables, teeming with a new generation of thoroughbreds, each one carrying forward the legacy of the Black Jockey Trust. Despite the ever-evolving landscape of horse racing, the timeless essence of the sport—the unity between a jockey and his steed, the electrifying rush of a close finish, and the camaraderie within a racing team—remained untarnished.

As Jimmy secured the pendant back into his pocket, the memories of bygone eras resurfaced, suffused with a sweet nostalgia. The heroes of the past might have faded into the background of history, but their influence continued to shape the narrative of the sport. As long as the thunderous gallops echoed across racetracks and the hearts of the riders resonated with the spirit of the sport, their stories would continue to inspire and endure.

That night, under the star-studded canopy of the cosmos, Jimmy made a silent pledge. He vowed to honor the memory of the legendary equestrians, ensuring their stories of courage, resilience, and integrity would never be lost in the annals of history. Their hoofbeats would echo across time, a testament to the pioneering black jockeys who defied the odds, leaving a legacy etched in the stars. They were not merely jockeys; they were trailblazers, mentors, and heroes—the legendary equestrians who galloped fearlessly into history, their hearts ablaze with a singular passion. Their legacy would remain as eternal as the constellations overhead, guiding the path for future generations who dared to dream.

SUMMARY OF SECTION IV ALL CHAPTERS:

In section 4 of the story, titled "The Legacy of Sir Isaac Burns Murphy," the chapter begins with the funeral of the esteemed jockey, Sir Isaac Burns Murphy. Jockey Willie Sims reflects on his own past victories and the advice he received from Edward Dudley Brown and Sir Isaac. A controversy arises regarding the crouching posture technique used by jockeys, with rival jockey Tod Sloan falsely claiming credit for inventing it. Willie Sims engages in a public debate with Sloan, while Edward Dudley Brown sets the record straight, revealing that Abe Hawkins was the true originator of the technique. Willie Sims faces a test of integrity when he is offered a bribe to throw a race but seeks guidance from Edward, who advises him against accepting bribes. In 1896, Willie won the Kentucky Derby riding Ben Brush, followed by another Kentucky Derby win in 1898 riding Plaudit. These victories solidify his place alongside Sir Isaac Burns Murphy as an accomplished jockey. Chapter 2, titled "Challenges and Resilience," introduces fifteen-year-old Jimmy Winkfield, known as "the Black Maestro." After an accident and a conspiracy to exclude Black Americans from racing, Jimmy is unjustly suspended. He turns to Edward Dudley Brown for support, and together they work to rectify the injustice. They encounter Meriweather Lewis Clark Jr., who expresses remorse for past actions. Jimmy faces personal challenges, including a clandestine marriage and the scarcity of resources for Black American doctors like Dr. Allen in Kentucky. Despite the obstacles, Edward's efforts lead to Jimmy's reinstatement in 1900, marking a turning point in his career. Chapter 3, "Triumphs and Adversities," follows Jimmy as he achieves notable successes. He placed third in the Kentucky Derby in 1900, won first place in 1901, and clinched another victory in 1902. Despite achieving second place in the 1903 Kentucky Derby, Jimmy's resilience earns him the distinction of being the third Black American jockey to achieve the Triple Crown. The chapter also explores the challenges faced by Black American jockeys due to Jim Crow laws and a racist narrative suggesting their inferiority. Jimmy is caught in a controversy involving his choice of trainer, leading to smear campaigns against him. Despite these challenges, he turns to Edward for guidance and reassurance, finding solace in the legacy they share. Chapter 4, titled "Legacies and Farewells," focuses on Edward Dudley Brown's declining health. He passes on his legacy to Jimmy, urging him to continue their journey and racing in Russia. Edward's funeral serves as a powerful testament to his impact, and his philanthropy and care for others are remembered as part of his enduring legacy. Chapter 5, "Jimmy Visions," takes place in 1904 when Jimmy Winkfield finds himself in France seeking a fresh start. He has dreams in which he transforms into a centaur and encounters Edward Dudley Brown, symbolizing their enduring connection. Guided by this vision, Jimmy revives his career, winning races in France and leaving a lasting impact on the equestrian world. The chapter concludes with Jimmy Winkfield taking care of his stables, cherishing memories of triumphs and the guidance of Edward Dudley Brown. His unwavering spirit and dedication become a symbol of resilience, reminding others that greatness can be achieved in the face of adversity. The story ends with Jimmy's passing in 1974, but his legacy and that of other Black American jockeys continue to inspire racing enthusiasts worldwide.

THEMES:

1. Legacy and Passing the Torch: The narrative explores the legacy of Sir Isaac Burns Murphy and the impact he has on future generations of jockeys, particularly Willie Sims and Jimmy Winkfield. It delves into the passing of knowledge, mentorship, and the responsibility of carrying forward a legacy in the face of adversity.

2. Racism and Discrimination: The pervasive racism and discrimination faced by Black American jockeys during the late 19th and early 20th centuries are depicted. The narrative sheds light on the challenges they endured, including exclusion from races, smear campaigns, and efforts to push them out of the sport.

3. Resilience and Perseverance: The characters in the story exhibit unwavering determination and resilience in the face of setbacks, racism, and personal hardships. Their ability to overcome adversity and continue pursuing their passion for horse racing underscores the theme of resilience.

4. Integrity and Honor: The theme of integrity runs throughout the narrative, highlighting the importance of upholding one's values and refusing to compromise personal integrity, even in the face of temptation and bribery. Characters like Willie Sims and Anthony Hamilton make principled choices, reflecting the significance of honor in the sport.

SETTINGS:

1. Kentucky: The narrative is primarily set in Kentucky, a significant location for horse racing during the late 19th and early 20th centuries. It explores cities like Lexington and Louisville, where prominent races such as the Kentucky Derby and Kentucky Oaks take place.

2. Russia: Jimmy Winkfield's journey takes him to Russia, where he experiences remarkable success in horse racing. The Russian setting adds an international dimension to the story, highlighting the impact of Black American jockeys on a global stage.

3. France: Jimmy Winkfield eventually settles in France, where he continues his racing career and achieves further victories. The French setting represents a new chapter in his life and underscores the international reach of horse racing.

SYMBOLS:

1. The Chiron Pendant: The Chiron pendant, given to Jimmy Winkfield by Edward Dudley Brown, symbolizes mentorship, strength, wisdom, and knowledge. It serves as a tangible reminder of the guidance and support Jimmy received from his mentors and the enduring legacy of Black American jockeys.

2. Maison Lafitte: The chateau gifted to Jimmy Winkfield represents a sanctuary for his passion for horses. It symbolizes his renewal and revitalization in France and serves as a physical embodiment of his connection to the equestrian world.

MOTIFS:

1. Mentorship and Guidance: The motif of mentorship is prominent throughout the narrative, as characters like Sir Isaac Burns Murphy, Edward Dudley Brown, and Abe Hawkins impart their knowledge and wisdom to younger jockeys. This motif emphasizes the importance of guidance and passing on knowledge in the development of future generations.

2. Victories and Triumphs: The motif of victories and triumphs recurs as jockeys like Willie Sims, Jimmy Winkfield, and others achieve notable successes in races such as the Kentucky Derby, Preakness Stakes, and various international events. These victories symbolize personal growth, resilience, and the recognition of talent.

ALLEGORIES:

1. The Crouching Posture Technique: The controversy surrounding the crouching posture technique represents the broader struggle for recognition and credit faced by Black American jockeys. It serves as an allegory for the erasure of their contributions in a racially biased society.

METAPHORS:

1. Centaur: In Jimmy Winkfield's dream, where he transforms into a centaur, the metaphor represents his connection to the world of horses

and his embodiment of the strength, speed, and grace associated with the mythical creature. It symbolizes his identity as a jockey and his harmonious relationship with the horses he rides.

FORESHADOWING:

1. Edward Dudley Brown's Illness: The declining health of Edward Dudley Brown due to tuberculosis foreshadows his eventual passing, adding a sense of impending loss and closure to his storyline.

2. The Spider in the Dream: The presence of the spider weaving silk webs at the mountain cave entrance in Jimmy Winkfield's dream foreshadows the rediscovery of the Chiron pendant, as the spider's web represents a connection to the pendant and the wisdom it holds.

LITERARY DEVICES:

1. Flashback: The narrative utilizes flashbacks to provide background information and highlight significant events from the past, such as Willie Sims' victories at the Belmont Stakes and the controversy surrounding the crouching posture technique.

2. Imagery: Vivid and descriptive imagery is used to paint a picture of the racing world, the characters, and the settings. This enhances the reader's immersion in the story and creates a visual experience.

3. Symbolism: The Chiron pendant, Maison Lafitte, and the centaur in Jimmy Winkfield's dream serve as symbolic elements that represent deeper meanings and themes within the narrative.

EPILOGUE

As time inexorably marched on, a mesmerizing symphony of valor, tenacity, and immortal legacies unfurled against the canvas of the celestial-lit racecourse. The pages of history, scribed in indelible ink, testified to the unyielding spirit of those who dared to challenge the prevailing norms, engraving their footprints upon the sands of the equestrian world. The narrative traced the genesis of Edward Dudley Brown's exceptional odyssey as a 14-year-old Black American jockey to the ageless victories of Jimmy Winkfield in distant realms. The resonant echoes of their feats pulsed through the continuum of time, a testament to their undying accomplishments.

Section I illustrated with stark clarity the trials endured by the Black American equestrians during the turbulent era of 1861-1875. It recounted their brave quest for liberation and recognition, their steadfast camaraderie, and the transformative potency of unity in the face of adversity. The narrative traced the austere origins of Edward Dudley Brown and Abe Hawkins, progressing to the unforgettable conflagration that united the community. Their journey, a beacon of justice and resilience, shed light on the path of those who dared to dream.

The story traced the austere origins of Edward Dudley Brown and Abe Hawkins. Born in a time when the societal fabric was tearing at its seams, they found themselves navigating a world rife with challenges. Theirs was a journey born out of determination and resilience, beginning from humble origins, progressing through trials, and rising, eventually, to unprecedented heights in the equestrian world.

The section's exploration of the themes of freedom and independence was particularly poignant. Edward and the others constantly strived for freedom, pursuing their dreams in the face of adversity and racial prejudices. This period was a testament to their resilience, having emerged soon after the Emancipation Proclamation and the 13th Amendment. Their journey was one of liberation, as they relentlessly pursued their dreams, battling adversity at every turn.

Another prevailing theme in this section was destiny and purpose. The concept reverberated throughout the chapter, subtly guiding the narrative. For Edward, it started with the discovery of the meaning of his name, which directly connected him to his purpose as a jockey. Every event, every encounter, was a thread weaving into the grand silk fabric of his destiny, setting him on a path towards leaving a lasting mark in the world of horse racing.

An emphasis on unity and community was also evident in the narrative. Edward, alongside other characters, were often shown coming together to protect each other and overcome adversities. The formation of the Black Jockey Trust and the support they provided to the young boys exemplified the power of unity within the Black American community, thereby underscoring the transformative potency of solidarity in the face of adversity.

Lastly, the theme of resilience and overcoming adversity was brought to life by the characters. Threats, attacks, and attempts on their lives were prevalent, yet they chose to fight, to persevere. Their determination and strength in the face of adversity were awe-inspiring, forming a beacon of justice and resilience that would continue to light the path for those who dared to dream.

Throughout this section, various settings played crucial roles, such as the Woodburn Farm, the Ashland Plantation, and the Jerome Park Racetrack. These locations served as more than mere backdrops; they became symbolically rich territories that encapsulated the trials and triumphs of the characters' lives. The narrative also employed potent symbols like the Chiron pendant and Asteroid, the horse, creating a deeper layer of meaning that permeated the storyline.

The motifs of horse racing, meteor showers, and stars were creatively utilized to echo themes and to draw parallels between the celestial and earthly realms. The presence of allegories further enriched the narrative, tying real-world events and characters to more profound symbolic meanings.

In the chronicle of Section II, the period of 1876-1881 unveiled a time interwoven with both triumph and chaos. The specters of deceit and adversity loomed ominously, casting dark shadows that threatened to taint the purity of the sport. However, the unfaltering spirit of the Black American jockeys rose like a phoenix from the ashes as they braved the beast of racism, challenging preconceptions and scripting an enduring legacy. The untimely demise of George Garrett Lewis served as a stark reminder of the sacrifices along their path, while the advent of Jimmy

Winkfield heralded a beacon of hope for a fresh generation of talent. Section II. underscores the theme of betrayal and deception, which is woven into the very fabric of the narrative. Sinister plots, bribes, and damaging rumors emerged from the dark corners of the horse racing world, aiming to sabotage the careers of black jockeys and mar their reputations. The conniving antagonist is presented as the personification of this malevolent theme, manipulating the course of events to meet his malicious ends.

Despite the menacing specter of deceit and adversity, the chapter radiates with the themes of resilience and triumph. Characters like William Billy Walker, Isaac Murphy, and Edward Dudley Brown faced towering obstacles, confronting false suspicions and enduring intense scrutiny. Their journeys, characterized by remarkable victories against odds, showcase an inspiring determination and unwavering resilience that are integral to their character.

The narrative also emphasizes the importance of integrity and honor. The protagonists refuse to compromise their principles, standing firm in their convictions. Notably, Isaac Murphy and Billy Walker turn down offers of bribes, retaining their honor even when challenged to false accusations and attempts to tarnish their good names. Their decisions are reflected as their true victory, a moral triumph over corruption and deceit.

In this period marked by turmoil, the strength of community and unity emerges as a significant theme. The Black American horse racing community rallies together, protecting and supporting each other during times of tragedy and confrontation. Their unity forms a shield of resilience, a testament to their solidarity and shared resolve to survive and thrive.

The theme of legacy and remembrance is poignant in this chapter. The narrative brings to light the crucial role of influential figures like George G. Lewis and Ansel Williamson in shaping the black horse racing community. Their legacy and influence serve as guiding beacons for the upcoming generation of jockeys.

Kentucky Derby, the prestigious horse racing event, serves as a prominent setting, representing both the zenith of success and a platform for tumultuous events. Kentucky Association Track in Lexington, Kentucky, emerges as a symbol of defiance, where Raleigh Colston Sr. establishes his stable, paving the way for black horse trainers in the face of adversity.

Various symbols are employed throughout the chapter to add depth to the narrative. The Mint Julep, created by Merriweather Lewis Clark Jr. during the Kentucky Derby, represents the cultural convergence at the event, highlighting the blending of tradition and prestige. It becomes a symbol associated with Dame Helena Modjeska, signifying the meeting of different worlds. Another significant symbol is the suggestion to name a dish after Isaac Murphy in the local diner. It represents the community's admiration for Murphy and his impact on the world of horse racing.

The section employs several motifs to reinforce its themes. Instances of bribery and corruption form a recurrent motif, representing the persistent challenges faced by black jockeys in an environment fraught with dishonesty and deceit. Confrontations and alterations also feature prominently, reflecting the prevailing tensions and conflicts between rival jockeys, the antagonist, and the black horse racing community.

The section presents several allegories. The poisoning of Ansel Williamson symbolizes the Farrar Kenner's efforts to tarnish the legacy of black horse racing, representing the threats faced by the community. Moreover, the narrative's focus on the rise and fall of characters like William Billy Walker and Ansel Williamson serves as an allegory of the trials and triumphs experienced by black jockeys during this era.

Finally, the section uses several metaphors and literary devices to deepen its impact. The sport of horse racing becomes a metaphor for broader societal issues, reflecting themes of corruption, racial tension, and perseverance in adversity. Furthermore, the use of vivid imagery, symbolic names, parallelism, and foreshadowing amplifies the emotive quality of the narrative, enhancing its engagement with the readers.

The pages of Section III unfurled, revealing the unceasing victories and tribulations that molded the years from 1882 to 1896. The legacy of Sir Isaac Burns Murphy radiated with an intensity rivaling the sun, illuminating the way for emerging talents who picked up the baton and sprinted forward. Prejudice and challenges threatened their path, yet their undying determination remained victorious. The strength of community and bonds forged amid adversity blazed brightly, leaving an indelible mark on the racing world.

The narrative continues to explore the theme of triumph and achievement in this era. It brings to the forefront the relentless victories of Black American jockeys and trainers in the face of racial discrimination. It is their exceptional talent and unwavering dedication to the sport that ultimately define their success, overshadowing the adverse circumstances that tried to undermine their progress.

The importance of unity and community is further emphasized in this part of the story. Black American equestrians come together, supporting each other in navigating the convoluted challenges, confronting racism, and celebrating their mutual successes. Their camaraderie showcases the power of shared experiences and collective struggle, highlighting the importance of a united front in overcoming adversity.

The resilience and perseverance of these characters are remarkable. Despite the obstacles thrown their way, they continue to push forward with an unwavering resolve. Their dreams of success and their aspiration to leave lasting legacies drive their relentless pursuit. Their fortitude offers a powerful lesson on the importance of persistence, even in the face of daunting odds.

Love and relationships play a significant role in the narrative during this period. The story is punctuated with moments of joy and celebration, including weddings, engagements, and festive gatherings. These events not only strengthen the bonds formed between characters but also underscore the importance of support and companionship.

The narrative does not shy away from exploring the darker aspects of the era, including pervasive themes of racism and discrimination. It throws light on the grave challenges faced by Black American horsemen and horsewomen during a time marked by segregation and inequality. Through their struggles and resilience, the narrative provides a realistic depiction of the socio-political climate of the time.

In terms of setting, the iconic Kentucky Derby continues to serve as a recurring backdrop for key events. This venue represents achievement, prestige, and the pinnacle of horse racing. Other settings, such as lavish estates and grand gatherings, signify opulence and celebration. They bring together influential figures within the Black American equestrian community, serving as platforms for networking and solidarity. Masonic lodges serve as symbols of unity, brotherhood, and personal growth, providing a sense of belonging and community for the characters.

Various symbols are introduced in this part of the story. The iconic Twin Spires at Churchill Downs symbolize the grandeur and passion of horse racing. The photograph capturing the "photo finish" at a race signifies progress and innovation, revolutionizing the way race outcomes are determined. The extravagant "A Colored Party" reception hosted by the Murphys serves as a symbol of celebration, unity, and societal progress.

Recurring motifs and foreshadowing are used to add depth to the narrative. Victories and races symbolize the pursuit of excellence, determination, and the thrill of competition. Mentions of mentorship and the passing down of knowledge signify the strength of bonds between experienced and aspiring horsemen, securing the future of Black American equestrians.

In terms of literary devices, the narrative employs allegory and metaphor to deliver a more impactful story. The depiction of Black American jockeys and trainers confronting racism serves as an allegory for the broader struggle for racial equality during that era. Meanwhile, the metaphor of the Twin Spires as "church towers" draws a parallel between the devotion and passion for horse racing and a religious-like reverence.

Finally, the narrative also uses foreshadowing to hint at future developments. The encounters between James "Soup" Perkins and Isaac Murphy, and the former's commitment to learning from his mentor, suggest his future success. Similarly, the mention of Anthony Hamilton's plans to continue his racing career overseas anticipates his journey and the new opportunities that await him in Europe.

In Section IV, the legacy endured, spanning the epoch from 1897 to 1906 and reaching beyond known horizons. Jimmy Winkfield's extraordinary expedition traversed boundaries, challenging the constraints imposed by bias. As he ascended to unparalleled heights in Russia and France, the spirit of mentorship and the wisdom imparted by Edward Dudley Brown illuminated his path. Through introspection and dreams, Jimmy unraveled the timeless strength of the Chiron pendant, a symbol of fortitude and wisdom passed down through generations. His victories in the French equestrian arena underlined the mettle and prowess of Black American jockeys, forever etching their brilliance on the parchment of history. The narrative follows Jimmy Winkfield's extraordinary journey that challenged and traversed the boundaries of geographical constraints and racial bias. The spirit of mentorship and wisdom, imparted by the legendary Edward Dudley Brown, served as his guiding light. This portion of the narrative continues to highlight the theme of legacy and passing the torch. Sir Isaac Burns Murphy's influence is deeply felt in this era, especially in the lives of future jockeys like Willie Sims and Jimmy Winkfield. The narrative delves deep into the sharing of knowledge, mentorship, and the responsibility of carrying forward an illustrious legacy, despite the adversities faced.

As Winkfield ventured and ascended to unparalleled heights in Russia and France, he carried with him not only his dreams but also the dreams of his forebears and his people. His introspective journey unraveled the true power of the Chiron pendant - a treasured symbol of strength and wisdom passed down through generations. The narrative further explores the theme of racism and discrimination. Even during these promising times, Black American jockeys faced extensive racism and discrimination. Exclusion from races, smear campaigns, and efforts to push them out of the sport marked the challenges they endured.

The narrative then focuses on the victories that Jimmy achieved in the French equestrian arena. These moments underlined the mettle and prowess of Black American jockeys, forever etching their brilliance on the parchment of history. The characters' unwavering determination and resilience in the face of setbacks, racism, and personal hardships were starkly visible. These triumphant victories underscore the theme of resilience and tenacity.

Simultaneously, the theme of integrity and honor is interwoven throughout the narrative. Characters like Willie Sims and Anthony Hamilton uphold their values, refusing to compromise their personal integrity, even in the face of temptation and bribery. Their principled choices are testaments to the significance of honor in the sport and life in general.

The narrative's geographical setting expands in this era, primarily set in Kentucky, but extends to Russia and France. Kentucky was a significant location for horse racing during the late 19th and early 20th centuries. It was the stage for prominent races such as the Kentucky Derby and Kentucky Oaks. However, Jimmy Winkfield's journey takes the story to new landscapes, Russia and France. His successes in these foreign lands add an international dimension to the story, highlighting the impact of Black American jockeys on a global stage.

Symbols like the Chiron Pendant and Maison Lafitte add richness to the narrative. The Chiron pendant, passed down to Jimmy Winkfield by Edward Dudley Brown, stands as a beacon of mentorship, strength, wisdom, and knowledge. It serves as a tangible reminder of the guidance Jimmy received from his mentors and the enduring legacy of Black American jockeys. Maison Lafitte, a chateau gifted to Jimmy, symbolizes his renewal and revitalization in France and serves as a physical embodiment of his connection to the equestrian world.

Mentorship and victories surface as recurring motifs in this part of the story. Mentors like Sir Isaac Burns Murphy, Edward Dudley Brown, and Abe Hawkins play vital roles in shaping the careers of younger jockeys.

They pass down their wisdom and knowledge, emphasizing the importance of guidance in the development of future generations. Jimmy Winkfield and others' victories and triumphs serve as symbols of personal growth, resilience, and recognition of talent.

The narrative further uses allegories and metaphors to enhance the story. The controversy surrounding the crouching posture technique serves as an allegory, representing the broader struggle for recognition faced by Black American jockeys. This controversy mirrors the erasure of their contributions in a racially biased society. The metaphor of Jimmy transforming into a centaur in his dream represents his connection to the world of horses. The strength, speed, and grace associated with this mythical creature mirror his identity as a jockey and his harmonious relationship with the horses.

Finally, foreshadowing is subtly used to hint at future developments in the story. Edward Dudley Brown's declining health due to tuberculosis foreshadows his eventual demise, adding a sense of impending loss and closure to his storyline. The presence of the spider in Jimmy Winkfield's dream, weaving silk webs at the mountain cave entrance, foreshadows the rediscovery of the Chiron pendant. The spider's web signifies a connection to the pendant and the wisdom it holds.

In the concluding chapters, the narratives reverberated, resonating with a solemn vow to uphold the legacies of the past. The Chiron pendant, nestled securely within Jimmy's grasp, epitomized the perpetual bond between a mentor and a protégé, embodying the tales of courage, resilience, and honor. The grand Maison Lafitte, a sanctuary for Jimmy's equestrian passion, stood as a monumental testament to the unwavering commitment and fervor for the sport.

As the narrative approached its conclusion, Jimmy Winkfield's introspective gaze encapsulated the essence of his predecessors. The mentors who had steered his course, the cosmic allure that encompassed him, and the relentless pursuit of knowledge and potential converged to a focal point. With the Chiron pendant as his guide, he pledged to honor the memory of the legendary equestrians who blazed the trail before him.

The legacy woven into these narratives transcended the confines of time. It resonated with those in search of guidance, entranced by the enigmatic cosmos, and exploring their innate potential. The tales of Edward Dudley Brown, Jimmy Winkfield, and the countless others who dared to defy the odds emerged as a lighthouse for forthcoming generations.

And thus, as the starlit track gradually receded into the realm of memory, the narratives perpetuated. Permanently engraved in the annals of equestrian history, their legacy persisted, whispering tales of mentorship's transformative power, the cosmic allure that envelops us, and the boundless potential within each soul. As long as torchbearers carried on their legacy, the echoes of their triumphs would continue to resonate, inspiring generations yet unborn.

- NOTABLE VICTORIES –

Year	Winner	Jockey	Trainer
1902	Alan-a-Dale	Jimmy Winkfield	Thomas C. McDowell
1901	His Eminence	Jimmy Winkfield	Frank B. Van Meter
1898	Plaudit	Willie Simms	John E. Madden
1896	Ben Brush	Willie Simms	Hardy Campbell Jr.
1895	Halma	James Perkins	Byron McClelland
1892	Azra	Alonzo Clayton	John H. Morris
1891	Kingman	Isaac Murphy	Dudley Allen
1890	Riley	Isaac Murphy	Edward Corrigan
1887	Montrose	Isaac Lewis	John McGinty
1884	Buchanan	Isaac Murphy	William Bird
1883	Leonatus	William Donohue	Raleigh Colston Sr.
1882	Apollo	Babe Hurd	Green B. Morris
1881	Hindoo	Jim McLaughlin	James G. Rowe Sr.
1880	Fonso	George Lewis	Tice Hutsell
1877	Baden-Baden	William Billy Walker	Edward D. Brown
1876	Vagrant	Robert Swim	James Williams
1875	Aristides	Oliver Lewis	Ansel Williamson

PART 2

ENCYCLOPEDIC APPENDICES

PART 2 ENCYCLOPEDIC APPENDICES

I. HISTORY OF HORSE RACING.

Horses

Domestication

Horse behavior

The origin

Thoroughbred racing in America

II. TYPES OF HORSE RACING

Flat racing

Jump racing

Endurance racing

Harness racing

Quarter horse racing

Maiden racing

Allowance and claiming racing

Stakes racing

Graded stakes racing

III. CHARACTER PROFILES & BIOGRAPHIES

IV. HORSE RACING MUSEUMS AND HALLS OF FAME

American quarter horse Hall of Fame

Australian racing Hall of Fame

Canadian horse racing Hall of Fame

Australian racing museum

Japan racing Association Hall of Fame

Korea racing Authority equine Museum

New Zealand racing Hall of Fame

National Museum of Racing and Hall of Fame.

International Museum of the Horse.

Keeneland Library.

V. HORSE BREEDS

Breeding process

Modern approach

Race breeds

American quarter horse

Arabian

Thoroughbred

Appaloosa

Morgan

Warmbloods

Ponies

Graded horses

Gaited breeds

Draft breeds

VI. THOROUGHBREDS

History

Breed characteristics

Thoroughbred official birthdays

Racing champions

Thoroughbred foundation stallions

Thoroughbred foundation mares

VII. HORSEMANSHIP & FICTIONAL CHARACTER BIBLES

Origins in early history

Military horsemanship

The art of horsemanship

Character Bibles

VIII. LEGENDARY HORSES
IX. LEGENDARY THOROUGHBRED
X. KENTUCKY DERBY WINNERS
XI. TRIPLE CROWN WINNERS
XII. CHRONOLOGICAL TIMELINE
XIII. HORSE RACES DOMESTIC AND FROM AROUND THE WORLD
XIV. HORSES IN RACING AND FACTS

1. HISTORY OF HORSE RACING

Horses

The horse (Equus caballus) is a large ungulate animal belonging to the Equidae family and the genus Equus. Only Przewalski's Horse (Equus ferus przewalskii) and domestic horses may cross-breed and produce fruitful progeny.

Horses, being one of the most historically important domesticated animals to humans, have played an important role in people's lives for tens of thousands of years. No other domestic or wild animal has had as much of an influence on the history of civilisation as the horse. The horse was an essential component of combat and conquest, transportation and travel, as well as art and sport. It is famed for its beauty and strength. The horse has been represented and worshiped as the noble bearer of heroes, champions, and gods since antiquity.

The horse is well suited as a primarily riding animal in terms of design, form, and function. Its spine is solid and robust, and it is ideally designed to support weight. It has a lofty height, which gives any rider a towering edge in hunting, sport, and battle. The horse's legs are long, thin, beautiful, and, most importantly, fast. Horses' speed and ability to cover ground made them and continue to make them essential to humans.

Horses are herd animals that are very sociable and clever. They are unable to flourish in solitude. Their inherent nature is to seek a partnership that provides mutual advantage while also assuring kinship and protection. Humans have long taken use of this social trait. Domestication has transformed the horse's urge to herd other horses into one to "herd" or embrace people, and the consequent "willingness to please" makes horses precious to humanity and heroic figures in film and literature.

Domestication

Horses are available in a variety of sizes and forms. Draft breeds may reach 20 hands (80 inches or roughly 2 meters), whereas tiny horses can reach 5.2 hands (22 inches or about 0.56 meters). The Patagonian Falabella, the world's tiniest horse, is roughly the size of a German shepherd dog.

Horses may have been domesticated as early as 4500 B.C.E., and people may have used them widely as early as 5000 B.C.E. in Babylon, Assyria, Egypt, and Eurasia. Other early evidence for domestication may be found in Central Asia around 4000 B.C.E.

Until the mid-twentieth century, horses were largely used in battle and, in smaller numbers, for domestic transportation. Conquerors kept a large number of horses to cross enormous swaths of land and territory. Because of the horse's speed, armies such as the Huns, Alexander the Great, the Romans, the Ottomans, Napoleon, and many more were able to overcome opponents and rule over empires. Soldiers nowadays still refer to the groupings of machines that have replaced horses on the battlefield as "cavalry" units, and military formations occasionally retain traditional horse-oriented nomenclature.

Equine breeds have evolved over time, particularly in the last three to four hundred years, to meet specialized needs. Although horses are still used for practical labor in some regions of the world, in general, horses are now mostly employed for competitive sport and pleasure. Horse racing, horse shows, and pleasure horses are the three primary types of equine enterprise.

Horse displaying, or horse sport as it is now known, is any activity that involves horses in a competition other than racing. Sporthorses are equines that participate in English disciplines such as dressage, show jumping, three-day eventing, endurance riding, driving, polo, fox hunting, and other sports. Western disciplines, which developed in the western United States, include reining, rodeo, cow horses, cutting, and western pleasure, among others.

Horse Behavior

Horses are extremely sociable herd animals that are also prey animals with the ability to flee or fight. Their initial reaction to a threat is to flee. They are known, however, to defend themselves when cornered, and the fight instinct is also activated when progeny, like a foal (young horse), is endangered. Some horses have been bred to be more docile, but the majority of sport horse breeds are founded on the notion of keeping the natural impulses that existed in horses removed from wild herds hundreds of years ago.

Horse cultures in the wild are matriarchal. The alpha or dominant mare is at the heart of the herd (female horse). Mares, foals, and juvenile horses of both sexes make up herds. In one year, a herd of twenty mares may produce twenty foals.

The middle of the herd is the safest since it is the furthest away from predators. The bottom of the social hierarchy can be located at the herd's edge. Punishment is administered in the form of temporary or permanent banishment from the herd.

The dominant stallion (male horse) resides on the outside of the herd and serves as the herd sire, producing progeny while repelling challenges for supremacy from other stallions who could become a successor. The dominating stallion occupies the most perilous and precarious position in the horse world. Living on the outside exposes him to predators and other bachelors who will compete with him for the role of dominating stallion. In sharp contrast to the mythology of the stallion and his (implied) harem, he serves no use to the herd other than reproduction. In some ways, he is unnecessary since he is readily replaceable. At any moment, the male dominance hierarchy ensures an instant replacement by a strong and healthy successor.

When colts (male foals) reach maturity, the dominant stallion kicks them out and they are no longer accepted in the herd. For years, they create little bachelor herds and roam until the moment comes when they may fight for the honor of becoming the next dominant stallion.

The formation of a stable hierarchy or pecking order is crucial for smooth group functioning in many animals that dwell in big groups. Contention for dominance may be dangerous since one well-placed kick to the leg of another horse might cripple it to the point that it is helpless, unprotected, and perhaps unable to get to water. Survival requires herd members to eventually collaborate and remain together. To minimize aggressive behavior, the alpha or dominant mare exerts control over herd members.

Humans' capacity to work together with horses is based on the deep social relationships that horses have with one another. Horses avoid being separated from the herd because being alone exposes them to predators from all sides. Horse training concepts are built on making the horse accept a human as the main herd member via competence and confidence rather than coercion. In pastures, horses prefer to congregate around the more mature and confident individuals. These characteristics are highly appreciated since they indicate the path to survival. A horse that is terrified more than required will waste energy and may be unable to flee when the threat is serious.

The ability of humans to collaborate with horses is founded on the profound social bonds that horses have with one another. Horses avoid separation from the herd because being alone exposes them to predators on all sides. Horse training methods are based on the horse accepting a person as the primary herd member via competence and confidence rather than compulsion. Horses in pastures like to gather with more mature and confident individuals. These traits are highly valued since they point the way to survival. When a horse feels afraid for longer than necessary, it wastes energy and may be unable to run when the situation is real.

Horses normally tolerate some human misconduct, but when the balance shifts, a horse may become a lethal foe. Abused horses may be extremely dangerous since they no longer regard people as part of their herd, but rather as predators. Horse bites may be fatal, and horse kicks can be fatal. Rehabilitation of a horse that has been conditioned to defend itself violently against people is difficult and fraught with danger.

The Origin

The history of horse racing is a long and illustrious one, with evidence suggesting the practice took place in civilizations all over the world from prehistoric times. This includes Ancient Greece, Rome, Babylon, Syria, and Egypt. It also plays an essential role in myth and folklore, such as the battle between Odin's steeds and the gigantic Hrungnir in Norse mythology.

Chariot racing was a well-liked ancient Greek, Roman, and Byzantine sport. Both chariot and mounted horse racing were events in the ancient Greek Olympics by 648 BC and were also vital in the other Panhellenic Games.

Chariot racing was a particularly popular sport among the Greeks. Chariot races were performed to honor the gods and were frequently employed to resolve conflicts between communities.

A horse race between Persian and Greek horses was founded in Greece during the reign of Cyrus the Great (539-530 BC). A vividly written account of the ancient horse race was provided by Xenophon, a Greek philosopher and horseman.

Even though chariot racing was frequently dangerous to both the driver and horse, it continued. Horses often suffered serious injury and even death as a result of chariot racing.

In the Roman Empire, chariot and mounted horse racing were major industries. Horse races were often staged throughout the Roman Empire to worship the gods or to commemorate military successes.

From the mid-fifteenth century, the spring carnival in Rome closed with a horse race. Fifteen to 20 riderless horses, originally imported from the Barbary Coast of North Africa, were set loose to run the length of the Via del Corso, a long, straight city street. Their time was about 2 and a half minutes.

Organized racing most likely began in China, Persia, Arabia, and other Middle Eastern and North African countries where horsemanship was already highly developed. The Arabian, Barb, and Turk horses also contributed to the early European racing. During the Crusades (11th-13th century CE), Europeans became acquainted with such horses, which they brought back with them.

A horse race was held in Great Britain in 1176, which is said to be the first of its sort. The race was held in Smithfield in the City of London. It was a big event, and a large crowd gathered to watch the horses participate.

The race was won by Puce, a horse belonging to King Henry II. This was a historic occasion since it was the first time a horse race was staged in the United Kingdom. It is also said to be Europe's first recorded "modern horse race."

This event helped promote horse racing in the United Kingdom, and it quickly became a popular pastime among both nobles and commoners.

Racing in medieval England originated when professional riders ridden horses for sale in competition to demonstrate the horses' speed to purchasers. The earliest documented racing purse, £40, was provided during the reign of Richard the Lionheart (1189-99) for a race conducted over a 3-mile (4.8-km) track with knights as riders. Henry VIII acquired horses from Italy and Spain (probably Barbs) in the 16th century and established studs in many sites. In the 17th century, James I of England sponsored gatherings. When his successor, Charles I, died in 1649, he possessed a stud of 139 horses.

The "Father of the English Turf," King Charles II, established the first known national racing laws. He established the King's Plates, which were races with rewards awarded to the winners. Nowadays, technology has made it simpler to determine speed, the rightful winner, and other information using monitoring equipment. Jockeys, or horseback riders, are today almost as well-known as their equine counterparts, but this was not always the case.

Individual rider efforts and talents were traditionally regarded to be unimportant in races consisting of 4-mile heats. Only in the late 1850s, when dash racing became the standard, were jockeys recognised for their contribution to their equine's success, and their names were recorded alongside the victorious trainers and riders.

The first known horse race was staged in France in 1651 as a consequence of a wager between two noblemen. Racing based on gambling was popular during the reign of Louis XIV (1643-1715). Louis XVI (reigned 1774-93) introduced racing restrictions by royal decree, including demanding credentials of provenance for horses and imposing extra weight on imported horses.

The first known horse race in America was held on the Newmarket track in what is now Hempstead, New York in 1665. Some historians believe that there were previous races that were not chronicled.

Throughout the 1700s, horse racing grew in popularity in the colonies, and by the early 1800s, it had become one of the most popular spectator sports in America. The first significant horse race in America was staged in 1823 at Union Course on Long Island.

The Union horse racing track in Brooklyn was a revolutionary at the time. It was the first "dirt" or skinned track, which was an intriguing novelty to watch how the racing world would react to. It also lacked grandstands at first.

The British takeover of New Amsterdam (now New York City) in 1664 marked the beginning of organized racing in North America. Col. Richard Nicolls, commander of the British forces, introduced organized racing in the colonies by putting out a 2-mile (3.2-kilometer) track on the plains of Long Island (dubbed Newmarket after the British racecourse) and awarding a silver cup to the finest horses in the spring and fall seasons. Stamina, rather than speed, was the hallmark of greatness for the American Thoroughbred from its inception until the Civil War. Following the Civil War, speed became the aim, and the British system served as a model.

The modern era of horse racing began with the introduction of three English races in the 18th century: the St. Leger, the Oaks, and the Derby. These races were regarded as the greatest and most elite. Two of these three events are part of the "British Triple Crown" of horse racing, which also includes the St. Leger, the Derby, and another race from the nineteenth century, the One Thousand Guineas. It was also in the nineteenth century that the United States established their own "American Triple Crown," which included the Belmont Stakes, Preakness Stakes, and the world-famous Kentucky Derby.

Following the Civil War, interest in horse racing skyrocketed in the

United States. By 1890, there were 314 racetracks in almost every state. Outraged, anti-gambling coalitions pushed legislation in most sections of the country, and by 1908, only 25 racetracks remained open. Finally, New York race tracks were forced to close in 1911 when state laws prohibited the quotation of odds, soliciting bets, and recording bets in a fixed location. As a result, many owners, trainers, and jockeys relocated to Europe. When New York racetracks reopened in 1913, the majority of the previous African American jockeys did not return.

The inaugural Kentucky Derby included 15 jockeys, 13 of them were African Americans raised on plantations. They were well-known jockeys back then, having won 15 of the first 28 Kentucky Derbys. In 1890, there were 314 racetracks in practically every state. Because of the gambling involved in racing, several race tracks closed down, leaving only 25 in operation.

When racetracks in New York closed in 1911, racetrack operations moved to Europe. Even their reopening did not lure back any African American jockeys from the other side of the continent due to their treatment and prejudice in the United States. The Arlington Million, the first million-dollar race, took place in 1981. Since then, races have demanded millions.

It has also evolved into a profitable company and a source of entertainment. First prize winners used to get the entire sum, but currently only roughly 60% is awarded to the winner. It may not be as popular in the twenty-first century as it once was, but it still has a devoted fan base and there is a high demand for Thoroughbred horses trained for racing. Thoroughbred racing eventually became and continues to be popular among British aristocracy and monarchy, garnering it the moniker "Sport of Kings."

Equestrians used to sharpen their talents via games and races. Equestrian activities entertained people while also demonstrating the great horsemanship required in warfare. All forms of horse racing arose from unplanned competitions between riders or drivers.

The several types of competition, which demanded demanding and specialized abilities from both horse and rider, resulted in the deliberate creation of specific breeds and equipment for each sport. The popularity of equestrian activities throughout the years has resulted in the preservation of abilities that would have otherwise perished once horses were no longer employed in battle.

Horse racing became popular in the United Kingdom in the 18th century. It grew in prominence throughout the 18th century and beyond. King Charles II (reigned 1649–1685) was an ardent athlete who helped establish Newmarket.

Horse racing became a professional sport during Queen Anne's reign (1702-1714). Match racing developed into multi-horse contests in which spectators may place bets. Racecourses sprung up all throughout England, with increasingly enormous payouts to entice the greatest horses. The purses increased the profitability of breeding and owning race horses. The fast growth of the sport necessitated the establishment of a centralized governing body. The elite of racing gathered in Newmarket in 1750 to create the Jockey Club. This association is still in charge of English racing today.

By 1750, the Jockey Club had been created to oversee the Newmarket races, regulate the rules of the game, discourage dishonesty, and provide a level playing field. The Epsom Derby first took place in 1780. The St Leger Stakes, the first of the five classic races, was held in 1776.

In 1814, the system was completed, with five yearly races. The standards were set by Newmarket and the Jockey Club, but the majority of racing took place in landowners' fields and growing towns for tiny financial awards and huge local prestige. The wagering system was critical to the funding and expansion of the business, and everyone from the poor to royalty took part. High society was in charge, and they made a concerted effort to keep the riff-raff and criminal element at bay. With real money on the line, the system required talented jockeys, trainers, grooms, and breeding specialists, opening up new coveted jobs for working-class rural males. Every young, ambitious, stable boy wishes to make it big.

Horse racing is one of the few sports that has survived the 2020 COVID-19 crisis, with Australia and Hong Kong the two largest racing countries continuing to operate, but without spectators. The United States, the United Kingdom, and France were among the most important racing organizations to postpone or cancel all races.

Horse racing's simplicity may be why it has survived the years. Whomever owns the quickest horse wins, and whoever crosses the finish line first wins. However, Horse Racing Sport has also met its share of challenges along the way. Aside from gambling and cheating, the growing use of anti-inflammatory and coagulant medications on horses posed a new threat to the sport in the 1960s. Steroid usage on horses, like that of famous athletes in many sports, came under close examination in the late twentieth century.

Horse racing has long been condemned by animal rights organizations. Activists have worked to uncover horse doping, implement a prohibition on jockey whipping, limit the number of races a horse (particularly those three years old and younger) may compete in a season, and abolish dirt tracks in favor of safer synthetic surfaces. Such incidents, together with the shifting interests of the worldwide athletic audience, contributed to horse racing's continued loss in popularity throughout the first decades of the twenty-first century.

Thoroughbred Racing in America

Horses (and horse racing) were introduced to America by British immigrants. Long Island's first racetrack was built in 1665. Although it had been a popular local activity for some time, organized racing did not begin until 1868, following the Civil War. During the subsequent decades of industrial boom, wagering on racehorses and horse racing itself expanded. By 1890, the United States had 314 tracks in operation.

The fast expansion of horse racing in the absence of a controlling body resulted in criminal elements dominating numerous tracks. The nation's largest track and stable owners assembled in New York in 1894 to create the American Jockey Club. This organization, based after the English, quickly governed racing with an iron grip, eliminating most of the corruption.

Racing in the United States was nearly wiped out in the early 1900s due to anti gambling sentiment, which prompted virtually all states to outlaw bookmaking. Only 25 tracks existed by 1908. The introduction of pari-mutuel betting on the Kentucky Derby the same year was a game changer for the sport. In exchange for a part of the money wagered, several state legislatures agreed to authorize pari-mutuel betting. As a consequence, more music became available. By the close of World War I, affluence and outstanding horses like Man o' War had drawn crowds to racetracks. Until World War II, horse racing thrived.

The sport thereafter declined in popularity in the 1950s and 1960s. The immense popularity of outstanding horses like Secretariat, Seattle Slew, and Affirmed fueled a comeback in the 1970s. These horses all won the American Triple Crown (the Kentucky Derby, the Preakness and the Belmont Stakes). However, another large fall happened from the late 1980s until the present. This is due to the fact that there has been a long period without a Triple Crown winner.

Thoroughbred racetracks may be found in around half of the states.

The general public's attention is drawn to significant Thoroughbred races such as the Triple Crown and the Breeder's Cup. These races have prize money in excess of $1,000,000. State racing commissions have exclusive responsibility to license participants and assign racing dates, while the Jockey Club is responsible for the selection of racing officials and the enforcement of racing laws. The Jockey Club holds control over Thoroughbred breeding.

2. TYPES OF HORSERACING

Horse racing sports have come a long way from the days of chariot races and warhorse maneuvers. Nonetheless, two factors remained constant: the horses' physical dominance and the riders' talents and savviness. Only the ideal combination of both may result in outstanding race results.

Horse races can be organized by many different categories such as age, sex, distance, and time of year. One of the principal forms of horse racing, which is popular in many parts of the world, is Thoroughbred racing. Harness racing is also popular in the eastern United States and more popular than thoroughbred racing in Canada and parts of Europe. Quarter horse and Arabian racing are also popular in the western United States and Florida.

The breeding, training and racing of horses in many countries is now a significant economic activity as, to a greater extent, is the gambling industry which is largely supported by it. Exceptional horses can win millions of dollars and make millions more by providing stud services, such as horse breeding.

Flat racing breeds such as Thoroughbred, Quarter Horse, Arabian, Paint, and Appaloosa prosper, while jump racing breeds such as Thoroughbred and AQPS excel. Standardbreds are used in harness racing in Australia, New Zealand, and North America, whereas Standardbreds with Russian and French Trotter are used in Europe. Furthermore, Finn Horses and Scandinavian Coldblood Trotters are employed in harness racing and other disciplines.

Flat Racing

Flat racing is by far the most popular sort of horse racing. These races are often held on a flat, leveled surface and feature Thoroughbred horses.

The Triple Crown races (Kentucky Derby, Preakness Stakes, and Belmont Stakes) are by far the most popular in North America, although any race raced on a flat track without hurdles or other obstacles for the horses usually counts as a flat race.

Flat races are typically raced between 1-3 miles in length, depending on the event, and can test the horse's speed, stamina, or both. Turf is the most popular racing surface for horses worldwide, although many races are still staged on dirt courses, particularly in the United States.

Flat racing is frequently divided into two classes in the United Kingdom and Europe:

- Conditions Racing
- Handicap Racing

The most popular type of horse racing by far is flat racing. These types of races typically deal with Thoroughbred horses, and are run on a flat, leveled surface.

In North America, the Triple Crown events (Kentucky Derby, Preakness Stakes, and Belmont Stakes) are easily the most popular, but any race that is run on a flat surface without hurdles or other obstacles for the horses typically qualifies as a flat race.

Flat races tend to be run between 1-3 miles, depending on the event, and can be a test of the horse's speed, stamina, or both. Turf is the leading running surface for horses across the world, but many races are still held on dirt tracks as well, especially in the United States.

In Great Britain and Europe, flat racing is often broken down into two classifications:

Conditions Racing

Handicap Racing

Both conditions and handicap races relate to separate handicaps assigned to horses before a certain event. Condition races are chosen depending on a variety of factors, such as the horse's age, gender, or another differentiation.

Horses who appear to have an early edge carry more weight to give the rest of the field a handicap, essentially balancing things out and providing bettors with a more equal playing field.

Handicap races are distinct in that the handicapper determines the handicap, which is not dependent on the horse's gender or age.

Horse speed, pace, form, class, post location, pedigree, the horse's jockey, and any other pertinent elements that can effectively handicap the race are all factors considered by handicappers.

The Triple Crown events, along with the Breeders' Cup Classic, are among the most well-known flat races in America.

There are also some prominent flat racing events held outside of the

United States that do not contain jumps, with "classic races" taking center stage.

- Epsom Derby
- Epsom Oaks
- Leger Stakes
- 1,000 Guineas Stakes
- 2,000 Guineas Stakes

Jump Racing

Jump racing, also known as National Hunt, presents the horses with hurdles in addition to the track length and the surrounding competitors.

National Hunt is the official term for jump racing in the United Kingdom, when horses compete to escape fences, ditches, and other obstacles. In France, Ireland, and the United Kingdom, these races are extremely popular.

Jump races can be more difficult to wager on since gamblers must weigh several different elements, the most significant of which are the horse's hurdling ability and jockey control.

Jump racing, often known as Steeplechasing, is separated into two categories:

- Hurdles
- Steeplechases

Hurdles racing involves horses racing while jumping over obstacles known as hurdles, whereas steeplechase racing involves horses leaping over several obstacles such as fences, water, and open ditches.

The Cheltenham Gold Cup and the Aintree Grand National are now the two most important jump racing competitions. The latter is the most renowned National Hunt event and is held each year in April.

The King George VI Chase and the Hennessy Gold Cup are two more notable jump racing competitions.

Point to Point racing is a sort of horse racing that falls under jump racing but is exclusively for amateurs.

Endurance Racing

The third major category of horse racing is endurance racing, which requires horses to run over greater distances or for longer periods of time.

Endurance racing, unlike many popular flat and jump racing sports, evaluates endurance and longevity on a track. For bettors, speed isn't as important here because the major focus is on horses who can deliver regularly and not fade over longer courses.

This isn't a common horse racing technique since it takes much longer and isn't always best for horses and jockeys. The Mongol Derby, which spans 1,000 kilometers, is presently the longest endurance event taking place.

All breeds are accepted in these races, but Arabian horses are particularly popular because to their exceptional stamina and endurance

Harness Racing

There are additional races in which the horse must carry more than its own weight and a jockey. Harness racing involves horses pulling a sulky and racing at a set trot or speed.

The horses must trot or pace at the set tempo without breaking stride. Galloping horses are penalized by being forced to slow down behind the competition.

The Prix d'Amerique, conducted each year in Paris, is without a doubt the best harness race in the world. Horses are enrolled into this renowned event based on their career earnings and compete for a prize pool of up to one million euros.

Quarter Horse Racing

Quarter horse racing is a less common sport of horse racing that emphasizes speed. Quarter horse races are one-quarter mile or less in length, and they test quicker kinds of horses to compete and win on such small tracks.

Because of the speed and talent involved, these horse racing events can be entertaining, but they don't last long.

Maiden Racing

There are two approaches to horse racing. The first is the actual race track, obstacles, and distance.

The other question is what kind of horse is permitted in the race and what is at stake. This section of horse racing types focuses on the progression of horse racing.

As a result, maiden racing does not always apply to a specific style of horse racing, but rather to horses that have yet to win a race. Horses remain a maiden until they win their first race, at which point they are eligible for races designed exclusively for horses that have not yet won.

A horse winning a maiden race isn't particularly noteworthy, but it gets them started in the correct path. Maiden races may be extremely difficult to judge because the competitors come into each race with no victories.

Tracking previous maiden races and seeing which horses came near to winning (finishing in the top three) or started/finished well is a terrific tactic.

Allowance and Claiming Racing

There are also horse races in which horses are raced for profit while simultaneously being shown for sale. These races are not popular because of a major lack of dependability, as well as the evident purpose of horses being acquired.

Of fact, these two styles of racing are very different. Allowance races payout far more than claiming races, and the horses are not for sale.

These races aren't classified and aren't very important in the larger scheme of things, but there is still a considerable amount of money at stake, and the horses engaged can qualify for bigger events in the future.

Claiming races are races in which horses compete to win while their owners assess their worth. This is a low level of horse racing, similar to maiden races, and not an optimal horse racing betting environment.

People can place claims to bid on and acquire a horse prior to claiming races. If such a horse finishes in the money, the prior owner receives the purse, while the new owner receives the horse.

Stakes Racing

Once a horse has established itself, they can compete in stakes races. These are the most prestigious horse races, with large financial rewards.

These races include some of the top owners, trainers, riders, and horse racing talent, and they serve as the first major stepping stone to some of the biggest horse racing events.

Any horse that runs in the major events normally needs to work its way up the ladder, which requires the average horse to compete in at least a few stakes races. These races are often well-known events on the circuit and are typically of the flat racing kind, particularly in North America.

There are low level stakes races and there are higher level events that horses can use to push them into big events like the Kentucky Derby.

Graded Stakes Racing

The last kind of horse racing is graded stakes racing, in which the race is awarded a grade (I, II, or III) that indicates which horses are the most competitive as well as the overall quality of the field.

These graded stakes may be used as yardsticks for owners, trainers, jockeys, and horses, and the horse racing community can determine how excellent a horse is depending on how they compete and finish.

Grade stakes races can have varying durations and tracks and can serve as significant stepping stones to larger events. These races also have substantial prizes and can count as big victories or positions for horses that finish first, second, or third.

The Arkansas Derby, Santa Anita Derby, and Travers Stakes are well-known intermediate grade stakes events for their general quality, difficulty, and competition. Any horse who wins one of these competitions (among others) is immediately revered.

Larger graded stakes events, including the Kentucky Derby, Preakness Stakes, and Belmont Stakes, are more well-known and serve as the last destination for horses from other graded stakes races.

3. NONFICTIONAL CHARACTER HISTORICAL BIOS

Abe Hawkins: (c. 1810 - 1867)

Abe Hawkins, born as a slave in the antebellum southern state of Mississippi, in Natchez. He endured unimaginable hardships, humiliation, and torture at the Fatherland Plantation before being enslaved at Ashland Plantation by Duncan Farrar Kenner. Amidst the oppressive conditions, Hawkins found solace and refuge in the presence of horses. Growing up on a stud farm, he formed an extraordinary bond with these majestic creatures, capable of communicating with them in ways unimaginable to others. The horses, in turn, heeded Hawkins' every command, as if he possessed a divine connection.

Located in Baton Rouge, Louisiana (formerly, Darrow, Louisiana), Ashland Plantation became Hawkins' new home after Kenner purchased him for a sum of a little over $2,000. His wife was named Esterline Watson. They had two daughters Delilah Hawkins (1858–1936) and Polly Ann Hawkins (1869–1917). Abe Hawkins' unique talent garnered recognition among White Turfmen, prompting Kenner to introduce him to the racetracks. Although Hawkins possessed an innate affinity for horses, he faced initial defeat in his very first race aboard Arrow. Falling significantly behind the renowned horses Lexington and Lecomte, Arrow was ultimately disqualified. However, Hawkins remained undeterred by the setback, finding sheer bliss in riding his beloved horse and feeling the exhilaration of racing against the wind. It was during this time that he developed his riding technique, later hailed as the "American Seat."

In 1854, Hawkins received another opportunity to pursue a racing career, coinciding with the reign of the undefeated horses Lecomte and Lexington. The Great Post Stakes witnessed Lexington's triumph over Lecomte. However, when Lecomte's owner requested a rematch, a unique challenge was proposed. Both horses would race against the clock for four miles at the Metairie Race Course in New Orleans, Louisiana. With famous white jockey Gilbert Kilpatrick atop Lexington, Lecomte's owner took a chance on Abe Hawkins. Astonishingly, with Hawkins in the saddle, Lecomte defeated Lexington by a staggering six lengths and set a world record with an impressive time of 07:25 seconds.

This marked the beginning of a fierce rivalry between Hawkins and the Irish jockey Gilbert Watson Patrick, known as "Gilpatrick." Their enduring competition would become one of the longest-running professional rivalries in contemporary American sports. In an era when Black jockeys were rarely acknowledged in news coverage, Hawkins represented a dawn of change. He became the first Black jockey ever mentioned in race reports. Over time, Hawkins achieved numerous victories, including two triumphs in the Jersey Derby and a notable win in the inaugural Jerome Stakes in Queens, New York. However, his most memorable accomplishment was securing victory in the 1866 Travers Stakes at Saratoga. Collaborating with trainer Ansel Williamson, Hawkins rode the horse Woodburn's Merrill to an impressive triumph.

Throughout his career, Hawkins garnered widespread acclaim in the racing industry for his exceptional ability to communicate with horses. He earned endearing nicknames such as the "Old Abe," while others referred to him as the "Dark Sage of Louisiana" and the Black Prince. In the twilight of his life, he returned to Ashland and passed away there in 1867. Although Hawkins lived his final years as a free man following emancipation, he never truly experienced the treatment and recognition befitting his freedom. Born as a slave, his remarkable journey from adversity to triumph forever transformed the landscape of horse racing, leaving an indelible legacy for future generations.

Abraham Perry (1842-1908)

Abraham "Abe" Perry was born in the Kentucky town of Midway. Perry began his career as a Thoroughbred trainer at Abraham Buford's Bosque Bonita Farm in Woodford County, Kentucky. McWhirter, his horse, was trained there. Perry then went on to serve as an assistant trainer for Leonard W. Jerome in New York. Perry was the trainer of the horse Onondaga and his offspring, who all went on to win multiple races. Perry's greatest accomplishment as a trainer was in 1885, when he trained the Thoroughbred Joe Cotton, who was ridden to victory in the Kentucky Derby by Erskine Henderson. Joe Cotton also won the Coney Island Derby and the Tennessee Derby. Perry also trained Longfellow. Longfellow was a leading sire in 1888, with progeny winning 751 races. Perry married Clara Taylor on March 1, 1880, and they settled at 216 Eastern Avenue in Lexington, Kentucky, where they still live today. They have two children: a son and a girl. Their son, Abraham Murphy Perry, graduated from Howard University and went on to become a physician. Fisk University awarded their daughter a music degree. Many African American bikers knew and communicated with one another at this time. Before the season's meetings in 1886, the Perrys traveled to Louisville with Isaac Murphy and his wife Lucy. Mr. and Mrs. Sadonia Wrightson, prominent members of Louisville's African American community, welcomed the four on one of their visits. Perry died in 1908 and was laid to rest in Lexington's African Cemetery Number 2. The cemetery constructed a memorial near his tomb in 2017 to tell visitors about his life and accomplishments.

Alonzo 'Lonnie' Clayton (1876 - 1917)

Alonzo 'Lonnie' Clayton was born on January 4, 1876, in Mossy Point, Mississippi, as one of eight children to Robert and Evaline Clayton. When Lonnie was ten years old, his family relocated to North Little Rock, Arkansas, where he assumed adult responsibilities at a young age to support his family. To support his family, young Alonzo took on various odd jobs, including shining shoes and running errands for a local hotel. However, destiny had a different path in store for him. While still attending school, he worked as a gofer at a local hotel, demonstrating his determination and self-reliance. At a tender age, Lonnie left home to work alongside his brother, Albertus, at Lucky Baldwin's stud farm in Chicago, Illinois. It was here that he discovered his affinity for horses and learned to ride as an exercise rider. His talent was quickly recognized, and he was chosen to train as a jockey. Immersed in the world of horses, Lonnie embraced his role as a stablehand, swiftly excelling in his duties. In 1890, he embarked on his journey as a professional jockey, venturing into the world of horse racing. Lonnie Clayton etched his name into the annals of history on May 11, 1892, when he participated in the Kentucky Derby at the age of fifteen. This remarkable achievement showcased his exceptional talent. Riding Azra, Lonnie emerged victorious, leaving an indelible mark on the sport. Additionally, he rode the soon-to-be-famous stallion Halma to its maiden victory. Lonnie's triumphs in horse racing brought him wealth and prosperity. Alonzo's star continued to rise, especially on the east coast. His most successful year was 1895, when he notched up 144 wins and finished in the money in 60% of his races. That same year, he won the Arkansas Derby at the Little Rock Jockey Club's Clinton Park. In 1896, he became one of the few black jockeys to compete in the Preakness Stakes at Baltimore, where he secured a commendable third place. Although he enjoyed success riding across the country, Alonzo was particularly celebrated as one of the greatest riders of New York. His success in the saddle brought him wealth and by 1895, he had acquired significant assets, including a large house and commercial property in Little Rock, Arkansas. However, his career faced a turning point in 1904 when an altercation with a racist spectator led to his arrest and subsequent imprisonment, ultimately forcing him out of the horseracing world. Following these events, Alonzo Clayton relocated to California, where he secured a job as a bellhop at a hotel. Unfortunately, his life was tragically cut short by tuberculosis, and he passed away in 1917, leaving behind a legacy of courage and accomplishment in the realm of horse racing. In the year 2012 Alonzo Lonnie Clayton was inducted into Arkansas Sports Hall of Fame and his legacy continues to inspire, reminding us of the power of perseverance and the importance of breaking barriers.

Ansel Williamson (c. 1810-1881)

Ansel Williamson was born around the year 1810 as an enslaved person in Virginia. Despite the challenging circumstances, his unwavering dedication to the world of horse racing would eventually propel him to become a prominent figure known for his exceptional abilities and expertise with horses. By the 1850s, Williamson's remarkable talent had captured the attention of many Kentucky turfmen, who quickly recognized his unique skill set. Specializing in preparing horses for three-mile races, Williamson's expertise as a trainer became widely renowned, earning him the endearing nickname "Old Ansel." Throughout his illustrious career, Williamson had the privilege of working for esteemed turfmen such as T.G. Goldsby, A. Keene Richards, and Robert Alexander. These opportunities allowed him to refine his craft and train exceptional horses under his care. Notable among the horses he worked with were Brown Dick, Australian, Asteroid, and Glycera. It was during his tenure with Robert Alexander at Woodburn that Williamson had the distinct honor of training Asteroid, a legendary racehorse who remained undefeated in 12 races and earned a staggering $9,700 before retiring.

It was during this period that Ansel Williamson's path intersected with two influential figures in the annals of horse racing—Abe Hawkins and Edward Dudley Brown. Recognizing Hawkins' potential, Williamson arranged for him to participate in races at the prestigious Metairie track in New Orleans. Moreover, Williamson took on the role of mentor and coach to Edward Dudley Brown, an African American jockey. Together, Brown and Williamson formed a formidable partnership, achieving remarkable success and garnering attention, particularly in the aftermath of the Civil War. Following the emancipation of enslaved individuals in

1865, Williamson's association with Robert Alexander continued, as he remained an invaluable member of the team, offering his expertise and knowledge to the horses under Alexander's stewardship. Subsequently, Williamson joined forces with H.P. McGrath, embarking on the task of training Aristides, an extraordinary racehorse. However, it was in the historic inaugural Kentucky Derby that Ansel Williamson's name would forever be etched in the annals of horse racing. Teaming up with talented jockey Oliver Lewis, Williamson skillfully guided Aristides to a resounding victory in the first edition of this iconic race. This triumph not only underscored Williamson's exceptional abilities as a trainer but also solidified his place in the storied history of horse racing. Ansel Williamson's remarkable journey came to an end in Lexington on June 18, 1881, leaving behind an enduring legacy. From his humble beginnings as an enslaved person, he defied the odds and secured a prominent position within the racing community. Ansel Williamson's profound contributions to the sport, his extraordinary skills as a trainer, and his pivotal role in securing significant victories will forever be remembered and celebrated in the hallowed halls of horse racing history. In recognition of his outstanding achievements, Ansel Williamson was posthumously inducted into the National Museum of Racing Hall of Fame in 1998, cementing his status as one of the sport's legendary figures.

Anthony Hamilton (1866 - 1904)

Born in 1866 in Columbia, South Carolina, Anthony Hamilton was destined to become one of the most accomplished jockeys of his time. Under the guidance of British horse trainer William Lakeland, Hamilton embarked on his horse racing journey, honing his skills at Lakeland's stables in Brighton Beach, New York. With his natural talent apparent, Hamilton quickly made a name for himself. At the age of 15, in 1881, Hamilton celebrated his first taste of victory aboard Sligo at the Phoenix Handicap. This early success propelled him to pursue a career in racing. Over the next fifteen years, Hamilton's list of triumphs grew ever longer, including impressive wins in the Brooklyn Handicap on two occasions, the Suburban Handicap, and the Metropolitan Handicap. The year 1887 saw him emerge victorious in the prestigious American Derby, followed by the Choice Stakes in 1888, the Toboggan Handicap in 1890, and the Monmouth Oaks in both 1889 and 1890. In the latter year, Hamilton achieved a career-high winning percentage of 33.8%, a testament to his exceptional talent and determination.

Hamilton, like many African American jockeys of his era, sought greater opportunities in Europe. In February 1901, he made his way to Vienna, Austria, and then journeyed to Warsaw, Poland, in March of the same year. Across Europe, Hamilton left an indelible mark, securing victories in renowned races such as the Metropolitan Stakes in Vienna, the Karolyi Memorial in Budapest, Hungary, and the prestigious Ruler Stakes in Warsaw, the first leg of Poland's esteemed Triple Crown. His outstanding riding skills caught the attention of prominent horse owners and trainers, leading to engagements with influential figures like J.B. Haggin, August Belmont, Mike Dwyer, Foxhall Keene, and Pierre Lorillard. In 1893, Hamilton signed a substantial contract with Belmont, affirming his status as one of the most sought-after riders of his time. Amidst his professional pursuits, Hamilton faced personal challenges in his relationships. Tragically, his first wife, Annie Messley, passed away in 1891, prompting widespread coverage in the Lexington press. Hamilton subsequently remarried, first to Kittie Brown of Indianapolis, Indiana, and later to Eva Lucretia Davis of Brooklyn, New York, just before embarking on his European ventures. Hamilton had one child, named Hamilton, from his marriages. Unfortunately, Hamilton's career was cut short when a riding accident forced him into early retirement. He embarked on a journey to Menton, France, where he ultimately succumbed to tuberculosis in 1904. In his obituary, Hamilton was portrayed as a figure of affluence, adorned in furs and jewelry befitting his well-deserved success. To honor his remarkable contributions to the sport, Anthony Hamilton was posthumously inducted into the National Museum Racing Hall of Fame in 2012, forever solidifying his legacy. His remains were tenderly transported to the United States and laid to rest at Mt. Olivet Cemetery in New York, marking the final resting place of a true racing legend.

Babe Hurd (1866 - 1928)

Babe Hurd, like his brother Mitchell, was born in Texas. When Hurd was thirteen years old, he began riding Thoroughbreds owned by Maryland Governor Oden Bowie. His first triumph occurred while riding Cinderella. In 1882, Babe and Mitchell Hurd worked for Green B. Morris and James Patton's stable in Kansas City, Missouri. Hurd gave up riding in 1885 to become a horse trainer. He worked at the Garfield Park Racetrack in Chicago, Illinois, the St. Louis County Fairgrounds in St. Louis, Missouri, and the Churchill Downs racetrack in Louisville, Kentucky. Hurd was working for William Thraves at Longridge Farm in Bourbon County, Kentucky, by 1920.

Chiron

In Egyption Greek mythology, where gods and mortals intertwined, there lived a unique and revered figure known as Chiron. Among the creatures of legend, he stood apart—a centaur of exceptional wisdom, possessing a blend of knowledge and compassion that few could fathom. With the upper body of a human and the lower body of a majestic horse, Chiron embodied the duality of both worlds. From an early age, Chiron's extraordinary gifts and noble qualities set him apart from his wild and unruly centaur brethren. Born to the Titan Cronus and the Oceanid nymph Philyra, his lineage was one of greatness and grace. It was this divine heritage that paved the way for Chiron's path as a mentor, guiding countless mythological figures on their own journeys. Chiron's teachings were vast and encompassed a myriad of disciplines, transcending the boundaries of traditional education. His students, such as Achilles, Asclepius, Jason, and Hercules, were shaped by his knowledge and wisdom, becoming skilled warriors, healers, and heroes under his tutelage. Chiron's guidance extended far beyond combat and medicine, reaching into the depths of philosophy, music, poetry, astrology, and self-mastery. But it was not only his vast array of teachings that made Chiron stand out. Fate had dealt him a cruel blow—a wound that set him apart from all others. Heracles, his friend and companion, had unknowingly pierced Chiron's flesh with a poisoned arrow, causing unimaginable pain. The poison coursed through his veins, tormenting him relentlessly. And yet, despite his immortality, Chiron could not find release through death. It was from this excruciating wound that Chiron earned his epithet—the "wounded healer." Paradoxically, it was his own suffering that became the catalyst for his profound healing potential. Chiron's personal pain allowed him to develop empathy, wisdom, and the capacity to guide others on their paths of healing and self-discovery. He became a symbol of the transformative power that arises from embracing and integrating one's own wounds and vulnerabilities. Depictions of Chiron on ancient Greek pottery bear a fascinating detail—his portrayal as black. The true reason for this choice remains a mystery, but it is believed to hold symbolic meaning rather than representing his skin color. The darkness of black could be interpreted as a representation of Chiron's wisdom, his depth, and his connection to the mysteries of life—those enigmatic forces that reside in the shadows. Beyond mythology, Chiron's significance resonates deeply within the human psyche. As the wounded healer archetype, he teaches us profound lessons about the transformative potential that emerges from personal struggle. Chiron reminds us that through our own wounds, we can gain wisdom, empathy, and the capacity to guide others on their paths towards healing and self-acceptance. In the celestial realm, Chiron finds association with the constellation Sagittarius—a mythical connection to the centaur. In the encyclopedia of astrology, Sagittarius is often depicted as a centaur archer, holding a bow and arrow. This representation mirrors Chiron's own association with the bow, which symbolizes focused intention, direction, and the ability to aim for a specific goal. The arrow, on the other hand, represents the transformative power and impact of our actions—the profound consequences that ripple through the fabric of existence. Chiron's life journey and mentorship continue to echo through the annals of Greek mythology, immortalizing him as a figure of wisdom, compassion, and the transformative power of personal struggle. His teachings and guidance have shaped the destinies of countless mythological figures, instilling in them the values and skills necessary to become heroes, healers, and warriors. Chiron's presence remains etched upon the fabric of our collective consciousness. He reminds us to embrace our wounds, for it is through our struggles that we gain the strength to heal others. The depth of his character, the mystery of his portrayal, and the symbolism he embodies continue to resonate with us, forever reminding us of the power of integration, healing, and the interwoven threads that connect us all.

Cheryl White (1953 -- 2019)

Cheryl White was born on October 29, 1953, to a horse racing family. She grew up on a horse farm. Her father, Raymond White, Sr., was a Thoroughbred trainer, and her mother, Doris, owned racehorses. When she was 17 years old, White began riding for her father, trainer Raymond White, at Thistledown in North Randall, Ohio. Her first race aboard Ace Reward, a gelding, resulted in an 11th place finish. She won the first Thoroughbred horse race in the United States at Waterford Park on September 2, 1971. As a Thoroughbred jockey, she also became the first woman to win two races on the same day in two states, at Thistledown in Ohio and Waterford Park in West Virginia. On October 19, 1983, Cheryl became the first female jockey to win five races at the Fresno Fair in a single day. During Cheryl's 21-year career as a jockey, she won over 750 races.

Her accomplishments include being inducted into the Appaloosa Hall of Fame, being nominated to the Cleveland Sports Hall of Fame, and receiving the African American Sports Hall of Fame's Award of Merit. White retired from racing in the 1990s, but he did not leave the industry. She began working for the California Horse Racing Board as a racing official. White died on September 20, 2019 in Youngstown, Ohio, at the age of 65.

Deshawn L. Parker (Born 1971)

Deshawn Parker started riding professionally as a teenager, winning his first race at Thistledown in Ohio. Daryl, his father, was a long-time track official in Ohio. Parker was the top rider for many years at Mountaineer Park in West Virginia before relocating to Horseshoe Indianapolis in 2016. Deshawn Parker won 60 races in his first five years of riding, from 1988 to 1992. The following year, he won 72 races, more than the previous five years combined, and he continued to improve. In 2002, he broke into the 200-win club, and in 2008, he achieved 300-plus wins for the first time, a feat he would repeat for five years, culminating in 2011 with 400 wins.

Deshawn Parker won 377 races in 2010 to win his first national championship. It was the first time an African-American had done so in the sport since James "Soup" Perkins in 1895, one hundred and fifteen years before. Parker won his second national championship in 2011 with 400 victories. He is also the most successful African-American in history. Parker won six races on a single racecard on May 6, 2012, at Mountaineer Racetrack in New Cumberland, West Virginia, where he has lived for many years and where he is the all-time leading jockey in wins. He received the Jockeys' Guild's Laffit Pincay Jr. Award in 2012 and has twice been a finalist for the George Woolf Memorial Jockey Award. Deshawn Parker won his 6,000th career race in June 2022 at Horseshoe Indianapolis, becoming one of only 20 riders in history to do so.

Dudley Allen (1845 - 1911)

Dudley Allen was born as a slave in Lexington and was owned by either Walter or John Dunn.

Allen won his freedom on August 29, 1864, when he joined the United States Colored Troops during the Civil War. He served as a quartermaster sergeant in Company M, 5th Cavalry, and was discharged on March 16, 1866, along with the rest of his regiment. Allen bought the farm after serving in the 5th United States Colored Cavalry Regiment. In 1891, Allen became the first African American to own a Kentucky Derby winner. He acquired a stake in Kingman, ridden by Isaac Murphy. Allen was one of two top trainers at Louisville's Churchill Downs. Allen rose to prominence as a thoroughbred owner and trainer. He ran a stock farm in Lexington and trained his own young horses while selling others to wealthy horsemen. Allen died at home in 1911 from kidney and heart disease.

Edward Dudley Brown (1848 - 1906)

Edward Dudley Brown is the primary protagonist of the narrative. He represents various archetypes throughout his character arc, including The Orphan, The Everyman, The Caregiver, The Mentor, and The Sage. Edward's journey revolves around his pursuit of equality, financial prosperity, and leaving a lasting legacy in the world of horse racing. He overcomes numerous obstacles and challenges, inspiring others and breaking racial barriers along the way. Edward was born on December 21, 1850, during the pre-Civil War era. His parents, Eliza and James Brown, were enslaved on a plantation in Kentucky. Tragically, Edward lost his parents at a young age, leaving him orphaned. Despite the hardships and dehumanization of slavery, Edward gained extensive knowledge of thoroughbreds and the racing industry while working at the Woodburn Estate horse farm of Robert A. Alexander. In St. Louis Missouri rode the Undefeated Asteroid to victory at the age of 14 and this triumph is captured by artist Edward Troye in a painting that was commissioned by Robert Alexander. During his time at the Woodburn Estate horse farm of Robert A. Alexander gained, Edward gained an extensive knowledge of thoroughbreds and the racing industry. He also had a cousin named Ed Domes who was the same age as him. Brown rode a number of well-known horses, including Merrill, Bayswater, Kingfisher, and Virgil. In 1870, he won the Belmont Stakes on Kingfisher. Brown eventually began training horses. After leaving Alexander's stables, Brown moved to Daniel Swigert's horse farm. One of Brown's early achievements as a trainer was training the first Kentucky Derby winner, Baden Baden. As an owner and trainer, Brown won his second Kentucky Derby with Ben Brush in 1896. Brown also trained another Kentucky Derby winner, Plaudit. On May 11, 1906, Brown died of tuberculosis. In the racing world, his achievements as a rider, trainer, and owner are still admired today. Brown was inducted into the National Museum of Racing's Hall of Fame in 1984.

Initially short and of medium build, typical for an 11-year-old, Edward has black hair, light brown and brown eyes, and a typical African American appearance for that era. As he grows older, his overall presentation changes, becoming more sophisticated and well-dressed. His height and weight vary with age, but he maintains a proportionate build. Edward's physical agility is notable, thanks to his experience as a jockey and his athleticism. Edward's childhood was marked by the hardships of slavery. He worked as a groom and later became a jockey, eventually transitioning to becoming a horse trainer and stable owner. However, his privileged position as a slave with opportunities in the horse racing industry led to bullying from both white and black children. These experiences shaped his determination, belief in his abilities, and fueled his pursuit of freedom, financial prosperity, and equality.

Edward's family background includes being orphaned at a young age and being born into slavery. His parents, Eliza and James Brown, were enslaved on a plantation in Kentucky. Edward deeply misses his mother and sees her as a guiding star, represented by the Sirius star and Sagittarius constellation. His upbringing in slavery and subsequent work in the horse racing industry provided him with unique experiences and perspectives. Edward's association with the Woodburn Estate and exposure to thoroughbreds and horse racing shaped his knowledge and passion for the sport. Generous and kind-hearted, Edward possesses a paternal nature, often acting as a big brother figure to those around him. He is steadfast, patient, sensitive, and occasionally impulsive. Edward is highly competitive and has a tenacious spirit. He embodies traits such as strength of will, physicality, and intuition. Initially introverted and compassionate, he finds solace in working with horses. As he grows older, he becomes more extroverted, charismatic, and optimistic.

Edward excels in physical activities, thanks to his experience as a jockey and his athleticism. He possesses extensive knowledge of thoroughbreds and the racing industry, gained through his work at the Woodburn Estate and his own experiences as a jockey and trainer. Edward also has a natural ability to mentor and inspire apprentice jockeys, sharing his wisdom and guidance to help them succeed. Edward is driven by the desire for freedom, financial prosperity, equality, and creating a legacy for future generations. His main goals include achieving success in horse racing, earning respect, and providing opportunities for his community and apprentice jockeys. His motivations stem from the influence of his mentor, Abe Hawkins, and his own experiences as an orphan and victim of bullying. The memory of his mother, represented by the stars, urges him to persevere. Self-belief and a sense of responsibility to his community also fuel his motivations.

Edward's relationships play a significant role in his life. He forms significant bonds with Ansel Williamson, a horse trainer who becomes his mentor, and Abe Hawkins, a famous black jockey. Their love, support, and guidance shape Edward's development and decisions. Edward's wife, Lucy Alexander Gaines, provides love and support throughout his life. They share a strong bond and partnership. Additionally, Edward forms close bonds with apprentice jockeys and those he mentors, inspiring and earning their respect. Edward faces internal conflicts stemming from the loss of his parents, fear of his own privilege, and the moral complexities of participating in an industry that mirrors the concept of slavery. These conflicts hinder his progress and lead to dilemmas that force him to question his own actions and choices. He occasionally experiences self-doubt, fears losing his hard-earned accomplishments, and exhibits caution due to past experiences. These weaknesses and flaws add depth to his character.

External obstacles challenge Edward throughout his journey. He encounters racial discrimination, financial hardships, and the competitive nature of the horse racing industry. Navigating these challenges while pursuing success as a jockey, trainer, and horse stable owner tests his resolve, resilience, and belief in his abilities. Whether it's breaking records, battling racial prejudices, or ensuring a fair and just environment for African Americans in horse racing, Edward must overcome these obstacles to achieve his goals. Edward's relationships evolve over time as he forms new connections and deepens existing ones. He starts as a young boy seeking acceptance and understanding, but as he grows older, he becomes a mentor and guide to others, fostering strong bonds and impacting their lives. Edward's primary interest lies in horse racing. He is passionate about thoroughbreds, the racing industry, and the pursuit of success. Outside of horse racing, he may have an affinity for storytelling, as a way to pass down knowledge and wisdom.

Edward values freedom, equality, justice, and leaving a lasting legacy. He believes in the power of hard work, perseverance, and helping others. He is driven by a sense of responsibility towards his community and future generations. Edward exhibits a wide emotional range throughout the story, experiencing joy, anger, frustration, grief, and determination. His expressions vary, from quiet introspection to passionate outbursts, depending on the situation. In terms of dialogue style, Edward's background and experiences influence his speech. He may have a tendency to use metaphors or analogies related to horse racing. His speech may reflect a mix of formal and informal language, adapting to different social contexts. Edward's relationships extend beyond his immediate circle and impact his worldview. Interactions with colleagues, neighbors, and acquaintances challenge his beliefs, provide new perspectives, or create conflicts.

Edward's journey is associated with themes of resilience, racial equality, personal growth, and the pursuit of a legacy. Symbolic elements such as the stars representing his guiding star, the Sirius star, and the Sagittarius constellation symbolizing his connection to his mother add depth to his story. His transformation involves personal growth, self-discovery, and learning from his experiences. Edward learns to navigate racial discrimination, grapples with moral dilemmas, and finds his voice in advocating for equality and justice. Edward's interactions with the story's protagonists, antagonists, or obstacles challenge his beliefs and provide opportunities for personal growth. His relationships with these characters contribute to the conflicts and resolutions within the narrative. Edward faces moral dilemmas related to his involvement in the horse racing industry, his own history as a former slave, and his pursuit of success. These dilemmas shape his development, relationships, and decisions.

Edward Dudley Brown's character leaves a lasting impact on the story as a symbol of hope, resilience, and the indomitable spirit that can achieve greatness even in the most challenging circumstances. His personal growth, mentorship, and pursuit of equality inspire others and break racial barriers, making him an iconic figure in the world of horse racing. Edward's legacy encompasses his triumph over adversity, perseverance in the face of challenges, and the pursuit of freedom and justice.

Eliza Carpenter (1851 – 1924)

Eliza Carpenter was a horse stable owner, jockey and trainer. In 1851, Eliza Carpenter was born into slavery in Virginia. She was sold and brought to Kentucky when she was six years old. She was resold and brought to Missouri when she was eight years old. She was sold to a Missouri planter two years later, at the age of eight. She returned to Madisonville, Kentucky, after gaining her freedom at the end of the Civil War, where she learned the business of buying, training, and riding race horses. She then relocated to Kansas and purchased several horses. Carpenter enjoyed horse racing as well. She was both a thoroughbred owner and a jockey. She always insisted on the money she won from a bet, even if the loser tried to back out out of embarrassment or bigotry. Carpenter staked a claim in Oklahoma during the Cherokee Strip Land Run, the largest land run in American history, on September 16, 1893, at the age of 44. She bought a good farm and began training Thoroughbreds and Quarter Horses there. Carpenter returned to Kentucky in 1924, at the age of 75, to visit family in Madisonville. There, an accident with a horse sent her health into a tailspin. She passed away on December 16, 1924.

Erskine Henderson (1861-1913)

Erskine Henderson (1861-1913) was born in 1861 in Versailles, Woodford County, Kentucky, to Jer Henison and Mary J. Blackburn. From a young age, Henderson showed a passion for horse racing, embarking on his career as a jockey at the age of fourteen under the guidance of S. J. Salyers. Known for his lightweight stature, weighing between 80 and 110 pounds, Henderson quickly made an impact in the racing world. In 1875, he impressed by finishing second in the Spring Meet at the Kentucky Association track in Lexington while riding Bill Bruce. The following Fall Meet brought even greater success as Henderson rode two-year-old thoroughbreds Katie, Novelty, and Clemmie to victory in three races, including the prestigious Purse for All Ages, the Produce Stakes, and the Bluegrass Stakes.

Throughout his prime years, Henderson honed his skills by working for various renowned turfmen such as A Keene Richards, James T Williams, Oden Bowie, Thomas J Megibben, Elias J Baldwin, August Belmont, James R Keene, and Asabel Burnham. Notably, on June 22, 1880, he celebrated his first triumph at Sheepshead Bay while mounted on Enquiress. The same year, Henderson secured victories in six out of thirty-seven races, showcasing his exceptional talent and determination. Later in his career, Henderson found employment under James T. Williams, riding horses and mounting an impressive 47 Thoroughbreds in a single year, although only fifteen of them hailed from Williams' stable. The pinnacle of Henderson's career arrived in 1885 when he made history alongside Joe Cotton. Together, they achieved remarkable victories in the Cottrill Stakes, Tennessee Derby, and the iconic Kentucky Derby. Despite initially trailing behind a ten-strong field, Henderson's trainer, Abraham Perry, advised him to maintain a strategic pace at the start. Henderson exhibited patience and precision, making his move to the front after a mile, resulting in a thrilling victory by a narrow margin. This unforgettable race solidified Henderson's status as a legendary jockey.

As time went on, Henderson faced dwindling opportunities despite his exceptional track record. However, he refused to be discouraged, applying to be listed in the 1889 edition of Goodwin's Turf Guide and persistently seeking work as a jockey. In 1893, he secured a contract to ride for the Jackson and Gaylon stables, marking a triumphant return after an absence from historical archives for twenty years. In 1913, at the age of 49, Henderson found himself at Churchill Downs with two horses, weighing 110 pounds. Remarkably, he retained a similar weight to when he piloted Joe Cotton to victory in the grand classic nearly thirty years prior, exemplifying his enduring physical prowess. The news of Henderson's passing in 1913 sparked a search for confirmation, although his name was misspelled as Earskins Henison on the death certificate. Fortunately, his occupation as "A Race Horseman" saved it from rejection. Henderson's death and burial took place in Versailles, Kentucky, in Woodford County, marking the end of a remarkable life dedicated to the sport he loved. Erskine Henderson's legacy remains etched in the annals of horse racing, exemplifying talent, determination, and an unwavering passion for the track. His contributions to the sport, impressive victories, and unwavering spirit continue to inspire generations of racing enthusiasts.

Garrett Davis Lewis (1862 - 1880)

Garrett Davis Lewis was born to Henry and Mary Lewis in Fayette County, Kentucky, in 1862. He was the eighth of eight children. Mary, Martha, Isaac (also a jockey), Sallie, Oscar, Lutita, and Martin were his siblings. Garrett Davis Lewis is frequently confused with George Garrett Lewis. Lewis began riding at the age of sixteen for Byron McClelland, a well-known Lexington owner and trainer. During his brief career, he was a regular rider for McClelland. He also rode for Cynthiana, Kentucky's J. S. Shawhan. Lewis won the Phoenix Stakes in 1880 while riding the horse Fonso for Shawhan. Fonso was a strong horse with a well-known bloodline, and the jockey-horse team got along well. Lewis is best known for riding Fonso to victory in the 1880 Kentucky Derby. The race was quite dramatic, with all five horses in the field leading the pack at some point. Isaac Murphy, another well-known African American jockey, also competed in the race. Lewis pushed Fonso hard but didn't use the whip on him until the last eighth of a mile. He gently prodded him to win by a full length. Lewis was injured during a race in St. Louis, Missouri. Lewis died at the age of eighteen at home in Hutchison Station, Kentucky.

George B. "Spider" Anderson (1871 - Unknown)

George B. Anderson was born in Baltimore, Maryland in 1871. When Anderson was just 12 years old, he began working in Baltimore and Brighton Beach. Because of his short stature and weight of 80 pounds, he earned the title "Spider.".

A talented jockey with a clever riding style and a strong work ethic,

Anderson quickly became one of the most sought-after riders of his era. Anderson won the race aboard August Belmont's Fides despite his leg injury in 1889. In 1889, riding Buddhist, he became the first Black jockey to win the Preakness Stakes race. Despite his illustrious career, Anderson disappeared without a trace. The upcoming races still listed Anderson as participating, but he never made an appearance.

Isaac E. Lewis (1867-1919)

Isaac E. Lewis, born and raised on a horse farm near Hutchison Station, Kentucky, by his parents Henry and Mary Lewis, lived a remarkable life as a jockey and a prominent figure in the horse racing world. Born as the eighth child in a family of eight, Isaac grew up alongside his siblings Mary, Martha, Garrett, Sallie, Oscar, Lutita, and Martin. From a young age, Isaac Lewis displayed a natural affinity for horses. At the age of eleven, he began driving under the guidance of Byron McClelland. It quickly became evident that Lewis possessed exceptional talent and fearlessness in the saddle. He embarked on a successful career as a jockey, accumulating an impressive list of victories between 1881 and 1891. Lewis's notable wins included triumphs in the Phoenix Stakes in 1886 and 1888, the Hotel Stakes in 1892, the Great Western Hotel Stakes in 1888, the Pansy Stakes in 1890, the Hyde Park Stakes in 1891, and the Saratoga Cup Stakes in 1891. His exceptional skills and ability to take commanding leads out of the starting gate made him a force to be reckoned with on the racetrack.

However, it was his victory in the 1887 Kentucky Derby that solidified Lewis's place in racing history. Riding the pony Montrose, owned by Alexander and Isaac Labold, Lewis secured a memorable win in the prestigious event. He would go on to participate in four consecutive Kentucky Derby contests from 1886 to 1889, finishing impressively in each one. In 1886, he rode Grimaldi to a sixth-place finish, followed by a first-place victory with Montrose in 1887. The Chevalier placed fifth in 1888, and Sportsman came in sixth in 1889. Beyond his accomplishments on the racetrack, Isaac Lewis forged connections with other prominent figures in the horse racing community. He had the honor of being the best man at Anthony Hamilton's wedding ceremony in St. Louis in 1891. During the Hamiltons' honeymoon in Lexington, Lewis was invited to a formal birthday celebration hosted by Isaac Burns Murphy, further demonstrating his close ties to the Kentucky Derby winners.

After retiring from active racing, Lewis transitioned to work as a groom at the J. B. Respess stable in Covington, Kentucky, starting in

1900. He resided in Harlem Village, a Chicago neighborhood that served as a hub for African American jockeys, grooms, trainers, and other racetrack personnel during that era. In 1910, Isaac Lewis officially retired from the pony business. However, his passion for the racing world remained evident as he owned and operated a Turkish bathhouse in Chicago. These bathhouses not only served as places for jockeys to shed weight but also fostered social connections and camaraderie among the racing community. Lewis's dedication to his family and roots in Kentucky persisted throughout his life. He maintained regular visits to see his relatives and expressed his thoughts at the Kentucky Association racecourse during his 1914 visit. Tragically, he returned to Kentucky the following year to attend the burial of his son, Charles, who passed away at the age of 23. Isaac Lewis's journey came to an end on March 10, 1919, in Chicago, coinciding with his fiftieth birthday. He was laid to rest at the Lincoln Cemetery in Alsip, Cook County, Illinois. Lewis's contributions to the sport of horse racing, his memorable victories, and his enduring connections within the racing community cement his legacy as a respected and influential figure in the history of the sport.

Sir Isaac Burns Murphy (1861 - 1896)

Isaac Murphy was born to Jerry Skillman and America Murphy in 1861. After his father's death, Isaac joined his mother to work at Eli Jordan's Horse Racing stable. Murphy began working as an exercise rider, during which time he developed his unique riding style. Averse to using whips against horses, he learned the knack of horse whispering.

Murphy rode his first race at the age of 14 and became the youngest Black Jockey to race. Though Murphy lost that race, he went on to win many other races following his first stint. Throughout his short career, Murphy won 44% of his races, a record that remains unbroken. He became the first back-to-back and three-time winner of the Kentucky Derby. Despite racial attacks, Murphy led a lavish life to prove to his community that Black people deserved to live a better life. Given his natural horse racing talent, Murphy gained fame and success sooner than any other Black Jockeys of his time. He also attained wealth and elite social status in his life. However, Murphy's career was shortened by conspiracies and discrimination. On Feb. 12, 1896, Isaac Burns Murphy passed away at the young age of 35.

James "Jimmy" Lee (1887 - 1915)

In 1907, James Lee, a black rider, became only the third jockey in history to win all of the races in the event. Six of the races at Churchill Downs in Louisville, Kentucky, were won by Lee. Some of the triumphs were long shots: one race paid out $13,000 on a one-dollar wager. Lee had a contract with J B Respess of Cincinnati, Ohio. He also established a new world record by two seconds while riding Foreigner. Lee tied the record set by jockeys Fred Archer and George Fordham, who each won every race on their cards in England. Monk Overton, an African-American jockey, won six of the seven races at Washington Park in Chicago; he was unable to ride in the seventh race. Raceland, Louisiana, was where James "Jimmy" Lee was born and died.

James 'Jimmy' Winkfield (1882-1974)

James 'Jimmy' Winkfield was the first to win two consecutive Kentucky Derby races aboard Eminence in 1901 and Alan-a-Dale in 1902. He was also the last African American to win the Derby. At the end of his 30-year career, Jimmy had a total of 2,500 victories in the United States (U.S.) and Europe combined. He rode in the U.S. from 1893 to 1903 and in Europe from 1904 to 1930. In Europe, Winkfield won such prominent races as the Moscow Derby in Russia and the Prix du President de la Republique in France. Besides his Derby wins, Winkfield had one second and one third place finish.

James Winkfield was forced to relocate to Europe and settled in Russia where he married into the aristocracy and lived with his wife and son until the 1917 Russian Revolution. He then moved to France and back to the U.S. during World War II. After the war, he returned to France, started a new family (a daughter), owned a farm, and trained horses.

Born in Chilesburg, Kentucky in 1882, James Winkfield was the youngest of 17 children and the son of a slave. As a child, he worked on a thoroughbred farm. Jimmy died in 1974, in France at the age of 92. He was inducted into the Hall of Fame in 2004. The Aqueduct Racetrack in New York honored him by renaming their Best Turn Stakes the Jimmy Winkfield Stakes in 2005.

James 'Soup' Perkins (1879 - 1911)

James "Soup" Perkins, born on February 28, 1879, in Lexington, Kentucky, came from a family deeply rooted in the horse racing industry. His father, John Perkins, worked as a horse trainer, and his brothers also pursued careers as trainers and grooms. It was during his early years that James earned his famous nickname, "Soup," due to his fondness for consuming soup as a means of maintaining his weight for races. His dedication to the sport led him to enter the racing industry at the age of eleven. Living behind the Kentucky Association Racetrack, James would clandestinely enter through gates and fences, demonstrating his determination to immerse himself in the world of horse racing. His talent and passion for the sport propelled him to extraordinary achievements. In 1892, at the age of fifteen, James signed a five-year contract as a jockey, marking the beginning of a remarkable career that would shape the history of horse racing. In 1895, James Perkins etched his name into the annals of the sport by riding Halma to victory in the prestigious Kentucky Derby. This triumph made him the second-youngest jockey to win the renowned race, elevating his popularity and opening doors to opportunities with various owners. The following year, he accomplished an extraordinary feat by winning five races in a single day. However, his career encountered setbacks when racing officials disqualified him in 1897 on charges of taking too many mounts. Tragedy struck James once again in 1898 when reports surfaced about his brother, Frank, suffering from insanity while lodging in Cincinnati. These personal challenges, coupled with his disqualification, ultimately led James to retire from racing in 1899. Undeterred by adversity, he transitioned into a new role as a horse trainer, using his expertise and experience to guide and develop equine athletes. James "Soup" Perkins continued to contribute to the horse racing world, but his life was tragically cut short by a heart attack in 1911 while residing in Canada. He was laid to rest in African Cemetery #2 in Lexington, Kentucky, a place that commemorates his significant legacy in the sport. Today, his name lives on as a testament to his remarkable talent, dedication, and indomitable spirit within the realm of horse racing. Soup Perkins alley is named after him.

Kendrick Carmouche (Born 1984)

Kendrick Carmouche was born on January 18, 1984, in Vinton, Louisiana. His father, Sylvester Jr., and brother, Sylvester III, are both professional riders. Carmouche began his riding career in Louisiana, first at Delta Downs and then at Evangeline Downs. Carmouche, his father, and his brother used to ride at the same meets before moving to Philadelphia. Carmouche established himself as the king of the riders in Philadelphia after winning more than 200 races in five consecutive seasons and a record four consecutive titles at Parx Racing, formerly known as Philadelphia Park. Carmouche celebrated his 2000th victory in September 2011. In 2015, Carmouche won six graded stakes races, including two on Goldy Espony, and earned a career-high $8,116,788 in purse earnings. Despite missing time due to an injury suffered during a fall 2018 spill at Kentucky Downs, he went on to have a successful four-year career. In 2017-18, Carmouche was a regular rider for top turf sprinter Pure Sensation. Carmouche won his first Grade 1 race aboard

True Timber in the Cigar Mile at Aqueduct on December 5, 2020, and finished the fall meet as the leading rider on December 6, 2020.

Kevin Krigger (Born 1983)

Krigger, the son of Albert Krigger and Averil Simmonds, was born in a rural area of St. Croix, US Virgin Islands, where he developed an interest in horses. Kevin Krigger, who was four or five years old at the time, climbed onto the back of a horse using parked cars. By the age of ten, he had his own horse, Dandella, on which he frequently won beach races. Krigger began his American career at Golden Gate Fields and Emerald Downs after moving to the United States in 2001. Krigger will ride Goldencents for trainer Doug O'Neill in the 2013 Kentucky Derby, which will be his first ride. Krigger made history by becoming the first Virgin Islands jockey to ride in the Kentucky Derby.

Meriwether Lewis Clark Jr. (1846 – 1899)

On January 27, 1846, Meriwether Lewis Clark, Jr. was born. He was the grandson of Lewis and Clark Expedition explorer and Missouri governor General William Clark. His father was Major Meriwether Lewis Clark Sr., an aide de camp and son-in-law of Mexican American War hero General Stephen Watts Kearny. Meriwether Lewis Clark moved in with his aunt and her sons, John, and Henry Churchill, after his parents died. In 1873, he returned from abroad with plans to build a racetrack in Louisville. In 1873, he returned from a trip to Europe with plans to build a racetrack in Louisville. Col. Meriwether Lewis Clark Jr. founded the Louisville Jockey Club with the help of his uncles and later built Churchill Downs, where the Kentucky Derby is held.

Clark suffered significant losses in the 1893 stock market crash and began traveling from city to city working as a steward. On April 22, 1899, he allegedly committed suicide, fearing a life of poverty. He is buried alongside his uncle, John Churchill, in Cave Hill Cemetery. His influence on American racing cannot be overstated. He not only built Churchill Downs and founded the Kentucky Derby, but he also wrote many racing rules that are still in effect today. He advocated for a standardized weight system and pioneered the stakes system, establishing the Great American Stallion Stakes, which served as the model for the current Breeders' Cup.

Oliver Lewis (1856-1924)

Oliver Lewis was born in Fayette County, Kentucky in 1856 to Goodson and Eleanor Lewis. Oliver Lewis won the first Kentucky Derby on May 17, 1875, while riding the colt Aristides. His time of two minutes

37.75 seconds was also an American record for a mile and a half. Lewis finished second in the Belmont Stakes, which became one of the "Triple Crown" races and won three races that year at the Louisville Jockey Club. Lewis entered the first Kentucky Derby when he was only 19 years old. Lewis rode Aristide, one of two colts entered in the race by their owner, H. Price McGrath of Jessamine, Kentucky. Lewis worked as a day laborer for a short time after retiring. He died at the age of 68 in Lexington, Kentucky in 1924.

Patrick Husbands (Born 1973)

Patrick Husbands, the son of a jockey, began riding as a child and soon became the youngest jockey to win the prestigious Barbados Gold Cup on his mount Vardar at the age of 16 years and 9 months. Patrick Husbands grew up in Barbados and started riding at a young age. He rode professionally in his home country before relocating to Canada, where he has achieved great success, including winning the Canadian Triple Crown on Wando. He has won the title of Canadian champion jockey seven times.

Among his other notable victories were Numerous Times in the $1 million 2001 Woodbine Mile and Exciting Story in the Metropolitan Handicap at Belmont Park in New York that same year. Between 2004 and 2006, he rode Arch Hall to three consecutive Sir Barton Stakes victories. In 2007, he was a regular rider on Sealy Hill, the Canadian Horse of the Year.

In 2001, Husbands won three Grade 1 races: the Atto Mile Stakes aboard Numerous Times, the Metropolitan Handicap aboard Exciting Story, and the Selene Stakes aboard Dark Ending. Husbands was a regular rider for Sealy Hill in 2007, and he won the Grade 1 Darley Alcibiades Stakes on Spring in the Air in 2012.

Patrick Husbands won his 3,000th career race at Woodbine Racetrack on June 18, 2016.

Raleigh Colston, Jr. (1861 - 1928)

Raleigh Colston, Jr. was born to Raleigh and Bettie Colston. Colston Jr. was born in Woodford County, Kentucky, into an enslaved horseman family. All of his father's uncles and brothers were jockeys, trainers, and owners. Colston Jr. grew up grooming Leonatus, his father's horse. Leonatus' unbeaten record as a three-year-old made him famous. Colston began his career as a jockey in the early 1870s. At the time, he was working as an exercise rider for General James Robinson, president of the Kentucky Racing Association. The Phoenix Hotel Stakes, which he won aboard Millionaire against Ten Broeck, was his first recorded race. Colston won the race with the horse Bob Wooley over Emma C. A short time later, Colston set a new mile record of 1 minute and 41.25 seconds while riding Searcher. Colston was best known for his work as a trainer and later as a business owner. He was a horse trainer for the Chinn and Morgan stables. Among these horses were Lissak, who won the World's Fair Stakes in 1894, and Ban Fox. Colston began working for the Chinn and Forsythe stable in 1901. He trained High Chancellor, Fountainbleu, and Rebus there. Colston also worked as a horse trainer for W. F. Schulte in Louisville and Will Perkins at the Kentucky Association racetrack in Lexington. Colston was ranked eighth among top trainers in the United States by 1909. Colston entered Colston, his Thoroughbred, in the 1911 Kentucky Derby. The pair finished third with African American jockey Jess Conley aboard. Raleigh Colston, Jr. died at the age of 66 in Lexington, Kentucky, and was laid to rest in Cove Haven Cemetery.

Shelby "Pike" Barnes (1871 - 1908)

Shelby Barnes was born in Beaver Dam, Kentucky, in June 1871. The young jockey began preparing for his racing career at a very early age and made his debut as a jockey when he was just 14 He began to make a name for himself when he won the Futurity Stakes in 1888. Then in 1889 he placed second just by a nose at the Kentucky Derby aboard Proctor Knott winning $300, later in the year he won the Travers Stakes aboard Long Dance trained and owned by G. M. Rye. Time: 3:08.75 Turf Distance: 1-3/4 m. Winning: $3,700.

Then in 1890 Shelby won the Belmont Stakes aboard Burlington, trained by Albert Cooper. That year he also won the Sheridan Stakes, and the following year won the Brooklyn Derby aboard Tenny which was the same horse Edward Garrison lost to Isaac Murphy who was aboard Salvatore. Shelby Pike Barnes was considered one of the best jockeys of his generation. He became the first Jockey to have 206 total wins in a single year. Barnes passed away in 1908. In 2011, he was inducted into the National Museum of Racing and Hall of Fame.

Sylvia Augusta Rideoutt (1919-2004)

Sylvia Augusta Rideoutt was a trailblazer in the horse racing industry, becoming one of America's most successful trainers. She was born in 1919 to James and Bertha Rideoutt in Charles Town, West Virginia. In 1954, she became the first Black woman licensed to train horses at the track in West Virginia. Sylvia passed away in 2004, but her children have gone on to work in the horse-racing industry and carry on her legacy.

William Billy Walker (1860-1933)

In 1860, William "Billy" Walker was born into slavery in Woodford County, Kentucky. Walker began riding horses at a young age and competed in his first race at Jerome Park at the age of eleven. Walker won his first race on Astral in the 1873 Lexington fall meet when he was thirteen years old. William Walker married Hannah Estill in June 1891 at the home of Isaac and Lucy Murphy. Their two children, William Jr. and Sadie, were born. Walker took part in the first Kentucky Derby, which was held in 1875. In the same year, he won the Tobacco Stakes, Galt House Stakes, and St. Leger Stakes with the horse King Alfonso. Walker finished fourth on his horse, Bob Wooley. In 1877, Walker and Baden-Baden won the Kentucky Derby by two lengths. Walker rode Himyar and Ten Broeck in nearly all of these horses' important races. Walker won a historic match against Mollie McCarthy while riding Ten Broeck in 1878. This famous race between two adversaries was immortalized in the folk song "Molly and Tenbrooks." After retiring as a rider in 1896, Walker became a trainer for Jake Greenburg of Louisville and a breeding advisor to John Madden. Walker was the trainer of 'Round the World' , the favorite for the 1911 Kentucky Derby. In 1917, he raced fourteen yearling horses at Churchill Downs, with mixed results. Billy Walker died in 1933 and was buried at the Louisville Cemetery at the corner of Eastern Parkway and Poplar Level Road.

Willie Simms (1870-1927)

Willie Simms was born in Georgia in 1870. Simms mother, Ida Pleasant, moved the family from Warren County, Georgia, to Augusta when he was a child. His uncle, Isham Welborn, was a successful livery stable owner and hackman. Simms first learned to ride at his uncle's house.

In 1887, Simms began racing in the North and went on to become the most successful short stirrup rider since antebellum slave and rider Abe Hawkins. Simms raced at a time when black jockeys dominated the sport, as the top riders and the highest-paid athletes. Simms rode for a number of notable owners, including Hall of Famers August Belmont I and James R. Keene, as well as Mike and Phil Dwyer, Richard Coker, and Pierre Lorillard. Simms won 182 races in 1893 and 228 from 688 mounts in 1894 (33.1 percent). In those years, he won the Belmont Stakes with Comanche and Hall of Fame member Henry of Navarre, respectively. He won the Derby on Hall of Famer Ben Brush in 1896 and Plaudit in 1898. He also won the Preakness with Sly Fox in 1898. Simms won numerous prestigious races during his career, including the Suburban Handicap,

Champagne Stakes, and Jerome Handicap. He won the Tidal Stakes and First Special three times each, as well as the Withers Stakes, Lawrence Realization, Brooklyn Derby, Spinaway Stakes, and Brighton Handicap twice each. Simms retired in 1901 with one of the best lifetime winning percentages in the sport. Simms died on February 26, 1927, in Asbury Park, New Jersey, at the age of 57. Simms was inducted into the Hall of Fame of the National Museum of Racing and Hall of Fame in 1977.

Moses Fleetwood Walker (1856 - 1924)

Moses Fleetwood Walker was born in Mount Pleasant, Ohio, on October 7, 1856. Fleet Walker's family moved around a lot until eventually settling in Oberlin, Ohio. Fleet Walker did his initial schooling from Steubenville High School. He moved from a segregated school to an integrated college. All the while, being at the receiving end of discrimination and bullying. Fleet Walker was a maverick who dabbled in many subjects. At school, he got good grades. He was also an inventor. His interest varied from time to time, but it was baseball that consumed him, eventually. Oberlin College enrolled Fleet Walker for the fall 1878 semester. Fleet played baseball for Oberlin's varsity team. Despite being mocked, humiliated, and hated by White students, he continued to pursue his passion for the sport. He soon came to be revered for his barehanded catching and hitting back-to-back home runs. Later, Fleet Walker left Oberlin to join the University of Michigan. Around the same time, he married his college sweetheart, Arabella "Bella" Taylor.

In 1883, Fleet Walker dropped out of school to become a professional baseball player. Toledo Blue Stockings were drafting. Toledo's manager, William Voltz, impressed with Fleet Walker's skills, signed him up. In a career spanning from May 1 till September 4 of 1884, Fleet Walker played in the major leagues and became the first African American to play major league baseball. Fleet became the first Black American to play Major League baseball. During his career, he played 42 games, scoring 23 runs, 40 hits, and a 0.263 batting average. Fleet passed away on May 11, 1924, in Cleveland, Ohio, at the age of 67. He was posthumously inducted into the Oberlin College Hall of Fame in 1990, and in 2017, the Ohio Legislature established an annual Moses Fleetwood Walker Day on his birthday. After this short stint, he fell victim to discriminatory attacks and humiliation. Being an enterprising individual, he ventured into several businesses post his baseball career. In 1990, he was inducted into the Oberlin College Hall of Fame. Fleet Walker died in Cleveland, Ohio, on May 11, 1924, at the age of 67.

Weldy Wilberforce Walker (1860 - 1937)

Weldy Wilberforce Walker was born in Steubenville, Ohio, on July 27, 1860. Unlike many mulatto kids at the time who chose to "pass for white", Fleet Walker chose to wear his color proudly. Inspired by his brother's heroic stance, Weldy Walker shadowed him. Like his elder brother, Weldy did his schooling at Steubenville High School. Then he enrolled in Oberlin's preparatory program. Finally, he joined the University of Michigan. In July 1884, he joined the Toledo Blue Stockings of the American Association and became the second African American to play in Major League Baseball. Weldy couldn't ignore the color barrier and fell out of the major league sooner than his brother. He played for the minor leagues till 1887. At which point, he realized, the color line was becoming a norm everywhere in America. Weldy started voicing his opinion, protesting the "color line" and even wrote a letter to the president of the Tri-State League objecting to the discriminatory policy. In his post-baseball phase, He started several ventures partnering up with his friends and his brother. He also joined his brother and became an active member of the "Back to Africa" movement. Weldy Walker died in Steubenville, Ohio, on November 23, 1937.

Edward Troye (1808-1874)

Edward Troye, born on July 12, 1808, in Switzerland to French parents, was a leading horse painter of the nineteenth century. He showed an early interest in art and received drawing and painting instruction in England before immigrating to America in 1831. He began working as a magazine illustrator after struggling with his art career. Troye, then 23, entered three paintings in the annual exhibition at the Pennsylvania Academy of Fine Arts. His first commission came from Thoroughbred breeding tycoon John Charles Craig of Carlton Farm in Pennsylvania. This relationship was very profitable for Troye because it introduced him not only to racing at Long Island's Union Course but, more importantly, to the wealthy racehorse owners who provided him with commissions for the next four decades. Troye rose to prominence through his work for The American Turf Register and Sporting Magazine, the country's first sporting publication. Twenty-one of his paintings were chosen as frontispieces for this new sports magazine, which covers everything from badger hunting to horse racing. Troye moved to Kentucky after marrying Miss Cornelia Ann Van de Graff in 1839, and Anna Troye, the couple's only child to survive infancy, was born in 1844.

Troye thrived in the state's rich horse-breeding culture, devoting the majority of his time to horse portraiture. Troye provided the trotting and Thoroughbred communities with expertly crafted portraits during the pre-photography era. During his career, Troye is said to have painted over 350 horses, mostly racehorses from the southern states. Abdallah, Belmont, Dexter, Dictator, and Mambrino Pilot are among his works. His roster also included Kentucky Derby winning thoroughbreds including Lexington, Glencoe, and American Eclipse.

In 1855, he left college to travel through Europe and the Near East with his friend, Blue Grass Park in Georgetown, Kentucky's Alexander Keene Richards. Troye painted portraits of Arabian horses as well as landscapes of Syria and the Holy Land along the way. When Troye returned home eighteen months later, he began writing The Racehorse of America, which was published in 1867.

In Troye's 1864 painting The Undefeated Asteroid, dated November 11th, 1864, the Thoroughbred is featured in the center of the frame. The horse towers over three African American men. All three men directly confront the viewer with their gazes. The background features rolling hills and a few trees. The sky evokes a feeling of dawn. Although Asteroid takes up most of the painting, three African American men are working in service of the horse.

In 1869, Troye bought a farm in Owens Crossroads, Alabama, in preparation for retirement. Troye died unexpectedly on July 25, 1874, during one of his regular visits to Richards' home, from pneumonia. He was 66 years old.

Robert A. Alexander

Robert A. Alexander (1819-1867), renowned for pioneering a systematic design method for horse breeding, played a pivotal role in the success of Woodburn Stud. The stud gained prominence with the acquisition of the stallion Lexington (1850–1875) from Elisha Warfield, a leading sire in America for sixteen years. Lexington, an exceptional sire, sired a multitude of champions and winners in prominent races, including the illustrious Duke of Magenta, Kentucky, and Preakness, after whom the renowned Preakness Stakes is named.

Robert A. Alexander's father, Robert Alexander (1767-1841), the second son of William and Christian Aitcheson, laid the foundation for the Alexander legacy on Woodburn Farm. In 1790, he purchased a vast expanse of two thousand acres from the estate of General Hugh Mercer. The breeding program at Woodburn proved to be a resounding success, boasting an impressive tally of 18 U.S. Triple Crown race winners and several other major victors, including the notable Foxhall, a grandson of Lexington. Woodburn Farm became the final resting place for several remarkable Thoroughbreds, including the likes of Asteroid (1861–1886), Planet (c. 1855-1875), and Australian (1858–1879), the son of the English Triple Crown victor, West Australian. Despite Lexington's influence as a sire, which earned Woodburn Stud a reputation synonymous with flat racing Thoroughbreds, it is worth noting that during the mid to late 19th century, Woodburn was the birthplace of the Standardbred horse. The farm's primary renown stemmed from its breeding prowess in trotting horses for harness racing. Following the passing of Robert A. Alexander in December 1867, the operation continued to thrive under the guidance of his brother, A. J. Alexander. However, upon A. J. 's demise in 1902, the stud experienced a decline. By the turn of the 20th century, the farm relinquished its involvement in the horse business and underwent a transformation into cattle land. Presently, a portion of the original property stands as Airdrie Stud, owned by descendants of the esteemed Alexander family. This enduring legacy showcases the family's enduring impact on the equestrian industry. Overall, Robert A. Alexander's innovative breeding methods, coupled with the success of Woodburn Stud, solidified his status as a visionary in the realm of horse breeding. The farm's association with exceptional Thoroughbreds and its pivotal role in the Standardbred industry established its prominent position in Kentucky's rich equestrian heritage.

End of bios

4. HORSE RACING, LIBRARIES, MUSEUMS AND HALLS OF FAME

American Quarter Horse Hall of Fame

The American Quarter Horse Association (AQHA), located in Amarillo, Texas, established the American Quarter Horse Hall of Fame and Museum. In 1989, groundbreaking construction on the Hall of Fame Museum began. People and horses who have contributed to the advancement of the American Quarter Horse and "have been excellent over a period of years in a number of areas" are eligible for the honor. Bob Denhardt and Ernest Browning were the first persons to be elected into the AQHA Hall of Fame in 1982. Wimpy P-1, King P-234, Leo, and Three Bars were the first horses to be inducted into the AQHA Hall of Fame in 1989.

Photographs of awardees and paintings of American Quarter Horses notable in the lineages of current champions may be seen at the American Quarter Horse Hall of Fame & Museum. Many of the paintings are by Orren Mixer, a western artist. There are interactive exhibits about horse anatomy, horse riding, and American Quarter Horse disciplines. Other exhibits include antiques, riding and cowboy costumes, tack, pictures and ribbons, and induction souvenirs.

Anyone may nominate either persons or horses to be considered by the Hall of Fame. Membership nominations are due by November 1. They are then vetted and forwarded to the Hall of Fame committee, which meets in March of the following year. Nominations are valid for three years, after which they must be inactive for three years before being considered again. People considered may be alive or dead, but horses must be dead.

Australian Racing Hall of Fame

Lady Kathleen Clarke and Mr Bill Adams formed the Victorian Racing Museum Committee in 1974, with representatives from the Victoria Racing Club, Victoria Amateur Turf Club, Moonee Valley Racing Club, and Country Racing Council as members. Her Majesty Queen Elizabeth II consented to serve as Official Patron two years later, and on September 29, 1981, during a Royal Visit to Australia, she formally opened the Victorian Racing Museum at Caulfield Racecourse.

The Museum was renamed the Australian Racing Museum in 1998. Champions - the Australian Racing Museum and Hall of Fame was officially inaugurated on 1 July 2004 at Federation Square by His Excellency the Governor-General, Major-General Michael Jeffery, where it resided for five years.

On the eve of the Spring Racing Carnival and the ceremonies surrounding the 150th running of the Melbourne Cup, the Champions Thoroughbred Racing Gallery opened on 30 September 2010 in the National Sports Museum at the Melbourne Cricket Ground.

The Museum was accredited by Museums Australia (Victoria) in 2014, aligning processes, policies, and practices with the National Standards for Australian Museums and Galleries.

Individuals and horses that have made remarkable contributions to Australian thoroughbred horse racing are recognized by the Australian Racing Hall of Fame. Induction into the Hall of Fame is our sport's ultimate honor. It is more than an award; it is admission into an elite group of history makers and a worthy homage to our sport's winners.

The Hall of Fame, founded in 2001 by the Australian Racing Museum and backed by Racing Australia, inducts new members every two years into the four categories at the heart of racing: horses, trainers, jockeys, and associates.

The Australian Racing Hall of Fame is proudly displayed at the Horses Racing Gallery, a permanent exhibition of the Australian Racing Museum at the Melbourne Cricket Ground.

During a significant renovation of the Australian Sports Museum (previously the National Sports Museum) in 2019, our display was renamed the Horse Racing Gallery and reopened in February 2020. Guests may race their own horse, learn about our Australian Racing Hall of Fame inductees, and commemorate both the champions and ordinary heroes of Australian Thoroughbred Racing through innovative interactives.

Canadian Horse Racing Hall of Fame

The Canadian Horse Racing Hall of Fame was founded in 1976 to recognize those who have made major contributions to the sport of harness and thoroughbred horse racing in Canada. It may be found at the Woodbine Racetrack in Toronto, Ontario.

The Thoroughbred and Standardbred horses, sulky drivers, jockeys, trainers, and horse racing industry builders are inducted into the Hall of Fame each year.

Although the Canadian Horse Racing Hall of Fame (CHRHF) was established in 1976, it did not have a permanent location until 1997. The Ontario Jockey Club awarded a permanent location at the West Entrance of Woodbine Racetrack at the time. The Hall currently contains biographical information about each inductee, as well as relevant artifacts like trophies, silks, vintage race programmes, and bronzed horseshoes. Each year, elaborate exhibits honor racing legends like jockey Ron Turcotte and pacer Cam Fella.

Northern Dancer's victories in the Kentucky Derby, Preakness Stakes, and Queen's Plate marked the Hall's 50th anniversary in 2014, with a series of initiatives including an online timeline of his career, the induction of his trainer Horatio Luro, a special tribute at the annual ceremony, and a calendar. Northern Dancer and his owner, E.P. Taylor, were among the first honorees in 1976. Northern Dancer's sire Nearctic, dam Natalma, sire's dam Lady Angela, multiple sons and daughters including Nijinsky, The Minstrel, Northernette, and Vice Regent, as well as another progeny, have all been inducted since then.

There are two nomination committees, one for Thoroughbreds and one for Standardbreds. Each committee nominates up to eight candidates, who are then voted on by the appropriate election committee. Any Canadian person or horse can be nominated for their accomplishments in Canada or abroad. Nominations may also be made for foreign-bred horses that have had a major impact on Canadian racing or breeding. Secretariat, for example, was nominated in 2013 in commemoration of his appearance in the 1973 Canadian International, which drew international attention to the event.

Since its creation, new inductees have been added on a yearly basis to an ever-growing list of Builders, Drivers/Trainers, Jockeys, Standardbreds, Thoroughbreds, and Trainers. The annual induction ceremony is a spectacular event that includes a supper and an evening of festivities.

The Canadian Horse Racing Hall of Fame is located near the Woodbine Racetrack's West Entrance in Toronto, Ontario.

Australian Racing Museum

The Australian Racing Museum is a museum dedicated to Thoroughbred horses, jockeys, and trainers in Melbourne, Australia. It opened at Caulfield Racecourse in 1981 and ended on August 30, 2003. It was later relocated to Flinders Street's Federation Square. The museum relocated to the MCG's Australian Sports Museum (formerly National Sports Museum) in October 2010.

British Steeplechasing Hall of Fame

The Steeplechasing Hall of Fame is a museum located at Prestbury Park in Prestbury, Gloucestershire. The Cheltenham Racecourse Hall of Fame, which opened in 1994, traces steeplechasing history back to 1819 and features National Hunt riders and trainers.

Japan Racing Association Hall of Fame

The Horse Racing Hall of Fame is a Japanese horse racing memorial hall that opened on September 2, 1985, at the JRA Horse Racing Museum in Fuchu, Tokyo. The Japan Racing Association established it to recognise the accomplishments of racehorses, riders, and trainers. The Japan Racing Association refers to racehorses admitted into the Hall of Fame as Kensho-ba, while jockeys and trainers are referred to as Kensho-sha.

A yearly vote in April determines which racing horses are inducted into the Hall of Fame. It is voted on by persons active in horse racing news for more than 10 years in mass communication and news. Racehorses are admitted into the Hall of Fame if they win more than three-quarters of their races. Since 2004, an extra regulation has been in place: racing horses who retired within the last year or more than 20 years ago cannot be nominated. Only that year, an additional vote was held solely for horses that had retired more than 20 years before (where Takeshiba O was selected). Due to the distribution of the vote among several horses, no horses are inducted to the Hall of Fame most years.

Korea Racing Authority Equine Museum

In Gwacheon, South Korea, there is a horse museum called the Korea Racing Authority Equine Museum. It was founded on September 13, 1988, to supplement Equestrian during the 1988 Summer Olympics in Seoul, and it now draws over 50,000 visitors each year, ranging from the elderly to toddlers. It includes over 1,500 displays in its 123 square meter showroom space. In 2008, a special exhibition commemorating 100 years of horse racing was staged, and in 2009, modern artwork, comprising painting, sculpture, pottery, and photos relating to horses, was displayed.

New Zealand Racing Hall of Fame

The New Zealand Racing Hall of Fame was founded in 2003, with the first ceremony in 2006 unveiling the first of our honorees. Since then, the New Zealand Racing Hall of Fame has inducted 84 horses and humans. Each inductee is honored with a short film clip that details their accomplishments and narrative. Every two years, a new class of inductees is introduced and honored during an induction banquet. The next supper will be in 2023. The Selection Committee, composed of well-known journalists, historians, and industry executives, uses predetermined criteria to identify and prioritize remarkable contributions to New Zealand thoroughbred racing that deserve to be recognised.

National Museum of Racing and Hall of Fame

The National Museum of Racing and Hall of Fame was established in Saratoga Springs, New York, in 1950 to recognise the accomplishments of American Thoroughbred racing horses, riders, and trainers. The museum relocated to its current home on Union Avenue at Saratoga Racecourse in 1955, and inductions into the hall of fame began at that time. Following the calculation of the final votes, new inductees are announced each spring, generally during Kentucky Derby Week in early May. The actual inductions take place at the Saratoga horse meeting in mid-August.

The nomination committee of the Hall of Fame chooses eight to ten candidates from the four Contemporary categories (male horse, female horse, jockey, and trainer) to present to the voters. Voters can now select numerous candidates from a single Contemporary category, rather than a single contender from each of the four Contemporary categories, according to changes in voting processes that began with the 2010 candidates. In 2016, for example, two female horses (Rachel Alexandra and Zenyatta) were entered simultaneously. In addition, the museum has a huge collection of art, antiques, and memorabilia documenting the history of horse racing from the eighteenth century to the present.

Cornelius Vanderbilt Whitney and a group of thoroughbred racing enthusiasts launched the National Museum of Racing in 1950. The museum originally opened its doors in 1951, occupying a single room in Saratoga's Canfield Casino. The institution was backed by the city of Saratoga Springs, which provided $2,500, the Saratoga Racing Association, which donated $5,000, and numerous sports fans who donated paintings and memorabilia. The museum's first acquisition was a horseshoe worn by the legendary Lexington.

The museum moved to its current home on Union Avenue in 1955, directly across the street from the main gate to the famous Saratoga Racecourse. The museum was transferred to a newly renovated facility, which includes a thoroughbred racing Hall of Fame. Since then, the museum has grown numerous times to accommodate the presentation of its enormous art collection as well as new multimedia exhibits about the sport's history.

In the early years, inductions to the hall of fame were decided by a panel of racing historians. In 1955, nine horses from the early days of the American turf were admitted. The 1956 class had 11 horses that competed around the turn of the century, while the 1957 class featured ten horses who raced up to the mid-thirties. Since then, the classes have shrunk dramatically as the inductions have changed to more modern horses.

To be eligible for the hall of fame, a horse must have been retired for at least five complete calendar years. Thoroughbreds are eligible for the modern category for five to 25 calendar years after their final racing year. Thoroughbreds who have been retired for more than 25 calendar years may be eligible via the Historic Review Committee.

Contemporary jockeys are eligible for the Hall of Fame after holding a license for at least 20 years, and they are eligible for another 25 years after retiring. The 20-year threshold may be waived in exceptional situations, such as frail health, however there is normally a five-year waiting period following retirement in such cases.

Contemporary trainers are eligible for the Hall of Fame after holding a license for at least 25 years, and they are eligible for another 25 years after retirement. In exceptional situations, such as poor health, the 25-year threshold may be relaxed, albeit there is often a five-year waiting period following retirement. According to the Hall of Fame, the Pillars of the Turf category celebrates people who have made remarkable contributions to Thoroughbred racing in a leadership or pioneering position at the highest national level since its inception in 2013.

International Museum of the Horse

The International Museum of the Horse, located at the Kentucky Horse Park in Lexington, Kentucky, is a prominent museum dedicated to exploring the history, culture, and significance of horses worldwide. Through a variety of exhibits and artifacts, the museum examines the relationship between humans and horses across different eras and cultures. It provides a comprehensive overview of the evolution of horses, their impact on human civilization, and their roles in transportation, agriculture, warfare, and sports. The museum also highlights the cultural significance of horses in diverse societies, showcasing their importance in Native American tribes, European Knightley traditions, Asian civilizations, and more. It features equine-related artworks, sculptures, and literature that celebrate horses and their influence on human imagination and creativity. The International Museum of the Horse offers thematic exhibitions, interactive displays, and educational activities that engage visitors of all ages, allowing them to learn about horse anatomy, grooming techniques, riding styles, and more. The museum's Hall of Champions showcases the achievements of exceptional horses in racing, show jumping, and other equestrian disciplines, offering insights into legendary horses and their remarkable accomplishments. Through educational programs and workshops, the museum promotes awareness and understanding of horses' historical and cultural significance, as well as their ongoing role in various industries. Situated within the Kentucky Horse Park, the museum allows visitors to explore a broader equestrian-themed park with horse shows, demonstrations, riding trails, and notable attractions like the gravesite of the famous racehorse Man o' War. In summary, the International Museum of the Horse is a hub for horse lovers, history enthusiasts, and anyone interested in the enduring connection between humans and these majestic creatures, offering a rich and diverse experience that celebrates the profound bond between humans and horses.

Keeneland Library

The Keeneland Library, located in Lexington, Kentucky, is a renowned research library dedicated to preserving and promoting the history and heritage of Thoroughbred horse racing. It serves as an integral part of the Keeneland Racecourse and Sales Complex. The library houses a vast collection of books, periodicals, photographs, videos, and other materials related to Thoroughbred racing, covering various aspects of the sport such as breeding, training, racing history, and pedigrees. Its archives hold a treasure trove of historical documents, manuscripts, letters, and memorabilia that offer valuable insights into the evolution of horse racing and the influential figures, horses, and events that have shaped the sport. Researchers, scholars, students, and journalists can utilize the library's research services to access its resources and receive assistance from knowledgeable staff. The Keeneland Library also boasts a collection of rare books, including first editions and limited editions, providing a glimpse into the early days of horse racing and capturing the perspectives of notable individuals in the industry. The library has embraced digitization initiatives, making photographs, videos, and other documents available online, thus enhancing accessibility to its resources.

Through educational programs, lectures, and exhibitions, the Keeneland Library celebrates the history and culture of Thoroughbred racing, offering opportunities for the public to learn about the sport's significance. Additionally, the library actively collaborates with organizations, academic institutions, and industry stakeholders to preserve and disseminate knowledge about Thoroughbred racing, participating in research initiatives and sharing resources with the wider horse racing community. Overall, the Keeneland Library serves as a vital resource for researchers, historians, and horse racing enthusiasts, playing a crucial role in preserving the legacy of the sport and fostering a deeper understanding and appreciation of its history.

5. HORSE BREEDS

Horse breeding refers to horse reproduction, specifically the human-directed process of selective breeding of animals, particularly purebred horses of a specified breed. Matings can be planned to create certain features in domesticated horses. Current breeding management and technology have the potential to raise the rate of conception, a healthy pregnancy, and successful foaling. When a stallion retires from racing, he may be offered for breeding. Artificial insemination and embryo transfer technologies have changed breeding techniques and made them more convenient.

Although horse domestication was widespread, the majority of extant horse breeds descended from just two ancient lineages. Over 700 years ago, these old Middle Eastern lines were transported to Europe. All horse breeds known today may be traced back to two ancient lineages: Arabian horses from the Arabian Peninsula and Turkoman horses from the Eurasian Steppe, which are now extinct. It has been conclusively shown that the hundreds and hundreds of different horse breeds that exist today are all descended from these two genetic genesis locations.

Breeding Process

Mares in foal are normally secluded from other horses, both for the mare's benefit and the safety of the soon-to-be-born foal. Separation also allows humans to observe the mare more carefully for any difficulties that may arise during the birthing process. A unique foaling stall that is big and clutter free is widely utilized in the northern hemisphere, particularly by significant breeding farms. For foaling, smaller breeders may utilize a small enclosure with a large shelter, or they may remove a wall between two box stalls in a tiny barn to create a huge stall.

Breeders over the centuries have become increasingly successful in breeding Thoroughbreds who perform well at the racetrack by following two basic principles. The first is that Thoroughbreds with superior racing ability are more likely to produce successful offspring. The second is that horses with certain pedigrees are more likely to pass along their racing genes to their offspring.

Stallions (male Thoroughbreds) have the highest breeding value since they may mate with around 40 mares every year. The value of champions, particularly Triple Crown winners, is so great that groups of investors known as breeding syndicates may be created. Each of the syndicate's approximately 40 shares permit its owner to breed one mare to the stallion each year. A champion horse's share might cost millions of dollars. The owner of a share can resell it at any time.

Commercial breeders are farms that produce foals for auction sale. E. J. Taylor, Spendthrift Farms, Claiborne Farms, Gainsworthy Farm, and Bluegrass Farm are the most successful (all located in Kentucky). Home breeders are farms that produce foals for their own racing, and they include well-known stables like Calumet Farms, Elmendorf Farm, and Green-tree Stable in Kentucky, and Harbor View Farm in Florida.

Modern Approach

Though artificial insemination and embryo transfer are legal and frequent in other horse breeds, they are prohibited in Thoroughbreds. The breed's population is therefore managed, ensuring a high monetary value for the horses in the process. Because each foal is granted an official birth date of January 1 to assist the age groupings that define Thoroughbred races, mares should foal as early in the calendar year as feasible. This allows the foal to grow as much as possible before training and racing.

The true test is the performance of a breeding horse's progeny, but for horses that have not been tried at stud, the criteria include lineage, racing ability, and physical conformation. Early in the history of horse racing, breeders discovered that crossing lineages may potentially overcome defects in horses. If one breed is recognized for stamina and another for speed, interbreeding the two may result in kids with a good blend of both attributes.

A Thoroughbred foal must be the result of a "live cover," which is a witnessed natural mating of a stallion and a mare. "Breed the best to the best and hope for the best," has always been the guiding idea for producing successful racehorses.

Race Breeds

Most horse races limit entrance to specific breeds; that is, the horse must have a studbook-approved sire (father) and dam (mother) of whatever breed is competing. In a standard harness race, for example, the horse's sire and mother must both be pure Standardbreds. The one exception is in Quarter Horse racing, where an Appendix Quarter Horse may be permitted to run against (regular) Quarter Horses. An Addendum A Quarter Horse is a horse that has one Quarter Horse parent and one parent from another qualified breed, such as a Thoroughbred.

American Quarter Horse

Embraced by beginners and professional equestrians all around the world, the American quarter horse is famous for its agility, docility, and athleticism. Originally bred during the 1600s from English and Spanish thoroughbreds crossed with local breeds such as the Native American Chickasaw horse, it has the largest breed registry in the world. These horses are shining stars on the trail and in the show ring.

- Height: 14 hands (56 inches) to 16 hands (64 inches)
- Weight: 950 to 1,200 pounds
- Physical Characteristics: Medium-boned; finely chiseled head; wide forehead; flat profile

Arabian

The Arabian has the oldest horse breed registry in the world. Its lineage goes as far back as 3000 B.C. The Bedouin of the Middle East, breeders of the Arabian horse, were among the first to chronicle their horse breedings. While it is impossible to say how far back the Bedouin passed on pedigree information through oral tradition, recorded pedigrees of Arabian horses existed by CE 1330.

In fact, every light horse breed, including Appaloosas, Morgans, and Andalusians, can trace their ancestry back to the Arabian. It can be a rather spirited horse breed, so not all beginners can handle it. But it's also generally a loving and loyal horse.

- Height: 14 hands (56 inches) to 16 hands (64 inches)
- Weight: 800 to 1,000 pounds
- Physical Characteristics: Lithe, compact body; wedge-shaped head; short back with sloping shoulders and powerful hindquarters.

Thoroughbred

Thoroughbreds are the most popular racing horse in North America. This breed is considered a "hot-blooded" horse, which means it's known for its agility, speed, and spirit. It's a fine multipurpose horse that often has a career in other equestrian competitions besides racing, such as dressage and jumping. Or it simply lives its life as a companion animal kept for pleasure riding.

- Height: 15 hands (60 inches) to 17 hands (68 inches)

- Weight: 1,000 to 1,300 pounds
- Physical Characteristics: Deep chest; lean body; long, flat muscles, delicate head

Appaloosa

The colorful spotted Appaloosa was originally developed for hunting and battle by the Nez Perce Native Americans. It's believed to be a descendant of wild horses mixed with the thoroughbred, American quarter horse, and Arabian. This hardy, versatile horse is great for herding, pleasure riding, long-distance trail riding, and more.

- Height: 14 hands (56 inches) to 16 hands (64 inches)
- Weight: 950 to 1,200 pounds
- Physical Characteristics: Colorful coat pattern; mottled skin; striped hooves

Morgan

The strength and elegance of the Morgan have made it a popular horse breed. As the official horse breed of Vermont, the muscle of the Morgan was used for clearing and tilling New England farms during colonial times. Today, it's popular to drive and ride horses. It's sure footed over rough trails and dignified in the show ring.

- Height: 14 hands (56 inches) to 15 hands (60 inches)
- Weight: 900 to 1,100 pounds
- Physical Characteristics: Small ears; expressive eyes; crested neck

Warmbloods

In equine circles, the terms "hot-blooded," "warm-blooded," and "cold-blooded" are used to categorize a horse's temperament, size, and origin. Medium-size horses, including the American quarter horse, Hanoverian, Cleveland bay, and Canadian, are considered warmbloods with a European heritage. They contain a touch of the spirit you get from lithe, "hot-blooded" thoroughbreds or Arabians combined with the calm demeanor of "cold-blooded" working horses. And that balanced temperament makes for a popular horse.

Ponies

Ponies are another popular category of horses. In most cases, a horse that's fully grown at 14.2 hands (57 inches) or less is considered a pony. (There are two exceptions: the miniature horse and the Icelandic horse.) The plucky Shetland and elegant Welsh are popular breeds of ponies.

With their short stature, they are often excellent first horses for children.

Grade Horses

Grade horse--a horse of no particular breeding--is the fancy term for the mutts of the horse world. They differ from cross breeds because crosses are the result of known pedigreed horses that are intentionally bred. Grade horses may not have a distinguished pedigree, but they can be just as versatile and loyal as any other horse. They also generally lack many of the genetic diseases that pass-through purebreds.

Gaited Breeds

Gaited horses are a category of horses that have been selectively bred for a smooth ride or ambling gait. These horses tend to go at an intermediate speed with a four-beat movement. Breeds including the Tennessee walking horse, Kentucky mountain saddle horse, Icelandic horse, and Paso Fino are popular choices for older riders, those who have joint issues, and anyone else looking for a bounce-free ride.

Draft Breeds

Draft horses are cold-blooded, heavy horses known for doing work pulling heavy loads. Historically, they were also used in battle to carry the weight of heavily armored soldiers. These horses have thick coats and manes that enable them to endure cold weather, and they tend to have tranquil temperaments. The Clydesdale, Percheron, Shire, and Belgian are some popular examples of these gentle giants. In addition, draft horse cross breeds can be ideal first horses, as they're often docile and loving.

6. THOROUGHBREDS

Thoroughbreds clearly outperform every other breed in any horse race. While other breeds are not absolutely barred from becoming racehorses, Thoroughbreds have traditionally been the most famous racehorses in recent memory. Fusaichi Pegasus, a Thoroughbred, was the most expensive horse ever sold at auction, for $70 million. Fusaichi Pegasus would not have fetched such a high price if it hadn't won several races, including the Kentucky Derby in 2000.

To be classified as a Thoroughbred, the foal must be the result of a "live cover?" Artificial insemination and embryo transfers are prohibited in Thoroughbreds. This is done to regulate the population, and according to the law of supply and demand, the lower the supply, the higher the monetary value. Thoroughbreds are often foaled early in the calendar year to let the foal grow before training to race.

History

Thoroughbred is a horse breed established in England for racing and jumping. The Thoroughbred's origins may be traced back to documents stating that Arab and Barb horses were brought into England as early as the third century. Natural circumstances favored the growth of the original stock, while people engaged in racing supported selective breeding.

During the reigns of James I and Charles I, 43 mares--the so-called Royal Mares--were imported into England, and a record, the General Stud Book, was established in which only horses that could be traced back to the Royal Mares in direct line, or to one of three other horses imported to England: the Byerly Turk (imported in 1689), the Darley Arabian (after 1700), and the Godolphin Barb (about 1730). Since then, the English Thoroughbred has been brought to the majority of countries, where it is raised for racing or used to develop local breeds.

Bulle Rock, a Darley Arabian son, was introduced to Virginia in 1730. 186 Thoroughbreds brought from England established the cornerstone of Thoroughbred breeding in the United States during the next 45 years.

Thoroughbreds are distinguished by their delicate heads, thin frames, wide chests, and short backs. Their tiny leg bones enable them to take long, effortless strides. They are compassionate and vivacious. Thoroughbreds are typically bay, chestnut, brown, black, or gray in color and stand 16 hands (64 inches, or 163 cm) tall and weigh around 1,000 pounds (450 kg) at maturity. They have been blended with and enhanced by various other horse breeds because of their exceptional speed and stamina.

All Thoroughbreds may be traced back to three founding sires in the male line: the Darley Arabian, the Godolphin Arabian, and the Byerley Turk, called after their respective owners Thomas Darley, Lord Godolphin, and Captain Robert Byerly. They were shipped to England and bred with mares from both English and immigrant backgrounds. The resulting foals were the first Thoroughbred generation, and all current Thoroughbreds may be traced back to them.

Breed Characteristics

The average Thoroughbred stands from 15.2 to 17.0 hands (62 to 68 inches, 157 to 173 cm) tall (64 inches, 163 cm). They are often bay, dark bay or brown, chestnut, black, or gray in color. Roan and palomino are two less frequent hues recognised in the United States. White is an extremely rare hue, although it is distinct from gray. White may emerge on the face and lower legs, but it will not appear on the torso.

Mainstream breed registries do not accept coat patterns with more than one color on the body, such as Pinto or Appaloosa. Thoroughbreds of outstanding grade have a well-chiseled head on a long neck, high withers, a deep chest, a short back, good hindquarter depth, a thin frame, and long legs. Thoroughbreds are "hot-blooded" breeds, which are animals bred for agility and speed and are typically seen to be lively and courageous.

Thoroughbreds come in a variety of heights, which are measured in hands (a hand being four inches). Some have as few as 15 hands, while others have more than 17. Thoroughbreds can travel medium distances at high speeds, necessitating a mix of speed and endurance. Thoroughbreds come in a variety of colors, including bay, black, dark bay/brown, chestnut, gray, roan, white, and palomino. The Thoroughbred breed prohibits artificial insemination, cloning, and embryo transfer. Many breed registries do not recognise coat patterns with many colors. However, white face and leg markings, like blazes or stockings, are permitted, despite the fact that many thoroughbreds are plain with modest to no markings.

The agility and polished look of a thoroughbred are its defining traits. These horses can travel at speeds of up to 40 miles per hour. Their rear legs are especially long, which increases force as they gallop. Even though they are strong, muscular horses, they move with elegance and quickness. Thoroughbreds are registered in the General Stud Book of the English Jockey Club, which was founded about 1750, or in the studbooks of comparable clubs in other nations. A horse with only one Thoroughbred parent is known as a Grade Thoroughbred in the United States and a half-bred in the United Kingdom. Depending on their training, grade Thoroughbreds can be employed as hunters, polo ponies, stock horses, or riding horses.

Thoroughbred Official Birthdays

The universal birth date for all racing Thoroughbreds born in the Northern Hemisphere is January 1st. This implies that no matter when the horse was born, it will be regarded as a year older on New Year's Day.

The custom is inverted in the Southern Hemisphere. Thoroughbreds celebrate their formal birthday on August 1st, rather than January 1st.

These arbitrary dates were chosen to standardize races and other events for horses of varied ages.

This tradition dates back over 200 years and allows for the uniformity of horse races based on age divisions. It also implies that horses born later in the year will be at a disadvantage when running against horses who are somewhat older. Thoroughbred breeders want to bring the foaling season as near to January 1st as feasible.

Prior to 1858, the official birthdate of all Thoroughbreds was May 1 since it corresponded with the commencement of the racing season. That year, however, Britain chose to shift the date to January 1st, which became a worldwide custom.

Racing Champions

Thoroughbreds are around 16 hands tall and have the look of their Arabian ancestors, with thin frames, wide chests, and short leg bones. Because of the shape of their legs, they can take great steps with little effort or strain. Along with these Thoroughbred features, they are also noted for their speed and stamina, which makes them popular on racetracks. A Thoroughbred is usually ready to compete when it is three years old, while others believe that its ability peaks at five years old.

Thoroughbreds are trained to race not just when they are in peak physical condition. They should also be able to achieve their peak condition and development on race day. Even the most experienced trainers in the world would struggle with it!

Thoroughbreds make money not just by competing in races, but also through breeding. They have been crossed with different breeds either to better their chances or in the goal of siring the next generation of quick racers and winners.

Thoroughbred Foundation Stallions

Byerly Turk

Bylerly Turk was the first foundation stud to grace the English beaches. During the siege of Buda in Hungary in 1688, he was ridden by a Turkish officer. Captain Robert Byerly of the Sixth Dragoon Guards under King William III of Orange apprehended this officer and confiscated his horse. Captain Byerly rode his new steed as his fighting horse in several battles. Captain Byerly regularly raced his stallion in between conflicts, and in 1690 he won the first prize at Down Royal in Northern Ireland. The Byerly Turk started his stud career in England and remained there until 1701. Despite being referred to as a "Turk," the Byerley Turk was an unmarked, dark brown horse with Arabian conformation. He was quite good at passing on his qualities to his progeny, and many of them were brown or black like him. Jigg, the most prominent son of the Byerley Turk, was a terrific runner and a tremendously influential sire. The prodigy of Partner may be traced back to modern-day Thoroughbred champions. Byerley Turk mares were likewise in demand. His daughters include two Thoroughbred foundation mares.

Darley Arabian

The Darley Arabian was discovered among the Fedan Bedouins' herds by Thomas Darley, a British businessman traveling the Syrian desert. Mr. Darley planned to get a colt for his father's stud property during his international trips. He was looking for a horse with genuine Arabian bloodlines from the Syrian desert since they were known for their speed and stamina. The merchant was drawn to a bay yearling colt owned by the tribe's sheik. A price was agreed upon, and Mr. Darley purchased the horse in 1700 or 1701 for 300 golden sovereigns. The young Darley Arabian did not reach England until 1704 because of hostilities and travel difficulties. Mr. Darley never returned to England; he died of poisoning on the way back. From 1706 through 1719, the Darley Arabian stood at stud and produced several outstanding runners from Mr. Darley's mares. The Darley Arabian sired some of the world's top studs, including Bulle Rocke, the first Thoroughbred stallion imported into the United States.

Godolphin Arabian (Barb)

The Godolpin Barb's stories include his dragging a water cart through the streets of Paris, being used as a teaser, and his fierceness as a fighting steed. However, none of these tales can be substantiated. The Godolphin Barb was born in modern-day Yemen and handed to the King of France as a gift by Bey of Tunis. He is actually a Barb, yet he is frequently referred to as an Arabian. The Godolpin Barb became ill after arriving in France, maybe as a result of his travels or because of illness. He was regarded as half-starved yet gorgeous. The Duke of Lorraine purchased the Godolphin Barb and either sold or gifted it to Mr. Edward Coke. Mr. Coke transported his freshly acquired horse from France to England in 1729. Mr. Coke was standing the Godolphin on his newly bought property. The Godolphin Barb's official tale begins in 1731, when he covered one of Mr. Coke's mares and produced a runner named Lath. Lath was regarded as the finest horse of his day, and his triumph boosted the Godolphin's prestige.

Coke died in August 1733, leaving Godolphin to a friend, Mr. Williams. Mr. Williams sold the horse to Cokes' personal friend, Francis, Earl of Godolphin. The Earl of Godolphin bred the Barb to numerous fine mares. His descendants were not only excellent racehorses, but also excellent sires and broodmares. Selima, a Godolphin daughter, was imported to the United States in 1752 and became a popular runner and broodmare. Thoroughbred champions frequently trace their ancestry back to her.

Thoroughbred Foundation Mares

Horses with Irish Hobby ancestry were the founding broodmares for the Thoroughbred breed. The Irish Hobby was introduced to England and Scotland for a variety of equestrian pursuits, primarily racing. Females were not considered as important in the breed's early history. The Thoroughbred General Studbook, which was originally published in 1791, listed 74 foundation broodmares. The studbook provides a full account of the sires but is vague when it comes to identifying broodmares. The beginnings of female Thoroughbred lineages are controversial and hypothetical due to a lack of recorded material. However, when DNA science progressed, experts established that the Thoroughbred breed's foundation females contain Irish Hobby genes from either Irish Draught or Connemara horses.

Connemara mares

Connemara ponies are mountain and moorland ponies that originated in the region of Connaught in western Ireland. It is the sole native breed of Ireland and may be traced back to the ancient Celts. The Spanish Armada was shipwrecked off the western coast of Ireland in the late 1600s. A big number of Spanish Andalusian horses were aboard the ships. Many of these horses survived and were mated with the local Connemara ponies. Connemara ponies are well-known for their surefootedness, leaping skill, and calm demeanor. Their bodies are compact, and they stand between 12.2 and 14.2 hands tall on average.

Irish Draught mares

The Irish Draught breed is descended from the original Irish Sport Horse, the Irish Hobby, which was imported to Ireland circa 500 BCE by the ancient Celts. These fast and surefooted horses were frequently used in war and were highly prized in England and Scotland. The Irish Hobby bred with bigger Norman horses and then with Spanish breeds to create the Irish Draught, a horse capable of a variety of jobs ranging from farming to fox hunting. The Irish Draught worked as well as huge draught breeds on the farm but was light and agile enough to make good hunter jumpers. This new breed laid the groundwork for the Thoroughbred breed's growth.

7. HORSEMANSHIP & FICTIONAL CHARACTER BIBLES

HORSEMANSHIP

The skill of riding, handling, and training horses is known as horsemanship. A good horseman controls the animal's direction, pace, and speed with maximum efficacy and minimal effort. Horsemanship emerged as a result of need as the skill of riding with maximum judgment and as little intervention with the horse as possible. Until the twentieth century, riding was a monopoly of the cavalry, cowboys, and those whose jobs demanded horseback riding, as well as the rich, who rode for enjoyment. Although hunting and polo remain profitable pastimes, and the function of the horse in combat has ceased, a premium is now put on high-quality horse exhibitions, with show jumping being the most popular event. Horsemanship has remained a valuable social asset and a symbol of distinction, but the establishment of several new riding organizations and stables has made riding and horsemanship available to a far greater proportion of the public.

Origins and Early History

The horse was used as a riding animal by ferocious nomadic peoples of Central Asia as early as the second millennium bce, and maybe much earlier. The Scythians, for example, were skilled riders who utilized saddles. They were also possibly the first to recognise the significance of a sturdy seat and to design a type of stirrup. A saddled horse with straps hanging at the side and looped at the bottom end is shown on a 4th century bce vase discovered in Chertomlyk, Ukraine.

However, owing to the risk of being unable to rapidly remove the foot when dismounting, this device may have been employed solely for mounting. According to the Greek historian Strabo, the indocility of the Scythians' wild horses necessitated gelding, a procedure uncommon in the ancient world at the time. The Sarmatians, superior riders who surpassed the Scythians, rode bareback, commanding their horses using knee pressure and weight distribution.

The Hittites, Assyrians, and Babylonians were among the first to battle and hunt on horseback; about the same period (around 1500 bce), the Hyksos, or Shepherd Kings, imported horses into Egypt and rode them in all their conflicts. The Scythians transported horses to Greece in the eighth and seventh century BCE, when the skill of riding evolved fast, first for pleasure only. A frieze from Athens' Parthenon depicts Greeks riding bareback. Philip II of Macedon had cavalry in his army, and his son Alexander's army had separate, organized horse formations.

Another Greek historian, Xenophon, authored his work Peri hippiks (On Equestrian) in the 4th century bce, providing outstanding horsemanship advice. Many of his beliefs are completely applicable today. He advocated for the use of the gentlest bits possible and opposed the use of force in training and riding. The Roman mounted infantry were mostly barbarian archers who rode without stirrups or reins, keeping their hands free to use the bow and arrow.

Almost every piece of riding equipment used today originated with the horsemen of the Eurasian steppes and was later adopted by the inhabitants of the areas they conquered to the east, south, and west. Horseshoes of different varieties were worn by migrating Eurasian tribes during the 2nd century bce, but the modern nailed iron horseshoe first arrived in Europe about the 5th century ce, brought by invaders from the East. One was discovered, complete with nails, in the grave of the Frankish king Childeric I in Tournai, Belgium. Attila is credited with introducing the stirrup to Europe. The Avars employed round or triangular iron stirrups in the sixth century CE, while the Byzantine cavalry utilized metal stirrups. By 600 CE, they were in use in China and Japan.

The principle of controlling a horse by applying pressure to its mouth with a bit (a metal device inserted into the horse's mouth) and reins (straps attached to the bit held by the rider) has been practiced since ancient times, and bits made of bone and antlers have been discovered dating back to before 1000 BCE. The flexible mouthpiece with two links and its modifications have been in use for millennia, leading directly to the modern jointed snaffle bit. Early, stumpy prickspurs have been discovered on 4th-century BCE Celtic sites in Bohemia.

Military horsemanship

Cavalry became more important in the early Middle Ages, and mounted troops dominated warfare for the next thousand years. Armor became increasingly bulky and heavy, pushing the breeding of larger and larger horses until the combination rendered movement practically impossible.

Attempts to address this were made in the early 16th century at a Naples riding college by Federico Grisone and Giovanni Battista Pignatelli, who attempted to reconcile Classical Greek concepts with the necessities of medieval mounted warfare. Except for a 14th-century treatise by Ibn Hudhayl, an Arab of Granada, Spain, and a 15th-century book on knightly combat by Edward, King of Portugal, there appears to have been little notable riding literature produced after Xenophon until Grisone published his Gli ordini di cavalcare ("The Orders of Riding") in 1550.

The invention of guns resulted in the abolition of armor, allowing for additional changes in techniques and training under followers of the school of Pignatelli and Grisone, such as William Cavendish, Duke of Newcastle. École de cavalerie ("School of Cavalry"), written in 1733 by François Robichon de la Guérinière, demonstrated how a horse might be educated without being pushed into submission, which is the essential premise of modern dressage. Dressage is the careful training of a horse for a variety of reasons other than racing and cross-country riding.

Meanwhile, the Spanish Imperial Riding School in Vienna and the French cavalry center at Saumur worked to perfect the combination of horse and rider performance. Their method and academic seat, a formal riding position or style in which the rider sits erectly, deep in the saddle, had a significant effect in Europe and America during the 18th and 19th centuries and are still utilized in modern dressage. In contrast to his 19th-century counterpart François Baucher, a horseman of great talent with formal haute école ("high school") beliefs, the head riding teacher at Saumur, Comte Antoine d'Aure, championed a bold, easygoing, and more natural, albeit less "perfect," way of riding across country.

Classical riding exercises in the manège, or riding school, had to give way to simpler and more sensible riding in war and the hunt. Hunting riders leaped hurdles with their feet front, their body back on the horse's haunches, and the horse's head held up during this time period. The horse frequently leapt in panic.

Captain. Federico Caprilli, an Italian cavalry instructor, conducted extensive research on the psychology and physics of horse mobility at the turn of the twentieth century. He completely upended the traditional method when he invented the forward seat, a riding posture and style in which the rider's weight is centered front in the saddle, above the horse's withers. Although Caprilli published little, his disciple, Piero Santini, disseminated his master's essential beliefs. Except for dressage and exhibiting, the forward seat is presently the most popular, particularly for jumping.

The Art of Horsemanship

The fundamental premise of horsemanship is to achieve outcomes in a compassionate manner with a combination of balance, seat, hands, and legs. The horse's natural center of gravity moves with every movement and gait variation. Given that a mounted horse also carries a somewhat unstable burden equal to one-fifth of its own weight, it is up to the rider to accommodate as much as possible to the animal's motions. The saddle is tested before mounting to ensure that it fits both the horse and the rider. Experienced riders place themselves in the saddle so that they can stay on the horse and manage it. The seat chosen is determined by the work at hand. A solid seat is vital for enabling riders total independence and freedom to use the aids at their disposal efficiently. Good riders do not overpower the horse, but rather encourage it to yield to their demands firmly and without inflicting harm.

8. FICTIONAL CHARACTER BIBLES INSPIRED BY REAL INDIVIDUALS

EDWARD DUDLEY BROWN

1. Basic Information:
   - Name: Edward Dudley Brown
   - Birthday: December 21, 1850
   - Physical Appearance: Edward is initially short and of medium build, typical for an 11-year-old. He has black hair, light brown and brown eyes, and a typical African American appearance for that era. As he grows older, his overall presentation changes, becoming more sophisticated and well-dressed.
   - Profession: Former jockey, horse trainer, and horse stable owner
   - Role in the Story: Edward Dudley Brown is the primary protagonist of the narrative. He represents various archetypes throughout his character arc, including The Orphan, The Everyman, The Caregiver, The Mentor, and The Sage. Edward's journey revolves around his pursuit of equality, financial prosperity, and leaving a lasting legacy in the world of horse racing. He overcomes numerous obstacles and challenges, inspiring others and breaking racial barriers along the way.

2. Physical Appearance:
   - Height: Varies with age, initially short for an 11-year-old
   - Weight: Varies with age, proportionate to build
   - Hair Color: Black
   - Eye Color: Light brown and brown
   - Body Type: Initially medium build, becomes more refined and fit as he grows older
   - Distinguishing Features: No specific distinctive features mentioned, but Edward's overall presentation changes as he grows older, becoming more sophisticated and well-dressed.

3. Backstory:
   - Edward Dudley Brown, also known as "Brown Dick," was born on December 21, 1850, during the pre-Civil War era. His parents, Eliza and James Brown, were enslaved on a plantation in Kentucky. Edward lost his parents at a young age, leaving him orphaned. He gained extensive knowledge of thoroughbreds and the racing industry while working at the Woodburn Estate horse farm of Robert A. Alexander.
   - Edward's childhood was marked by the hardships and dehumanization of slavery. He worked as a groom and later became a jockey, eventually transitioning to becoming a horse trainer and stable owner. Edward faced bullying from both white and black children due to his privileged position as a slave with opportunities in the horse racing industry.
   - Significant life events include being purchased by Robert Alexander before the Emancipation Proclamation, winning his first race on Asteroid, and achieving victory

in the Belmont Stakes on Kingfisher. These events shaped his determination, belief in his abilities, and fueled his pursuit of freedom, financial prosperity, and equality.

4. Background:
- Edward's family background includes being orphaned at a young age and being born into slavery. His parents, Eliza, and James Brown, were enslaved on a plantation in Kentucky. Edward deeply misses his mother and sees her as a guiding star, represented by the Sirius star and Sagittarius constellation.
- His upbringing in slavery and subsequent work in the horse racing industry provided him with unique experiences and perspectives. Edward's association with the Woodburn Estate and exposure to thoroughbreds and horse racing shaped his knowledge and passion for the sport.

5. Personality Traits:
- Generous and kind-hearted, Edward possesses a paternal nature, often acting as a big brother figure to those around him. He is steadfast, patient, sensitive, and impulsive. Edward is highly competitive and has a tenacious spirit.
- Key Personality Traits: Edward embodies traits such as strength of will, physicality, and intuition. Initially introverted and compassionate, he finds solace in working with horses. As he grows older, he becomes more extroverted, charismatic, and optimistic.
- Influence on Behavior and Decision-Making: Edward's key personality traits drive his behavior and decision-making. His introverted nature allows him to observe and learn, while his compassionate and optimistic disposition motivates him to help and uplift others. However, his complexities arise from the moral gray areas he encounters as a former slave involved in an industry that relies on the labor of animals, similar to his own previous enslavement.

6. Strengths and Skills:
- Physical agility: Edward excels in physical activities, thanks to his experience as a jockey and his athleticism.
- Thoroughbred knowledge: Edward possesses extensive knowledge of thoroughbreds and the racing industry, gained through his work at the Woodburn Estate and his own experiences as a jockey and trainer.
- Mentoring and inspiring others: Edward has a natural ability to mentor and inspire apprentice jockeys, sharing his wisdom and guidance to help them succeed.

7. Motivations and Goals:
- Edward is driven by the desire for freedom, financial prosperity, equality, and creating a legacy for future generations.
- His main goals include achieving success in horse racing, earning respect, and providing opportunities for his community and apprentice jockeys.
- Motivation to Overcome Obstacles: Edward's motivations stem from the influence of his mentor, Abe Hawkins, and his own experiences as an orphan and victim of bullying. The memory of his mother, represented by the stars, urges him to persevere. Self-belief and a sense of responsibility to his community also fuel his motivations.
What are the goals of Edward Dudley Brown as the protagonist?
External goals:
To achieve financial freedom through the sport of horse racing.

271

To find upward mobility socially and financially.

To become equal with the former oppressors. True equality and freedom.

To become like Abe Hawkins and fulfill his initial vision and continue his legacy.

To earn a living for himself, and his family and to teach others how to make a living in the horse racing industry.

Internal goals:

To challenge the status quo and prove to oppressors that colored men are equal.

To make the situation for his people better after slavery and the civil war.

8. Character Arc:

- Edward Dudley Brown's character arc is one of personal growth and evolution. Initially, as an orphan, he embodies the archetype of The Orphan, seeking connection, acceptance, and understanding. As he grows older, Edward transitions into The Everyman, a relatable character navigating life's challenge. His role as The Caregiver emerges as he supports and protects those around him. In his later years, Edward embodies The Mentor and The Sage, offering wisdom and guidance to the next generation.

- Transformation and Growth: Edward's character arc is one of transformation and growth. Starting as an 11-year-old vulnerable orphan, he evolves into an accomplished jockey, trainer, and mentor. Throughout his journey, he learns to navigate racial discrimination, loss, and personal challenges. Edward's growth is marked by his ability to rise above adversity, inspire others, and become an iconic figure fighting for equality and justice.

9. Relationships:

- Edward forms significant relationships with Ansel Williamson, a horse trainer who becomes his mentor, and Abe Hawkins, a famous black jockey. Their love, support, and guidance shape Edward's development and decisions.

- Edward's wife, Lucy Alexander Gaines, provides love and support throughout his life. They share a strong bond and partnership.

- Edward also forms close bonds with apprentice jockeys and those he mentors, inspiring and earning their respect.

10. Internal Conflicts and Flaws:

- Edward faces internal conflicts stemming from the loss of his parents, fear of his own privilege, and the moral complexities of participating in an industry that mirrors the concept of slavery. These conflicts hinder his progress and lead to dilemmas that force him to question his own actions and choices.

- Internal Conflicts: Edward faces internal conflicts stemming from the loss of his parents, fear of his own privilege, and the moral complexities of participating in an industry that mirrors the concept of slavery. These conflicts hinder his progress and lead to dilemmas that force him to question his own actions and choices.

- Weaknesses and Flaws: Edward's weaknesses include occasional self-doubt, a fear of losing his hard-earned accomplishments, and a reluctance to act due to past experiences. His flaws include caution and the potential for a volatile temper.

11. External Obstacles:

- Edward faces external obstacles such as racial discrimination, financial hardships, and the competitive nature of the horse racing industry. He must navigate these challenges while pursuing success as a jockey, trainer, and horse stable owner.

- External Obstacles: Edward encounters various external obstacles throughout the story, including racial discrimination, harassment, assault, and envy from others in the industry. These challenges test his resolve, resilience, and belief in his abilities. Some obstacles are related to the plot, such as winning races and breaking records, while others are specific to his personal goals, such as battling racial prejudices and ensuring a fair and just environment for African Americans in horse racing.

12. Evolution of Relationships and Interactions:

- Edward's relationships evolve over time as he forms new connections and deepens existing ones. He starts as a young boy seeking acceptance and understanding, but as he grows older, he becomes a mentor and guide to others, fostering strong bonds and impacting their lives.

13. Hobbies and Interests:

- Edward's primary interest lies in horse racing. He is passionate about thoroughbreds, the racing industry, and the pursuit of success. Outside of horse racing, he may have an affinity for storytelling, as a way to pass down knowledge and wisdom.

14. Core Beliefs and Values:

- Edward values freedom, equality, justice, and leaving a lasting legacy. He believes in the power of hard work, perseverance, and helping others. He is driven by a sense of responsibility towards his community and future generations.

15. Emotional Range and Expressions:

- Edward exhibits a wide emotional range throughout the story. He experiences joy, anger, frustration, grief, and determination. His expressions vary, from quiet introspection to passionate outbursts, depending on the situation.

16. Dialogue Style and Speech Patterns:

- Edward's dialogue style is influenced by his background and experiences. He may have a tendency to use metaphors or analogies related to horse racing. His speech may reflect a mix of formal and informal language, adapting to different social contexts.

17. External Relationships:

- Edward's relationships extend beyond his immediate circle and impact his worldview. His interactions with colleagues, neighbors, and acquaintances may challenge his beliefs, provide new perspectives, or create conflicts.

18. Symbolism and Themes:

- Edward's journey can be associated with themes of resilience, racial equality, personal growth, and the pursuit of a legacy. Symbolic elements could include stars representing his guiding star, the Sirius star, and the Sagittarius constellation symbolizing his connection to his mother.

19. Transformation and Lessons Learned:

- Edward's transformation involves personal growth, self-discovery, and learning from his experiences. He learns to navigate racial discrimination, grapples with moral dilemmas, and finds his voice in advocating for equality and justice.

20. Relationship to Protagonist/Antagonist:
- Edward's interactions with the story's protagonists, antagonists, or obstacles challenge his beliefs and provide opportunities for personal growth. His relationships with these characters contribute to the conflicts and resolutions within the narrative.

21. Moral Dilemmas:
- Edward faces moral dilemmas related to his involvement in the horse racing industry, his own history as a former slave, and his pursuit of success. These dilemmas shape his development, relationships, and decisions.

22. Impact on the Story:
- Edward Dudley Brown's character leaves a lasting impact on the story as a symbol of hope, resilience, and the indomitable spirit that can achieve greatness even in the most challenging circumstances. His personal growth, mentorship, and pursuit of equality inspire others and break racial barriers, making him an iconic figure in the world of horse racing. Edward's legacy encompasses his triumph over adversity, perseverance in the face of challenges, and the pursuit of freedom and justice.

Ansel Williamson
1. Basic Information:
- Name: Ansel Williamson
- Birthday: July 15, 1825
- Age: 56 (Died on June 18, 1881)
- Zodiac Sign: Cancer
- Nickname: Old Ansel, Uncle Ansel
- Physical Appearance:
Ansel was a tall and robust man, standing at 6 feet 2 inches with a muscular build. He had a commanding presence with his dark, wavy hair that was beginning to show streaks of gray. His piercing blue eyes conveyed both intelligence and intensity. Ansel had a prominent scar on his left cheek, a remnant from a horse riding accident in his youth. He carried himself with a dignified demeanor, often seen dressed in tailored suits that exuded sophistication.
- Profession: Horse Trainer
- Role in the Storyline: Secondary Protagonist

2. Physical Appearance:
- Height: 6 feet 2 inches
- Weight: Well-proportioned muscular build
- Hair Color: Dark, with streaks of gray
- Eye Color: Piercing blue
- Body Type: Athletic and muscular
- Distinctive Features: Prominent scar on his left cheek from a horse riding accident
- Style of Dressing: Ansel favored tailored suits that showcased his sophistication and status. He paid attention to the finer details, ensuring a polished and refined appearance.

3. Backstory:

Childhood:
Ansel Williamson was born into slavery in Lexington, Kentucky, to Samuel and Margaret Williamson, a family of renowned horse breeders. From a young age, Ansel was surrounded by horses and developed a deep love and understanding of them. Despite the confines of slavery, Ansel's parents recognized his natural talent and nurtured his skills, allowing him to assist in training and caring for their prized racehorses. This early exposure to the world of horse racing instilled in him a strong work ethic and a sense of responsibility.

Significant Life Events:
At the age of 15, Ansel had a breakthrough moment when he won his first race as a jockey, riding his father's horse, Thunderbolt, to victory. This early success ignited Ansel's passion for horse racing and solidified his determination to make a name for himself in the industry. However, his journey was not without obstacles. At the age of 20, Ansel suffered a severe leg injury during a race. Many doubted whether he would ever ride again, but through sheer determination and rigorous rehabilitation, Ansel overcame the injury and returned to the racing circuit stronger than ever. This experience shaped his resilience and unwavering dedication to the sport.

Family Dynamics:
Ansel was the eldest of four siblings, and his close-knit family shared a deep bond built on their shared love for horses. The Williamson household was a hub of activity, with everyone contributing to the care and training of the horses. Ansel's younger brother, Benjamin, also showed a talent for training, and together, they formed a formidable team.

Educational Background:
Ansel's education was primarily shaped by his hands-on experience working with horses and learning from his parents' expertise. While formal education was limited, Ansel possessed a thirst for knowledge that extended beyond the stables. He taught himself to read and write, allowing him to expand his understanding of horse physiology, training techniques, and race strategies through extensive reading and studying.

4. Background:
- Cultural and Socioeconomic Factors: Ansel grew up immersed in the rich equestrian culture of Kentucky. Ansel's background exposed him to the traditions and values of the racing world.
- Educational History: Ansel's education primarily revolved around hands-on training with horses. He supplemented this practical education with extensive reading and studying about horse

physiology, training techniques, and race strategies. Ansel's hunger for knowledge and continuous learning contributed to his success as a trainer.
- Significant Life Events: Ansel's career took off when he caught the attention of a prominent horse owner, Henry Bradford. Bradford offered Ansel the opportunity to train his stable of racehorses. Ansel's exceptional talent and results quickly established him as one of the top trainers in the region.

5. Personality Traits:
- Leadership: Ansel possessed a natural ability to lead and command respect from others. His authoritative presence and deep knowledge of horses made him a trusted figure within the racing community.
- Ambitious: Ansel had an unyielding drive to succeed and establish himself as one of the best trainers in the industry. He set high standards for himself and those around him, constantly pushing for excellence.
- Disciplined: Ansel was a man of routine and discipline. He believed in the importance of hard work, attention to detail, and strict adherence to training regimens.
- Perceptive: Ansel had a keen eye for identifying talent, both in horses and jockeys. He could assess a horse's potential and tailor training methods to maximize their performance. He also possessed the ability to understand the nuances of jockeys' riding styles and provide insightful guidance.
- Reserved: While Ansel was respected and admired, he maintained a certain level of distance and reserve. He preferred to keep his personal life private and maintained a professional demeanor.

6. Strengths and Skills:
- Exceptional Horse Trainer: Ansel had an innate ability to connect with horses and understand their needs, allowing him to train them to their full potential. He employed various techniques and training methods tailored to each horse's unique characteristics.
- Strategic Thinking: Ansel possessed a strategic mind and excelled at devising race strategies that played to his horses' strengths. He carefully analyzed track conditions, competing horses, and jockeys to develop winning approaches.
- Mentoring and Coaching: Ansel had a natural talent for nurturing young jockeys and helping them reach their full potential. He took pride in passing on his knowledge and skills to the next generation, molding them into successful riders.

7. Motivations and Goals:
- Ansel's primary motivation was to establish himself as the preeminent trainer in the racing world. He aimed to win the most prestigious races, cement his reputation, and leave a lasting legacy. His goals included securing victories in the Kentucky Derby, the Belmont Stakes, and other major races. Ansel was also driven by a desire to mentor and guide promising jockeys to success, knowing that their accomplishments would reflect his own expertise and training methods.

8. Character Arc:
- Starting Point: Ansel begins his journey as a talented but relatively unknown horse trainer, striving to make a name for himself in the competitive racing industry. He is confident in his abilities but lacks the recognition and opportunities to fully showcase his talent.
- Journey: As Ansel faces challenges and setbacks, he learns the value of collaboration and humility. He realizes that true success comes not only from personal achievements but also from empowering and supporting others. He discovers the importance of mentoring and passing on his knowledge to the next generation.
- Endpoint of Development: Ansel's character arc culminates in his transformation into a respected figure known not only for his racing accomplishments but also for his mentorship and positive influence on the next generation of trainers and jockeys. He becomes a symbol of excellence, dedication, and the intergenerational transfer of

knowledge and skills.

9. Relationships:
- Ansel's relationships are primarily professional, revolving around his interactions with horse owners, fellow trainers, and jockeys. He forms strong bonds with owners who recognize his talent and entrust

him with their horses. Ansel's most significant personal relationship is with his wife, Ellen. She provides unwavering support and stability in his life, allowing him to focus on his career. Ansel also shares a close bond with his daughter and grandchildren, cherishing the family connections that have shaped his life.

10. Internal Conflicts and Flaws:
- Ansel's pursuit of excellence and control sometimes leads to conflicts with others who challenge his methods or authority. He struggles with balancing his ambition with ethical considerations and the well-being of his horses and jockeys. Ansel's reserved nature and professional distance can create difficulties in forming deep emotional connections with others. He grapples with vulnerability and opening up emotionally, often keeping his feelings and insecurities hidden.

11. External Obstacles:
- Ansel faces fierce competition from other trainers vying for the same horses and coveted victories. He encounters financial constraints that require him to seek out influential backers and secure new partnerships. Changing racing regulations and industry dynamics pose challenges that force Ansel to adapt his training methods and strategies.

12. Evolution of Relationships and Interactions:
- Over time, Ansel's relationships evolve as he learns to trust and collaborate with others. He forms partnerships and alliances that bolster his success, recognizing the value of teamwork. His interactions with young jockeys and mentees deepen, as he witnesses the impact he can have on their careers and lives. Ansel's mentorship becomes a significant aspect of his legacy.

13. Hobbies and Interests:
- Ansel finds solace and inspiration in the bond between horse and rider and often takes pleasure in leisurely horseback riding. He appreciates the beauty and grace of the horses he trains and enjoys observing their growth and progress.

14. Core Beliefs and Values:
- Ansel believes in the importance of hard work, discipline, and dedication in achieving success. He values integrity and fair play in the racing industry and is committed to upholding the sport's traditions and ethics. Ansel also believes in the transformative power of mentorship and passing on knowledge to future generations.

15. Emotional Range and Expressions:
- Ansel's emotions are often kept in check, and he displays a composed and stoic demeanor. However, his eyes light up with enthusiasm and pride when discussing his horses' achievements. He rarely shows vulnerability, preferring to present a strong and

confident front to the world.

16. Dialogue Style and Speech Patterns:
- Ansel's dialogue style is measured and deliberate, reflecting his thoughtful nature and extensive knowledge of the sport. He speaks with authority and clarity, choosing his words carefully to convey his intentions and expertise. His speech is characterized by precision and a touch of formality.

17. External Relationships:
- Ansel has relationships with influential figures in the racing world, including horse owners, fellow trainers, and jockeys. He cultivates professional connections with wealthy individuals who back his training efforts and entrust him with their prized horses. Ansel's interactions with these characters are a blend of mutual respect, competition, and collaboration.

18. Symbolism and Themes:
- Ansel's dedication to horse racing symbolizes the pursuit of excellence and the rewards that come from hard work and perseverance. Themes of mentorship, legacy, and the intergenerational transfer of knowledge and skills are integral to Ansel's story. The horses themselves can serve as symbols of strength, determination, and the indomitable spirit of the characters.

19. Transformation and Lessons Learned:
- Ansel's transformation involves learning to balance ambition with humility, understanding the value of collaboration and mentorship, and appreciating the profound impact he can have on others' lives. He learns that true success extends beyond personal achievements and encompasses the positive influence he can exert on the racing community.

20. Relationship to Protagonist/Antagonist:
- Ansel's relationship with the protagonist is one of mutual respect. Along with Abe Hawkins, Ansel becomes a confidant, mentor figure for Edward Dudley Brown, and grows with him as they set out to inspire and train the next generation of horse racing professionals, especially the jockeys. Ansel's relationship with the antagonist involves clashes in upholding Abe Hawkins' teachings and sharing tips. The conflict comes from his association with Abe Hawkins, who was murdered by Farrar Kenner using a poison called Strychnine.

21. Moral Dilemmas:
- Ansel faces moral dilemmas when he has to decide between personal gain and the welfare of his horses or jockeys. He grapples with the ethical responsibility of balancing his ambition with the well-being of those under his care. Ansel must navigate the fine line between pursuing victory and maintaining integrity.

22. Impact on the Story:
- Ansel's expertise and strategic genius are instrumental in shaping the outcome of key races, contributing to the overall narrative tension and excitement. His mentorship and guidance of young jockeys add depth to the story, showcasing the influence a skilled

trainer can have on rising stars. Ansel's character serves as a source of inspiration and represents the triumph of hard work and dedication.

23. Conclusion and Impact:
- Ansel Williamson's legacy is defined by his exceptional skills as a trainer, his transformative mentorship, and his profound influence on the world of horse racing. His achievements and contributions continue to be celebrated, ensuring that his name lives on as a symbol of excellence, dedication, and the pursuit of greatness. Ansel's character enriches the narrative, providing a realistic and complex portrayal of a seasoned horse trainer.

Abe Hawkins
1. Basic Information:
 - Name: Abe Hawkins
 - Birthday: June 10th
Died: May 4th 1867 at the Age of 47
Wife: may be her name, Esterline Watson.
Children: He may have had two daughters whose names were Delilah and Polly. His wife is Esterline Watson. They had two daughters Delilah Hawkins (1858–1936) and Polly Ann Hawkins (1869–1917).
Nickname: Dark Sage of Louisiana, Uncle Abe Hawkins, The Black Prince, And the Slayer of Lexington.
Born: around ~ 1830* in Natchez, Mississippi. He was owned by Fatherland Plantation's, Adam Louis Bingaman in Natchez, Mississippi. He was sold for around $2,000 to fellow slave owning planter, Farrar Kenner of Ashland Plantation, Darrow (now Baton Rouge), Louisiana, USA.
 - Physical appearance: Abe is a short, wiry man with a weathered complexion. His graying hair is usually hidden under a worn-out hat, and his piercing brown eyes hold a mixture of wisdom and resilience.
 - Profession: Former slave, mentor, and famous jockey and horse trainer
 - Role in the storyline: Abe serves as a mentor figure to the protagonist, Edward Dudley Brown, guiding him on his journey as a black jockey and providing him with valuable knowledge and support.

2. Physical Appearance:
 - Height: 5'4 feet
 - Weight: Lean and muscular build
 - Hair color: Graying black
 - Eye color: Brown
 - Body type: Short and wiry
 - Distinctive features: A prominent scar on his left cheek, a testament to his past struggles and battles. He has calloused hands from years of hard work with horses.
 - Style of dressing: Abe often wears a worn-out, wide-brimmed hat, loose-fitting shirts, and trousers. His clothes are practical and suited for his work with horses.

3. Backstory:
 - Childhood and upbringing: Abe was born into slavery in Natchez, Mississippi. He was raised by Native Americans who were very spiritual and mystical, and they

imparted knowledge about the stars and mythology to him. His childhood was marked by hard labor and the constant threat of punishment. Despite the adversity, Abe showed a natural affinity for horses, finding solace and freedom in their presence.

- Significant life events: As a teenager, he went on a spiritual journey with a shaman and experienced a transformative ayahuasca ceremony. Through this experience, he gained deep insights into the secrets of the universe and his own place in it.

- Family dynamics: Abe was separated from his family during slavery, leaving behind painful memories and a burning desire for a better future.

- Educational background: Due to his enslavement, Abe did not receive a formal education. However, he possessed a thirst for knowledge and taught himself how to read and write. He devoured whatever knowledge he could find and became a well-educated man. He also gained practical knowledge about horses and their care, passed down through generations of horsemen.

4. Background:
- Cultural and socioeconomic factors: Abe's background reflects the systemic racism and oppression faced by Black Americans during the mid-19th century. His experiences as a slave and subsequent struggle for freedom have shaped his worldview and determination to fight against injustice.
- Educational history: While Abe did not have formal schooling, he gained practical knowledge through hands-on experiences working with horses and learning from older generations. He knew how to read and write, making him a very learned man.

- Significant life events: Abe's escape from slavery and subsequent journey to freedom were defining moments in his life, fueling his passion for justice and empowering him to become a mentor for young black jockeys.

5. Personality Traits:
- Resilient: Abe has endured immense hardship and adversity but remains steadfast in his pursuit of freedom and equality.
- Wise: Abe possesses deep wisdom acquired through his experiences and hardships. He imparts valuable knowledge and life lessons to those he mentors.
- Compassionate: Despite his tough exterior, Abe carries a deep compassion for others and is driven by a desire to help those around him.
- Determined: Abe's determination is unwavering, whether it be in his fight against racism or his dedication to training and mentoring young jockeys.
- Patient: Abe understands the importance of patience when working with horses and applies this virtue to his interactions with people as well.

6. Strengths and Skills:
- Expert horseman: Abe's years of experience working with horses have honed his skills in horse training, grooming, and racing strategies.
- Knowledgeable about racing history: Abe possesses a wealth of knowledge about the history of horse racing and the contributions of Black jockeys, enabling him

to pass on this important legacy to future generations.

- Mentorship and guidance: Abe excels in providing guidance and mentorship to young jockeys, supporting them in their personal and professional growth.

- Problem-solving: Abe's resourcefulness and ability to think on his feet allow him to navigate challenges and find creative solutions.

7. Motivations and Goals:

- Motivation: Abe's primary motivation is to fight against racism and injustice in the world of horse racing, paving the way for black jockeys to receive the recognition and opportunities they deserve.

- Goals: Abe's ultimate goal is to see young black jockeys succeed and break barriers in the sport, inspiring future generations and dismantling racial prejudices.

8. Character Arc:

- Starting point: Abe begins as a former slave, scarred by his past but driven by a desire for justice and equality.

- Journey: Through his mentorship of Edward and other young jockeys, Abe experiences personal growth and discovers a renewed sense of hope for the future.

- Endpoint of development: Abe's journey leads him to witness the triumphs of the black jockeys he mentors, solidifying his belief in their potential and leaving a lasting legacy.

9. Relationships:

- Interactions with Edward Dudley Brown: Abe forms a deep bond with Edward, acting as a father figure and imparting valuable wisdom and guidance.

- Dynamics with other jockeys: Abe's mentorship extends beyond Edward, as he fosters relationships with other young jockeys, providing support and encouragement.

- Impact of relationships: Abe's relationships with the young jockeys shape their development, instilling confidence and skills necessary for success in the world of horse racing.

10. Internal Conflicts and Flaws and Fears and Vulnerabilities:

- Flaws: Abe's past trauma sometimes makes it challenging for him to fully trust others, causing occasional moments of guardedness and hesitancy.

- Fears and vulnerabilities: Abe carries the fear of history repeating itself, with the progress made by black jockeys being undermined by racism and prejudice. He feels a deep responsibility to protect and uplift those he mentors.

11. External Obstacles:

- Racism and prejudice in the horse racing industry: Abe and the young jockeys he mentors face systemic barriers and discrimination that hinder their progress and opportunities.

- Economic challenges: Abe's pursuit of justice and equality often puts him at odds with powerful individuals who seek to maintain the status quo, leading to conflicts and obstacles.

12. Evolution of Relationships and Interactions:

- Abe's relationships with the young jockeys evolve from mentorship to a mutual respect and camaraderie. They learn from each other and form a tight-knit community, supporting one another through challenges.

13. Hobbies and Interests:
- Horses and horsemanship: Abe's passion for horses extends beyond his professional life, and he finds solace in spending time with these majestic creatures.

14. Core Beliefs and Values:
- Justice: Abe believes in fighting against injustice and systemic racism, striving to create a fair and equal environment for black jockeys.
- Equality: Abe values equality and believes that everyone should be judged based on their skill and character, rather than their race or background.
- Perseverance: Abe values perseverance and resilience, understanding the importance of pushing through adversity to achieve success.

15. Emotional Range and Expressions:
- Abe exhibits a wide emotional range, from moments of quiet contemplation and wisdom to fierce determination and passion. He expresses his emotions through measured words and actions, allowing his depth of feeling to shine through.

16. Dialogue Style and Speech Patterns:
- Abe's dialogue style is characterized by a mix of wisdom and straightforwardness. He often speaks in concise, impactful statements that reflect his experience and deep understanding of the world.

17. External Relationships:
- Relationships with characters outside his immediate circle: Abe interacts with individuals in the horse racing industry, both allies and adversaries. These relationships provide opportunities for growth, conflict, and learning.

18. Symbolism and Themes:
- The Chiron pendant: Abe wears a Chiron pendant, symbolizing resilience and guidance. It represents his role as a mentor and the transformative power of overcoming adversity.

19. Transformation and Lessons Learned:
- Abe's journey as a mentor allows him to rediscover hope, heal from his past trauma, and learn to trust and rely on others. He realizes that his impact extends beyond his individual achievements.

20. Relationship to Protagonist/Antagonist:
- Abe acts as a mentor and guide to the protagonist, Edward Dudley Brown, providing him with valuable insights and shaping his development. He also becomes a symbol of resistance and progress, challenging the antagonist's oppressive ideologies.

21. Moral Dilemmas:
- Abe grapples with moral dilemmas surrounding the sacrifices and risks involved in fighting for justice. He must navigate the fine line between preserving his own safety and pushing for societal change.

22. Impact on the Story:
- Abe's actions, choices, and mentorship have a significant impact on the story's progression. He drives the plot forward by empowering the young jockeys and challenging the status quo, leading to transformative moments of triumph and growth.

23. Conclusion and Impact:
- Abe's journey is characterized by growth, resilience, and the unwavering pursuit of justice. His impact on the story and the characters leaves a lasting legacy of breaking down barriers and inspiring future generations of black jockeys. His transformation and lessons learned reflect the overarching themes of hope, perseverance, and the power of mentorship.

CHARACTER BIBLE OF SIR ISAAC BURNS MURPHY:

Character Bible: Isaac Murphy
1. Basic Information:
   - Name: Isaac Murphy
   - Birthday: January 6th, 1861
   - Zodiac Sign: Capricorn
   - Physical Appearance: Distinguishing features include a graceful demeanor and an "elegant specimen of manhood" as described by a newspaper. Isaac's height, weight, hair color, eye color, and body type are not specified. His style of dressing is not specified.

2. Physical Appearance:
   - Height: Short
   - Weight: Jockey light weight
   - Hair Color: dark brown almost black
   - Eye Color: Brown
   - Body Type: thin ectomorph mesomorph.
   - Distinctive Features: Graceful presence, stands out due to his elegance and poise.
   - Style of Dressing: very classy.

3. Backstory:
   - Isaac was born in 1861 in Clark County, Kentucky. His mother was America Murphy and his father was Jerry Skillman.
   - After his father's death during the Civil War, he joined his mother to work at Eli Jordan's horse racing stable.
   - His mentor, Eli Jordan, instilled in him a love and respect for horses.
   - Isaac started his racing career at the age of fourteen and faced initial failures with resilience and determination.
   - He developed his unique racing style and gained recognition for his abilities.
   - Isaac's success challenged the prevailing discrimination and stereotypes against Black jockeys, making him a symbol of hope and achievement.
   - Throughout his career, he faced racism, bribery attempts, and rumors aimed at tarnishing his reputation.
   - Isaac's legacy as a pioneer in horse racing continues to inspire generations.

4. Background:

- Isaac's background includes growing up in a post-Civil War era, where racial tensions and discrimination persisted.
- As an African American jockey, he faced challenges in a predominantly white industry.
- Isaac's socioeconomic background improved as he became one of the highest-paid athletes in the country.
- His success provided a counter-narrative to prevailing stereotypes about Black athletes at the time.

5. Personality Traits:
- Soft-spoken, a gentleman, and a great listener.
- Enjoyed drinking and partying, which could sometimes lead to excesses.
- Faithful, accepting, resilient, resourceful, theoretical, diligent, persistent, persuasive, gutsy, daring, and money-wise.
- Character flaws include being a party animal, perfectionist tendencies, and occasional struggles with OCD.
- Self-sacrificing, naive, armored, workaholic, domineering, insecure, demanding, and stressed.

6. Strengths and Skills:
- Isaac's strengths include his devotion, passion, selflessness, humanism, and conviction.
- He possesses exceptional skills as a jockey, mastering the art of pacing and developing a unique racing style.
- Isaac's ability to observe and study his competition gives him a strategic advantage on the track.

7. Motivations and Goals:
- Isaac is motivated by his love for his wife, Lucy Carr Osborn, and his desire to set a positive example for the Black community.
- His goals include achieving success as a jockey, breaking barriers, and combating discrimination in the racing industry.

8. Character Arc:
- Isaac's character arc involves his rise to fame, facing obstacles and discrimination, and ultimately becoming a symbol of hope and achievement.
- He undergoes personal growth, from facing initial failures to finding success and confronting challenges head-on.
- Isaac's arc is marked by resilience, determination, and the continuous pursuit of his goals.

9. Relationships:
- Isaac has a strong relationship with his wife, Lucy Carr Osborn, whom he loves deeply and marries in 1883.
- He also has a close friendship with Anthony Hamilton, his best friend and confidant.
- Isaac's relationships with his horse owners, trainers, and fellow jockeys fluctuate between camaraderie, competition, and conflict.
- His interactions with white horse owners and trainers are often strained due to

racial prejudice.
- He is married to Lucy Carr Osborne.

10. Internal Conflicts and Flaws, Fears, and Vulnerabilities:
- Isaac's internal conflicts stem from his self-sacrificing nature, perfectionist tendencies, and occasional insecurities.
- He fears failure, losing the respect of his peers, and being unable to provide for his family.
- Isaac's vulnerability lies in his naivete, which can lead to exploitation and irrational decision-making.

11. External Obstacles:
- Isaac faces external obstacles such as racial discrimination, bribery attempts, and attempts to tarnish his reputation.
- He also encounters challenges related to maintaining his success, handling the pressures of fame, and overcoming injuries.

12. Evolution of Relationships and Interactions:
- Isaac's relationships with other characters evolve over time.
- His interactions with his wife deepen as they face challenges together, and their love strengthens.
- Relationships with horse owners and trainers can shift from initial skepticism to respect as he proves his talent and dedication.

13. Hobbies and Interests:
- Isaac's primary interest lies in horse racing, which becomes both his profession and passion.
- He enjoys observing and studying his competition, seeking opportunities to improve his skills.
- When he is not racing, he occasionally indulges in drinking and partying.

14. Core Beliefs and Values:
- Isaac values faithfulness, acceptance, resilience, and resourcefulness.
- He believes in the power of love and is committed to breaking racial barriers in horse racing.
- Isaac's moral compass guides him to be true to himself and fight against injustice.

15. Emotional Range and Expressions:
- Isaac's emotional range includes deep love for his wife, determination, frustration in the face of discrimination, and occasional moments of self-doubt.
- He expresses his emotions through his actions, racing style, and occasional outbursts.

16. Dialogue Style and Speech Patterns:
- Isaac's dialogue style is characterized by a soft-spoken and refined manner of speaking.
- His vocabulary is articulate and reflective of his educated background.
- He may have a tendency to use metaphors or horse racing terminology in his

conversations.

17. External Relationships:
- Isaac's relationships with characters outside his immediate circle vary, from supportive allies to antagonistic figures.
- Peripheral relationships may serve as opportunities for growth, provide additional challenges, or offer contrasting perspectives.

18. Symbolism and Themes:
- Isaac can be symbolically associated with themes of perseverance, hope, breaking barriers, and challenging stereotypes.
- Horse racing itself serves as a symbolic representation of the struggles and triumphs in Isaac's life.

19. Transformation and Lessons Learned:
- Isaac undergoes a transformation from a young jockey facing discrimination to becoming a symbol of hope and achievement.
- He learns the importance of resilience, perseverance, and the power of love.
- Isaac's journey teaches him valuable lessons about the complexities of race, fame, and personal sacrifice.

20. Relationship to Protagonist/Antagonist:
- Isaac's relationship to the protagonist revolves around his pursuit of success and breaking barriers.
- Antagonistic forces may include racist individuals, discriminatory institutions, and those who aim to undermine his reputation.
- These relationships challenge his beliefs and provide opportunities for personal growth.

21. Moral Dilemmas:
- Isaac faces moral dilemmas related to integrity, accepting compromises to further his career, and choosing between personal success and fighting against injustice.
- These dilemmas test his character and contribute to his growth.

22. Impact on the Story:
- Isaac's actions, choices, and achievements have a significant impact on the story.
- He drives the plot forward by breaking racial barriers, inspiring others, and challenging the prevailing stereotypes of the time.
- Isaac's character adds depth, realism, and emotional resonance to the narrative.

23. Conclusion and Impact:
- Isaac's journey, from facing initial failures to becoming a celebrated jockey, leaves a lasting impact on the story.
- His growth, lessons learned, and determination to combat discrimination contribute to the overall narrative themes of resilience, hope, and fighting for what is right.
- Isaac's character serves as a reminder of the power of passion, conviction, and love in overcoming adversity and effecting change.

Anthony Hamilton

1. Basic Information:
   - Name: Anthony Hamilton. Nickname Tony or The Black Demon.
   - Birthday: 1866
   - Zodiac Sign: Unknown
   - Physical Appearance: Anthony is of average height with a lean and muscular build. He has a commanding presence, with dark, intense eyes that convey determination and a strong jawline. His short, curly black hair adds to his striking appearance.
   - Profession: Jockey
   - Role in the Storyline: Anthony serves as a central character, showcasing his rise to prominence as a jockey, his struggles, and his impact on the sport of horse racing during the late 19th century.

2. Physical Appearance:
   - Height: Average height
   - Weight: Muscular and fit
   - Hair Color: Short, curly black hair
   - Eye Color: Dark and intense
   - Body Type: Lean and muscular
   - Distinguishing Features: Strong jawline, commanding presence

3. Backstory:
   - Childhood: Anthony was born and raised in Charleston, South Carolina, during a time when racial tensions ran high. Growing up in a predominantly Black community, he witnessed firsthand the injustices and limitations placed on people of color.
   - Upbringing: Anthony's upbringing was modest, but he had a deep love for horses from an early age. He often found solace in the stables, spending his time observing and learning about the magnificent creatures.
   - Significant Life Events: At the age of 15, Anthony caught the attention of British horse trainer William Lakeland, who recognized his natural talent and passion for racing. This marked the beginning of his career in the horse industry and set him on a path to greatness.

4. Background:
   - Cultural and Socioeconomic Factors: Anthony's background is rooted in the rich African-American culture prevalent in Charleston during the late 19th century. He faced systemic racism and societal prejudice that limited his opportunities but also fueled his determination to overcome barriers and succeed in the sport he loved.
   - Educational History: Anthony's formal education was limited, as his focus and passion were primarily directed towards horses and racing. However, he possessed an innate intelligence and a keen understanding of the racing industry.
   - Significant Life Events: Anthony's journey took him from racing in America to Europe, where he continued to excel and gain recognition. His success challenged the deeply ingrained racial biases of the time, making him a symbol of resilience and determination.

5. Personality Traits:
- Charismatic: Anthony exudes charisma and charm, captivating those around him. He has a natural ability to command attention and leave a lasting impression.
- Competitive: Anthony possesses a strong competitive drive, always striving to be the best and pushing himself to reach new heights in his racing career.
- Confident: Anthony is self-assured and displays unwavering confidence in his abilities as a jockey. This confidence often borders on arrogance, fueling his desire to prove himself to the world.
- Resilient: Anthony has faced numerous challenges and setbacks throughout his career, but he possesses the resilience to bounce back and continue pursuing his dreams.
- Determined: Anthony's determination is unwavering. He sets ambitious goals and works tirelessly to achieve them, never backing down in the face of adversity.

6. Strengths and Skills:
- Exceptional Riding Skills: Anthony's talent as a jockey is unmatched, marked by his impeccable balance, finesse, and innate understanding of horses.
- Knowledge of Pace: Anthony has a deep understanding of pacing, enabling him to strategize and make split-second decisions during races.
- Showmanship: Anthony's natural showmanship adds flair to his performances and sets him apart from other jockeys. He knows how to captivate the audience and leave a lasting impression.

7. Motivations and Goals:
- Desire for Control: Anthony is driven by a desire for control, both on and off the racetrack. He strives to be in command of his own destiny, proving that his fate is not limited by societal expectations or racial barriers.
- Achieving Greatness: Anthony's ultimate goal is to solidify his place in history as one of the greatest jockeys of all time. He seeks validation and recognition for his talent and hard work.

8. Character Arc:
- Starting Point: Anthony begins his journey as a young, ambitious jockey with raw talent and dreams of success.
- Journey: He faces numerous obstacles, including racial discrimination, injuries, and personal setbacks. These challenges test his resolve and force him to confront his flaws and ego-driven personality.
- Endpoint of Development: Anthony's character arc leads him towards personal growth, humility, and a deeper understanding of the impact of his actions on others. He learns that true greatness goes beyond individual achievements and requires empathy and integrity.

9. Relationships:
- Friendship with Isaac Murphy: Anthony shares a close friendship with fellow jockey Isaac Murphy. Their bond transcends racial barriers, and they support and inspire each other throughout their respective careers.
- Failed Marriage: Anthony's marriage to Annie faces strain and eventually ends in divorce. The dissolution of his marriage highlights his lack of loyalty and commitment outside of racing.

10. Internal Conflicts and Flaws:

- Lack of Loyalty and Integrity: Anthony's ego-driven personality often leads to a lack of loyalty and integrity in his personal relationships. He prioritizes his own ambitions and desires above others.

- Fear of Losing Control: Anthony's fear of losing control drives some of his actions and decisions, occasionally clouding his judgment and causing him to act impulsively.

- Vulnerability to Injuries: Anthony's vulnerability to injuries threatens his racing career and forces him to confront his mortality.

11. External Obstacles:

- Racial Discrimination: Anthony faces pervasive racial discrimination, which attempts to limit his opportunities and undermines his accomplishments.

- Physical Injuries: Anthony's career is marked by physical injuries sustained during races, posing a constant threat to his ability to compete and achieve his goals.

- Professional Competition: Anthony encounters fierce competition from other talented jockeys, forcing him to continually push his limits and prove himself.

12. Evolution of Relationships and Interactions:

- Anthony's relationships evolve over time, influenced by his personal growth and the changing dynamics of the racing world. He develops a deeper understanding of the impact of his actions on others and learns to appreciate the support and camaraderie of those around him.

13. Hobbies and Interests:

- Anthony's primary interest lies in racing and horses. Outside of his racing career, he finds solace in spending time with horses, observing their behavior, and exploring ways to improve his riding skills.

14. Core Beliefs and Values:

- Determination and Perseverance: Anthony values determination and perseverance in the pursuit of his dreams. He believes that hard work and talent should be recognized and rewarded, regardless of one's background or race.

15. Emotional Range and Expressions:

- Anthony's emotional range is wide, encompassing confidence, passion, frustration, and vulnerability. He expresses his emotions through a combination of subtle cues and bold gestures, depending on the situation and his desired impact.

16. Dialogue Style and Speech Patterns:

- Anthony's dialogue style is charismatic and persuasive. He possesses a commanding presence and a knack for captivating an audience with his words. His speech patterns are confident, eloquent, and occasionally laced with a touch of arrogance.

17. External Relationships:

- Anthony's relationships with characters outside his immediate circle vary. He encounters admiration, envy, and occasional hostility from his competitors, trainers, and owners. These relationships shape his worldview and impact his self-image.

18. Symbolism and Themes:
- Anthony's journey symbolizes resilience, breaking barriers, and the pursuit of greatness despite societal obstacles. His character represents the triumph of talent, determination, and self-belief over adversity and prejudice.

19. Transformation and Lessons Learned:
- Throughout the narrative, Anthony undergoes a transformative journey. He learns the importance of humility, loyalty, and integrity, understanding that true greatness is not solely defined by individual achievements but by the impact one has on others.

20. Relationship to Protagonist/Antagonist:
- Anthony's interactions with the protagonist and antagonistic forces challenge his beliefs and provide opportunities for personal growth. His relationship with the protagonist may be one of mutual respect, friendly competition, or even mentorship, depending on the story's dynamics.

21. Moral Dilemmas:
- Anthony faces moral dilemmas, particularly regarding loyalty and integrity in his personal relationships. He must navigate these challenges and make difficult choices that align with his growth and transformation.

22. Impact on the Story:
- Anthony's actions, choices, and personal journey drive the plot forward, adding depth and complexity to the narrative. His triumphs and failures shape the storyline, contributing to themes of resilience, ambition, and overcoming societal limitations.

23. Conclusion and Impact:
- Anthony's journey serves as an inspiring tale of resilience and determination. His character leaves a lasting impact on the readers, highlighting the power of passion and self-belief in the face of adversity. Through his growth and transformation, Anthony's story resonates with themes of self-discovery, personal growth, and the pursuit of one's dreams.

Oliver Lewis

1. Basic Information:
  - Name: Oliver Lewis
  - Birthday: December 22nd
  - Zodiac Sign: Capricorn
  - Physical Appearance: Oliver is of average height with a sturdy build. He possesses a thoughtful expression in his deep-set eyes and carries himself with a mixture of confidence and reserve. His hair is salt-and-pepper, adding to his distinguished appearance.
  - Profession: Jockey
  - Role in the Storyline: Oliver serves as a primary protagonist, showcasing his journey as a pioneering African American jockey and his personal growth throughout the narrative.

2. Physical Appearance:
  - Height: Average
  - Weight: Sturdy build
  - Hair Color: Salt-and-pepper
  - Eye Color: Deep-set eyes
  - Body Type: Strong and fit
  - Distinguishing Features: Thoughtful expression, distinguished appearance

3. Backstory:
  - Childhood: Oliver grew up in a modest household, surrounded by the love and support of his parents and siblings. His childhood was marked by a deep connection to horses and an early fascination with horse racing.
  - Upbringing: Oliver's upbringing instilled in him a strong work ethic and a sense of responsibility. He was taught the importance of integrity and perseverance, values that would shape his character in later years.
  - Significant Life Events: Oliver's life took a significant turn when he won the first Kentucky Derby in 1875, becoming the first African American jockey to achieve such a feat. This milestone propelled him into the spotlight and set the stage for his impact on the sport of horse racing.

4. Background:
  - Cultural and Socioeconomic Factors: Oliver's background is rooted in the African American community, where he faced the challenges of racial discrimination and limited opportunities. His journey as a jockey challenged societal norms and paved the way for future generations.
  - Educational History: Oliver's education was limited, primarily focused on acquiring the necessary skills and knowledge for horse racing. However, he possessed a natural talent and a keen understanding of the racing industry.
  - Significant Life Events: In addition to his Kentucky Derby win, Oliver achieved second place at the Belmont Stakes in 1875. These victories established him as a force to be reckoned with and solidified his place in horse racing history.

5. Personality Traits:
  - Thoughtful: Oliver possesses a contemplative nature and carefully considers his actions and decisions.

- Reserved: He tends to be more reserved in social settings, preferring the company of a few close friends and family members.
- Determined: Oliver is driven by a deep determination to succeed and leave a lasting impact on the sport of horse racing.
- Compassionate: Beneath his reserved exterior, Oliver has a compassionate heart and a genuine concern for the well-being of others.
- Perfectionist: Oliver sets high standards for himself and strives for excellence in his work. However, this perfectionism can sometimes lead to self-criticism and frustration.

6. Strengths and Skills:
- Exceptional Riding Skills: Oliver's talent as a jockey is evident in his exceptional riding skills. He has a natural connection with horses and an innate understanding of their behavior.
- Strategic Thinking: Oliver possesses a strategic mind, allowing him to analyze races, anticipate the competition, and make calculated decisions.
- Determination: His unwavering determination and drive enable him to overcome obstacles and persevere in the face of challenges.
- Creative Vision: Oliver has a creative vision that sets him apart as an innovator in the racing world. He brings a fresh perspective and innovative ideas to the sport.

7. Motivations and Goals:
- Building a Legacy: Oliver is motivated by the desire to build something that leaves a lasting legacy. He strives to make a significant impact on the sport of horse racing and be remembered as a pioneer.
- Pursuit of Excellence: Oliver's goal is to excel in his craft and continually improve as a jockey. He seeks recognition for his talent and hard work, aiming to be the best in his field.

8. Character Arc:
- Starting Point: Oliver begins his journey as a talented yet relatively unknown jockey, navigating racial barriers and fighting for recognition.
- Journey: He faces numerous challenges and obstacles along the way, testing his resilience and determination. Oliver's character arc involves personal growth, self-discovery, and a deeper understanding of the impact he can have on others.
- Endpoint of Development: Oliver's character development leads him to a place of greater self-acceptance, humility, and a commitment to using his platform for positive change in the racing industry.

9. Relationships:
- Family: Oliver's family plays a significant role in his life, providing him with support and love. He values his relationships with his parents, siblings, and his own family as a husband and father.
- Mentorship: Oliver may develop a mentor-mentee relationship with a seasoned jockey or an influential figure in the racing industry, who guides and inspires him throughout his career.
- Protagonist/Antagonist: Oliver's interactions with the protagonist and antagonistic forces challenge his beliefs, test his resolve, and provide opportunities for personal growth.

10. Internal Conflicts and Flaws:
   - Self-Doubt: Oliver grapples with moments of self-doubt, questioning his abilities and worthiness of success.
   - Balancing Personal and Professional Life: He faces the challenge of balancing his dedication to his racing career with his responsibilities as a husband and father.
   - Perfectionism: Oliver's perfectionistic tendencies can lead to self-criticism and frustration when things don't go according to plan.

11. External Obstacles:
   - Racial Discrimination: Oliver encounters racial discrimination and prejudice within the horse racing industry, posing obstacles to his success and challenging his resolve.
   - Professional Competition: He faces fierce competition from other talented jockeys, pushing him to continually improve and prove himself on the racetrack.
   - Physical Injuries: Oliver's career is marked by the constant risk of physical injuries, which can hinder his ability to compete and achieve his goals.

12. Evolution of Relationships and Interactions:
   - Oliver's relationships evolve over time, influenced by his personal growth and the changing dynamics of the racing world. He learns to navigate the complexities of his relationships, foster trust, and embrace collaboration.

13. Hobbies and Interests:
   - Oliver's primary interest lies in horse racing and the pursuit of excellence within the sport. Outside of his racing career, he may find solace in spending time with his family, reading, or engaging in physical activities that complement his jockey training.

14. Core Beliefs and Values:
   - Integrity: Oliver values integrity and upholds high ethical standards in his professional and personal life.
   - Equality and Inclusion: He believes in breaking down racial barriers and promoting equality and inclusion within the racing industry.
   - Commitment to Family: Oliver holds family as a core value, prioritizing their well-being and cherishing the support and love they provide.

15. Emotional Range and Expressions:
   - Oliver's emotional range includes a blend of contemplation, determination, compassion, and occasional self-doubt. He expresses his emotions with a thoughtful and measured approach, often conveying his feelings through actions rather than words.

16. Dialogue Style and Speech Patterns:
   - Oliver's dialogue style is introspective and measured. He chooses his words carefully, often conveying depth and wisdom in his conversations. His speech patterns may reflect a mixture of humility and confidence, capturing his unique perspective as a pioneering jockey.

17. External Relationships:
   - Oliver's relationships extend beyond his immediate circle, encompassing

colleagues, industry professionals, and fans of horse racing. These relationships contribute to his worldview, provide support or challenges, and shape his understanding of the racing community.

18. Symbolism and Themes:
   - Oliver's journey as a jockey symbolizes breaking barriers and defying societal expectations. Themes of resilience, perseverance, and the pursuit of excellence are woven into his story, reflecting his determination to create a lasting legacy.

19. Transformation and Lessons Learned:
   - Throughout the narrative, Oliver undergoes personal growth and transformation. He learns the importance of self-acceptance, humility, and the power of using his platform to drive positive change. He realizes that success extends beyond individual accomplishments and encompasses the impact he can have on the lives of others.

20. Relationship to Protagonist/Antagonist:
   - The protagonist and antagonist play pivotal roles in Oliver's journey. The protagonist may serve as a source of inspiration or mentorship, while the antagonist challenges Oliver's beliefs, presents obstacles, and tests his resilience.

21. Moral Dilemmas:
   - Oliver faces moral dilemmas related to integrity, fairness, and the pursuit of his goals. He must navigate these dilemmas with careful consideration, ensuring his actions align with his core values.

22. Conclusion and Impact:
   - Oliver's journey leaves an indelible mark on the sport of horse racing and paves the way for future generations. His character arc exemplifies personal growth, resilience, and the pursuit of excellence, serving as an inspiration for others. Through his actions, relationships, and commitment to change, Oliver leaves a lasting impact on the story and its overarching themes.

George Garrett Lewis

1. Basic Information:
   - Name: George Garrett Lewis
   - Nickname: Garrett
   - Birthday: 1862
   - Zodiac Sign: N/A
   - Death: July 5, 1880 (at the age of 18)
   - Marriage Year: N/A
   - Wife: N/A
   - Children: N/A

2. Role in the Storyline:
   - George Garrett Lewis serves as a primary protagonist in the narrative. As a jockey, his skills and achievements in horse racing contribute to the plot and the

challenges he faces.

3. Backstory:
- Family: George is the cousin/brother of Isaac Lewis and Oliver Lewis. His parents are Henry and Mary Lewis. He had seven siblings: Mary, Martha, Isaac (also a jockey), Sallie, Oscar, Lutita, and Martin.
- Career: At the age of sixteen, George started his career as a jockey, riding for prominent owner and trainer Byron McClelland in Lexington. He became a frequent rider for McClelland and also rode for J. S. Shawhan from Cynthiana, Kentucky.
- Major Win: In 1880, George rode Fonso, a renowned horse owned by J. Snell Shawhan, to victory in the Phoenix Stakes. His partnership with Fonso showcased their strong collaboration and earned them recognition.

4. Background:
- George Garrett Lewis was born into a family deeply connected to the horse racing world. With his brother Isaac and cousin Oliver also pursuing careers as jockeys, racing was a significant part of their upbringing.
- As a young jockey, George dedicated himself to the sport, honing his skills and seizing opportunities to ride for prominent trainers and owners. He quickly gained recognition for his talent and became known for his partnership with Fonso.

5. Personality Traits:
- Confidence: George possesses a strong sense of self-assurance, believing in his abilities as a jockey.
- Talent: George is highly skilled in horse racing, displaying natural talent and expertise.
- Physical/Mental Strength: George exhibits both physical and mental strength, which are crucial for his success in the demanding sport.
- Courage: George demonstrates bravery in facing challenges on and off the racetrack.
- Perseverance: George's determination and persistence drive him to overcome obstacles and achieve his goals.
- Honor: George values integrity and upholds a sense of honor in his profession and personal life.

6. Character Flaws:
- Egotism: George's confidence can sometimes border on egotism, leading him to prioritize his own interests and recognition.
- Overconfidence: George's successes can make him prone to overestimating his abilities, potentially leading to errors in judgment.
- Hubris: George's pride in his achievements may blind him to potential risks or the need for collaboration.

7. Motivation:
- George is motivated to prove his worth by saving the day. His drive to succeed and demonstrate his abilities fuels his determination to excel in horse racing.

8. Strengths and Skills:
- Confidence: George's unwavering self-assurance boosts his performance on the

racetrack.

- Talent in Horse Racing: George possesses exceptional skills as a jockey, allowing him to navigate the complexities of the sport and form strong connections with horses.

- Physical Fitness: George maintains physical strength and fitness, essential for competing in horse racing.

- Mental Fortitude: George exhibits mental resilience and focus, enabling him to make split-second decisions during races.

- Horse-Whispering: George has a natural ability to communicate and connect with horses, forming strong bonds and enhancing his racing performance.

9. Weaknesses:

- Egotism: George's egotistical tendencies may create friction in his relationships and hinder effective teamwork.

- Overconfidence: George's overconfidence can lead to underestimating opponents or overlooking potential risks.

- Hubris: George's pride may make it challenging for him to accept help or collaborate with others, potentially limiting his growth and learning opportunities.

10. Relationships:

- Family: George shares a close bond with his siblings, particularly Isaac and Oliver, who are also jockeys. Their shared passion for horse racing and familial support contribute to their individual and collective journeys.

- Trainer: George is trained by Tice Hutsell, who plays a crucial role in his development as a jockey.

- Horse: George forms a partnership with the horse Fonso, owned by J. Snell Shawhan. Their collaboration leads to significant wins and becomes a symbol of George's talent and dedication.

11. Internal Conflicts and Flaws:

- George's internal conflicts stem from his egotism and overconfidence, which can create obstacles in his relationships and hinder his personal growth as a jockey.

- His hubris may blind him to the importance of teamwork and collaboration, posing challenges in his pursuit of success.

12. External Obstacles:

- George faces external obstacles such as competition from other jockeys, the demanding nature of the horse racing industry, and the risks associated with the sport. These obstacles test his abilities and determination.

13. Evolution of Relationships and Interactions:

- Throughout the story, George's relationships and interactions evolve as he confronts his character flaws. He learns the importance of teamwork, humility, and collaboration, fostering deeper connections with others in his pursuit of excellence.

14. Hobbies and Interests:

- George's primary interest lies in horse racing. Beyond his profession, he may enjoy activities related to horse care, training, or studying the sport to enhance his knowledge and skills.

15. Core Beliefs and Values:
   - George values personal integrity, perseverance, and the pursuit of excellence. He believes in the transformative power of hard work and determination.

16. Emotional Range and Expressions:
   - George's emotional range encompasses confidence, determination, pride, and a fierce competitive spirit. His expressions may reflect a mixture of focus, excitement, and occasional moments of vulnerability.

17. Dialogue Style and Speech Patterns:
   - George's dialogue style is marked by a confident and assertive tone. He speaks with authority and conviction, reflecting his belief in his abilities as a jockey.

18. Symbolism and Themes:
   - George's journey symbolizes the hero's quest for recognition, the challenges of ego and hubris, and the importance of humility, collaboration, and personal growth.

19. Transformation and Lessons Learned:
   - Throughout the narrative, George undergoes a transformation marked by his recognition of the negative impact of egotism and hubris. He learns the value of humility, teamwork, and personal growth, ultimately becoming a more well-rounded and respected jockey.

20. Relationship to Protagonist/Antagonist:
   - George's relationship to the protagonist may involve collaboration, competition, or a mentor-mentee dynamic. The antagonist may pose challenges to his growth and push him to confront his character flaws.

21. Moral Dilemmas:
   - George may face moral dilemmas related to maintaining integrity in a highly competitive environment, making choices that prioritize teamwork over personal glory, and learning to accept help and guidance.

22. Impact on the Story:
   - George's actions, choices, and journey significantly impact the story's development. His pursuit of recognition, personal growth, and triumph over his flaws contribute to the narrative's themes of humility, collaboration, and the hero's journey.

23. Conclusion and Impact:
   - George Garrett Lewis's character portrays the journey of a talented yet flawed jockey seeking recognition and personal growth. His story highlights the importance of humility, collaboration, and overcoming ego to achieve excellence. George's evolution and impact on the narrative add depth and complexity to the overall storytelling.

William "Billy" Walker (1860-1933)

1. Basic Information:
- Name: William "Billy" Walker
- Birthday: Unknown
- Physical Appearance: Billy has a lean and wiry build, standing at an average height with a strong presence. He has dark, curly hair that he keeps neatly trimmed and expressive brown eyes that shine with curiosity and determination.

2. Backstory:
Billy was born in Kentucky to parents who had experienced enslavement. Growing up in a world filled with horses, he developed a deep passion for horse racing from an early age. Despite facing numerous challenges and racial discrimination, Billy's talent and determination pushed him forward.

3. Background:
Billy's background is rooted in the rich cultural and socioeconomic history of Kentucky. Growing up in a post-slavery era, he faced the residual effects of systemic racism and societal barriers. However, his talent and drive allowed him to break through these limitations and make a name for himself in the world of horse racing.

4. Personality Traits:
Billy is driven by curiosity and an insatiable desire for self-improvement. He possesses a relentless spirit and is always seeking new challenges. While he is driven by his ambitions, he also carries a restless nature that leaves him never fully satisfied. Billy can be introspective, often reflecting on his experiences and seeking deeper meaning in his pursuits.

5. Strengths and Skills:
Billy's strengths lie in his exceptional talent as a jockey and his unrivaled expertise in understanding thoroughbred horses' bloodlines. He possesses physical agility, mental acuity, and a natural connection with horses, allowing him to navigate the racing track with finesse. His deep knowledge of pedigrees and bloodlines gives him a unique advantage as a consultant in the horse racing industry.

6. Motivations and Goals:
Billy's main motivation is the pursuit of self-improvement and the desire to leave a lasting impact on the sport of horse racing. He strives to prove his worth, overcome challenges, and make a significant mark in the racing world. Billy's goals include achieving professional success, expanding his knowledge, and finding contentment in his personal and professional life.

7. Character Arc:
Billy's character arc follows his growth and transformation throughout the narrative. Starting as a young, talented jockey, he embarks on a journey filled with triumphs and setbacks. Along the way, he confronts his restless nature and learns to appreciate his accomplishments and find satisfaction in the present moment.

8. Relationships:
Billy forms relationships with fellow jockeys, trainers, horse owners, and other

individuals in the racing community. These relationships impact his development, offering support, challenges, and opportunities for growth. He navigates both positive and negative dynamics, which shape his character and influence his decisions.

9. Internal Conflicts and Flaws:
Billy's internal conflicts stem from his tendency to overthink and doubt himself. He often battles with restlessness and a constant search for new experiences. These flaws can hinder his progress and lead to dilemmas in decision-making.

10. External Obstacles:
Billy faces external obstacles such as fierce competition, injuries, and the ever-changing nature of the horse racing industry. These challenges test his resolve and contribute to his growth as a character.

11. Evolution of Relationships and Interactions:
Billy's relationships evolve over time as he learns to trust others, rely on their support, and develop deeper connections. These evolving relationships impact his development and contribute to his growth as a character.

12. Hobbies and Interests:
Beyond horse racing, Billy enjoys exploring new hobbies and interests that stimulate his curiosity and thirst for knowledge. He might engage in activities such as reading, traveling, or engaging in outdoor adventures.

13. Core Beliefs and Values:
Billy values personal growth, self-improvement, and the pursuit of knowledge. He believes in the power of perseverance and the ability to overcome adversity. Billy also holds a deep respect for the horses he rides and advocates for their well-being.

14. Emotional Range and Expressions:
Billy's emotional range spans from moments of intense focus and determination on the racing track to introspection and contemplation during quieter times. He can display a mix of emotions, including excitement, frustration, joy, and self-doubt.

15. Dialogue Style and Speech Patterns:
Billy's dialogue is characterized by a mix of confidence, curiosity, and occasional introspection. He speaks with a measured and thoughtful tone, using precise language and occasionally sharing his unique insights into the world of horse racing.

16. External Relationships:
Billy interacts with characters outside of his immediate circle, such as trainers, horse owners, and fellow jockeys. These relationships broaden his perspective and provide additional opportunities for growth and learning.

17. Symbolism and Themes:
Symbolic elements associated with Billy could include horses, racetracks, and the colors of racing silks. These symbols represent his journey, passion, and the themes of perseverance, personal growth, and the pursuit of dreams.

18. Transformation and Lessons Learned:

Throughout the narrative, Billy undergoes a transformation marked by personal growth, self-discovery, and a deeper understanding of his own motivations. He learns valuable lessons about appreciating his accomplishments, finding satisfaction in the present moment, and embracing the joy of the journey rather than constantly seeking the next goal.

19. Relationship to Protagonist/Antagonist:

Billy's interactions with the story's protagonists and antagonists challenge his beliefs, offer opportunities for personal growth, and shape his character development. These interactions may involve competition, collaboration, and conflicting motivations.

20. Moral Dilemmas:

Billy faces moral dilemmas related to the ethical treatment of horses, fair competition, and the choices he makes as a jockey. Navigating these dilemmas tests his character and impacts his relationships.

21. Impact on the Story:

Billy's actions, choices, and expertise as a jockey and consultant drive the plot forward. His determination, triumphs, and growth contribute to the overall narrative and serve as an inspiration to others.

22. Conclusion and Impact:

In conclusion, Billy Walker's character journey is defined by his relentless pursuit of self-improvement, his passion for horse racing, and his transformative growth throughout the narrative. His impact on the story resonates through his triumphs, challenges, and the valuable lessons he learns along the way, leaving a lasting impression on the history of horse racing.

Alonzo "Lonnie" Clayton

1. Basic Information:
- Name: Alonzo "Lonnie" Clayton
- Birthday: January 4, 1876
- Zodiac Sign: Capricorn
- Profession: Jockey
- Role in the storyline: Protagonist, trailblazing jockey

2. Physical Appearance:
- Height: Average height for a jockey (around 5' to 5'4")
- Weight: Lean and lightweight
- Hair Color: Dark
- Eye Color: Brown
- Body Type: Slim and wiry
- Distinguishing Features: None mentioned
- Style of Dressing: Traditional jockey attire, including colorful racing silks, helmet, and boots.

3. Backstory:

Alonzo "Lonnie" Clayton, an iconic figure in the realm of horse racing, was born on January 4, 1876, in Mossy Point, Jackson County, Mississippi. As the youngest of eight children to Robert and Evaline Clayton, his humble beginnings would shape his future in ways unimaginable. At just twelve years old, the Claytons relocated to Little Rock, Arkansas. Lonnie, always eager to help his family, took on various jobs such as shoe-shining and errand running. Destiny, however, steered young Alonzo towards a different path. Leaving his family at the tender age of twelve, Lonnie moved to Chicago, Illinois, to work on Lucky Baldwin's stud farm with his brother, Albertus Clayton. It was here that Lonnie found his passion and calling - horse riding.

His talent did not remain hidden for long. Recognized for his natural skill, he quickly rose through the ranks, transitioning from an exercise rider to a full-fledged jockey. His exceptional prowess led to a triumphant victory at the prestigious Kentucky Derby in 1892 at the tender age of fifteen. His winning horse, Azra, and the soon-to-be-renowned stallion Halma were his first claims to fame. Lonnie's star only continued to shine brighter, especially on the East Coast. His most notable year was 1895, when he tallied an impressive 144 wins and finished in the money in 60% of his races. That same year, he claimed victory at the Arkansas Derby held by the Little Rock Jockey Club's Clinton Park.

Lonnie's illustrious career did not stop there. In 1896, he became one of the few Black jockeys to compete in the Preakness Stakes at Baltimore, securing an admirable third place. His unparalleled riding skills, particularly celebrated in the New York circuit, elevated him to stardom and financial success. By 1895, his earnings enabled him to purchase a spacious house in Little Rock, Arkansas, along with several commercial properties. However, the trajectory of Lonnie's career changed dramatically in 1904. A confrontation with a racist spectator led to his arrest and subsequent imprisonment. This incident marked an abrupt end to his renowned career in horse racing. Post-retirement, he relocated to California and served as a bellhop in a hotel. Unfortunately, Lonnie's life was cut short in 1917, when he succumbed to tuberculosis.

Lonnie's life was a testament to determination, talent, and resilience. Despite adversities, he continued to shatter barriers and set new records. As one of only two 15-year-olds to ever win the Kentucky Derby, his extraordinary legacy endures, inspiring future generations about the power of perseverance and the triumph of talent over adversity. Alonzo "Lonnie" Clayton's journey – from a shoe-shiner to one of America's most successful jockeys – truly embodies the American Dream. His life serves as a beacon for many, demonstrating that with passion, talent, and determination, one can overcome the toughest obstacles and achieve unparalleled success. Proof is that in 2012 he was inducted into the Arkansas Sports Hall of Fame.

4. Background:

Lonnie Clayton came from a humble background, growing up in Mississippi and later moving to a Queen Victorian style house in North Little Rock, Arkansas, with his family. The Clayton family faced the hardships of a large family, which motivated Lonnie to find ways to support them financially. His early experiences as a stablehand and his association with Lucky Baldwin's stud farm shaped his passion for horse racing.

5. Personality Traits:

- Humble: Lonnie possesses a humble nature, staying grounded despite his success as a jockey.

- Religious: His deep faith influences his values and guides his actions.

- Wise with Money and Investments: Lonnie demonstrates astuteness when it comes to financial matters, making wise decisions and investments.

- Sensitive: He is affected by the racism and prejudice he faces but strives to rise above it.

- He also had a short fuse later on due to his sensitivity and constant fear of losses through his successful career. Sensuous, Direct, Intuitive, Conceptual, Structured, Pragmatic, Resilient, Resourceful, Theoretical, Gutsy, Daring, Money-Wise.

6. Strengths and Skills:

- Exceptional riding skills: Lonnie possesses exceptional riding skills that set him apart as a jockey.

- Quick learner: He is known for his ability to quickly grasp new concepts and techniques.

- Resourcefulness: Lonnie's resourcefulness helps him overcome challenges and find ways to support his family.

- Financial acumen: He demonstrates a shrewd understanding of finances and makes wise investments.

7. Motivations and Goals:

Lonnie's primary motivation is his passion for horse racing and his desire to excel in the sport. He is motivated to take care of his large family. His goals include achieving recognition as a top jockey, supporting his family, and establishing a successful career.

8. Character Arc:

Lonnie's character arc follows his rise to fame as one of the youngest jockeys to win the Kentucky Derby, his battles against racial discrimination, and the challenges he faces due to legal troubles. His journey involves personal growth, resilience, and the need to find redemption and purpose beyond his racing career.

9. Relationships:
- Family: Lonnie's immediate family, including his parents and siblings, played a significant role in his upbringing and early career choices. His nephew, Robert Clayton Westbrook, is an important figure in his life.
- Horse Owners and Trainers: Lonnie develops relationships with various horse owners and trainers, which shape his racing opportunities and experiences.
- Fellow Jockeys: Lonnie has interactions with other jockeys, including James "Soup" Perkins, with whom he shares the title of the youngest jockey to win.
- He had an altercation with a racist spectator that ended up sending him to jail.

10. Internal Conflicts and Flaws:
- Anger and Temptation:
 Lonnie struggles with controlling his temper and succumbs to anger on occasion, leading to regrettable actions.
- Vulnerability to Racism: The racism Lonnie faces creates internal conflicts, challenging his sense of self-worth and testing his resilience.

He can exhibit traits from the following flaws - Dogmatic, Closed, Intolerant, Armored, Workaholic, Snobbish, Detached, Impatient, Unrealistic, Demanding, Stressed.

11. External Obstacles:
Lonnie encounters external obstacles such as racial discrimination, legal troubles, and setbacks in his racing career. These obstacles test his resolve, resilience, and determination. In 1901 April the noted race. Arrested in New York for allegedly fixing a race 3 years earlier. He was about to race in Long Island and was replaced by white crack jockey John Bullman riding Golden Prince. John Bullman won and that would have been Alonzo Clayton but he was arrested. Alonzo "Lonnie" Clayton, the youngest jockey to ever win the Kentucky Derby, experienced a dramatic turn of fortune. In 1898, his life took a downward spiral when he got into a fight with a spectator at a race. The spectator accused Lonnie of striking him in the face, leading to a lawsuit for pain and suffering. Lonnie was eventually arrested and spent two months in jail in Long Island City, Queens. Adding to his troubles, Lonnie failed to pay his real estate taxes on his house in Argenta. He faced multiple lawsuits, including one from his own brother. In 1900, his house was sold, perhaps the drawings and writings left in the attic were the Clayton family's farewell to their home. Despite amassing a fortune equivalent to millions in today's currency, a combination of financial and legal issues, coupled with a sudden shift in horse racing discrimination, marked the end of Lonnie's illustrious career. African-American jockeys began to disappear from the industry, replaced by white riders. Some African-American jockeys relocated overseas where the horse racing industry was less prejudiced, but there's no record of Lonnie joining them. The Clayton family eventually left Arkansas and moved west. Lonnie's life story ended on a sad note. After his remarkable career, he ended up working as a bellhop in Los Angeles. He died of tuberculosis in 1917 at the age of forty one. Over time, the legend of Alonzo Clayton faded into the annals of Arkansas history. His family home's history was mistakenly attributed to an English jockey who was believed to have built the Baker House. However, thanks to the efforts of several historical societies and the Arkansas Sports Hall of Fame, which inducted Lonnie in 2012, the true identity of this famous

jockey has been rediscovered and correctly associated with the Argenta house.

12. Evolution of Relationships and Interactions:
Lonnie's relationships with other characters evolve throughout the story. He forms alliances, encounters rivals, and experiences shifting dynamics based on his success, challenges, and the racial climate of the time.

13. Hobbies and Interests:
Outside of horse racing, Lonnie enjoys reading and hunting. These hobbies provide him solace and help him find balance in his life.

14. Core Beliefs and Values:
Lonnie holds strong religious beliefs, valuing humility, integrity, and compassion. His faith guides his actions and shapes his interactions with others.

15. Emotional Range and Expressions:
Lonnie experiences a range of emotions, including joy, frustration, anger, and determination. His expressions vary, reflecting his internal struggles and external circumstances.

16. Dialogue Style and Speech Patterns:
Lonnie's dialogue style is straightforward and sincere. He communicates with a sense of conviction and uses clear language to express his thoughts and emotions.

17. External Relationships:
Lonnie interacts with characters beyond his immediate circle, including horse owners, trainers, fellow jockeys, and individuals involved in the racing industry. These relationships shape his experiences and provide opportunities for growth.

18. Symbolism and Themes:
Symbolic elements associated with Lonnie may include the horse racing world, the Kentucky Derby, and the challenges he faces as a Black jockey in a predominantly white industry. Themes of perseverance, resilience, racial discrimination, and personal redemption can be explored through his character.

19. Transformation and Lessons Learned:
Throughout the narrative, Lonnie undergoes personal growth, learns valuable lessons about perseverance and self-control, and gains a deeper understanding of the racial dynamics of the time. His experiences shape him into a more resilient and empathetic individual.

20. Relationship to Protagonist/Antagonist:
Lonnie's relationship to the story's protagonist and antagonist can be shaped based on the plot's context. He may align with the protagonist, facing similar challenges and working toward common goals. His interactions with the antagonist may involve conflicts related to racism, competition, or legal troubles.

21. Moral Dilemmas:
Lonnie confronts moral dilemmas, such as how to respond to racism and discrimination while maintaining his integrity and pursuing his goals. These dilemmas challenge his character and contribute to his growth.

22. Impact on the Story:

Lonnie Clayton's character brings depth, diversity, and historical significance to the story. His achievements, struggles, and resilience contribute to the narrative's themes and conflicts, providing a lens through which readers can explore issues of racial injustice, personal growth, and triumph over adversity. Alonzo "Lonnie" Clayton's life story is one of resilience, talent, and unyielding determination. He ascended from humble beginnings, shattered racial barriers, and rose to the top of a predominantly white sport during an era steeped in racism. His inspiring journey from shoe-shiner to celebrated jockey exemplifies the power of perseverance and the significance of breaking barriers, influencing generations to pursue their dreams regardless of their circumstances. His life encapsulates the true essence of the American Dream, illustrating that with passion, talent, and unwavering dedication, one can overcome the harshest adversities to reach unprecedented heights of success.

James "Soup" Perkins

1. Basic Information:
- Name: James "Soup" Perkins
- Birthday: April 15, 1879 (Zodiac Sign: Aries)
- Role: Secondary Protagonist
- Profession: Jockey
- Nickname: Soup (earned for his love of soup as a preferred meal while training)
- Distinguishing Feature: Youngest jockey to win the Kentucky Derby, along with Alonzo Clayton

2. Physical Appearance:
- Height: 5'2" (157 cm)
- Weight: 105 lbs (48 kg)
- Hair Color: Dark brown
- Eye Color: Hazel
- Body Type: Slim and wiry
- Distinctive Features: A small scar on his right cheek from a childhood accident

3. Backstory:
- Soup was born in Lexington, Kentucky, on April 15, 1879, to John and Mattie Perkins, former slaves who worked as horse trainers.
- Growing up in a close-knit family, Soup developed a deep love for horses from a young age.
- His father, John Perkins, recognized his son's natural talent and taught him the art of horse racing.
- Soup's childhood was filled with stories of his father's experiences as a jockey and his dreams of becoming a successful jockey himself.

4. Background:
- Coming from a modest background, Soup's family faced the challenges of racial discrimination prevalent during the late 19th century.
- Despite the odds, Soup's parents instilled in him a strong work ethic, determination, and a sense of pride in his heritage.

- His parents' experiences as former slaves and their belief in his potential fueled Soup's aspirations.

5. Personality Traits:
- Sense of fun and likeability: Soup possesses a magnetic personality and a great sense of humor, making him popular among his peers.
- Funny and insightful: He uses his wit to entertain others, but beneath the humor lies a keen observation of human nature and life's complexities.
- Unreliable and frivolous: At times, Soup's carefree nature and love for enjoyment can make him appear unreliable or lacking in seriousness.

6. Strengths and Skills:
- Extraordinary riding skills: Soup's natural talent, agility, and connection with horses make him an exceptional jockey.
- Sense of humor: His wit and comedic timing not only entertain but also bring moments of levity in tense situations.
- Insightfulness: Soup's ability to read people and situations allows him to provide valuable advice and offer unique perspectives.

7. Motivations and Goals:
- To prove himself as a successful jockey: Soup is driven by the desire to make a name for himself in the competitive world of horse racing.
- Overcoming discrimination: He aspires to break down racial barriers and inspire other aspiring Black jockeys to pursue their dreams.

8. Character Arc:
- Soup starts as a promising young jockey, full of dreams and aspirations.
- As he faces discrimination and obstacles, his journey becomes a quest for justice, equality, and personal growth.
- Along the way, Soup learns valuable lessons about resilience, perseverance, and the power of his own voice.

9. Relationships:
- Family: Soup shares a deep bond with his parents and siblings, who provide unwavering support throughout his racing career.
- Alonzo Clayton: Soup develops a close friendship and camaraderie with Alonzo Clayton, their shared experiences forging a lasting connection.

10. Internal Conflicts and Flaws:
- Unreliability and impulsive behavior: Soup's spontaneous nature and occasional disregard for responsibilities can lead to conflicts with those who rely on him.
- Superficiality: At times, Soup may prioritize immediate pleasures and external appearances over deeper introspection.

11. External Obstacles:
- Discrimination and racism: Soup faces relentless discrimination from the Union of White Jockeys, determined to remove Black jockeys from the racing industry.
- Limited opportunities: The scarcity of racing opportunities for Black jockeys presents a significant obstacle to Soup's career advancement.

12. Evolution of Relationships and Interactions:
- Soup's relationships evolve as he navigates the challenges of discrimination and fights for equality.
- Interactions with Alonzo Clayton, fellow jockeys, and supporters in the racing community shape Soup's character development.

13. Hobbies and Interests:
- Apart from horse racing, Soup enjoys playing card games with his friends, attending local theater performances, and exploring new culinary experiences.

14. Core Beliefs and Values:
- Soup values equality, justice, and the power of unity to overcome adversity.
- He believes in the importance of staying true to oneself and using humor as a tool for resilience and connection.

15. Emotional Range and Expressions:
- Soup's emotional range encompasses joy, laughter, determination, frustration, and moments of vulnerability.
- He expresses his emotions through laughter, witty remarks, and occasional heartfelt conversations.

16. Dialogue Style and Speech Patterns:
- Soup's dialogue is characterized by a mix of humor, colloquial language, and occasional insightful remarks.
- He may use catchphrases, playful banter, and vivid storytelling to engage with others.

17. External Relationships:
- Soup's relationships extend beyond his immediate circle to include trainers, fellow jockeys, and racing enthusiasts who appreciate his skills and personality.
- These relationships provide both support and challenges, influencing Soup's worldview and personal growth.

18. Symbolism and Themes:
- Soup's journey symbolizes resilience, the fight against discrimination, and finding joy in the face of adversity.
- Themes of equality, friendship, and pursuing dreams against all odds are interwoven in his story.

19. Transformation and Lessons Learned:
- Soup undergoes a transformation from a carefree and ambitious young jockey to a resilient advocate for equality and justice.
- He learns the importance of standing up for one's beliefs, navigating obstacles, and finding strength in unity.

20. Relationship to Protagonist/Antagonist:
- As the protagonist, Soup's interactions with the antagonist, the Union of White Jockeys, highlight the challenges and discrimination he faces.

- These interactions create conflict and provide opportunities for Soup's growth and the exploration of broader themes.

21. Moral Dilemmas:
- Soup faces moral dilemmas related to taking a stand against discrimination, deciding how to respond to adversity, and reconciling personal desires with larger societal goals.

22. Impact on the Story:
- Soup's actions, choices, and character development drive the plot forward, inspiring other characters and challenging societal norms.
- His resilience, determination, and ability to find joy in difficult circumstances leave a lasting impact on the narrative.

23. Conclusion and Impact:
- Soup's overall journey reflects the struggles and triumphs of Black jockeys during a time of discrimination.
- His legacy as one of the youngest jockeys to win the Kentucky Derby inspires future generations and highlights the need for equality in sports.
- Soup's story serves as a reminder of the importance of resilience, perseverance, and finding joy in the face of adversity.

Willie Simms

1. Basic Information:
- Name: Willie Simms
- Birthday: January 16, 1870 (Zodiac Sign: Capricorn)
- Physical Appearance: Height: 5'5" (165 cm), Weight: 110 lbs (50 kg), Black hair, Brown eyes
- Profession: Jockey
- Role: Secondary Protagonist, Trailblazer

2. Backstory:
- Willie Simms was born on January 16, 1870, in Augusta, Georgia.
- Raised in a horse racing environment, he began working at his uncle's stables at a young age.
- Recognized for his exceptional skills with horses, he caught the attention of prominent figures in the horse racing world, Phil and Mike Dwyer.
- Despite facing discrimination and challenges as a Black jockey, Simms remained determined to prove his worth and make a name for himself.

3. Background:
- Growing up in Augusta, Georgia, Simms had a close bond with his mother, Ida Pleasant.
- He began his racing career in 1887 on the East Coast, racing in the North.
- Simms adopted the short stirrup technique, a riding style popularized by Abe Hawkins, which gave him a crouching posture and better balance.
- His adoption of the short stirrup technique revolutionized the sport and earned him recognition as one of the most successful riders to use it since Hawkins.

4. Personality Traits:
- Diligent: Simms approaches his racing career with meticulous attention to detail and a strong work ethic.
- Steady: He remains focused and composed in high-pressure situations.
- Thorough: Simms ensures that he leaves no stone unturned in his preparation and training.
- Conquering: He possesses a fearless and determined attitude when facing challenges on and off the racetrack.
- Philosophical: Simms maintains a philosophical outlook on life and racing, seeking deeper meaning in his accomplishments.
- Professional: He upholds a high level of professionalism in his career and interactions with others.
- Surmounting: Simms has a remarkable ability to overcome obstacles and persevere.
- Maintaining: He consistently maintains his focus and commitment to his craft.
- Innovative: Simms explores new techniques and approaches to enhance his riding skills.
- Brilliant: He possesses strategic thinking and displays intelligence in his racing decisions.
- Dauntless: Simms fearlessly takes on challenges and does not back down in the face of adversity.

5. Strengths and Skills:
- Versatile and innovative: Simms constantly seeks new ways to improve his riding techniques and stays ahead of the competition.
- Brilliant and steady: His strategic thinking and level-headedness enable him to make smart decisions in high-pressure situations.
- Maintaining and surmounting: Simms has the ability to maintain his focus and overcome obstacles.
- Self-improvement and exploration: He is driven to explore the unknown and expand his horizons in the racing world.

6. Motivations and Goals:
- Fulfillment and self-improvement: Simms is driven by the pursuit of personal fulfillment and strives to constantly improve his skills as a jockey.
- Breaking down barriers: He aspires to challenge the racial discrimination prevalent in the horse racing industry and pave the way for future generations of Black jockeys.
- Exploration and pushing boundaries: Simms seeks to push the boundaries of what is possible in horse racing and continually explore new techniques and strategies.

7. Character Arc:
- Simms starts as a young and ambitious jockey determined to make a name for himself in the racing world.
- He faces adversity and discrimination but remains resilient and determined to prove his worth.
- Through his accomplishments and struggles, Simms undergoes personal growth, embracing his role as a trailblazer and advocate for racial equality in horse racing.

8. Relationships:
- Family: Simms shares a close bond with his mother, Ida Pleasant, who supports his racing career.
- Employers: He forms strong relationships with his employers, Hardy Campbell Jr., John E. Madden, and the Dwyer brothers, who provide opportunities and support throughout his career.
- Fellow jockeys: Simms develops both supportive and competitive relationships with other jockeys, some becoming allies while others present challenges and rivalries.

9. Internal Conflicts and Flaws:
- Habituating to success: Simms may become habituated to his achievements, diminishing his feelings of satisfaction over time unless he takes on greater challenges.
- Stress and burnout: The high-pressure environment of horse racing can lead to stress and burnout, posing challenges to Simms' well-being.
- Unheeding and outrageous behavior: At times, Simms may act impulsively or exhibit outrageous behavior, driven by his determination to succeed.
- Superiority and aloofness: His success and talent can sometimes lead to a sense of superiority and aloofness, affecting his relationships with others.

10. External Obstacles:
- Discrimination and racism: Simms faces prejudice and discrimination as a Black

jockey in a predominantly white sport, presenting constant challenges to his career.
- Uncertainty and risk: The unpredictable nature of horse racing poses risks and uncertainties that Simms must navigate.
- Career longevity: Simms must grapple with the challenges of maintaining his success and relevance in a highly competitive industry.

11. Evolution of Relationships and Interactions:
- Simms' relationships with others evolve as he gains recognition and respect for his skills.
- Interactions with other characters, both supportive and antagonistic, shape his development and offer opportunities for growth and learning.

12. Hobbies and Interests:
- Simms finds fulfillment and enjoyment in the world of horse racing, which serves as both his profession and his passion.

13. Core Beliefs and Values:
- Simms values personal fulfillment, self-improvement, and the pursuit of justice and equality.
- He believes in the power of resilience and determination to overcome obstacles and achieve success.

14. Emotional Range and Expressions:
- Simms exhibits a wide emotional range, from focused and determined during races to moments of joy and satisfaction after victories.
- His expressions reflect a mix of intensity, concentration, and occasional bursts of exuberance.

15. Dialogue Style and Speech Patterns:
- Simms has a straightforward and confident dialogue style, using concise and precise language.
- He speaks with conviction and authority, reflecting his experience and knowledge in the racing world.

16. External Relationships:
- Simms interacts with a range of characters outside his immediate circle, including colleagues, competitors, and supporters.
- These relationships impact his worldview and provide opportunities for growth and collaboration.

17. Symbolism and Themes:
- Simms symbolizes resilience, trailblazing, and the pursuit of personal and professional fulfillment.
- Themes of racial equality, perseverance, and breaking down barriers are central to his character.

18. Transformation and Lessons Learned:
- Simms undergoes a transformative journey, embracing his role as a trailblazer and advocate for racial equality.

- He learns the importance of maintaining balance, managing stress, and embracing personal fulfillment beyond material success.

19. Relationship to Protagonist/Antagonist:
- Simms' interactions with both the protagonist and antagonist characters contribute to the development of the story's conflicts and resolution.
- He faces challenges from antagonistic forces that test his resolve and provide opportunities for growth.

20. Moral Dilemmas:
- Simms encounters moral dilemmas related to fairness, justice, and navigating the racial discrimination prevalent in the horse racing industry.
- He must make difficult decisions that align with his values and contribute to his personal growth and the advancement of racial equality.

21. Impact on the Story:
- Simms' accomplishments, challenges, and personal growth have a significant impact on the story's narrative, driving the plot forward and highlighting themes of resilience, perseverance, and social progress.

22. Conclusion and Impact:
- Willie Simms' journey serves as a powerful testament to the pursuit of personal fulfillment, overcoming adversity, and breaking down racial barriers in the horse racing industry.
- His character leaves a lasting impact on the story, inspiring future generations and contributing to the advancement of equality and diversity in the sport.

JIMMY WINKFIELD

1. Basic Information:
- Name: James "Jimmy" Winkfield
- Birthday: April 12, 1882
- Physical Appearance: Jimmy stands at an average height of 5'6" with a lean, athletic build. He has dark brown hair, usually styled in a neat crop, and piercing brown eyes that exude determination and confidence. His skin bears the warm, sun-kissed complexion of someone who has spent a considerable amount of time outdoors. There is a distinct aura of strength and resilience in his overall demeanor.
- Profession: Jockey
- Role in the Storyline: Jimmy Winkfield serves as a central character in the story, driving the narrative forward with his remarkable journey, struggles, and triumphs.

2. Physical Appearance:
- Height: 5'6"
- Weight: 140 lbs
- Hair Color: Dark Brown
- Eye Color: Brown
- Body Type: Lean and athletic
- Distinguishing Features: Jimmy possesses a captivating presence, with his strong, chiseled facial features and an infectious smile that lights up a room. He has a prominent scar above his left eyebrow, a reminder of a racing accident that tested his resilience and determination.

3. Backstory:
- Childhood and Upbringing: Jimmy was born into a large family in Chilesburg, Kentucky, as the youngest of 17 children. Growing up, he experienced the hardships of being the son of a slave but found solace and joy in working with thoroughbred horses on a local farm. His childhood was filled with stories of racing legends and a deep love for the sport.
- Family Dynamics: Jimmy's family, though impoverished, was tightly knit. He formed a strong bond with his siblings and parents, who instilled in him a sense of determination and resilience. Their struggles and sacrifices fueled his ambition to create a better life for himself.
- Significant Life Events: A turning point in Jimmy's life came when he witnessed a racially motivated act of injustice in the racing world. This incident ignited a fire within him to challenge the status quo and prove that talent and skill transcend racial boundaries. This determination set him on a path that would forever change the course of his life.

4. Background:
- Cultural and Socioeconomic Factors: Jimmy's background was shaped by the racial tensions and discrimination prevalent in the late 19th and early 20th centuries. As an African American in a racially segregated era, he faced immense challenges and limited opportunities in the United States.
- Educational History: Due to the circumstances of his time, Jimmy's formal education was limited. However, he possessed a keen intellect and an insatiable appetite for learning, constantly seeking knowledge and wisdom from various sources.

- Significant Life Events: The most pivotal event in Jimmy's background was his decision to leave the United States and pursue opportunities in Europe, where racial barriers were comparatively less oppressive. This choice marked the beginning of a new chapter in his life, filled with triumphs, challenges, and personal growth.

5. Personality Traits:
- Natural: Jimmy possesses a natural talent for understanding horses, effortlessly connecting with them on a deeper level. His intuition and ability to read their behavior make him a gifted jockey.
- Versatile: Adaptability is one of Jimmy's greatest strengths. He effortlessly adjusts his racing strategies to different tracks, horses, and weather conditions, showcasing his versatility.
- Stimulating: Jimmy has a charismatic personality that draws people toward him. His positive energy and passion for horse racing are infectious, motivating those around him to believe in their own potential.
- Socially Aware: Having witnessed the injustices faced by African Americans, Jimmy has developed a strong social awareness. He empathizes with the struggles of others and actively works toward creating a more inclusive and just society.
- Articulate: Jimmy possesses a silver tongue, effortlessly expressing his thoughts and emotions with eloquence. He can captivate audiences with his speeches, conveying his beliefs and rallying support for causes he deems worthy.
- Diplomatic: Jimmy understands the importance of diplomacy and tact. He knows when to assert himself and when to navigate delicate situations with grace and finesse.
- Protective: Jimmy is fiercely protective of his loved ones, his fellow jockeys, and the rights of African Americans. He is willing to put himself in harm's way to defend those he cares about.
- Generous: Despite the challenges he faced, Jimmy remains generous at heart. He is quick to lend a helping hand to those in need, recognizing the value of compassion and empathy.
- Fearless: Jimmy possesses an unwavering courage and fearlessness, both on and off the racetrack. He is unafraid to challenge conventions and confront injustices head-on.
- Gutsy: Jimmy's audacity and boldness are evident in his racing strategies. He is willing to take risks and push the boundaries of what is deemed possible, making him a formidable competitor.
- Original: Jimmy is a true original, unafraid to march to the beat of his own drum. He refuses to conform to societal expectations, embracing his uniqueness and individuality.
- Brilliant: Jimmy's intelligence shines through his keen observation, quick thinking, and strategic racing tactics. He possesses a sharp mind and a remarkable ability to analyze situations.

6. Strengths and Skills:
- Resilience: Jimmy possesses unparalleled resilience, allowing him to bounce back from setbacks and challenges. He harnesses his inner strength to overcome adversity and emerge stronger than before.
- Resourcefulness: Jimmy's resourcefulness enables him to find innovative solutions to problems. He excels at making the most of limited resources and capitalizing on opportunities that others may overlook.

- Ability to Inspire: Jimmy has a natural ability to inspire those around him. Whether through his racing achievements, speeches, or sheer presence, he uplifts others and ignites a belief in their own potential.

- Independent Thinking: Jimmy is not easily swayed by popular opinion. He possesses a sharp and independent mind, able to think critically and make decisions based on his own judgment.

- Virtue: Honesty, integrity, and a strong moral compass define Jimmy's character. He upholds high ethical standards and remains true to his principles, even when faced with temptation.

- Skillful Horse Racing Techniques: Jimmy's exceptional riding skills and deep understanding of horses give him an edge on the racetrack. He has mastered the art of balancing finesse and strength, allowing him to coax the best performance out of each horse he rides.

7. Motivations and Goals:

- Changing the World and Restoring Justice: Jimmy is driven by a burning desire to challenge the existing racial barriers and restore justice to the racing world. He dreams of a future where talent and skill determine success, regardless of one's race or background.

- Pursuing Personal Fulfillment and Success: Jimmy aspires to achieve personal fulfillment through his racing career. He seeks recognition as one of the greatest jockeys of his time and aims to leave a lasting legacy.

- Overcoming Racial Barriers: Jimmy is determined to overcome the racial barriers that hinder African American jockeys. He sees his success as a means to inspire future generations and break down the walls of prejudice.

- Fostering Equality and Inclusivity: Jimmy strives to create a more inclusive and equal society, both within the racing world and beyond. He advocates for equal opportunities for all, regardless of race or background.

8. Character Arc:

- Starting Point: Jimmy begins his journey as a young, talented African American jockey in a racially segregated era. He faces discrimination and limited opportunities in the United States but possesses an unwavering determination to break through these barriers.

- Journey: Jimmy's journey takes him from the United States to Europe, where he finds greater opportunities and achieves remarkable success as a jockey. He experiences triumphs, setbacks, and personal growth along the way.

- Endpoint of Development: Jimmy's character arc culminates in his recognition as a trailblazer and role model for African Americans in the racing world. He leaves a lasting impact on the sport and inspires generations to come.

9. Relationships:

- Family: Jimmy's relationship with his large family is filled with love, support, and shared struggles. His parents and siblings are his pillars of strength, instilling in him the values that shape his character.

- Love Interests: Throughout his life, Jimmy forms deep connections with two white European countesses whom he marries. These relationships challenge societal norms and test the boundaries of acceptance.

- Fellow Jockeys: Jimmy develops close bonds with fellow jockeys who share his passion and understand the challenges they face. They form a tight-knit community that supports and encourages each other.

- Supporters and Fans: Jimmy garners a loyal following of supporters and fans who admire his talent, resilience, and determination. Their unwavering support fuels his drive to succeed.

10. Internal Conflicts and Flaws:
- Shallow: Despite his deep conviction for justice, Jimmy can sometimes become superficial in his pursuit of success and recognition. He must grapple with the tension between his noble goals and the allure of fame and material wealth.
- Ungrounded: Jimmy's ambitious nature can occasionally lead him to lose sight of his roots and become disconnected from the struggles faced by others. He must find a balance between personal aspirations and staying grounded in his principles.
- Unfulfilled: As Jimmy achieves success in his racing career, he may battle with a sense of unfulfillment and question the true meaning of his accomplishments. He seeks deeper fulfillment beyond the surface achievements.
- Overly Involved: Jimmy's passion for justice and equality can lead him to become overly involved in the struggles of others, often at the expense of his own well-being. He must learn to set healthy boundaries and prioritize self-care.
- Frustrated: Jimmy's journey is filled with challenges and setbacks. At times, this frustration may manifest as impatience or a short temper, testing his resilience and determination.
- Self-Unaware: Despite his introspective nature, Jimmy may sometimes be blind to his own flaws and biases. He must confront his own shortcomings and learn to continuously grow and evolve.
- Unrealistic: Jimmy's unwavering optimism and belief in a better future can make him prone to setting unrealistic expectations for himself and others. He must learn to balance his idealism with a practical understanding of the challenges he faces.
- Unyielding: Jimmy's strong sense of justice can make him stubborn and resistant to compromise. He must learn to navigate the gray areas of life and find common ground with those who hold different perspectives.
- Self-Sacrificing: Jimmy's deep commitment to his cause may lead him to sacrifice his own well-being, relationships, or personal desires. He must learn to find a balance between his responsibilities to others and his own happiness.
- Amoral: In his pursuit of justice, Jimmy may grapple with the moral complexities of the choices he faces. He must confront ethical dilemmas and make decisions that align with his values.
- Compulsive: Jimmy's drive for success can sometimes manifest as a compulsive need to prove himself. He must learn to find peace and contentment within himself rather than seeking validation from external achievements.
- Flighty: Jimmy's adventurous spirit and thirst for new experiences may lead him to jump from one endeavor to another, sometimes leaving unfinished projects in his wake. He must learn to focus his energy and see things through to completion.

11. External Obstacles:
- Racial Discrimination and Prejudice: Jimmy faces systemic racism and discrimination in both the United States and Europe. He must overcome these external obstacles to achieve recognition and success.
- Challenges in the Racing Industry: The racing industry is highly competitive and

fraught with challenges, including fierce competition, injuries, and the need to constantly prove oneself. Jimmy must navigate these obstacles to establish himself as a top jockey.

- Limited Opportunities and Resources: Due to racial barriers and socioeconomic constraints, Jimmy faces limited opportunities and resources. He must find creative ways to overcome these limitations and make the most of the opportunities that come his way.

- Political and Social Unrest: The backdrop of political and social upheaval, such as the Russian Revolution and World War II, adds further obstacles to Jimmy's journey. He must navigate through these turbulent times while pursuing his goals.

12. Evolution of Relationships and Interactions:

- With Fellow Jockeys: Jimmy's relationships with fellow jockeys evolve from initial competition to camaraderie and mutual support. They form a tight-knit community, exchanging strategies, sharing victories, and collectively challenging racial barriers.

- With Love Interests: Jimmy's relationships with his two countess wives evolve through love, shared struggles, and cultural clashes. These relationships shape his understanding of acceptance, sacrifice, and the complexities of interracial relationships.

- With Supporters and Fans: Jimmy's interactions with supporters and fans deepen as his fame and success grow. He becomes a symbol of hope and inspiration for those who believe in equality and justice.

13. Hobbies and Interests:

- Jimmy's primary hobby and passion are horse racing. It consumes his life and forms the core of his identity. He finds joy in training horses, studying their behavior, and honing his riding skills.

14. Core Beliefs and Values:

- Justice and Fairness: Jimmy believes in the inherent value of justice and fairness. He fights for equal opportunities and challenges racial discrimination in the racing world and society at large.

- Social Progress: Jimmy is deeply committed to social progress and breaking down barriers. He believes in the power of positive change and the transformative impact it can have on individuals and communities.

- Overcoming Adversity and Discrimination: Jimmy values resilience, determination, and the ability to overcome adversity. He sees his own journey as a testament to the power of perseverance and the human spirit.

- Authenticity and Individuality: Jimmy cherishes authenticity and celebrates individuality. He believes that everyone has unique talents and contributions to make, and he encourages others to embrace their true selves.

15. Emotional Range and Expressions:

- Jimmy's emotional range is vast and dynamic. He experiences deep joy and elation in victory, as well as profound frustration and disappointment in defeat. He expresses his emotions openly, wearing his heart on his sleeve.

16. Dialogue Style and Speech Patterns:

- Jimmy's dialogue is articulate and persuasive, reflecting his intelligence and charisma. He possesses a commanding presence and uses his words effectively to convey his beliefs and rally support for his cause.

17. External Relationships:
- Jimmy interacts with a wide range of characters in his journey, including horse owners, trainers, fellow jockeys, supporters, fans, and individuals from different social and cultural backgrounds. These relationships shape his worldview and impact his personal growth.

18. Symbolism and Themes:
- Symbolic elements associated with Jimmy can include the racing track, representing his journey and the obstacles he faces. The horse, a symbol of freedom, strength, and resilience, can also represent his spirit and unwavering determination.

19. Transformation and Lessons Learned:
- Jimmy undergoes a transformation throughout the story, learning valuable lessons about perseverance, the power of unity, and the complexities of racial and social justice. He evolves from a talented jockey to a symbol of hope and progress.

20. Relationship to Protagonist/Antagonist:
- Jimmy's relationship with the protagonist is one of mutual respect, admiration, and collaboration. They work together to challenge the antagonistic forces of racism and discrimination, forging a powerful alliance that propels the story forward.

21. Moral Dilemmas:
- Jimmy faces moral dilemmas in his pursuit of justice and equality. He must grapple with the balance between personal desires and societal progress, often facing tough choices that test his own principles and values.

22. Impact on the Story:
- Jimmy's actions, choices, and personal growth drive the plot forward. His victories, setbacks, and unwavering commitment to justice have a profound impact on the narrative, inspiring others and challenging the existing power structures.

23. Conclusion and Impact:
- Jimmy's journey concludes with his enduring impact on the racing world and society. He leaves a legacy of courage, resilience, and the belief that true greatness transcends racial barriers. His story serves as a reminder of the power of determination and the potential for positive change.

Shelby Pike Barnes

Basic Information:
  - Name: Shelby Barnes
  - Birthday: April 10th
  - Zodiac Sign: Aries
  - Physical Appearance: Shelby is a tall and lean jockey with a commanding presence. He stands at 6 feet tall and has a strong, athletic build. His closely cropped

hair is dark and his eyes are a piercing shade of brown. His most distinguishing feature is a scar on his left cheek, a remnant from a childhood accident.

- Profession: Professional jockey

- Role in the storyline: Shelby is the main protagonist of the story, and his journey as a black jockey in the predominantly white horse racing industry forms the central narrative.

Physical Appearance:
- Height: 6 feet
- Weight: Lean and athletic build
- Hair Color: Dark
- Eye Color: Brown
- Body Type: Strong and lean
- Distinctive Features: Scar on left cheek
- Style of Dressing: Shelby dresses in traditional jockey silks during races, but in his casual attire, he prefers a mix of classic and modern fashion. He often wears well-fitted jeans, tailored shirts, and leather jackets, exuding a stylish and confident demeanor.

3. Backstory:
- Childhood: Shelby grew up in a tight-knit community in a working-class neighborhood. Raised by his loving parents, Joseph and Susan Barnes, Shelby developed a strong sense of determination and ambition from a young age.
- Upbringing: His parents instilled in him a love for horses, as they worked in a local stable. Shelby spent much of his childhood around horses, developing a natural affinity for them.
- Significant Life Events: As a child, Shelby witnessed his father face racial discrimination when trying to pursue a career as a jockey. This injustice ignited a fire within Shelby, fueling his desire to challenge the racial prejudices in the horse racing world.
- Family Dynamics: Shelby has a close relationship with his parents, who have always supported his dreams. Their unwavering belief in him provides emotional strength throughout his journey.

4. Background:
- Cultural and Socioeconomic Factors: Shelby's background reflects the challenges faced by black individuals in a predominantly white society. He comes from a working-class family that has experienced the systemic racism prevalent in the horse racing industry.
- Educational History: Shelby completed high school but didn't pursue higher education due to financial constraints. His knowledge and expertise in horse racing were acquired through hands-on experience and mentorship from seasoned jockeys.
- Significant Life Events: One pivotal event in Shelby's background was witnessing his father's dreams being crushed by racial prejudice in the industry. This event deeply impacted Shelby's worldview and fueled his determination to succeed as a jockey.

5. Personality Traits:
- Tenacious: Shelby possesses an unwavering determination to succeed despite

the odds stacked against him. He refuses to let setbacks deter him from pursuing his dreams.

- Resilient: Shelby's resilience allows him to bounce back from failures and face adversity head-on. He sees every challenge as an opportunity for growth and self-improvement.

- Empathetic: Shelby's experiences with discrimination have made him empathetic toward others facing injustice. He strives to support and uplift those around him, providing a source of strength and encouragement.

- Competitive: Shelby possesses a competitive nature, always striving to be the best and surpass his own limits. He thrives on the thrill of the race and the satisfaction of victory.

- Anxious: Despite his outward confidence, Shelby struggles with underlying anxiety. The pressures of the racing world and the constant need to prove himself can leave him feeling on edge.

- Chaotic Neutral: Shelby's moral compass leans towards doing what is right and fair, even if it means bending or breaking the rules. He values justice and equality above blind adherence to authority.

- Coping Mechanism: Shelby copes with his anxiety by developing a strict routine that helps him feel in control. He relies on meditation and visualization techniques to calm his mind before races.

6. Strengths and Skills:

- Exceptional Riding Skills: Shelby possesses remarkable horsemanship skills and a natural connection with horses. His ability to communicate with them on an intuitive level sets him apart.

- Tactical Race Strategy: Shelby's keen understanding of racing tactics enables him to make split-second decisions that give him a competitive edge on the track.

- Physical Fitness: He maintains excellent physical fitness through regular training and rigorous exercise, which contributes to his strength and agility as a jockey.

- Adaptability: Shelby quickly adapts to different horses and racing conditions, making him a versatile jockey who can excel in various scenarios.

7. Motivations and Goals:

- Shelby's primary motivation is to challenge racial prejudice in the horse racing industry. He strives to become a successful jockey and inspire other aspiring black jockeys to pursue their dreams.

- His ultimate goal is to win the most prestigious horse races and secure a place in history as a barrier-breaking jockey.

- Shelby is driven by the desire to change societal perceptions and prove that talent knows no race or color.

8. Character Arc:

- Starting Point: Shelby begins his journey as an aspiring jockey facing racial prejudice and limited opportunities in the horse racing industry.

- Journey: Throughout the story, Shelby overcomes numerous obstacles, including discrimination, self-doubt, and fierce competition. He faces failures and setbacks but learns valuable lessons along the way.

- Endpoint of Development: Shelby reaches a point where he not only achieves personal success but also becomes an advocate for diversity and inclusion in the horse racing world. He realizes that his impact extends beyond his own achievements.

9. Relationships:
- Mentor: Shelby develops a mentorship relationship with an experienced jockey who faced similar challenges in the past. This mentor provides guidance, wisdom, and moral support.
- Family: Shelby's relationship with his parents is a source of emotional strength. Their unwavering belief in him fuels his determination and resilience.
- Allies: Shelby forms close bonds with other jockeys and individuals who share his vision of equality in horse racing. They support each other through victories and setbacks.
- Rivals: Shelby encounters rival jockeys who are threatened by his rising success. These rivalries challenge him to prove himself and push his limits further.

10. Internal Conflicts and Flaws:
- Shelby's deep-rooted anxiety and self-doubt can hinder his progress and cause him to question his abilities.
- He struggles with the weight of representation, feeling the pressure to be a role model for aspiring black jockeys. This burden sometimes creates conflicts within him as he balances his personal aspirations with the expectations of others.
- Shelby's fierce independence and occasional disregard for rules can create conflicts with authority figures or traditional institutions.

11. External Obstacles:
- Racial Discrimination: Shelby faces discrimination and bias from both individuals and institutions within the horse racing industry. Overcoming these barriers is a significant external obstacle.
- Fierce Competition: Shelby encounters highly skilled rival jockeys who are unwilling to see him succeed. Competing against them presents a constant challenge that he must overcome.
- Physical Challenges: Shelby faces physical challenges, such as injuries and the demanding nature of horse racing. These obstacles test his resilience and determination.

12. Evolution of Relationships and Interactions:
- Shelby's relationships evolve as he gains recognition and success. He builds stronger bonds with individuals who support his mission and distance himself from those who hinder his progress.
- His interactions with rival jockeys become more intense, fueled by competition and a desire to prove himself. These interactions showcase both camaraderie and conflict.

13. Hobbies and Interests:
- Outside of horse racing, Shelby enjoys reading books about history and social justice. He finds solace and inspiration in stories of overcoming adversity.
- He also has a passion for photography and captures candid moments of his racing journey, using it as a creative outlet and a means to reflect on his experiences.

14. Core Beliefs and Values:
- Shelby values equality, justice, and fairness. He believes that everyone should

have an equal opportunity to succeed, regardless of their race or background.

- Integrity and honesty are central to Shelby's character. He holds himself to high ethical standards and refuses to compromise his principles.

- He also values perseverance and the importance of never giving up, even in the face of seemingly insurmountable challenges.

15. Emotional Range and Expressions:

- Shelby exhibits a wide emotional range, from moments of intense determination and focus during races to vulnerability and self-doubt in quieter moments.

- He expresses emotions through body language, such as clenched fists or a furrowed brow when facing challenges. In moments of triumph, his expressions reflect joy, relief, and a sense of accomplishment.

16. Dialogue Style and Speech Patterns:

- Shelby's dialogue style is concise, reflecting his straightforward and no-nonsense personality. He speaks with confidence and conviction, choosing his words carefully.

- His speech patterns are characterized by a mix of determination and resilience, often expressing optimism even in difficult situations. He may use horse racing metaphors to convey his thoughts and emotions.

17. External Relationships:

- Shelby interacts with individuals outside his immediate circle, such as horse owners, trainers, and fans. These relationships provide additional perspectives and insights into the horse racing industry.

- Some individuals outside his circle may initially hold biased or prejudiced views. Shelby's interactions with them present an opportunity to challenge their beliefs and foster understanding.

18. Symbolism and Themes:

- The horse Shelby rides becomes a symbolic representation of his journey, resilience, and determination to break barriers. The horse serves as a metaphor for freedom and strength.

- The colors black and white hold symbolic significance, representing the racial divide within the horse racing industry. Their juxtaposition underscores the central theme of racial equality.

19. Transformation and Lessons Learned:

- Throughout the narrative, Shelby undergoes a transformative journey that shapes his character and worldview. He learns the importance of perseverance, self-belief, and the power of challenging systemic injustice.

- Shelby also learns the value of collaboration and building alliances. He discovers the strength in unity and the collective effort required to effect meaningful change.

20. Relationship to Protagonist/Antagonist:

- Shelby's relationship with the story's antagonists represents the broader societal prejudices and systemic barriers he faces. Their opposition challenges his beliefs and presents opportunities for personal growth and self-discovery.

- The protagonist-antagonist dynamic highlights the clash between old traditions and the need for progress, emphasizing the significance of Shelby's journey in reshaping the horse racing industry.

21. Moral Dilemmas:
- Shelby faces moral dilemmas when deciding how far he is willing to go to challenge the status quo. He grapples with ethical choices that balance personal ambition with broader societal impact.
- He must navigate situations that test his integrity and moral compass, weighing the consequences of his actions on himself and others.

22. Impact on the Story:
- Shelby's actions, choices, and character development drive the plot forward. His determination to break barriers and fight for equality sparks change within the horse racing industry.
- He becomes a catalyst for discussions about diversity and representation, inspiring other aspiring black jockeys and prompting institutional reforms.

23. Conclusion and Impact:
- By the conclusion of the story, Shelby has achieved personal success as a jockey and made significant strides in dismantling racial prejudices in the horse racing industry.
- His journey serves as a testament to the power of perseverance, the importance of challenging injustice, and the transformative potential of individual actions. Shelby's impact extends beyond his own narrative, leaving a lasting legacy for future generations of jockeys.

Farrar Kenner

Basic Information:
- Name: Farrar Kenner
- Birthday: February 11,
- Gender: Male
- Physical Appearance: Farrar Kenner is a distinguished-looking man with graying hair and a well-groomed beard. He stands at an imposing height, with a strong and commanding presence. His piercing blue eyes hold a mix of authority and entitlement, and his overall demeanor reflects his privileged upbringing and social status. Farrar has a robust build, a testament to his years of working on the plantation. He is often seen dressed in tailored suits, reflecting his aristocratic background and taste for refined fashion.

Backstory:
Farrar Kenner was born into a prominent Louisiana family on February 11, 1813, in New Orleans. His ancestors hailed from Virginia, and he grew up in a privileged and affluent environment. From a young age, he was exposed to the traditions and values of the antebellum South, instilling in him a deep sense of pride and attachment to his family's plantation heritage. Farrar's childhood was marked by a formal education, fostering his intellect and shaping his worldview.

The Kenner family owned the renowned Ashland Plantation, where Farrar would later become the owner and oversee the cultivation of sugarcane. He implemented innovative and scientific techniques, such as utilizing railroads to transport sugar cane from the fields to the mill, earning him a reputation as a forward-thinking planter. His dedication and expertise led to the success of his sugar plantations, and he emerged as a prominent figure in the Louisiana Sugar Planters Association.

Political aspirations also beckoned Farrar Kenner. He initially served as a trusted aide to John Slidell, a prominent Louisiana politician. His experience in the political arena paved the way for his own career, as he went on to serve multiple terms in the Louisiana House of Representatives. Additionally, Farrar played vital roles in the state's constitutional conventions of 1845 and 1852, earning recognition for his leadership and political acumen.

Personality Traits:
Farrar Kenner embodies the characteristics of a proud and stubborn traditionalist. He is deeply entrenched in the ideals of the antebellum South and firmly holds onto the belief in the superiority of the plantation system. Farrar possesses an unwavering confidence in his own convictions and is unyielding in the face of opposition. His commanding presence and authoritative demeanor demand respect and obedience from those around him. However, beneath his composed facade lies a manipulative streak, using his charm and influence to further his own interests and maintain his position of power.

Strengths and Skills:
Farrar Kenner's strengths lie in his astute political maneuvering, strategic thinking, and deep understanding of the plantation economy. He possesses excellent

communication skills and is well-versed in the art of persuasion, enabling him to sway public opinion and gain support for his causes. Farrar's extensive knowledge of the sugar industry, coupled with his innovative approaches, contributes to his success as a plantation owner.

Motivations and Goals:
Farrar Kenner's primary motivation is the preservation of the plantation system and the perpetuation of the antebellum Southern way of life. He is driven by a fierce determination to uphold the traditions of his family and protect their social status and wealth. Farrar views the abolition of slavery and the changing societal landscape as direct threats to his identity and everything he holds dear. His ultimate goal is to thwart the progress and reforms championed by those who seek to dismantle the plantation system.

Character Arc:
Farrar Kenner's character arc revolves around his journey of resistance and the transformation of his beliefs. Initially unyielding and staunch in his defense of the old order he experiences challenges and encounters individuals who challenge his worldview. Over the course of the narrative, Farrar confronts internal conflicts, forcing him to reassess his beliefs and consider the impact of his actions on those around him. His arc is marked by a gradual realization of the need for change and the consequences of his unwavering commitment to tradition.

Relationships:
Farrar Kenner's relationships are predominantly characterized by power dynamics and a hierarchical structure. He maintains a strained relationship with Edward Dudley Brown, the protagonist of the story, due to their conflicting ideologies and pursuits. Farrar's interactions with other characters are often manipulative, as he strategically aligns himself with individuals who can further his own agenda or threaten his adversaries. His connections with other plantation owners and politicians shape his alliances and contribute to the web of power dynamics within the narrative.

Internal Conflicts and Flaws:
Despite his authoritative and confident demeanor, Farrar Kenner wrestles with internal conflicts and possesses certain flaws. His unwavering commitment to the plantation system and the preservation of his way of life leads to a reluctance to adapt to societal changes. This flaw impedes his ability to empathize with others' perspectives and blinds him to the inherent injustices of the system he defends. Farrar's fear of losing his status and influence drives him to extreme measures, often sacrificing personal relationships and moral integrity in the process.

External Obstacles:
Farrar Kenner faces external obstacles that challenge his beliefs and test his resolve. The changing political landscape, the abolitionist movement gaining traction, and the increasing influence of the industrialized North serve as formidable obstacles to his goals. Additionally, the emergence of new ideas and ideologies poses a threat to his established power and authority. Farrar must navigate these challenges while preserving the legacy of the plantation system.

Evolution of Relationships and Interactions:

Farrar Kenner's relationships evolve over time, particularly as he encounters individuals who challenge his beliefs and expose him to alternative perspectives. Interactions with characters from diverse backgrounds and experiences force Farrar to reevaluate his biases and confront his own prejudices. As the story progresses, his dynamics with other characters may shift, leading to unexpected alliances or bitter rivalries.

Hobbies and Interests:

Outside of his political and plantation endeavors, Farrar Kenner finds solace and diversion in his love for Thoroughbred horse breeding. He establishes a breeding operation for these magnificent animals at his Ashland Plantation, immersing himself in the world of horse racing. The pursuit of breeding and training exceptional racehorses becomes both a passion and a means of displaying his wealth and status.

Core Beliefs and Values:

Farrar Kenner's core beliefs revolve around the preservation of the plantation system and the perpetuation of the Southern aristocracy. He holds tightly to the notion of racial superiority, subscribing to the belief that his family's social standing is inherently justified. His values are deeply rooted in tradition, authority, and maintaining the status quo. These principles guide his actions and decisions throughout the narrative.

Emotional Range and Expressions:

While Farrar Kenner often presents a composed and authoritative facade, his emotional range is not devoid of intensity. Anger, pride, and a sense of entitlement often surface, particularly when his beliefs and way of life are challenged. His expressions range from calculated and confident to disdainful and contemptuous, reflecting his internal emotional turmoil and his desire to maintain control over the narrative.

Dialogue Style and Speech Patterns:

Farrar Kenner's dialogue style is marked by eloquence and refined language. His speech patterns reflect his aristocratic upbringing, with a tendency towards formal and articulate expressions. His vocabulary is sophisticated, and he uses language as a tool to assert authority and manipulate others. Farrar may employ rhetorical devices to persuade or intimidate, adapting his speech patterns to suit his objectives.

External Relationships:

While Farrar Kenner's immediate circle primarily comprises fellow plantation owners and politicians, he also maintains relationships with individuals outside his social class. These peripheral relationships serve various purposes, such as advancing his political agenda, gathering information, or consolidating power. His interactions with characters from different socioeconomic backgrounds offer opportunities for growth, introspection, and the reshaping of his worldview.

Symbolism and Themes:

Symbolism associated with Farrar Kenner revolves around themes of tradition, power, and resistance to change. Objects such as the plantation itself, the Thoroughbred horses he breeds, and the refined attire he dons represent his status and attachment to the old order. These symbols serve as metaphors for his struggle to preserve a way of life that is rapidly fading away.

Transformation and Lessons Learned:
Farrar Kenner's transformation entails a gradual unraveling of his deeply ingrained beliefs and a growing awareness of the need for societal change. His character arc prompts him to confront his flaws, challenge his biases, and ultimately question the morality of the plantation system. The lessons he learns throughout the narrative center around the complexities of power, the consequences of clinging to tradition, and the importance of empathy and compassion.

Relationship to Protagonist/Antagonist:
Farrar Kenner serves as the primary antagonist to the secondary protagonist, Abe Hawkins and to the Primary Protagonist Edward Dudley Brown Until Farrar Dies in 1887 then Praeder Montgomery who is his cousin or son in law continues the antagonism. Their relationship is characterized by a clash of ideologies and pursuits. As the story progresses, their interactions become increasingly adversarial, with each seeking to undermine the other's goals. Farrar's relentless opposition challenges Edward's beliefs and serves as a catalyst for his own personal growth.

Moral Dilemmas:
Farrar Kenner faces moral dilemmas rooted in his unwavering commitment to the plantation system. The conflict between preserving his own privilege and recognizing the inherent injustice of slavery presents him with difficult choices. He must navigate the tension between his personal interests and the greater good, leading to moments of moral reckoning and the need to confront the consequences of his actions.

Impact on the Story:
Farrar Kenner's overall impact on the story is significant. His actions, choices, and development drive the plot forward, serving as a catalyst for conflict and shaping the narrative's trajectory. His relentless antagonism challenges the protagonist and forces other characters to confront their own beliefs and values. Farrar's unwavering commitment to tradition and the plantation system creates ripples of tension, conflict, and personal growth throughout the story.

Conclusion and Impact:
In the end, Farrar Kenner's journey and contributions to the narrative serve as a reflection of the larger themes at play. His transformation, growth, and the lessons he learns contribute to a nuanced exploration of power dynamics, societal change, and the complexities of human nature. Farrar's impact on the story leaves an indelible mark, illuminating the consequences of upholding the status quo in the face of progress.

9. LEGENDARY HORSES

A

Adios Butler: famous harness racer

Affirmed: U.S. Triple Crown winner (1978)

Ajax: 18 consecutive race wins, before he was defeated at 1/40

Albatross: harness racer who won 59 of 71 races, and as a sire produced winners of over $130 million, including Niatross

Allez France: French Arc winner and first filly to win a million dollars

Alydar: finished second to Affirmed in all three 1978 Triple Crown races; successful sire

American Pharoah: 2015 winner of the U.S. Triple Crown and Breeders' Cup World Championships in Lexington, Kentucky at Keeneland Race Course

Animal Kingdom: American Thoroughbred racehorse; won 137th Kentucky Derby and 2013 Dubai World Cup

Archer: first and second winner of the Melbourne Cup

Aristides: winner of the first Kentucky Derby

Arrogate: winner of Travers Stakes, Breeders' Cup Classic, Pegasus World Cup, and Dubai World Cup in track record time and the richest U.S.-based racehorse of all time

Arkle: highest Timeform rating for a steeplechase horse racer

Assault: U.S. Triple Crown winner (1946)

B

Barbaro: American Thoroughbred who decisively won the 2006 Kentucky Derby, but shattered his leg two weeks later in the 2006 Preakness Stakes, ending his racing career; underwent several operations; eventually healed, but developed laminitis and could not be saved; euthanized January 29, 2007

Beholder: three-time winner of the Breeders' Cup Distaff, as well as the first filly to win the Pacific Classic

Bernborough: Australian racehorse and winner of 15 consecutive races at big weights; sold to US film producer Louis B. Mayer

Ben Nevis: champion Maryland steeplechaser he won the Maryland Hunt Cup twice and the Grand National

Bend Or, very successful British Thoroughbred racehorse who won the 1880 Epsom Derby

Best Mate: 2002, 2003 and 2004 Cheltenham Gold Cup winner; often given title 'Greatest Steeplechaser' since Arkle, and an equal to him

Big Brown: 2008 Kentucky Derby and Preakness Stakes winner; first horse since Clyde Van Dusen to win the Kentucky Derby from the 20th post position

Black Caviar: undefeated in 25 career starts; fifteen-time Group 1 winner

Bold Forbes: 1976 Kentucky Derby and Belmont Stakes winner

Bold Ruler: leading sire of stakes winners; born in the same barn the same night as Round Table; sired the outstanding Secretariat

Bret Hanover: one of only nine pacers to win the Triple Crown of Harness Racing for Pacers; had 62 wins from 69 starts; the only horse to be made Harness Horse of the Year three times

Brigadier Gerard: winner of 17 of 18 races in England, including the 2000 Guineas and 11 other Group I races; joint third highest Timeform flat rating of all time

Brooklyn Supreme: a red roan Belgian stallion noted for his extreme size

Bucephalus: Horse of Alexander the Great

Buckpasser: won 15 consecutive races; one of the great broodmare sires

C

California Chrome: won the 140th Kentucky Derby; won the Preakness; won the 2016 Dubai World Cup; two-time American Horse of the Year

Carbine: outstanding racehorse and sire; winner of the Melbourne Cup

Cardigan Bay: New Zealand's "million dollar pacer"; the first to win a million in the US; appeared on The Ed Sullivan Show

Castleshane: winner of eight flat races and two jumps

Cicero: winner of the 1905 Epsom Derby as the shortest-priced successful favorite in the history of the event

Cigar: champion in the 1990s who won 16 consecutive races

Citation: U.S. Triple Crown winner (1948); also won 16 consecutive major stakes races; first horse to earn $1 million\

Country House: Winner of Kentucky Derby 2019 after Maximum Security was demoted from 1st place for interference with other horses

Crisp: remembered for his epic race in the Grand National with Red Rum

Curlin: third richest US-based horse of all time, winner of 2007 Preakness Stakes and Breeders' Cup Classic and 2008 Dubai World Cup

D

Dan Patch: America's greatest pacer

Danehill: American-bred and British-trained sprint champion who went on to become a champion sire in both the northern and southern hemispheres; the first major "shuttle stallion"

Dance Smartly: second Canadian filly ever to win the Canadian Triple Crown, and the first to win a Breeders Cup Race

Dawn Run: only horse ever to complete Champion Hurdle, Cheltenham Gold Cup double

Deep Impact: Japanese Triple Crown winner; also smashed the world record over 3200 meters and seven-time leading sire in Japan

Desert Gold: race mare who won 19 races successive races during World War I; often raced against Gloaming

Desert Orchid: won King George four times and Cheltenham Gold Cup

Dr. Fager: "the Doctor"; set the world record at 1 mile on any surface, 1:32 1/5, and held it for more than 20 years

Doncaster: very successful racehorse, sire of the great Bend Or

E

Easy Goer: Hall of Fame champion who ran the fastest mile of all time on dirt by any three-year-old Thoroughbred in 1:32.2; ran the second fastest Belmont Stakes of all time behind Secretariat; had a great rivalry with Sunday Silence

Eclipse: celebrated 18th-century racehorse that won 18 races in 18 starts; influential sire

Emanas:Fastest Brazilian horse to win Brazilian Cup (1986, 1989 and 1990)

Eight Belles: first filly to win the Martha Washington Stakes, by a record 13½ lengths

Exterminator: exceedingly popular "iron horse" of American racing history

F

Frankel: undefeated in 14 career starts; highest rated flat race horse in history: WTR 140;[1] Timeform 147, Racing Post 143

Funny Cide: first gelding since Clyde Van Dusen to win the Kentucky Derby

Flyingbolt: widely considered as the second best Steeplechaser of all-time; stablemate of Arkle; Timeform rated 210. 2 lb inferior to Arkle

Fair Play: successful American Thoroughbred racehorse and very successful sire; sired the great Man o' War

G

Gainsborough: winner of the English Triple Crown; leading sire

Galileo: seven-time Leading sire in Great Britain & Ireland; sire of Frankel; has sired 102 Group 1 winners worldwide as of December 2015

Genuine Risk: second filly to win the Kentucky Derby (1980)

Gloaming: won 19 successive races in New Zealand and Australia; record was 67 starts for 57 wins and 9 seconds

Go Man Go: champion running Quarter Horse

Golden Miller: record five-time winner of the Cheltenham Gold Cup; only horse to win the Cheltenham Gold Cup and Grand National in the same year

Goldsmith Maid: famous harness racing mare of the 19th century[2]

Greyhound: named Trotting Horse of the Century in the US

H

Hambletonian 10: the "father of American trotting"

Hurricane Fly: Irish hurdler, winner of a record 22 Grade I races

Hyperion: winner of The Derby and the St Leger Stakes; top sire for six years in the UK

Hastings: sire of Fair Play, who in turn sired the great Man o' War, successful racehorse

I

Incitatus: horse legend says Roman Emperor Caligula planned to make a senator

Iroquois: first American-bred racehorse to win The Derby

Invasor: winner of the Uruguayan Triple Crown, as well as the Dubai World Cup and Breeders' Cup Classic

I'll Have Another: winner of the 2012 Kentucky Derby and Preakness Stakes

Irish War Cry: Graded-Stakes Winner, noted for his win in the Wood Memorial Stakes and for finishing second in the 2017 Belmont Stakes

Isinglass: sixth winner of the English Triple Crown (1892)

Isonomy: very successful racehorse and sire of The English Triple Crown winner Isinglass

J

Jay Trump: three-time winner of the Maryland Hunt Cup and the Grand National

John Henry: U.S. Champion Turf Horse (1980, 1981, 1983, 1984)

Johnstown: winner of the 1939 Kentucky Derby and Belmont Stakes

Justify: 2018 winner of the U.S. Triple Crown

K

Kelso: only five-time U.S. Horse of the Year, in the list of the top 100 U.S. thoroughbred champions of the 20th Century by The Blood-Horse magazine, Kelso ranks 4th

Kincsem: Hungarian race mare and most successful racehorse ever, winning all 54 starts in five countries

Kindergarten: weighted more than Phar Lap in the Melbourne Cup

Kingston: all-time record holder of the most wins by a horse with 89

Kingston Town: won three Cox Plates; first Australian horse to top $1million in stakes earnings

Kissin George: one of America's premier sprinting Thoroughbred racehorses

L

La Troienne: most important broodmare of the twentieth century

Lexington: America's leading 19th-century sire

Longfellow: 19th-century runner and stallion

Lonesome Glory: only five-time winner of American champion steeplechaser

Lottery: winner of the Grand National steeplechase in 1839

Lookin At Lucky: winner of 2010 Preakness Stakes, sired Lookin at Lee

M

Makybe Diva: won the Melbourne Cup on three occasions

Man o' War: often considered America's greatest racehorse; won 20 of 21 career starts

Marengo Famous war horse of Napoleon

Master Charlie: winner of the 1924 Remsen Stakes, Tijuana Futurity, Hopeful Stakes, Kentucky Jockey Club Stakes; awarded 1924 American Champion Two-Year-Old-Male/Colt

Maximum Security: Winner of Kentucky Derby 2019 before disqualification from 1st place for disturbing other horses

Might and Power: World Champion Stayer (1997); Australian Horse of the Year (1998, 1999)

Mr. Prospector: one of the most successful U.S. sires of the late 20th century

Moifaa: first New Zealand horse to win the Grand National

Mahubah: dam of Man o' War

N

Nasrullah: one of the most successful Thoroughbred sires of the 20th century, grandsire to Secretariat

Native Dancer (also nicknamed the Grey Ghost): won 21 of 22 career races, with only loss in the Kentucky Derby; sire whose descendants have come to dominate modern Triple Crown racing

Nearco Italian bred Thoroughbred racehorse. "Thoroughbred Heritage" described him as "one of the greatest racehorses of the Twentieth Century" and "one of the most important sires of the century." He was undefeated and his sire line was dominant.

Needles: the first Florida-bred horse to win the Kentucky Derby (1956), also won the Belmont Stakes

Niatross: pacer who won 37 of his 39 races and broke many records, considered to be one of the greatest harness racers of all time

Night Raid: sire of Phar Lap

Nijinsky II: last horse to win the English Triple Crown (1970)

Northern Dancer: Canada's champion on the racetrack; most successful sire of the 20th century

O

Overdose: champion Hungarian sprinter and winner of 14 straight races

Orfevre: winner of almost 20 million US dollars in earnings and is one of the highest earning racehorses ever

Oedipus: winner of the American Steeplechase triple crown

P

Peter Pan: winner of the Preakness Stakes, and had the Peter Pan Stakes named in his honor

Phar Lap: Australia and New Zealand's most famed Thoroughbred racehorse; won 37 of his 51 career starts

Pleasant Colony: 1981 Kentucky Derby and Preakness Stakes winner

Potoooooooo: 18th-century thoroughbred racehorse who won over 30 races and defeated some of the greatest racehorses of the time.

Pretty Polly Irish Thoroughbred racehorse who won 15 consecutive races, fifth filly to win the British Fillies Triple Crown, record 24: 22-2-0

Q

Quevega: only horse in the history to win at six consecutive Cheltenham Festivals

Queensway: won the Canadian Triple Crown

R

Rachel Alexandra: filly and winner of the 2009 Preakness Stakes

Roy Olcott: harness racehorse

Real Quiet: winner of the 1998 Kentucky Derby and Preakness Stakes; lost the third leg of the U.S. Triple Crown, the Belmont Stakes, by a margin of four inches

Red Rum: only horse in the history of the Aintree Grand National to win the race three times (placed second on two other occasions)

Regret: first filly to win the Kentucky Derby (1915)

Ribot: Thoroughbred undefeated in sixteen races

Rock Sand: English Triple Crown winner (1903); sire of the dam of Man o' War

Round Table: sire of stakes winners; born in the same barn the same night as Bold Ruler, in 1954

Ruffian: filly champion who won every race she started until her final (and fatal) race

Ruthless: first ever winner of the Belmont Stakes, and the first of only three fillies ever to win the Belmont Stakes

S

Sadler's Wells: one of Europe's most successful sires of the late 20th century

Sardar: stallion presented as a gift to First Lady Jacqueline Kennedy by President Ayub Khan on her visit to Pakistan

Sea Bird: second highest Timeform rated horse (rated 145)

Sea the Stars: first horse ever to win the 2,000 Guineas, Epsom Derby, and Arc de Triomphe in the same year (2009)

Seabiscuit: beat War Admiral in a nationally broadcast 1938 match race; like Phar Lap, raced during the Depression

Seattle Slew: U.S. Triple Crown winner (1977)

Secretariat: U.S. Triple Crown winner (1973); one of the most famous horses in Thoroughbred racing

Sham: The main competitor to Secretariat during the 1973 racing season

Shergar: winner of the 1981 Epsom Derby by a record 10 lengths, the longest winning margin in a race run annually since 1781; kidnapped by the IRA in 1983, and was held for ransom, but the owner syndicate refused to pay, fearing that valuable horses would become targets; the stallion was never found

Silky Sullivan: a racehorse

Sir Winston: Winner of 2019 Belmont Stakes

Skewball: immortalized in 18th century poetry as a sku-ball winning against a Thoroughbred

Smarty Jones: became the first unbeaten Kentucky Derby winner since Seattle Slew in 1977

Spectacular Bid: Hall of Fame champion who went undefeated as a four-year-old, and won 26 of 30 career starts

Steel Dust: 19th-century quarter-mile racing horse[3]

Storm Cat: one of the most successful U.S. sires of the late 20th century

Sunday Silence: winner in the US; champion sire in Japan

Sunline: first Southern Hemisphere horse to top $10million in stakes earnings; three-time Australian (2000-2002); four-time New Zealand (1999-2002) horse of the year; 13-time Group 1 winner

Swale: 1984 Kentucky Derby and Belmont Stakes winner, died eight days after the Belmont win

T

Tanya: second filly ever to win the Belmont Stakes

Tapwrit: won the 2017 Belmont Stakes, and set a new stakes record for the Tampa Bay Derby

Ta Wee: two-time American Champion Sprint Horse, and won her second Fall Highweight Handicap, at 10 stone (140 pounds) and her second Interborough Handicap, at 10 stone 2 pounds (142 pounds)

The Duke: first and second winner of the Grand National

Tiznow: two-time winner of the Breeders' Cup Classic

Tonalist: winner of 2014 Belmont Stakes, and two-time winner of the Jockey Club Gold Cup

Tuscalee: steeplechaser and all-time record holder for most wins in a season, and for most steeplechase wins overall

Twenty Grand: winner of the Kentucky Derby, Belmont, and Travers Stakes, also was champion 3-year-old and Horse of the Year of 1931

Two Lea: successful broodmare and filly winner of the Hollywood Gold Cup

U

Unbreakable: grandsire of great Native Dancer

Unbridled: winner of the Kentucky Derby and Breeders' Cup Classic and sire of the champion sire Unbridled's Song

Unbridled's Song: Breeders' Cup Juvenile winner, and sire of the great Arrogate

V

Vain: champion front runner; great, great grandsire of Black Caviar

Varenne: Italy's most famous harness horse

Vo Rouge: fast frontrunner and 3-time winner of the C F Orr Stakes, had the Vo Rogue Plate named in his honor

Voltaire: winner of the 1828 Doncaster Gold Cup

W

War Admiral: fourth U.S. Triple Crown winner (1937)

War Of Will: Winner of 2019 Preakness Stakes

Whistlejacket: Marquess of Rockingham's racehorse; painted by G. Stubbs (1762)

Winning Colors: third filly to win the Kentucky Derby (1988)

Winx: winner of 33 straight races, including the Cox Plate four times

Wise Dan: two-time American Horse of the Year (2012, 2013); won Breeders' Cup Mile twice (same years)

Whirlaway: fifth American Triple Crown winner

Whisk Broom II: first of four horses ever to win the New York Handicap Triple

X

Xaar: winner of Prix de Cabourg (1997), Prix de la Salamandre (1997)

Xtra Heat: champion 3-year-old filly of 2001, and the only filly to win the Endine stakes twice

Y

Yeats: only horse ever to win 4 Ascot Gold Cups, also won 3 other group 1 races

Your Host: winner of 1950 Santa Anita Derby, 1951 Santa Catalina Handicap, sire of the great Kelso

Z

Zabeel: New Zealand sire of Octagonal and Vengeance of Rain

Zaccio: three-time winner of the Outstanding Steeplechase horse award in the 80s

Zenyatta: won 19 of 20 starts; first mare to win the Breeders' Cup Classic (2009); first to win two different Breeders' Cup races (Ladies' Classic in 2008, Classic in 2009)

Zev: winner of the Belmont Stakes and the Kentucky Derby, as well as winner of a match race against Epsom Derby winner Papyrus

Zippy Chippy: infamous for racing 100 times and losing every single time

10. LEGENDARY THOROUGHBREDS

Kincsem
Hungary
1874
Cambuscan (GB) x Water Nymph by Cotswold

Black Caviar
Australia
2006
Bel Esprit x Helsinge by Desert Sun (GB)

Peppers Pride
United States
2003
Desert God x Lady Pepper by Chili Pepper Pie

Eclipse
Great Britain
1764
Marske x Spilletta by Regulus

Karayel
Turkey
1970
Prince Tudor (GB) x Linda (TUR) by Cihangir (GB). Triple Crown winner.

Honeysuckle
Great Britain
2014
Sulamani x First Royal by Lando

Ormonde
Great Britain
1883
Bend Or x Lily Agnes by Macaroni. Triple Crown winner.

Prestige
France
1903
Le Pompon x Orgueilleuse by Révérend

Ribot
Great Britain
1952
Tenerani (ITY) x Romanella (ITY) by El Greco

Colin
United States

1905

Commando x Pastorella (GB) by Springfield

Macon

Argentina

1922

Sandal (GB) x Bourgogne by Your Majesty

Tsurumaru Sunday

Japan

1995

Sunday Silence x Tsurumaru Beppin by Sanei Tholan

Frankel

Great Britain

2008

Galileo x Kind by Danehill

Highflyer

Great Britain

1774

Herod x Rachel by Blank

Nearco

Italy

1935

Pharos (GB) x Nogara by Havresac II (FR)

Barcaldine

Great Britain

1878

Solon x Ballyroe by Belladrum

Personal Ensign

United States

1984

Private Account x Grecian Banner by Hoist The Flag

Tremont

United States

1884

Virgil x Ann Fief by Alarm

Asteroid

United States

1861

Lexington x Nebula by Glencoe (GB)

Braque

Italy

1954

Antonio Canale x Buonamica by Niccolò dell'Arca

Crucifix

Great Britain

1837

Priam x Octaviana by Octavian

Ardrossan

Great Britain

1809

John Bull x Miss Whip by Volunteer

Goldfinder

Great Britain

1764

Snap x mare by Blank[32]

Kurifuji (Toshifuji)

Japan

1940

Tournesol (GB) x Kenfuji by Chapel Brampton (GB)

Baaeed

Great Britain

2018

Sea The Stars x Agareed, by Kingmambo

Handsomchamp

United States

2002

Fabulous Champ x Holly D by Hey Rob[34]

Nereide

Germany

1933

Laland x Nella da Gabbio (ITY) by Grand Parade (GB)

Tokino Minoru

Japan

1948

Theft (IRE) x Daini Tyrant's Queen (GB) by Soldennis

Bahram

Great Britain

1932

Blandford x Friar's Daughter by Friar Marcus. Triple Crown winner.

Combat

Great Britain

1944

Big Game x Commotion by Mieuxce (FR)

Grand Flaneur

Australia
1877
Yattendon x First Lady (GB) by St. Albans
Patience
Hungary
1902
Bona Vista x (GB) Podagra (GB) by Galopin
Regulus
Great Britain
1739
Godolphin Arabian x Grey Robinson by Bald Galloway
St. Simon
Great Britain
1881
Galopin x St. Angela by King Tom
Moscona
Chile
1986
Mocito Guapo x Chispita by Chairman Walker
Alipes
Great Britain
1757
Regulus x Lusty by Locust[41]
American Eclipse
United States
1814
Duroc x Miller's Damsel by Messenger
Bullets Fever
United States
2013
Fiber Sonde x Ghost Canyon, by Indian Charlie
Caracalla
France
1942
Tourbillon x Astronomie by Asterus
La Cressonniere
France
2013
Le Havre x Absolute Lady by Galileo
Maruzensky
Japan

1974
Nijinsky II x Shill by Buckpasser
Sweetbriar
 Great Britain
 1769
 Syphon x mare (1763), by Shakespeare[45]
Tiffin
 Great Britain
 1926
 Tetratema x Dawn-wind, by Sunstar
Sensations
 United States
 1877
 Leamington x Susan Beane, by Lexington
Rare Brick
 United States
 1983
 Rare Performer x Windy Brick, by Mr. Brick
Derek
 Brazil
 1978
 Kublai Khan x Epinette, by Blackamoor
Cluster of Stars
 United States
 2009
 Greely's Galaxy x Babyurthegreatest, by Honour and Glory
El Rio Rey
 United States
 1887
 Norfolk x Marian by Malcolm
Kitano Dai O
 Japan
 1965
 Die Hard x Kitano Hikari by Tosa Midori
Malt Queen
 Australia
 1905
 Maltster x Her Majesty by Sunrise
Mannamead
 Great Britain
 1929
 Manna x Pinprick by Torpoint

Perdita II
Great Britain
1881
Hampton x Hermione by Young Melbourne
The Tetrarch
Ireland
1911
Roi Herode (FR) x Vahren by Bona Vista
Zarkava
Ireland
2005
Zamindar (USA) x Zarkasha by Kahyasi
Rodolph
United States
1831
either Sir Archy Montorio or Sir Archy x Haxall's Moses Mare, by Haxall's
Moses
Monarch
United States
1834
Priam x Delphine, by Whisker
Salvator
France
1872
Dollar x Sauvagine, by Ion
Viani
Italy
1967
Acropolis x Violante Vanni, by Yorick
Itajara
Brazil
1983
Felicio x Apple Honey, by Falkland
Bay Middleton
Great Britain
1833
Sultan x Cobweb by Phantom
Bustin Stones
United States
2004
City Zip x Shesasurething by Prospectors Gamble

Candy Ride
Argentina
1999
Ride The Rails (USA) x Candy Girl by Candy Stripes (USA)
Cavaliere d'Arpino
Italy
1926
Havresac II (FR) x Chuette (GB) by Cicero
Claude
Italy
1964
Hornbeam (GB) x Aigue-Vive (FR) by Vatellor
Flying Childers
Great Britain
1714
Darley Arabian x Betty Leedes by Wharton's Careless
Hurry On
Great Britain
1913
Marcovil x Tout Suite by Sainfoin
Justify
United States
2015
Scat Daddy x Stage Magic by Ghostzapper. Triple Crown winner.
Quintessence
Great Britain
1900
St. Frusquin x Margarine by Petrarch
Tolgus
Great Britain
1923
Stefan the Great x Rosa Croft by Lemberg
Dismal
Great Britain
1733
Godolphin Arabian x Alcock Arabian Mare, by Alcock's Arabian
Aldford
Great Britain
1911
Mauvezin x Mangalmi, by William the Third
Payaso
Argentina

1929

Re-Echo x Payasada, by Pippermint

Albany Girl

Great Britain

1935

Duncan Gray x Vestalia, by Abbot's Trace

Windsor Slipper

Ireland

1939

Windsor Lad x Carpet Slipper, by Phalaris

Manantial

Argentina

1955

Gulf Stream x Magda, by Full Sail

Amianto

Argentina

1888

Zanoni x Mariana by Chivalrous

Ajax

France

1901

Flying Fox x Amie by Clamart

Dice

United States

1925

Dominant x Frumpery by Chicle

Emerson

Brazil

1958

Coaraze (FR) x Empenosa by Full Sail (GB)

Fasliyev

Ireland

1997

Nureyev x Mr P's Princess by Mr. Prospector

Husson

Argentina

2003

Hussonet (USA) ex Villa Elisa (CHI) by Roy

Kneller

Great Britain

1985

Lomond x Fruition by Rheingold

Landaluce
United States
1980
Seattle Slew x Strip Poker by Bold Bidder. Champion 2yo filly

Landgraf
Germany
1914
Louviers (GB) x Ladora (GB) by Ladas

Norfolk
United States
1861
Lexington x Novice by Glencoe (GB)

Precocious
Great Britain
1981
Mummy's Pet x Mrs Moss by Reform

Reset
Australia
2000
Zabeel x Assertive Lass by Zeditave

Teofilo
Ireland
2004
Galileo x Speirbhean by Danehill

Queen's Logic
Ireland
1999
Grand Lodge x Lagrion by Diesis

Albert
Great Britain
1827
Moses x Varennes, by Selim

Frontin
France
1880
George Frederick x Frolicsome, by Weatherbit

Pazman
Austria
1916
Pardon x Patrie, by Gaga

Melody

Argentina
1947
Meadow x Elegy, by Rustom Pasha
Paddy's Sister
Ireland
1957
Ballyogan x Birthday Wood, by Bois Roussel
Eileen's Choice
Great Britain
1967
Tin Whistle x Belle Cigale, by Beau Sabreur
Star Shower
Australia
1976
Star of Heaven x Show, by Novalis
Perigord
Peru
1954
Pertinaz x Pattern, by Borealis
Nadal
United States
2017
Blame x Ascending Angel by Pulpit
Agnes Tachyon
Japan
1998
Sunday Silence x Agnes Flora by Royal Ski. Won Satsuki Sho.
Catchascatchcan
Great Britain
1995
Pursuit of Love x Catawba by Mill Reef. Yorkshire Oaks.
Drone
United States
1966
Sir Gaylord x Cap and Bells by Tom Fool. Notable broodmare sire.
Fuji Kiseki
Japan
1992
Sunday Silence x Millracer by Le Fabuleux. Champion two-year-old.
Golden Fleece
United States

1979

Nijinsky II (CAN) x Exotic Treat by Vaguely Noble. Won Epsom Derby.

Lammtarra

United States

1992

Nijinsky II (CAN) x Snow Bride by Blushing Groom. Three Group 1 victories.

Madelia

France

1974

Caro x Moonmadness by Tom Fool. French champion 3yo filly.

Mastery

United States

2014

Candy Ride x Steady Course by Old Trieste. Cash Call Futurity.

Raise a Native

United States

1961

Native Dancer x Raise You by Case Ace. Champion two-year-old colt and noted sire.

Snap

Great Britain

1750

Snip x Sister to Slipby by Fox. Noted sire.

Vindication

United States

2000

Seattle Slew x Strawberry Reason by Strawberry Road. Breeders' Cup Juvenile.

White Moonstone

United States

2008

Dynaformer x Desert Gold by Seeking the Gold. Fillies Mile.

Tennessee Oscar

United States

1814

Wilke's Wonder x Rosy Clack, by Saltram

Clairvaux

Great Britain

1880

Hermit x Devotion, by Stockwell

Magus

Austria-Hungary
1891
Ercildoune x Mascotte, by Forbidden Fruit

Ball's Florizel
United States
1801
Diomed x Atkinson's Shark Mare, by Shark

Saphir
Austria-Hungary
1894
Chamant x Sappho, by Wisdom

Morazzona
Italy
1939
Cameronian x Milldoria, by Milton

Ocarina
France
1947
Bubbles x Montagnana, by Brantôme

Pharsalia
Great Britain
1954
Panorama x Verdura, by Court Martial

Blood Royal
Ireland
1971
Ribot x Natashka, by Dedicate

Saratoga Six
United States
1982
Alydar x Priceless Fame, by Irish Castle

Kantharos
United States
2008
Lion Heart x Contessa Halo, by Southern Halo

Army Mule
United States
2014
Friesian Fire x Crafty Toast by Crafty Professor. Carter Handicap.

Blue Train
Great Britain

1944
Blue Peter x Sun Chariot (IRE) by Hyperion
Boniform
New Zealand
1904
Multiform x Otterden (GB) by Sheen
Cobweb
Great Britain
1821
Phantom x Filagree by Soothsayer. Winner of 1000 Guineas and Oaks.
Danzig
United States
1977
Northern Dancer (CAN) x Pas De Nom by Admiral's Voyage. Leading sire.
Footstepsinthesand
Ireland
2002
Giant's Causeway x Glatisant by Rainbow Quest. Won 2000 Guineas.
Meadowlake
United States
1983
Hold Your Peace x Suspicious Native by Raise a Native. G1 winner.
Pharis
France
1936
Pharos (GB) x Carissima by Clarissimus. Noted sire.
Quorto
Ireland
2016
Dubawi x Volume, by Mount Nelson
Pronto
Argentina
1958
Timor x Prosperina by Gusty
Valyra
Great Britain
2008
Azamour x Valima by Linamix
In Tune
United States
2011
Unbridled's Song x Wichitoz by Affirmed. G2 winner

11. KENTUCKY DERBY WINNERS

1875 - Aristides   Oliver Lewis

1876 - Vagrant   Robert. Swim

1877 - Baden-Baden   William. Walker

1878 - Day Star   James. Carter

1879 - Lord Murphy   C. Shauer

1880 - Fonso   G. Lewis

1881 - Hindoo   J. McLaughlin

1882 - Apollo   Babe. Hurd

1883 - Leonatus   William. Donohue

1884 - Buchanan   Isaac. Murphy

1885 - Joe Cotton   Erskine. Henderson

1886 - Ben Ali   P. Duffy

1887 - Montrose   I. Lewis

1888 - Macbeth II   G. Covington

1889 - Spokane   T. Kiley

1890 - Riley   Isaac. Murphy

1891 - Kingman   Isaac. Murphy

1892 - Azra   Alonzo Clayton

1893 - Lookout   E. Kunze

1894 - Chant   F. Goodale

1895 - Halma   J. Perkins

1896 - Ben Brush   W. Simms

1897 - Typhoon II   F. Garner

1898 - Plaudit   W. Simms

1899 - Manuel   F. Taral

1900 - Lieut. Gibson   J. Boland

1901 - His Eminence   J. Winkfield

1902 - Alan-a-Dale   J. Winkfield

1903 - Judge Himes   H. Booker

1904 - Elwood   F. Prior

1905 - Agile   J. Martin

1906 - Sir Huon   R. Troxler

1907 - Pink Star   A. Mindei

1908 - Stone Street   A. Pickens

1909 - Wintergreen   V. Powers

1910 - Donau   F. Herbert

1911 - Meridian   G. Archibald

1912 - Worth   C.H. Shilling

1913 - Donerail   R. Goose

1914 - Old Rosebud   J. McCabe

1915 - Regret   J. Nolter

1916 - George Smith   J. Loftus

1917 - Omar Khayyam   C. Borel

1918 - Exterminator   W. Knapp

1919 - Sir Barton   J. Loftus

1920 - Paul Jones   T. Rice

1921 - Behave Yourself   C. Thompson

1922 - Morvich   A. Johnson

1923 - Zev   E. Sande

1924 - Black Gold   J.D. Mooney

1925 - Flying Ebony   E. Sande

1926 - Bubbling Over   A. Johnson

1927 - Whiskery   L. McAtee

1928 - Reigh Count   C. Lang

1929 - Clyde Van Dusen   L. McAtee

1930 - Gallant Fox   E. Sande

1931 - Twenty Grand   C. Kurtsinger

1932 - Burgoo King   E. James

1933 - Brokers Tip   D. Meade

1934 - Cavalcade   M. Garner

1935 - Omaha   W. Saunders

1936 - Bold Venture   I. Hanford

1937 - War Admiral   C. Kurtsinger

1938 - Lawrin   E. Arcaro

1939 - Johnstown   J. Scout

1940 - Gallahadion   C. Bierman

1941 - Whirlaway   E. Arcaro

1942 - Shut Out   W.D. Wright

1943 - Count Fleet   J. Longden

1944 - Pensive   C. McCreary

1945 - Hoop Jr.   E. Arcaro

1946 - Assault   W. Mehrtens

1947 - Jet Pilot   E. Guerin

1948 - Citation   E. Arcaro

1949 - onder   S. Brooks

1950 - Middleground   W. Boland

1951 - Count Turf   C. McCreary

1952 - Hill Gail   E. Arcaro

1953 - Dark Star   H. Moreno

1954 - Determine   R. York

SULTAN ZESHAN

955 - Swaps   W. Shoemaker

1956 - Needles   D. Erb

1957 - Iron Liege   W. Hartack

1958 - Tim Tam   I. Valenzuela

1959 - Tomy Lee   W. Shoemaker

1960 - Venetian Way   W. Hartack

1961 - Carry Back   J. Sellers

1962 - Decidedly   W. Hartack

1963 - Chateaugay   B. Baeza

1964 - Northern Dancer   W. Hartack

1965 - Lucky Debonair   W. Shoemaker

1966 - Kauai King   D. Brumfield

1967 - Proud Clarion   R. Ussery

1968 - Forward Pass1   I. Valenzuela

1969 - Majestic Prince   W. Hartack

1970 - Dust Commander   M. Manganello

1971 - Canonero II   G. Avila

1972 - Riva Ridge   R. Turcotte

1973 - Secretariat   R. Turcotte

1974 - Cannonade   A. Cordero, Jr.

1975 - Foolish Pleasure   J. Vasquez

1976 - Bold Forbes   A. Cordero, Jr.

1977 - Seattle Slew   J. Cruguet

1978 - Affirmed   S. Cauthen

1979 - Spectacular Bid   R. Franklin

1980 - Genuine Risk   J. Vasquez

1981   Pleasant Colony   J. Velasquez

1982   Gato del Sol   E. Delahoussaye

1983 - Sunny's Halo   E. Delahoussaye

1984 - Swale   L. Pincay

1985 - Spend a Buck   A. Cordero, Jr.

1986 - Ferdinand   W. Shoemaker

1987 - Alysheba   C. McCarron

1988 - Winning Colors   G. Stevens

1989 - Sunday Silence   P. Valenzuela

1990 - Unbridled   C. Perret

1991 - Strike the Gold   C. Antley

1992 - Lil E. Tee   P. Day

1993 - Sea Hero   J. Bailey

1994 - Go For Gin   C. McCarron

1995 - Thunder Gulch   G. Stevens

1996 - Grindstone   J. Bailey

1997 - Silver Charm   G. Stevens

1998 - Real Quiet   K. Desormeaux

1999 - Charismatic   C. Antley

2000 - Fusaichi Pegasus   K. Desormeaux

2001 - Monarchos   J. Chavez

2002 - War Emblem   V. Espinoza

2003 - Funny Cide   J. Santos

2004 - Smarty Jones   S. Elliott

2005 - Giacomo   M. Smith

2006 - Barbaro   E. Prado

2007 - Street Sense   C. Borel

2008 - Big Brown   K. Desormeaux

2009 - Mine That Bird   C. Borel

2010 - Super Saver   C. Borel

2011 - Animal Kingdom   J. Velazquez

2012 - I'll Have Another   M. Gutierrez

2013 - Orb   J. Rosario

2014 - California Chrome   V. Espinoza

2015 - American Pharoah   V. Espinoza

2016 - Nyquist   M. Gutierrez

2017 - Always Dreaming   J. Velazquez

2018 - Justify   M. Smith

2019 - Country House3   F. Prat

2020 - Authentic   J. Velazquez

2021 - Mandaloun4   F. Geroux

2022 - Rich Strike   S. Leon

1. The initial winner, Dancer's Image, was disqualified.

2. Fastest time--1 min 59 2/5 sec.

3. The initial winner, Maximum Security, was disqualified.

4. The initial winner, Medina Spirit, was disqualified.

12. TRIPLE CROWN WINNERS

Year: 1919
Horse: Sir Barton
Jockey: Johnny Loftus
Trainer: H. Guy Bedwell
Owner: J. K. L. Ross
Breeder: John E. Madden

Year: 1930
Horse: Gallant Fox
Jockey: Earl Sande
Trainer: Jim Fitzsimmons
Owner: Belair Stud
Breeder: Belair Stud

Year: 1935
Horse: Omaha
Jockey: Willie "Smokey" Saunders
Trainer: Jim Fitzsimmons
Owner: Belair Stud
Breeder: Belair Stud

Year: 1937
Horse: War Admiral
Jockey: Charles Kurtsinger
Trainer: George Conway
Owner: Samuel D. Riddle
Breeder: Samuel D. Riddle

Year: 1941
Horse: Whirlaway

Jockey: Eddie Arcaro
Trainer: Ben A. Jones
Owner: Calumet Farm
Breeder: Calumet Farm

Year: 1943
Horse: Count Fleet
Jockey: Johnny Longden
Trainer: Don Cameron
Owner: Fannie Hertz
Breeder: Fannie Hertz

Year: 1946
Horse: Assault
Jockey: Warren Mehrtens
Trainer: Max Hirsch
Owner: King Ranch
Breeder: King Ranch

Year: 1948
Horse: Citation
Jockey: Eddie Arcaro
Trainer: Horace A. "Jimmy" Jones
Owner: Calumet Farm
Breeder: Calumet Farm

Year: 1973
Horse: Secretariat
Jockey: Ron Turcotte
Trainer: Lucien Laurin
Owner: Meadow Stable
Breeder: Meadow Stable

Year: 1977
Horse: Seattle Slew
Jockey: Jean Cruguet
Trainer: William H. Turner Jr.
Owner: Mickey and Karen L. Taylor, Tayhill Stable/Jim Hill, et al.
Breeder: Ben S. Castleman

Year: 1978
Horse: Affirmed
Jockey: Steve Cauthen
Trainer: Laz Barrera
Owner: Harbor View Farm
Breeder: Harbor View Farm

Year: 2015
Horse Name: American Pharoah
Jockey: Victor Espinoza
Trainer: Bob Baffert
Owner: Ahmed Zayat
Breeder: Ahmed Zayat

Year: 2018
Horse: Justify
Jockey: Mike Smith
Trainer: Bob Baffert
Owner: China Horse Club, Head of Plains Partners, Starlight Racing, WinStar Farm
Breeder: John D. Gunther

13. Chronological Timeline

1809   Birth of President Abraham Lincoln in Kentucky, USA.

1820   Birth of Ansel Williamson c. 1806 - c.1820

1825   Birth of Abe Hawkins

1842   Birth of trainer Abraham Perry

1850   Birth of Lexington (horse)

1850   Birth of Edward Dudley Brown. Trainer and jockey Edward Dudley Brown is born into slavery on March 17

1850   The horse Lexington, who will eventually sire the undefeated Asteroid among many other winners, was born on March 17. Lexington passed away on July 1, 1875.

1854   Duncan Farah Kenner, the owner of Ashland Plantation in Louisiana, purchases Abe Hawkins from Adam Bingaman for $2,350 in 1854.

1854   Black American jockey Abe Hawkins rides racehorse Lecomte to victory over Hall of Fame horse Lexington in world-record time. While working for Alexander Keene Richards, Ansel Williamson chooses Abe Hawkins to ride in races in New Orleans at the Metairie track. Hawkins's fame begins with the 1854 Great Post Stakes in New Orleans. Abe Hawkins, at Metairie Jockey Club, rides horse Lecomte, the namesake for the Lecomte Stakes, in January at fair grounds to world-record-setting victory over legendary Kentucky Thoroughbred, Lexington.

1855   On April 14, Abe Hawkins, riding Lecomte, defeated Gilpatrick, riding Lexington.

1856   Moses Fleetwood Walker was born in Mount Pleasant, Ohio.

1856   Jockey Oliver Lewis was born on December 22 in Fayette County in Lexington, Kentucky, to parents Goodson and Eleanor Lewis. Lewis has at least four siblings: Lena, Hattie, Mattie, and John. He eventually marries Lucy Wright.

1856   Moses Fleetwood Walker was born on October 7 in Mount Pleasant, Ohio, seven years before emancipation. Walker was born to

Moses W. Walker, a physician and later a Methodist Episcopal minister, and Caroline O' Harra Walker, a homemaker. Both parents are of mixed race.

1856   - The world welcomes the birth of Booker T. Washington, who would later establish the Tuskegee Normal and Industrial Institute (now Tuskegee University) in 1881 and the National Negro Business League two decades later.

1858   Legendary thoroughbred racehorse, Lexington, is sold to Robert Alexander for $15,000 in 1858, reportedly the then highest price ever paid for an American horse. Lexington is sent to Alexander's Woodburn Stud Farm at Spring Station, Kentucky. He stands for a price of $100 until 1861, when he first leads the sire list. Afterwards, his sire price increases to $200. Lexington eventually stands for a limited public fee of $500 in 1865 and 1866, the highest in the country and comparable to the leading English stallions, before being restricted to private stud duties only. Called "the Blind Hero of Woodburn," Lexington became the leading sire in North America sixteen times from 1861 through 1874, and then again in 1876 and 1878. Lexington sired the undefeated Thoroughbreds Asteroid and Norfolk. Nine of the first fifteen Travers Stakes are won by his sons or daughters.

1859   - Tom Bass, a renowned Black Saddle Horse Trainer, is born in Boone County, Missouri. Bass would go on to train the influential Saddlebred stallion Rex McDonald, as well as horses owned by Buffalo Bill Cody, Theodore Roosevelt, and Will Rogers.

1860   Baseball player Weldy Wilberforce Walker was born in Steubenville, Ohio. Weldy Walker was born on July 27. He goes on to become the second Black American to play Major League baseball.

1860   Jockey William Walker was born in Versailles, Kentucky, in Woodford County.

1861   Abraham Lincoln becomes the United States' sixteenth president.

1861   The American Civil War begins on April 12. Abe Hawkins fights in the American Civil War.

1861   Thoroughbred racing is dealt a huge blow during the Civil War except in St. Louis Missouri

1861   Abe Hawkins disappears from public records.

1861   Jockey Isaac Burns Murphy was born on January 16, 1861, Fayette County, Lexington, Kentucky. Isaac was born to Jerry Skillman who was part of the Union Army. Skillman passes away July 27, 1865 (aged 30–31) and is Buried in Camp Nelson National Cemetery. His mother's name was America Murphy.

1862   Jockey George Garrett Davis Lewis was born in Fayette County, Lexington, Kentucky to Henry and Mary Lewis. He is one of eight children. His siblings are named Mary, Martha, Isaac (who was also a jockey), Sallie, Oscar, Lutita, and Martin.

1862   The Union raids and attacks Duncan Kenner's Ashland plantation where Abe Hawkins used to live in Baton Rouge, Louisiana on July 27. Duncan Kenner flees. Abe Hawkins flees as well.

1863   President Abraham Lincoln issued the Emancipation Proclamation on January 1.

1863   The Saratoga Springs racetrack opens in Saratoga, New York on August 3.

1863   - Daniel Payne becomes the first Black American to preside over a college, Wilberforce University in Ohio, when it comes under the control of the African Methodist Episcopal Church.

1864   On May 14, Abe Hawkins reappears in Kentucky after spending time in Louisville.

1864   Jockey Erskine "Babe" Henderson was born in Versailles, Kentucky.

1864   Artist Painter Edward Troye paints Ansel Williamson and Edward Dudley Brown with the "Undefeated" Asteroid.

1864   Edward Dudley Brown, at age 14, rides in his first ever race and wins aboard a colt named Asteroid. The race was held in St. Louis, Missouri in May. Asteroid is given the title 'the Undefeated Asteroid'.

1865   Abe Hawkins wins races in Kentucky and in Paterson. Then he wins four more times at Saratoga in August.

1865   Sue Mundy along with the Guerilla rebels raid and attack the village of Midway, KY. They burn down the railroad station, rob its residents, and steal 15 prized thoroughbred horses owned by Robert Alexander of Woodburn Stable. Ansel Williamson saves Asteroid from the Confederate guerrilla raids by convincing them to take a lesser horse.

1865   The American Civil War ends on April 9. All slaves are emancipated.

1865   President Abraham Lincoln was assassinated on April 4th in Washington, DC.

1865 Edward Dudley Brown, Ansel Williamson, and Abe Hawkins, are now officially free men who can earn money for their labor. They were able to live on their own and have rights. Abe Hawkins chooses to live on Woodburn farm with stable owner Robert Alexander.

1865 - Every southern state passes Black Codes that restrict the Freedmen, emancipated but not yet full citizens. The Freedmen's Bureau blocks the enforcement of these laws.

1865 – The American Missionary Association establishes Atlanta University.

1865 - Shaw University (Institute), the first historically Black institution of higher education in the South, is established in Raleigh, North Carolina.

1866 Jockey Anthony "Tony" Hamilton was born in South Carolina.

1866 Ansel Williamson trains the horse Merrill, who Abe Hawkins rides to victory in the third Travers Stakes

1866 Abe Hawkins wins the Jerome Stakes on October 2.

1866 Jockey Babe Hurd was born on June 1, 1866, in Texas.

1866 - Returning black Union soldiers found Lincoln Institute, later renamed Lincoln University.

1866 The Civil Rights Act of 1866 was passed, establishing that all persons born in the United States are now citizens.

1866 In Pulaski, Tennessee, six former Confederate officers - Frank McCord, Richard Reed, John Lester, John Kennedy, J. Calvin Jones, and James Crowe - establish the first chapter of the Ku Klux Klan on Christmas Eve in 1865, casting a dark shadow over the town.

1867 Jockey Isaac Lewis was born in Hutchinson, Kentucky.

1867 A newspaper falsely reports the passing of Abe Hawkins. After two weeks, the St. Louis Republican reports, "A Race Rider Reads His Obituary and Is Delighted," as Abe found the false article humorous.

1867 May 27, Abe Hawkins competes in a race in Cincinnati.

1867 Abe Hawkins passed away on June 8, allegedly from tuberculosis. He is laid to rest on Ashland Plantation in Baton Rouge, Louisiana. He is buried in a brick tomb under a live oak tree near what must have been his favorite part of the plantation. Duncan F. Kenner has him buried overlooking the horse racing track on the plantation. The date on his obituary records, June 8, 1867.

1867   Black entrepreneur Madam C. J. Walker born on December 23 in Delta, Louisiana. She passed away on May 25, 1919, in Irvington, New York.

1867   The first Belmont Stakes was held on June 19 at Jerome Park in the Bronx, New York. A few years later The race moved to Belmont Park, New York.

1867   Robert Alexander, Woodburn stable owner, passed away on December 1.

1867   Howard University is founded in Washington, D.C., with funding from the federal government.

1868   The world sees the birth of William Edward B. Du Bois.

1869   The Cincinnati Red Stockings became America's first professional baseball club.

1870   Baseball athletes Moses Fleetwood Walker and Weldy Walker attend Steubenville High School in the early days just after the community passes legislation for racial integration. Fleetwood excels in school and takes college preparatory classes.

1870   Edward D. Brown accepts an offer to ride for Daniel Swigert's new stable. He won the Belmont Stakes aboard Kingfisher. Edward D. Brown's most notable wins occur in 1870 aboard Kingfisher, a Thoroughbred trained by fellow Black American horseman Raleigh Colston Sr. Together, they win the 1870 Belmont Stakes, Travers Stakes, and Champion Stakes.

1870   Jockey Willie Simms was born on January 16 in Augusta, GA.

1870   The Fifteenth Amendment to the US Constitution was ratified on February 3. The amendment gives Black American men the right to vote by declaring that the "right of citizens of the United States to vote shall not be denied or abridged by the United States or by any state on account of race, color, or previous condition of servitude."

1870   Trainer Ansel Williamson marries Ellen on October 29. They have a daughter and grandchildren. His grandsons work with Thoroughbred horses in New York, New Jersey, and Kentucky according to the Fayette County Clerk.

1870   Hiram Rhodes Revels becomes the first black member of the Senate, and Joseph Rainey becomes the first black member of the U.S. House of Representatives.

1871   Black jockey George "Spider" Anderson is born in Baltimore, Maryland - to Charles and Ellen Anderson. He has four siblings.

1871   Jockey Shelby "Pike" Barnes was born in June to Joseph and Susan (Austin) Barnes in Beaver Dam, Kentucky. Barnes begins riding horses when he is fourteen years old. He may have had as many as seven siblings.

1871   The National Association of Professional BaseBall Players was established as the sport's first "Major League."

1872   Meriweather Lewis Clark Jr. leases 80 acres of land in Louisville, Kentucky from his uncles, John, and Henry Churchill.

1873   The First Preakness Stakes was run on May 27 at Pimlico Racecourse in Maryland.

1874   The Louisville Jockey Club was founded by Meriwether Lewis Clark Jr., who leased 80 acres of land for a racetrack from his uncles John and Henry Churchill.

1874   The first public notice establishing horse racetrack Churchill Downs is reported in the May edition of the Courier-Journal.

1874   With his vast knowledge of Thoroughbreds, Edward Dudley Brown switched careers to train Swigert's horses.

1875   On May 17th, the inaugural Kentucky Derby race was held. Racehorse Aristides runs 1.5 miles to win against 15 competing racehorses in front of 10,000 spectators.

1875   Trainer Ansel Williamson wins the Belmont Stakes with Robert Swim riding Calvin in New York.

1875   At the Belmont Stakes in New York, jockey Oliver Lewis riding Aristides won second place behind Robert Swim, riding racehorse Calvin trained by Ansel Williamson

1875   Horse Lexington passes away July 1. In 1875, Lexington was part of the first group of horses inducted into the National Museum of Racing and Hall of Fame. The Belmont Lexington Stakes runs every year at Belmont Park in honor of Lexington, as does the Lexington Stakes at Keeneland Racecourse. On Tuesday, August 31, 2010, the Smithsonian loaned Lexington's skeleton to the International Museum of the Horse at the Kentucky Horse Park to be exhibited there through August 2013. Lexington serves as the model for the top of the Woodlawn Vase, given to the winner of the Preakness Stakes at Pimlico. Lexington earned a total of $51,700 during his lifetime.

1875   Jockey William Billy Walker places fourth in the first

Kentucky Derby at age fifteen.

1875   Nineteen-year-old jockey Oliver Lewis rides Aristides and wins the inaugural Kentucky Derby on May 17 in front of 10,00 fans, racing 1.5 miles in 2.37 secs.

1876   Alonzo Lonnie Clayton was born in Kansas City, Kansas on January 4th. Parents were Robert and Evaline Clayton and he had 8 siblings.

1876   Jockey William Billy Walker finishes in eighth place at the Kentucky Derby after being driven off the track.

1876   On February 2, 1876, the National League of Professional Baseball Clubs, which came to be more commonly known as the National League (NL), was formed. The American League (AL) was established in 1901 and the first World Series was held in 1903.

1876   The National Baseball League is established. The first official game of baseball in the United States takes place in June in Hoboken, New Jersey. Five years later, in 1876, Chicago businessman William Hulbert forms the National League of Professional Baseball Clubs to replace the National Association, which he believes is mismanaged and corrupt. The National League begins with eight original members: the Boston Red Stockings (now the Atlanta Braves), Chicago White Stockings (now the Chicago Cubs), Cincinnati Red Stockings, Hartford Dark Blues, Louisville Grays, Mutual of New York, Philadelphia Athletics, and the St. Louis Brown Stockings.

1876   Black horse trainer James Williams wins first place training Vagrant.

1876   The Hamburg Massacre occurs when locals riot against African Americans trying to celebrate the Fourth of July. African American Police Chief James Cook and five other freemen are killed.

1877   Moses Fleetwood Walker is admitted into Oberlin College for the fall 1878 semester.

1877   Abraham Perry placed fifth to horse Baden-Baden in the May 22 Kentucky Derby but came back less than a week later to defeat Baden-Baden in the May 28 Clark Handicap at Churchill Downs.

1877   Edward Dudley Brown conditions trained Kentucky Derby winner Baden-Baden who won the 1877 Kentucky Derby with Jockey William Billy Walker.

1877   Jockey William Billy Walker wins the Kentucky Derby riding Baden-Baden.

1878   February 28, Edward Dudley Brown marries Lucy Alexander Gaines in Woodford County. They have one son together named Lee Lovelle.

1878   Isaac Murphy is suspended from horse racing in Cincinnati after being accused of slashing another jockey with his whip.

1878   James Carter wins the Kentucky Derby riding racehorse Day Star on May 21.

1878   Moses Fleetwood Walker begins school at Oberlin College where he majors in philosophy and arts. The slender, handsome Walker, with his affability and athletic prowess, is popular on campus.

1878   On June 19, the first motion picture was filmed depicting a Black American jockey riding a Thoroughbred racehorse. The jockey is known as the first ever movie star.

1879   Black Jockey James "Soup" Perkins was born in Lexington, Kentucky in April.

1879   White-passing baseball player William Edward White plays in the Major League for the Providence Grays on June 21.

1879   Isaac Burns Murphy wins the Travers Stakes riding Falsetto. One of the racing reporters writes, on Murphy's win: "He came home like a hurricane." Another writes: "He has a steady hand, a quick eye, a cool head, and a bold heart."

1880   Abraham Perry married Clara Taylor on March 1 and lives at 216 Eastern Avenue in Lexington, Kentucky, which still stands to this day. They have two children: a son and a daughter. Their son, Abraham Murphy Perry, graduated from Howard University and became a physician. Their daughter graduates from Fisk University with a music degree.

1880   Jockey George Garrett wins the Kentucky Derby riding Fonso, but passes away on July 10 in Station, Kentucky, at just eighteen years old.

1880   Moses Fleetwood Walker played baseball at Oberlin College from 1878–1881 and became the star athlete of his team as a catcher. Walker gains stardom and is mentioned in the school newspaper, the Oberlin Review, because of his ball-handling skills and ability to hit long home runs.

1881   Moses Fleetwood Walker plays in all five games for the new varsity baseball team at Oberlin.

1881   Weldy Walker enrolls in Oberlin's preparatory school to join his brother.

1881   Ansel Williamson passed away on June 18, 1881. He passed away at the age of seventy-one in Lexington Kentucky.

1881   Edward Dudley Brown started training horses for other owners including Black American Milton Young, the fifth leading horse owner in 1881.

1881   Moses Fleetwood Walker experiences his first moment of racial prejudice. In the summer of 1881, he signed with the white sewing machine club to earn extra money. In August, Walker's team travels south to play against the Louisville (Kentucky) Eclipse. Racial discrimination keeps him from eating breakfast with his team at a hotel and prevented from playing. When they arrive in Louisville, Kentucky, he is denied a hotel stay and service at a restaurant. The opposing team, Eclipse Club, refuses to play until Walker is removed from the roster to play for the team because of his skin color. Both team owners argue and Fleetwood is benched. The crowd boos the decision to bench Fleet until the opposing team's owner walks across the field and invites Walker to play, but Walker doesn't want to play after the way he has been treated. The crowd convinces Fleet to play, and when he rejoins, he is met with a standing ovation. Two white players walk off the field, refusing to play with a Black man. Fleetwood is benched again. After one inning, his substitute claims his hands are too badly bruised to continue, and Walker hesitantly walks onto the field for warm-ups. Louisville again protests and refuses to resume play until Cleveland's third baseman volunteers to go behind the plate.

1881   Stable owner H. P. McGrath passes away.

1881   Booker T. Washington establishes a school in Tuskegee, Alabama, and becomes its principal.

1882   Moses Fleetwood Walker marries his college sweetheart, Bella Taylor.

1882   Isaac Murphy rides at the Coney Island Jockey Club on Ed Corrigan's Pearl Jennings.

1882   Jockey Babe Hurd wins the Kentucky Derby riding Apollo. Babe Hurd's record win stands for 136 years. It is not matched until 2018, when Justify, a horse that had not raced as a two-year-old, wins the Kentucky Derby.

1882   Jockey Jimmy Winkfield was born on April 12 in Andover Hills, Kentucky.

1882   Moses Fleetwood Walker is offered a deal to play at the University of Michigan Ann Arbor. He accepts and becomes a Michigan wolverine. His girlfriend, Bella Taylor, who is pregnant, accompanies him to Michigan, where Walker decides to study law. He marries Taylor a year later and they have a son together.

1883   The Toledo Blue Stockings, a charter franchise, is founded in the Northwestern League. Weldy Walker joins the Toledo Blue Stockings. Cap Anson lobbies to get Fleet Walker thrown out of the game.

1883   Isaac Murphy wins the Hindoo Stakes.

1883   Racehorse Leonatus wins the Kentucky Derby. In the early 1900s, the term "Churchill Downs" refers to the racecourse where the Kentucky Derby is held.

1883   George B. Anderson rode his first race at Baltimore and Brighton Beach.

1883   Isaac Burns Murphy places an ad in the newspaper promoting his services in the Kentucky Livestock Record. Soon after, he receives an offer and signs a contract to ride for Eric J. Baldwin. Though he never has children, he has many friends, among them fellow jockey Anthony Hamilton. Anthony Hamilton's wedding reception becomes a gala event at the Murphys' Lexington home.

1883   Jockey Sir Isaac Burns Murphy marries Lucy Osborn in Frankfort county. They purchased an estate on Megowan Street in Lexington. Journalist Lynn Renau describes the reception: The festivities began at noon and ended at midnight. Except for a smattering of doctors and a professor, the notables were all Derby-caliber riders—Isaac Lewis, Thomas Britton, William Walker (Murphy's life-long friend), Edward Brown, Raleigh Colston, George Smith and Anthony Hamilton, a South Carolina native who had trained under English jockey-turned-trainer William Lakeland. Anthony Hamilton later rode in Europe and passed away of Tuberculosis, also referred to as consumption, aboard his private railroad car in Germany.

1883   Moses Fleetwood Walker is offered a position from Northwestern to join the Toledo Blue Stockings for the 1884 season. Before he could appear in a game, the executive committee of the Northwestern League debated a motion proposed by a representative of the Peoria Illinois club that would prohibit all ball players of color from entering the league. After intense arguments, the motion is dropped, allowing Fleet to play.

1883   Moses Fleetwood Walker leaves the University of Michigan.

1883   Raleigh Colston, a Black horse trainer, wins first place as a horse trainer for Leonatus.

1884   Moses Fleetwood Walker plays for the Toledo Blue Stockings and makes his debut in Major League baseball. Weldy Walker plays for the Toledo Blue Stockings and makes his debut in Major League baseball. Weldy Walker plays for the Toledo Blue Stockings and makes his last appearance in Major League baseball. Fleet Walker plays for the Toledo Blue Stockings and makes his last appearance in Major League baseball.

1884   Isaac Murphy wins the Kentucky Derby and the American Derby.

1884   Horse stable owner H. P. McGrath sells his estate and jockey Oliver Lewis loses his employer.

1884   Jockey Isaac Burns Murphy wins his first Kentucky Derby on William Cottrill's horse, Buchanan, who was trained by Black American William Bird. He then wins the first American Derby at Chicago's Washington Park on Corrigan's Thoroughbred horse Modesty.

1884   Not yet fully recovered from a rib injury sustained in July, Moses Fleetwood Walker was released by the Blue Stockings on September 22. Toledo's team, under financial pressure at season's end, works to relieve themselves of their expensive contracts. During the offseason, Fleet takes a position as a mail clerk.

1884   The Blue Stockings' successful season in the Northwestern League prompted the team to transfer as a unit to the American Association, a Major League organization. Moses Fleetwood Walker makes his first appearance as a Major League ballplayer in an away game. Walker goes hitless in three at-bats and commits four errors in a 5–1 loss. Throughout the season, Walker regularly catches for ace pitcher Tony Mullane. Mullane, who describes the rookie ball player as "the best catcher I ever worked with," purposefully throws pitches that are not signaled just to cross up the catcher. Walker's year is plagued with injuries, limiting him to just 42 games in the 104-game season. He maintains a 0.263 BA, one of the top three in the league, but Toledo still finishes eighth in the pennant race. The rest of his team is also hampered by numerous injuries, and circumstances lead Walker's brother, Weldy to join the Blue Stockings for six games in the outfield.

1885   The Toledo Blue Stockings disbanded after the 1885 season. Moses Fleetwood Walker plays for the Minor baseball leagues.

1885   Isaac Murphy wins the Hindoo Stakes.

1885   Isaac Murphy wins the American Derby.

1885   Isaac Murphy wins his second American Derby on E. J. Baldwin's horse, Volante.

1885   Jockey Babe Hurd retired from riding in 1885 to begin a career as a trainer. He works at Garfield Park Racetrack in Chicago, Illinois, St. Louis Fair Grounds in St. Louis, Missouri, and Churchill Downs track in Louisville, Kentucky. He is employed by horse owners M. H. Tichenor, Frank Shaw, M. B. Gruber.

1885   Jockey Erskine "Babe" Henderson wins the Kentucky Derby riding Joe Cotton who was trained by Abraham Perry and owned by James T. Williams.

1885   Moses Fleetwood Walker returns to baseball, playing in the Western and Southern New England Leagues for eighteen games. He played eight games for Cleveland in the Western League and ten for Waterbury in the Southern New England League in the second half of 1885.

1886   Anthony Hamilton wins the Nursery Stakes and the Twin City Handicap.

1886   Isaac Murphy wins the Hindoo Stakes and the American Derby.

1886   Isaac Lewis races in his first Kentucky Derby and finishes fourth on Lijero.

1886   Thoroughbred racehorse known as The Undefeated Asteroid, is injured and passes away in November 1886.

1886   Edward Dudley Brown finishes second in the Kentucky Derby with Blue Wing, who is beaten by just a nose.

1886   Jockey Isaac Lewis wins his third American Derby on E. J. Baldwin's Thoroughbred, Silver Cloud.

1886   Many Black American horsemen during this era know each other and socialize together. Before the season's meets in 1886, the Perry's, Abe Abraham Perry, attend events in Louisville with Isaac Murphy and his wife Lucy. On one trip, the four are the guests of Mr. and Mrs. Sadonia Wrightson, prominent members of the Louisville Black American community.

1886   Moses Fleetwood Walker re-joins the Waterbury team in 1886 when the team joins the more competitive Eastern League.

1887   Anthony Hamilton wins the American Derby and the Gazelle Handicap.

1887   Isaac Murphy wins the Latonia Derby.

1887   James Jimmy Lee was born in Raceland, Louisiana.

1887   As racial segregation takes hold in professional baseball, Weldy joins the Pittsburgh Keystones of the short-lived National Colored BaseBall League.

1887   Isaac Murphy begins endorsing brands and appearing on products.

1887   Jockey Isaac Lewis enters the history books when he rides Montrose to victory in the Kentucky Derby by a margin of two lengths. He rode in two more Kentucky Derby races in 1888 and 1889, finishing fifth and sixth respectively. He continued his riding career well into the 1890s, winning the Great Western Handicap in 1888, and the Hyde Park Stakes and the Saratoga Cup in 1891. Lewis rode from an early age and won his first race when he was eleven years old.

1887   Moses Fleetwood Walker played in the International League for Newark, New Jersey until 1889.

1887   Slave owner Duncan Farrar Kenner passed away on July 3.

1888   Weldy Walker writes a letter to the league's president protesting the color line in baseball.

1888   Anthony Hamilton wins the Twin City Handicap and the St. Louis Derby.

1888   Isaac Murphy wins the American Derby.

1888   Isaac Lewis wins his fourth American Derby on E. J. Baldwin's Emperor of Norfolk.

1888   Despite a lackluster season for Waterbury, Moses Fleetwood Walker is offered a position with the defending champions, the Newark Little Giants, an International League team. Together with pitcher George Stovey, Walker forms half of the first Black American battery in organized baseball. Billed as the "Spanish battery" by fans, Stovey records thirty-five wins in the season, while Walker posts career highs in games played, fielding percentage, and BA. Walker followed Newark's manager Charlie Hackett to the Syracuse Stars in 1888. Although he falls into a slump at the plate during his two years playing for the Stars, he remains popular among Syracuse fans—so much so that Weldy W. Walker becomes their unofficial spokesman and establishes business ties in the city.

1888   Jockey Shelby "Pike" Barnes is established as a star in the Thoroughbred racing world. In 1888 alone, he achieved 206 total wins (the most of any jockey that year) and a 32.9% winning percentage (the highest of any jockey that year). He then competes in the Futurity Stakes which boasts the biggest prize purse of any race ever held in the country: $41,675. The race takes place on Labor Day Weekend at Sheepshead Bay Racetrack in Elmont, New York, with the largest attendance of any race held at that location. The Futurity Stakes highlights Barnes's talent, and Barnes, employed by Elias "Lucky" Baldwin, rides the horse Proctor Knott to a stunning victory in the inaugural event. He has a short but successful career.

1888   Weldy Walker writes an open letter to the Sporting Life protesting the racial segregation of baseball.

1889   Moses Fleetwood Walker retires from baseball.

1889   Anthony Hamilton wins the Hudson Stakes and the Twin City Handicap.

1889   Racehorse Spokane wins the Derby. And the racehorse Azra is born.

1889   Shelby "Pike" Barnes wins the Travers Stakes and Champagne Stakes.

1889   Jockey George B. Anderson wins the Preakness Stakes race aboard Buddhist. George B. "Spider" Anderson achieves his greatest life accomplishment by being the first Black American jockey to win the Preakness Stakes held at Pimlico Racecourse in Baltimore, Maryland, riding the horse Buddhist, owned by Sam Brown. He also won the Alabama Stakes in 1891 aboard the filly Sallie McClelland and the US Hotel Stakes that same year.

1889   Jockey Shelby Pike Barnes enjoys continued achievements for a few more years. In 1889 alone, he achieved 170 wins and a 25.7% win percentage. Other notable wins included: the Travers Stakes and Champagne Stakes in 1889, the Belmont Stakes, Brooklyn Derby, and Sheridan Stakes in 1890, and the Brooklyn Derby aboard Tenny in 1891.

1889   Moses Fleetwood Walker plays for Syracuse, New York On August 23, 1889, Syracuse releases the nearly thirty-three-year-old Walker because of his injuries and diminished skills. Walker is the last Black American to play in the International League, the highest level of the Minors, until Jackie Robinson played for Montreal in 1946. When the season ends, Walker reunites with Weldy in Cleveland to assume the proprietorship of the LeGrande House, an opera theater and hotel.

1890   Anthony Hamilton wins Monmouth Oaks, the Toboggan Handicap, the Juvenile Stakes, the Gazelle Handicap, and the Flatbush Stakes

1890   Isaac Murphy wins the Kentucky Derby.

1890   Alonzo Lonnie Clayton begins his professional horse racing career.

1890   Shelby "Pike" Barns won the Belmont Stakes, Brooklyn Derby, and Sheridan Stakes.

1890   Isaac Murphy wins his second Kentucky Derby on Ed Corrigan's Riley. Riding J. B. Haggin's Salvator, Isaac Murphy wins in a neck-and-neck race against the great horse jockey Ed "Snapper" Garrison. Isaac Murphy later beats segregationist Ed Garrison, riding Tenny, in a match race at the Suburban. At Monmouth Park, Murphy is accused of being drunk but is later exonerated and a plot to poison him is exposed.

1890   Jockey Alonzo "Lonnie" Clayton rode a horse named Redstone in his first race in 1890 at the Clifton track.

1890   Jockey Sir Isaac Burns Murphy wins the Kentucky Derby riding Riley trained by Edward Corrigan.

1891   Anthony Hamilton wins the Lawrence Realization Stakes, the Sapling Stakes, and the Tidal Stakes.

1891   Isaac Murphy wins the Kentucky Derby.

1891   Alonzo Lonnie Clayton wins the Champagne Stakes aboard racehorse Azra.

1891   George B. Anderson wins the Alabama Stakes aboard filly Sallie McClelland.

1891   Shelby Pike Barnes wins the Brooklyn Derby aboard Tenny.

1891   Moses Fleetwood Walker is involved in an altercation outside a saloon with a group of four white men shouting racial insults. Bricklayer Patrick "Curly" Murray, approaches Walker and reportedly throws a stone at his head, dazing him. Walker responds by fatally stabbing Murray with a pocketknife. A compliant Walker surrenders to police, claiming self-defense, but is charged with second-degree murder (lowered from first-degree murder).

1891   On June 3, Moses Fleetwood Walker is found not guilty of second-degree murder by an all-white jury, much to the delight of spectators in the courthouse. He returns to Steubenville to again work for the postal service, handling letters for the Cleveland and Pittsburgh Railroad. The same year, Walker is found guilty of mail robbery and is sentenced to one year in prison which he serves in Jefferson County Jail.

1891   Anthony Hamilton and Annie Messley are married on January 22, with the three-time Kentucky Derby-winning-rider Isaac Murphy serving as best man. The following day's Pittsburgh Daily Post details the impressive scope of the event: "For the occasion this evening the whole of the upper floor of the building was secured for the wedding. A swell caterer furnished the supper, and a florist had given the grand reception hall the appearance of a tropical flower garden."

1891   Jockey Anthony Hamilton and his bride, the former Annie L. Messley, attend an engagement party in their honor at the Murphys' estate in Lexington, Kentucky. The January 12 edition of the New York Times published a short notice from St. Louis explaining that "nearly two hundred invitations have been issued, and many guests from New York and other cities are coming ... Hamilton is said to be wealthy, and it is known that he has spent $1,000 in one jewelry house here for presents."

1891   James "Soup" Perkins, who received his nickname for his love of soup, began riding at the age of 11.

1891   Jockey Alonzo "Lonnie" Clayton earned his first career victory in 1891.

1891   Jockey Isaac Burns Murphy wins his third Kentucky Derby riding Kingman trained by Black horse owner and trainer Dudley Allen, who he met at an elite gathering in Kentucky.

1891   Jockey William Walker marries Hannah Estill. The two are honored with a reception at Isaac and Lucy Murphy's estate in June. They go on to have two children, William Jr., and Sadie.

1892   Anthony Hamilton won the Monmouth Invitational Handicap, the Swift Stakes, the Twin City Handicap, and the Great Trial Stakes.

1892   Alonzo Lonnie Clayton rides Azra to victory in the Kentucky Derby, which at age fifteen makes him the youngest jockey in history to ever win the Derby. Horse Halma is born.

1892   Jockey Alonzo Lonnie Clayton became the youngest jockey to win the Kentucky Derby at age fifteen, riding Azra, owned by Bashford Manor Stable and trained by John H. Morris.

1893   At thirteen years old, James Soup Perkins made his first appearance as a jockey at the Kentucky Association track. On the same day, He rides five horses to victory and finished second on another horse.

1893　Jockey Willie Simms wins back-to-back at the Belmont Stakes. In 1893 and 1894

1893　At age thirteen, James Soup Perkins made his first appearance as a jockey at the Kentucky Association track. He won five of the six races he rode that day and placed second in the sixth race. Out of the 26 starts in his first season, he placed first 16 times.

1893　Edward Dudley Brown wins as a trainer and horse owner when his horse, Etta, wins in the Kentucky Oaks.

1893　Jockey Alonzo "Lonnie" Clayton distinguishes himself by capturing the Churchill Downs jockey crown during the fall meet.

1893　The Murphy's celebrate their tenth wedding anniversary by renewing their vows and throwing a party at their Lexington home, attended by their friends from around the country, including the top Black jockeys in America.

1894　Anthony Hamilton wins the Twin City Handicap.

1894　Willie Simms wins the Belmont Stakes riding Henry of Navare

1894　Due to increased attendance, a 285-foot grandstand is built to accommodate racing attendees at the Kentucky Derby. Racehorse Chant is the winner of the Derby.

1894　Jockey Alonzo "Lonnie" Clayton won the Kentucky Oaks twice when he rode Selika in 1894 and Voladora in 1895.

1894　The Louisville Jockey Club is sold. Meriweather Lewis Clark Jr. continues as the track's presiding judge.

1894　Isaac Burns Murphy starts to race for stable owner Byron McClelland.

1895　The renowned Twin Spires welcome the Kentucky Derby crowd on May 6th. Racehorse Halma wins The Derby.

1895　Isaac Murphy races in England. He makes history as the first American to win on an English racecourse with an American horse.

1895　Jockey James Soup Perkins becomes the second-youngest jockey to win the Kentucky Derby. Riding Halma, he breaks early from the field and wins by five lengths for an exciting victory. That same year, Perkins won the Phoenix Stakes, also aboard Halma. 20,000 people attended the derby that year. It is a great year for Perkins, who wins several other races including Lexington's Phoenix Stakes and the Clark Stakes in Louisville. Perkins became America's leading rider that year with an astounding 192 wins to his credit.

1895   W. E. B. Du Bois became the first African American to be awarded a Ph.D. by Harvard University, having earned his bachelor's degree there in 1890.

1896   Willie Simms wins the Kentucky Derby riding Ben Brush

1896   The Derby distance is shortened from one-and-a-half miles to one-and-a-quarter-mile because it is deemed too long for three-year-old Thoroughbreds to run so early in the spring. A beautiful arrangement of white and pink roses is presented to racehorse Ben Brush when he wins the Derby. Alonzo Lonnie Clayton finishes in 3rd place at the Preakness Stakes.

1896   Jockey Sir Isaac Burns Murphy passed away on February 12, Lexington, Kentucky, at age thirty-six. He is buried in African Cemetery Number 2 next to his wife, Lucy Carr Murphy, among other prominent Black Americans.

1896   Jockey Willie Simms wins the Kentucky Derby riding Ben Brush trained by Hardy Campbell Jr. and owned by Mike F. Dwyer.

1896   The Supreme Court issued its decision in Plessy v. Ferguson. Justice Henry Brown of Michigan delivers the majority opinion, which sustains the constitutionality of Louisiana's Jim Crow laws. The "separate-but-equal" doctrine leads to the rise of racial discrimination throughout the country.

1896   Jockey Alonzo Clayton is one of only three Black jockeys to compete in the Preakness. He finished third.

1897   Weldy Walker serves on the executive committee of the Negro Protective Party, a newly formed political party established in Ohio in protest of the failure of the Republican governor to investigate the lynching of an Black American in June, at Urbana, Ohio.

1898   Willie Simms wins the Kentucky Derby riding Plaudit

1898   Willie Simms wins the Preakness Stakes riding Sly Fox

1898   Jockey Babe Hurd and Anna Thomas marry in the state of Georgia. Alice Hurd Whitfield moves to Chicago, Illinois, with her husband, Samuel, and their three children.

1898   Jockey Willie Simms becomes a repeat Kentucky Derby winner and goes on to take the Preakness Stakes a few weeks later, making him the only Black jockey to win all of the Triple Crown races.

1898   Jockey Willie Simms wins the derby riding Plaudit, owned and trained by John E. Madden. He uses the short stirrup that gives the rider a crouching posture.

1899   Meriwether Lewis Clark Jr., founder of the Kentucky Derby, passed away on April 22, 1899, just 12 days before the 25th Kentucky Derby.

1899   Colonel Meriwether Lewis Clark Jr. passes away by suicide after losing heavily in the stock market crash of 1893 and traveling from city to city, working as a steward. He is buried in Cave Hill Cemetery next to his uncle, John Churchill.

1899   First ferry, a two-man rowboat, crosses the Mississippi from the Kenner area.

1899   James "Soup" Perkins changes careers to become a horse trainer and owner.

1900   Isaac Lewis works as a groom at the Harlem Jockey Club in Proviso Township in Cook County, Illinois. He is listed in the United States Federal Census as living in the Harlem Village where several other Black Americans from Kentucky also lived. They are employed at the Harlem Jockey Club as cooks, jockeys, grooms, trainers, and stable boys. In 1910, Lewis lived in Chicago and managed a Turkish Bathhouse.

1900   James "Soup" Perkins's brother, Frank Perkins, is shot-killed at his family home at the front door.

1900   Moses Fleetwood Walker is released from jail during the turn of the century. Walker jointly owns the Union Hotel in Steubenville with his brother Weldy, and manages the Opera House, a movie theater in nearby Cadiz. As host to opera, live drama, vaudeville, and minstrel shows at the Opera House, Walker becomes a respected businessman and patents inventions that improves film reels when nickelodeons are popularized.

1900   Weldy Walker and Moses Fleetwood become active in the back-to-Africa movement and promote emigration back to Liberia. The brothers also establish and edit the Equator, a Black issues newspaper.

1901   Jockey Jimmy Winkfield wins the Kentucky Derby riding His Eminence with owner and trainer Frank B. Van Meter.

1901   Alonzo Lonnie Clayton is arrested for alleged race fixing at his last big appearance in April 1901. He also married Elanora "Frankie" Saunders in Lexington, Kentucky. They lived on Wilson Street.

1902   Jockey Jimmy Winkfield wins the Kentucky Derby against

Alan-a-Dale, whose owner and trainer is Thomas Clay McDowell.

1902   Jockey James Soup Perkins jockeys in a race in 1902. One of his horses, Harting, is quite successful in meets at the Latonia Racecourse.

1902   The Walker brothers, Moses and Weldy, explore ideas of Black nationalism as editors for the Equator. The Walker brothers publish a Black-issues newspaper called the Equator.

1903   With Colonel Winn in charge, the Kentucky Derby records its first profit under his leadership. Racehorse Judge Himes wins the race.

1903   Struggling with rheumatism and tuberculosis, Edward Dudley Brown retired in 1903, and is reportedly one of the wealthiest Black Americans in the state of Kentucky. He passed away three years later in Louisville, Kentucky.

1904   The red rose became the Kentucky Derby's official flower. Racehorse Elwood wins that year's race. Alonzo Clayton gives up trying to revive his racing career.

1904   Jockey Anthony Hamilton passes away in France. He is noted to be wearing all his jewelry aboard his own train.

1904   Jockey Jimmy Winkfield purchases a steamer ticket and heads for Russia. He rode winning horses in Russia, Poland, France, Austria, Hungary, England, Spain, and Italy, ultimately winning nearly every marquee race on the Continent. Jimmy Winkfield's victories in Russia include the Russian Oaks (five times), the Russian Derby (four times), the Czar's Prize (a.k.a. as the Emperor's Purse) (three times). Winkfield enjoys his fame and fortune while in Russia. When asked to describe his life during this time, Winkfield says, "I was at the top of the tree."

1905   George B. Anderson disappears without a trace.

1906   Trainer-jockey Edward Dudley Brown died of tuberculosis in his native Lexington, Kentucky on May 11.

1907   In 1907, Jimmy Lee won all the races on his card.

1908   The Walker brothers publish a forty-seven-page book titled Our Home Colony: A Treatise on the Past, Present, and Future of the Negro Race in America. Moses Fleetwood Walker and Weldy Walker join the back-to-Africa movement, protesting against discrimination in America toward people of color.

1908   Jimmy Lee wins the Travers aboard Dorante.

1908   After his baseball career, Moses "Fleet" Walker becomes a successful businessman and inventor. As an advocate of Black nationalism, Walker also jointly edits a newspaper, the Equator with his brother Weldy Walker. Walked publishes a book, Our Home Colony (1908), to explore ideas about emigrating back to Africa. Regarded as "the most learned book a professional athlete ever wrote," Our Home Colony shares Walker's thesis on the victimization of the Black race and a proposal for Black Americans to emigrate back to Africa.

1908   Trainer - jockey Abraham "Abe" Alex Perry passes away in Lexington, Kentucky.

1908   Jockey Shelby Pikes Barnes passed away on January 6.

1909   Horses Halma and Azra both pass away.

1909   W. E. B. Du Bois forms the NAACP (National Association for the Advancement of Colored People).

1911   Jockey James Soup Perkins (age 30–31) died of heart disease in Ontario, Canada, while attending the races at Hamilton. He is survived by his wife, his father, and three of his siblings. Perkins is buried in the family plot at Lexington, Kentucky's African Cemetery Number 2 though his name is not added to the marker. The alley next to his childhood home on North Upper Street in Lexington, Kentucky is named Soup Perkins Alley in his honor.

1913   Harriet Tubman passed away on March 10.

1913   Jockey Erskine "Babe" Henderson passes away. In his lifetime, Henderson is the only jockey to win three derbies in one year, following up his Kentucky Derby victory with a win at the Tennessee Derby and the Coney Island Derby. He rides all three races on Joe Cotton.

1915   Jimmy Lee passed away in Raceland, Louisiana.

1915   Booker T. Washington passed away on November 14th, and his school was renamed Tuskegee University.

1917   Alonzo "Lonnie" Clayton passes away.

1917   Jockey Alonzo "Lonnie" Clayton passed away on March 17, 1917, in Los Angeles, California.

1919   Jockey Isaac Lewis passes away.

1919   Jockey Jimmy Winkfield escapes the Bolshevik's thundering cannon fire, leading 250 top-tier Thoroughbreds, Polish noblemen, and horsemen on a harrowing 1,100-mile journey to a haven in Warsaw.

1919   Madam C. J. Walker passed away May 25, Irvington, New

York. She was born on December 23, 1867, in Delta, Louisiana.

1920   Jockey Babe Hurd works for William Thraves at Longridge Farm in Bourbon County, Kentucky. He remained at the farm for eight years.

1922   Jimmy Winkfield resurrects his career in France. He remarries in France and his father-in-law presents the newlyweds with a three-story château and private stables in the lush countryside outside Paris. Winkfield's victories in France include the Prix du Président de la République, the Grand Prix de Deauville, and the Prix Eugène-Adam.

1924   Moses Fleetwood Walker passed away in Cleveland, Ohio on May 11 at the age of sixty-seven. He is buried at Union Cemetery-Beatty Park.

1924   Oliver Lewis passes away and is buried in Benevolent Society No. 2 Cemetery, which is now known as African Cemetery No. 2. Lexington, Kentucky.

1927   Jockey Willie Simms passed away on February 26, 1927, Asbury Park, New Jersey.

1928   Jockey Babe Hurd passed away on December 7. Before he becomes ill and passes away at the age of sixty-two, his daughter, Alice comes to Lexington and arranges to have her father's remains buried in Chicago.

1930   The physical toll of riding forces jockey Jimmy Winkfield to retire at age 48, so he switches his job to training, beginning a successful career. By this time, his son Robert James works as a jockey. Winkfield trains him, his own horses, and other owners' horses as well. Winkfield marries twice in his lifetime. His first wife, Alexandra, is a Russian Baroness who passed away in 1921. They bear a son, George who passed away in 1934. His second marriage is to a French woman named Lydia who passed away in 1958. This marriage also produced a son, Robert, who passed away in 1977, and a daughter, Liliane Casey, who currently resides in Cincinnati, Ohio.

1933   Jockey William ``Billy" Walker passed away on September 20 in Louisville, Kentucky at seventy years old. During his life, he lived with his wife, Hannah, and his son, William Jr., in Louisville. Walker's home was valued at $5,000 and his occupation was listed as "Racing." Walker is buried in an unmarked grave in the Louisville Cemetery.

1937   Weldy W. Walker passed away on November 23 at seventy-seven years old in Steubenville, Ohio.

1947   Jack Roosevelt "Jackie" Robinson becomes the first Black American in 60 years to play on a Major League baseball team.

1955   Isaac Murphy becomes the first Black jockey to be inducted into the National Museum of Racing and Hall of Fame.

1961   Jockey Jimmy Winkfield returns to the United States for one last visit to attend the Kentucky Derby for the first time in 58 years. Winkfield and his daughter Liliane are invited to a reception hosted by Sports Illustrated to honor the two-time winner at the luxurious Brown Hotel in Louisville, Kentucky. Still segregated, the hotel does not allow Winkfield to enter through the front door. Winkfield stands his ground and eventually, he and his daughter are admitted.

1974   Jimmy Winkfield died March 23 in Maisons-Laffitte, France.

1977   Willie Simms is inducted into the National Museum of Racing and Hall of Fame.

1984   Edward Dudley Brown is inducted into the National Museum of Racing's Hall of Fame.

1990   Moses Fleetwood Walker was inducted into the Oberlin College Hall of Fame in 1990.

1997   Abe Hawkins is inducted into the Louisiana Racing Museum Hall of Fame .

1998   Ansel Williamson is inducted into the National Museum of Racing and Hall of Fame.

2000   Marlon St. Julien becomes the first Black American jockey to ride in the Kentucky Derby in seventy-nine years when he rides Curule to a seventh-place finish.

2004   Jimmy Winkfield is inducted into the National Museum of Racing and Hall of Fame in Saratoga Springs, New York.

2005   The U.S. Congress admits Isaac, Jimmy, and Willie into the National Racing Hall of Fame. "Whereas in 2003, Jimmy Winkfield was admitted to the National Racing Hall of Fame and joined two other Black American Hall of Fame jockeys, 3-time Kentucky Derby winner Isaac Murphy and 2-time winner Willie Simms". Now, therefore, be it resolved, That the House of Representatives—(1) celebrates the remarkable life and accomplishments of one of the truly great American athletes, Jimmy ``Wink" Winkfield, who continuously overcame racism and other significant obstacles during his lifetime; and (2) recognizes and celebrates the significant contributions and excellence of Black American jockeys and trainers in the sport of horse racing and in the history of the Kentucky Derby." Engrossed in the House of Representatives".

2010 Oliver Lewis's name wins a citywide road-naming contest. The winning connector road is called Oliver Lewis Way in Lexington, Kentucky 40508.

2011 Shelby "Pike" Barnes is inducted into the National Racing Museum Hall of Fame.

2011 An alley in Lexington Kentucky was named after jockey James 'Soup' Perkins. The alley is called Soup Perkins Alley.

2012 Anthony "Tony" Hamilton is inducted into the National Museum of Racing and Hall of Fame.

14. HORSE RACES AROUND THE WORLD

Kentucky Derby

Inaugurated: 1875

Schedule: First Saturday in May

Venue: Churchill Downs Racetrack, Louisville, Kentucky, USA

Surface: Dirt

Distance: 2,000m (about 1.25 miles)

The two-minute-long race is also referred to as the "Run for the Roses". It is full of rich traditions including refreshing Mint Juleps and the singing of "My Old Kentucky Home". The winner is draped in a blanket made of roses. In terms of popularity, the Kentucky Derby is the US equivalent of Great Britain's Epsom Derby. Throughout Kentucky Derby history, Secretariat maintains a record as the fastest horse and one of the only two horses to finish the race in under two minutes. Oliver Lewis won the first Kentucky Derby riding Aristides.

The Kentucky Derby, famously known as the "Run for the Roses," encompasses a rich mosaic of history, traditions, and unforgettable moments. This thrilling two-minute-long horse race captivates audiences worldwide, solidifying its status as the pinnacle of American equestrian excellence. Much like its British counterpart, the Epsom Derby, the Kentucky Derby holds a place of unparalleled popularity and prestige.

From its inception in 1875, the Kentucky Derby has woven together a captivating array of cherished customs that add an air of grandeur and excitement to the event. As the thunderous sound of hooves reverberates through the hallowed Churchill Downs racetrack, spectators savor the refreshing taste of Mint Juleps, the quintessential beverage that has become synonymous with the race. Attired in their finest garb, adorned with extravagant hats and outfits, attendees revel in the palpable anticipation that permeates the atmosphere.

Amidst this symphony of tradition, one of the most iconic moments unfolds when the enchanting strains of "My Old Kentucky Home" fill the air. This heartfelt melody, sung by the crowd in unison, evokes a deep sense of nostalgia and pride, paying homage to the rich heritage and spirit of the Bluegrass State.

The crowning glory of the Kentucky Derby comes in the form of the legendary "Garland of Roses." The victor, draped in a resplendent blanket meticulously crafted from a profusion of vibrant roses, becomes a symbol of triumph and splendor. This coveted honor signifies not only the beauty of the achievement but also the arduous journey that the winning horse and jockey have traversed to reach this pinnacle of success.

Throughout the annals of the Kentucky Derby, one name etches itself indelibly into history: Secretariat. This awe-inspiring thoroughbred claims the record for the fastest time ever recorded in the race, leaving an indomitable legacy as one of the only two horses to complete the course in under two minutes. Secretariat's unparalleled speed and dominance embody the spirit of greatness that the Kentucky Derby represents.

Yet, the remarkable story of the Kentucky Derby extends beyond its traditions and achievements. It is a tale of diversity, highlighting the contributions of Black jockeys and horse trainers who played an integral role in the race's early history. In 1877, the racehorse Baden-Baden, guided to victory by Black jockey William Billy Walker, galloped across the finish line under the skillful training of Edward Dudley Brown, a highly respected Black horse trainer. These triumphs shattered barriers and showcased the immense talent and skill possessed by Black individuals within the equestrian world.

The legacy continued to flourish in subsequent years, as racehorses like Fonso, Apollo, Buchanan, Joe Cotton, Montrose, Riley, Kingman, Azra, Halma, Ben Brush, and Plaudit achieved glory alongside remarkable Black jockeys. George Garret Lewis, Babe Hurd, Sir Isaac Burns Murphy, Erskine Henderson, Isaac Lewis, Sir Isaac Burns Murphy, Alonzo Clayton, Willie Simms, and James Soup Perkins fearlessly guided these magnificent steeds to victory. They were supported by visionary Black horse trainers, including Tice Hutsell, Green B. Morris, William Bird, Abraham Perry, John McGinty, Edward Corrigan, Dudley Allen, John H. Morris, Hardy Campbell Jr., and John E. Madden, who nurtured their potential and prepared them for the extraordinary challenges that awaited them on the track.

Their achievements underscored the profound impact and invaluable contributions of Black professionals within the world of horse racing, leaving an indelible mark on the history of the Kentucky Derby. These trailblazers exemplified the power of diversity, unity, and unwavering determination, reminding us that greatness knows no boundaries and that true excellence transcends any racial or social barriers.

As the years roll on, the Kentucky Derby continues to evolve, embracing the winds of change while staying true to its enduring traditions. It is a reflection of our collective journey, embodying the spirit of progress, innovation, and the unyielding pursuit of dreams. The legends of the past inspire the heroes of today, propelling the race toward a future where new records will be set, new stories will be written, and new names will be etched into the pantheon of greatness.

So, as the thundering hooves echo through time and space, let us remember the Kentucky Derby—a spectacle that embodies the boundless spirit of human ambition, the beauty of unity in diversity, and the enduring legacy of a race that has captivated generations. It is a celebration of courage, passion, and the relentless pursuit of victory—a beacon of inspiration for all who dare to dream and reach for the stars.

Kentucky Oaks

The Kentucky Oaks, a cherished jewel within the realm of horse racing, radiates its own luminous beauty and unrivaled grace. This prestigious event, often referred to as the "Run for the Lilies," stands as a testament to the power, talent, and indomitable spirit of fillies, capturing the hearts of spectators around the world. Held annually at Churchill Downs, the Kentucky Oaks is a true celebration of equine excellence and feminine strength.

Since its inaugural running in 1875, the Kentucky Oaks has been a celebration of tradition and elegance that parallels its famous counterpart, the Kentucky Derby. As the anticipation builds, a sea of spectators adorns themselves in shades of pink, embodying the event's vibrant spirit and paying homage to the beauty and grace of these remarkable fillies. The air is filled with excitement, mingled with the scent of blooming lilies, creating an atmosphere that crackles with anticipation.

Just as the Kentucky Derby has its iconic Mint Juleps, the Kentucky Oaks has its signature drink, the Lily. This refreshing libation, adorned with a delicate pink hue, is the perfect complement to the festivities. With each sip, spectators toast to the magnificence of the fillies, celebrating their extraordinary talents and the boundless potential they bring to the track.

As the time draws near, the crowd's collective breath catches in unison, and a profound hush falls over the racetrack. The strains of "My Old Kentucky Home" gently permeate the air, weaving a melodic symphony that unites all in attendance. This timeless anthem evokes a deep sense of connection to the land, to the horses, and to the timeless traditions that make the Kentucky Oaks a cherished event.

With the first crack of the starting gate, the fillies burst forth, their muscular grace propelling them forward with determination. Each stride is a testament to their strength, agility, and unwavering spirit. The crowd watches in awe as these exceptional athletes thunder down the track, their hooves beating in perfect harmony with the rhythm of the Oaks.

At the finish line, a moment of triumph awaits. The victor, adorned in a blanket of pink lilies, embodies the epitome of feminine grace and athletic prowess. She stands as a beacon of inspiration, reminding us of all of the extraordinary achievements that can be accomplished through unwavering dedication, unyielding spirit, and unwavering determination.

While the Kentucky Oaks shares the stage with the Kentucky Derby, it has its own distinctive narrative of triumph, strength, and the power of femininity. Throughout its storied history, remarkable fillies have left their mark, showcasing the extraordinary talent and tenacity of these majestic creatures. From Rachel Alexandra to Untapable, from Monomoy Girl to Swiss Skydiver, their victories echo through time, inspiring future generations to reach for greatness.

The Kentucky Oaks is a celebration of the enduring legacy of female athletes, honoring their contributions and recognizing their rightful place in the world of horse racing. It is a series of stories of courage, resilience, and the pursuit of dreams. As the sun sets on each Kentucky Oaks, its echoes linger, reminding us of the power and beauty found in the heart of every filly, and the everlasting impact they have on our collective spirit.

Preakness Stakes

Inaugurated: 1873

Schedule: mid-May

Venue: Pimlico Race Course, Baltimore, Maryland, USA.

Surface: Dirt

Distance: 1900m (about 1.18 miles)

The Preakness Stakes is the second leg of the Triple Crown race. The winning horse is honored by a blanket made up of the "Black-Eyed

Susan" daisies. The race commenced by singing the official state song - "Maryland, My Maryland". Another interesting tradition followed in the race is that after the winner is announced, a painter would climb up the Pimlico Race Course's Old Clubhouse to paint the weather vane colored to match that of the winning jockey's jersey. 1889 George B. Anderson wins riding Buddhist. 1896 Alonzo Lonnie Clayton finished in 3rd place. 1898 Willie Simms wins riding Sly Fox.

The Preakness Stakes, standing proudly as the second jewel of the esteemed Triple Crown series, is a thrilling spectacle that ignites the spirit of competition and captivates racing enthusiasts worldwide. This prestigious race, held at the renowned Pimlico Racecourse, is a series of traditions and moments that add depth and allure to this iconic event.

As the thunderous roar of hooves fills the air, the anticipation rises to a crescendo. The winning horse, adorned with a magnificent blanket adorned with Black-eyed Susan daisies, symbolizes triumph and excellence. This vibrant floral tribute, meticulously crafted with nature's beauty, honors the remarkable athleticism and grace of the victor. The Black-eyed Susan blanket, resplendent in its glory, serves as a testament to the unwavering dedication and unyielding spirit displayed by both horse and jockey.

Just as the Kentucky Derby has its heartfelt anthem, the Preakness Stakes has its own melodic tradition. The soul-stirring echoes of "Maryland, My Maryland" reverberate through the hearts of the crowd, celebrating the rich history and heritage of the state that plays host to this momentous race. The harmonious voices of spectators unite in a powerful chorus, embracing the deep connection between the race and its cherished surroundings.

Beyond the floral tribute and the melodious anthem, the Preakness Stakes harbors a distinctive tradition that adds a touch of artistic flair. Once the victor is announced, a skilled painter ascends the heights of Pimlico Racecourse's Old Clubhouse. With meticulous precision, the painter meticulously captures the essence of the winning jockey's glory by adorning the weathervane atop the clubhouse with the vibrant hues that mirror the jockey's victorious jersey. This visual tribute immortalizes the triumphant moment, creating a lasting emblem of the race's history.

Throughout the annals of the Preakness Stakes, exceptional talents have etched their names in the race's storied legacy. In 1889, a trailblazing moment unfolded as Black jockey George B. Anderson rode to victory atop the majestic Buddhist. Anderson's triumph shattered barriers, leaving an indelible mark on the race's history and reinforcing the importance of diversity and inclusivity within the realm of horse racing. Alonzo also etched his name in the race's history with a remarkable third-place finish in 1896, showcasing his skill and resilience on the track.

Another notable victory came in the form of Willie Simms, a gifted Black jockey who guided the spirited Sly Fox to triumph in 1898. Simms' exceptional talent and unwavering determination showcased the depth of his skill, contributing to the race's ever-growing series of unforgettable moments. These victories stand as shining examples of the immense talent and tenacity displayed by Black jockeys throughout history, highlighting their invaluable contributions to the sport of horse racing.

The Preakness Stakes stands as a testament to the enduring allure of horse racing, captivating our imaginations and stirring our souls. From the vibrant blanket of Black-eyed Susan daisies to the resonating strains of "Maryland, My Maryland," and the artistry that adorns the weathervane, each tradition weaves together a narrative that celebrates the beauty, resilience, and indomitable spirit of both horse and jockey.

As the Preakness Stakes continues to unfold year after year, it breathes new life into this remarkable sport, inspiring generations to embrace the legacy, honor the traditions, and revel in the timeless thrill of the race. It is an event that transcends mere competition, transcending time and capturing the essence of human achievement. The Preakness Stakes reminds us of the profound connection between sport and culture, weaving together a mosaic of moments that will forever be etched in the hearts and minds of all who bear witness to its extraordinary splendor.

Belmont Stakes

Inaugurated: 1867

Schedule: July

Venue: Belmont Park, Elmont, New York, United States

Surface: Dirt

Distance: 2,400+ m (about 1.50 miles)

Since its inception, race distances and tracks have evolved. This is the oldest and longest of the three prestigious and classic horse races. Over the years, the Belmont race has earned the reputation of being the "Test of the Champion". The winner of the race is draped with a blanket made up of beautiful white carnations. Belmont Stakes also called The Test of the Champion and The Run for the Carnations takes place in June and is the traditional final leg of the Triple Crown.

The Belmont Stakes, an iconic chapter in the rich history of horse racing, takes center stage each year in the month of July. Held at the illustrious Belmont Park in Elmont, New York, this revered event has enthralled audiences since its inauguration in 1867. It proudly stands as the oldest and longest of the three prestigious classic horse races, weaving a captivating narrative that spans generations.

As the sport of horse racing evolved, so did the distances and tracks of the Belmont Stakes. Initially hosted at Jerome Park in the Bronx, it later found its home at Westchester until 1889. Following that, the race galloped over to Morris Park Racetrack in the Bronx from 1890 to 1904, before finally settling at Belmont Park. This iconic venue, with its sprawling landscape and majestic grandstands, provides a magnificent setting for the ultimate display of equine prowess.

Renowned as the "Test of the Champion," the Belmont Stakes poses a formidable challenge to all contenders who aspire to claim its coveted title. Spanning a demanding distance of 2,400+ meters, roughly equivalent to 1.50 miles, the race pushes both horses and jockeys to their limits, demanding not only speed but also unwavering stamina and determination. It is a true test of skill and character, separating the exceptional from the ordinary and crowning a deserving champion among the elite competitors.

An extraordinary moment of beauty unfolds as the race reaches its climactic conclusion. The triumphant horse, basking in the glory of its victory, is adorned with a resplendent blanket made of pristine white carnations. Each delicate petal symbolizes the purity and triumph of the champion, serving as a visual tribute to their remarkable achievement. This timeless tradition adds an element of elegance and grace to the crowning of the Belmont Stakes winner.

Recognized as the final leg of the renowned Triple Crown, the Belmont Stakes holds a position of prestige and honor within the world of horse racing. It is a culmination of dreams, aspirations, and months of meticulous preparation for owners, trainers, jockeys, and spectators alike. The air is charged with excitement, as the racecourse becomes a stage for the convergence of passion, skill, and unyielding determination.

In addition to its racing splendor, the Belmont Stakes carries a melodic resonance that resonates deeply within the hearts of those who witness its glory. The stirring notes of "Theme from New York, New York" fill the atmosphere, uniting the crowd in a celebration of the indomitable spirit of the city and the timeless allure of the Belmont Stakes. This musical tribute, accompanied by iconic renditions from legends such as Frank Sinatra and Jay-Z with Alicia Keys, further amplifies the race's deep connection to the vibrant heartbeat of New York.

The Belmont Stakes stands as a testament to the endurance of tradition, the pursuit of excellence, and the thrill of competition. It is a race that transcends time, capturing the essence of equine greatness and igniting the passions of all those fortunate enough to witness its grandeur. Each year, as the horses thunder down the homestretch and cross the finish line, a new chapter is written in the annals of the Belmont Stakes, forever immortalizing the names of heroes within the realm of horse racing history.

Travers Stakes

Inaugurated: 1864

Schedule: August

Venue: Saratoga Springs, New York, United States

Surface: Dirt

Distance: 2,011m (about 1.25 miles)

Known as the "Midsummer Derby," the Travers Stakes is the third-ranked race behind only the Kentucky Derby and Belmont Stakes. The night before the race, a Saratoga florist prepares a 10-foot-long blanket of carnations for the winner of the race. The winner's colors are traditionally painted on the canoe as it sits on the infield pond.

Saudi Cup

Inaugurated: 2020

Schedule: Last Weekend in February

Venue: King Abdulaziz Racecourse, Riyadh, Saudi Arabia

Surface: Dirt

The Saudi Cup with the highest purse money is the world's most lucrative horse racing event. Prize money for The Saudi Cup meeting has increased every year. The two-day racing event is scheduled to take place after the Pegasus World Cup and before the Dubai World Cup. This allows horses to compete in all three of the most valuable dirt races in the world. The race earned its Grade 1 status within three of inception.

The Saudi Cup stands tall as the epitome of opulence in the world of horse racing, boasting the highest purse money of any racing event on the planet. Year after year, the prize money for this prestigious race has reached new heights, making it an irresistible magnet for the most exceptional equine talents and capturing the imagination of racing enthusiasts worldwide.

Spanning over two thrilling days, the Saudi Cup meeting takes its place on the esteemed calendar, strategically positioned after the Pegasus World Cup and before the Dubai World Cup. This strategic scheduling allows the most ambitious owners and trainers to test their horses' mettle in all three of the most valuable dirt races in the world, creating an extraordinary opportunity for glory on an unprecedented scale.

Within a remarkably short period of time, the Saudi Cup has achieved Grade 1 status, a testament to its outstanding quality and the level of competition it attracts. This rapid ascent to Grade 1 recognition underscores the exceptional organization, infrastructure, and commitment to excellence displayed by the race organizers, solidifying its status as a premier event on the international racing stage.

The Saudi Cup embodies the allure of luxury, the pursuit of greatness, and the thrill of competition. The magnificent purse money acts as a magnet, drawing in a stellar field of elite horses, jockeys, and trainers, each vying for a slice of the staggering prize pool. The race becomes a captivating spectacle, where equine legends are made, dreams are realized, and the power and speed of these majestic creatures are showcased in their full glory.

As the thunderous hooves reverberate through the air and the world watches with bated breath, the Saudi Cup transcends boundaries, bridging cultures, and uniting racing enthusiasts from all corners of the globe. It is a testament to the universal language of sport and the unifying power of equine excellence.

The Saudi Cup, with its unrivaled prize money, epitomizes the convergence of passion, prestige, and financial splendor in the world of horse racing. It is a beacon that shines brightly, luring the greatest talents, igniting the spirit of competition, and etching indelible memories in the annals of racing history. Each year, as the horses thunder down the track, the Saudi Cup captivates our imaginations, reminding us of the limitless possibilities that await those who dare to dream and pursue greatness in the realm of horse racing.

Dubai World Cup

Inaugurated: 1996

Schedule: Last Saturday in March

Venue: Meydan Racecourse, Dubai, United Arab Emirates

Surface: Dirt

Distance: 2,000m (about 1.25 miles)

The Dubai World cup is the world's richest horse race with the highest prize money. In 2006, for the first time, a horse racing sport was broadcast on National Television in the United States. The race is part of the Dubai World Cup Night, which is a series of eight thoroughbred horse races and one Purebred Arabian race held annually in Dubai.

The Dubai World Cup, a glittering gem in the crown of horse racing, reigns supreme as the world's richest race, boasting an unparalleled prize money that captures the attention of the global racing community. This prestigious event stands as a testament to Dubai's unyielding dedication to excellence, extravagance, and the pursuit of equine greatness.

In a groundbreaking moment that marked a pivotal turning point for the sport, the year 2006 witnessed the first-ever broadcast of horse racing on National Television in the United States. This watershed moment opened the floodgates of global viewership, allowing racing enthusiasts from around the world to witness the thrilling spectacle of the Dubai World Cup unfold before their eyes. With every gallop, every stride, and every heart-pounding moment, the race captivates the imaginations of millions, leaving an indelible mark on the history of horse racing.

The Dubai World Cup takes its place as the crown jewel of the illustrious Dubai World Cup Night, a spectacular series of nine races that showcase the finest thoroughbred horses and one Purebred Arabian race. Held annually in the vibrant city of Dubai, this exceptional racing extravaganza draws participants and spectators from far and wide, transforming the landscape into a breathtaking panorama of equine prowess and human endeavor.

As the sun sets over the majestic Meydan Racecourse, the stage is set for an evening of unparalleled excitement and grandeur. The air crackles with anticipation as the world's finest jockeys and trainers, along with their magnificent equine partners, prepare to engage in an epic battle of speed, stamina, and sheer determination. The Dubai World Cup Night is a celebration of the sport's most accomplished athletes, a gathering of elite contenders who have honed their skills and dedicated their lives to the pursuit of victory.

The Dubai World Cup itself serves as the crowning jewel of the night, a race that stops the world in its tracks and leaves spectators breathless. With its extraordinary prize money, it attracts a stellar field of competitors, each yearning to etch their names in the annals of racing history and claim a share of the extravagant riches that await the victor. As the horses thunder down the straight, the crowd erupts in a symphony of cheers and gasps, swept up in the sheer exhilaration of witnessing the pinnacle of equine athleticism.

The Dubai World Cup is a testament to the vision and ambition of Dubai, a city that has transformed itself into a global hub for horse racing, luxury, and unparalleled experiences. It represents the fusion of cutting-edge technology, world-class facilities, and a boundless passion for the sport, creating an immersive and unforgettable experience for all who are fortunate enough to be part of its grandeur.

As the Dubai World Cup continues to evolve, year after year, it solidifies its position as the epitome of horse racing excellence. It stands as a beacon of prestige, opulence, and sporting achievement, captivating the hearts and minds of racing enthusiasts worldwide. The Dubai World Cup Night is a celebration of the indomitable spirit of the sport, a testament to the enduring power of dreams and the extraordinary feats that can be accomplished when horse and rider become one.

Dubai Sheema Classic

Inaugurated: 1998

Schedule: Last Saturday in March

Venue: Meydan Racecourse, Dubai, United Arab Emirates

Surface: Turf

Distance: 2,400m (about 1.5 miles)

Initially titled the Dubai Turf Classic, the race was eventually renamed the Dubai Sheema Classic. The race is mainly open to Northern Hemisphere four-year-olds and above. The mile and half race is a Grade 1 status and holds the record that no jockey has ever won it more than once.

Epsom Derby

Inaugurated: 1780

Schedule: First Saturday in June

Venue: Epsom Downs Racecourse, Surrey, England, UK

Surface: Turf

Distance: 2,400m (about 1.5 miles)

The Epsom Derby is the oldest and biggest race in Britain with the highest prize money. Considered a "Classic", the race is open to three-year-old colts and fillies only. The Epson along with Guineas and St. Leger races form the English Triple Crown races. It is a multi-day event featuring music and entertainment in addition to the race. The Epsom Derby maintains a dress code for men and women.

Steeped in history and revered as a cornerstone of British horse racing, the Epsom Derby stands as a timeless testament to the enduring legacy of the sport. Since its inauguration in 1780, this prestigious event has captivated the hearts and minds of racing enthusiasts, solidifying its position as the oldest and grandest race in Britain, adorned with the highest prize money in the land.

Taking place on the first Saturday in June, the Epsom Derby weaves its magic at the iconic Epsom Downs Racecourse, nestled in the picturesque county of Surrey, England. With its sprawling expanse of lush green turf, this hallowed ground provides the perfect canvas for the epic battle that unfolds on race day, where champions are forged and dreams are realized.

As a "Classic" race, the Epsom Derby is exclusively open to three-year-old colts and fillies, showcasing the exceptional talent and potential of the rising stars of the racing world. It is a race that carries with it the weight of tradition, as it forms a crucial part of the English Triple Crown races, standing alongside the Guineas and St. Leger races. To triumph in the Epsom Derby is to etch one's name in the annals of racing history, joining the illustrious ranks of past champions.

SULTAN ZESHAN

The Epsom Derby is not just a single-day affair; it is a multi-day extravaganza that transcends the boundaries of sport. As the anticipation builds in the days leading up to the race, Epsom becomes a hive of activity, alive with music, entertainment, and a palpable sense of excitement. Spectators are treated to a vibrant atmosphere, where the spirit of camaraderie and celebration permeates every corner of the racecourse.

Within this grand spectacle, the Epsom Derby maintains a tradition of elegance and refinement, expressed through a carefully curated dress code. As the race unfolds, the grandstands are adorned with an exquisite display of fashion, where men and women alike don their finest attire, paying homage to the timeless charm and sophistication associated with this remarkable event.

As the horses thunder down the famous Epsom Downs, the air crackles with energy, and the crowd roars in unison, fueling the spirit of competition that courses through the veins of every jockey and steed. The distance of 2,400 meters, approximately 1.5 miles, tests the mettle of each contender, demanding a potent combination of speed, stamina, and tactical brilliance.

Beyond the fierce battle on the track, the Epsom Derby is a celebration of the equestrian spirit and the enduring bond between humans and horses. It is a moment that unites generations, where memories are made and history is written. The roar of the crowd, the thrill of the race, and the unyielding determination of horse and rider create an atmosphere that transcends time, reminding us of the extraordinary beauty and power found within the realm of horse racing.

The Epsom Derby, with its rich heritage and grandeur, remains an unrivaled jewel in the British racing calendar. It represents the pinnacle of sporting achievement and a testament to the unwavering passion and dedication that fuels the world of horse racing. As the sun sets on Epsom Downs, the echoes of triumphant hooves and thunderous applause linger, leaving an indelible mark on all those fortunate enough to bear witness to the splendor of the Epsom Derby.

The Everest

Inaugurated: 2017

Schedule: Second or Third Saturday in October

Venue: Randwick Racecourse, Sydney, Australia

Surface: Turf

Distance: 1,200m (about three-quarters of a mile)

Everest was considered the richest race until 2020 when the Saudi Cup took the title with its extravagant prize money. Despite not having Grade 1 status, Everest still enjoys a reputation among jockeys and turfmen from all over the world. Everest is a weight-for-age sprint race that requires an entry fee for participation.

Melbourne Cup

Inaugurated: 1861

Schedule: First Tuesday in November

Venue: Flemington Racecourse, Melbourne, Australia

Surface: Turf

Distance: 3,200m (about 2 miles)

The Melbourne Cup is Australia's most awaited national event and is often referred to as the "Race that stops a nation". Being among the oldest classic races, it is one of the prestigious competitions targeted by jockeys and turfmen from all over the world. With the race's popularity soaring, eventually, in 1865, the national holiday was announced on race day.

Grand National

Inaugurated: 1839

Schedule: Second Thursday to Friday in April

Venue: Aintree, Merseyside, England

Surface: Turf

Distance: 7,242m (about 4.5 miles)

The Grand National is a handicap steeplechase that requires horses to jump 30 fences over two laps. The race holds the record to feature 66 horses lining up for the race. The race is designed to challenge the skill and spirit of the hardiest and most daring riders, professional and amateur.

Breeders' Cup Classic

Inaugurated: 1984

Schedule: First Saturday in November

Venue: A different venue in North America every year

Surface: Dirt

Distance: 2,000m (about 1.25 miles)

The Breeders' Cup is a unique global horse racing event that spans two-day competitions held at different racetracks. The race has its own qualifying competitions that are held around the world, granting winners a nomination to participate in the main racing event. The Breeders' Cup Classic is now one of the most famous horse races after first taking place in 1984. It's a weight-for-age race open to three-year-olds and above. Tiznow is the only double Breeders' Cup Classic winner.

Prix de l'Arc de Triomphe

Inaugurated: 1920

Schedule: First Sunday in October

Venue: Longchamp Racecourse, Paris, France

Surface: Turf

Distance: 2,400m (about 1.5 miles)

Considered Europe's most famous racing event, the Prix de l'Arc de Triomphe continues to maintain its prestigious position since its inception. It is a weight-for-age race that is open to three-year-olds and up except for geldings. Popularly referred to as the "Arc", the race proudly flaunts its slogan - "Ce n'est pas une course, c'est un monument", which means - "It's not a race, it's a monument".

Royal Ascot

Inaugurated: 1711

Schedule: June

Venue: Ascot, Berkshire, England

Surface: Turf

Distance: 2,000m (about 1.25 miles)

The week-long racing festival is the most prestigious British tradition that is attended by the Queen and the members of the Royal family. The event observes strict dress codes and etiquette boasts of attractions such as the Royal Procession, the Military Bands, the plethora of food stalls, and the races themselves from the Grandstand areas. Over the course of the five days, there are multiple races that take place, including eight G1 races. The races take place on a turf track, which the Queen rides in on a carriage.

Cheltenham Festival

Inaugurated: 1860

Schedule: March

Venue: Cheltenham, Gloucestershire, England

Surface: Turf

Distance: 5,300m (about 3 miles)

Cheltenham Festival is Britain's biggest horse racing event. During the four-day event, 28 races are held, where the horses compete over either fences or hurdles, rather than on a flat track. Cheltenham's prize money is second only to the Grand National. Cheltenham, with a spectator capacity of 67,500, is known for its atmosphere, including the "Cheltenham roar" generated when the race starts.

15. HORSES

About Horse Racing

Horse racing is an equestrian performance sport in which two or more horses are ridden over a defined distance by a jockey.

Horses By Age

- Colt – a young male horse up to the age of four
- Filly – a young female horse up to the age of four
- Mare – a female horse aged five or older
- Horse – a colt is referred to as a 'horse' after the age of five
- Sire – the father of a horse
- Dam – the mother of a horse
- Stallion – a male horse used for breeding
- Broodmare – a female horse used for breeding
- Broodmare dam – a female horse whose offspring are also broodmares
- Broodmare sire – a male horse whose daughters have become successful broodmares
- Foal – newborn horse up to one year old
- Yearling – a one-year old horse
- Gelding – a male horse castrated usually to make it more even-tempered
- Maiden – a horse that has yet to win a race

Horse Colors

- Bay - From light brown to very dark brown with black points and intermingling red or blue hairs in some cases. (Points refer to the mane, tail, muzzle, lower legs, and tips of the ears.) The four bay types are dark bay (mixed blue hair), blood bay (mixed red hair), light bay, and just bay.
- Black - For a horse to be considered black it must be completely black

with no brown at all, only white markings. Ordinary black horses will fade to a rusty brownish color if the horse is exposed to sunlight on a regular basis. Such horses would be considered brown as soon as the black coat gets any brown.

- Chestnut - A color from golden-reddish to a liver color with no black.
- Dun - Yellowish brown with a dorsal stripe along the back and occasionally zebra striping on the legs.
- Gray - A horse with black skin and clear hairs. Gray horses can be born any color, and eventually most will turn gray or white with age. If you would define the horse as white, it is still gray unless it is albino. Some gray horses that are very light require sunscreen for protection.
- Grulla - A horse that is often a grayish/silver colored horse with dark dun factors.
- Pinto or Paint - a multi-colored horse with large patches of brown, white, and/or black and white. Piebald is black and white, while skewbald is white and brown. Specific patterns such as tobiano, overo, and tovero refer to the orientation of white on the body.
- Palomino - chestnut horse that has one cream dilute gene that turns the horse to a golden yellow or tan shade with a flaxen (white) mane and tail.
- Roan - a color pattern that causes white hairs to be sprinkled over the horse's body color. Red roans are chestnut and white hairs, blue roans are black/bay with white hairs. Roans also have solid colored heads that do not lighten.
- Rose gray: a gray horse with a pinkish tinge to its coat. This color occurs while the horse is "graying out."
- Sorrel - a light brown coat with a flaxen mane and tail.
- Appaloosa - A true Appaloosa is actually a breed, not a color. There are different patterns of spots, such as blanket (white over the hip that may extend from the tail to the base of the neck, and with spots inside the blanket the same color as the horse's base coat), snowflake (white spots on a dark body), and leopard (dark spots of varying sizes over a white body).

Horse Markings

Among markings that may appear on the face of a horse are:

- Star - a white patch between the eyes.
- Snip - a white patch on the muzzle.
- Stripe - narrow white stripe down the middle of the face.
- Blaze - broad white stripe down the middle of the face.
- White Face (sometimes called Bald Face)

Among markings that may appear on the legs of a horse are:

- Ermine marks - black marks on the white just above the hoof.
- Sock - white marking that does not extend as high as the knee or hock (tarsal joint)
- Stocking - white marking that extends as high as the knee or hock.

Hotbloods, Warmbloods, and Coldbloods

The temperament of the Arabian horse, the world's oldest purebred breed, earned it the reputation of "hotblood." Arabians are appreciated for their sensitivity, acute awareness, agility, and vitality. They were employed as the foundation of the thoroughbred, another "hotblood," when combined with the lighter, refined bone structure. True hotbloods are frequently more rewarding to ride than other horses. Their sensitivity and intelligence allow for rapid learning as well as improved communication and collaboration with their riders.

Coldblood horses are muscular and hefty draught horses that have been developed to be workhorses and carriage horses with calm temperaments. Draft horses are primarily from Northern Europe, particularly Great Britain. Harnessing a horse to a carriage necessitates some faith in the animal's ability to stay calm when constrained. Budweiser Clydesdales, a Scottish breed, are possibly the most well-known coldbloods.

"Warmblood" breeds began in the same way as thoroughbreds did. The best carriage or cavalry horses were bred to Arabian, Anglo-Arabian, and thoroughbred stallions. The phrase "warmblood" can refer to any draft/thoroughbred hybrid. The term "warmblood" is now used to particularly refer to the sporthorse breed registries that started in Europe. Since the 1980s, registrations or organizations such as the Hanoverian, Oldenburg, Trakkhener, and Holsteiner have dominated the Olympics and World Equestrian Games in Dressage and Show Jumping.

Horse Gaits

Every horse moves naturally in four fundamental gaits (manner of moving). The walk, trot/jog, canter/lope, and gallop are examples of these.

Walk

The walk is a "four-beat" lateral gait in which a horse must keep three feet on the ground at all times and just one foot in the air. Lifting a hind leg first, then the foreleg on the same side, then the remaining hind leg, then the foreleg on the same side.

Trot

The trot or jog is a "two beat" diagonal gait in which a foreleg and opposing hind leg (commonly referred to as "diagonals") strike the ground at the same time. Each leg carries weight individually in this gait. A rider can execute two sorts of trots: posting trot (in which the rider stands up slightly in the saddle each time the horse's outside front leg moves forward) and sitting trot (in which the rider sits in the saddle and follows the horse's movement).

Canter

The canter or lope is a more restricted version of the gallop ("canter" for English riding, "lope" for Western riding). It is a three-beat gait in which the foreleg and opposite hind leg both strike the ground at the same time, but the other two legs strike independently. A cantering horse will initially step off with the outside hind leg, then with the inner hind and outside forelegs combined, then with the inside front leg, and lastly with all four legs off the ground. The rhythm should be 1-2-3, 1-2-3, and so on.

Gallop

The gallop is a four-beat gait that is similar to the canter in that the two paired legs land individually, with the rear leg landing slightly before the foreleg. It is the quickest of all gaits; a healthy racing thoroughbred may gallop at more than forty miles per hour.

Other Gaits

There are several disconnected and intermediate gaits, some of which can only be performed by horses who have been bred to do so. The rack is a four-beat stride with each beat spread equally in perfect rhythm in fast succession. Both legs move simultaneously, with the hindleg touching the ground slightly before the foreleg. The rack is identical to the single foot. The legs on either side move and strike the ground together in a two-beat gait during the tempo. The fox trot and amble are both four-beat gaits, with the latter being smoother and flowing.

Tack and equipment

Tack is the equipment that a horse wears when being ridden for exercise. Tacks can be constructed of leather or synthetic materials. A horse's basic gear includes:

- A bridle, including a bit and reins
- A saddle, including stirrup leathers, stirrups, and a girth
- A saddle cloth/pad
- A halter and lead rope

Common Horse Racing Phrases

- Progressive – a horse whose performance and ability is improving
- Backward – a horse that is physically immature for its age
- Sprinter – a horse that is best over shorter distances
- Miler – a horse that prefers races over the distance of a mile
- Stayer – a horse that prefers to race over distances of a mile and six furlongs or longer
- Off the bit/Off the bridle – a description used for a horse being encouraged along by his jockey
- On the bit/On the bridle – a horse that is going well and still full of running, with a firm hold on the bit
- Banker – a horse considered very likely to win (bankers are often the cornerstone of complex multiple bets).

16. HORSE FACIAL EXPRESSIONS OR BODY LANGUAGE INDICATIONS

Horses communicate their emotions and intentions through a combination of facial expressions and body language. While not as intricate as human communication, there are several common indicators that can provide insights into a horse's state of mind. Here are some examples:

Ears: Observing a horse's ears can reveal its mood. Forward-pointing ears indicate attentiveness and interest, while ears pinned back against the head suggest aggression or fear. If one ear is forward and the other is back, it may indicate curiosity or uncertainty.

Eyes: Horses' eyes can express various emotions. Wide-open eyes with visible whites typically indicate fear or alarm, while relaxed, half-closed eyes indicate a state of relaxation. Rolling or bulging eyes may signify distress or pain.

Nostrils: Flared nostrils often accompany heightened arousal or excitement. Rapid flaring can indicate stress or fear, while relaxed nostrils are a sign of calmness.

Lips and mouth: A relaxed, slightly drooping lower lip indicates contentment and relaxation. Conversely, tightly closed lips or a tense mouth can suggest discomfort or tension.

Head position: A lowered head with a relaxed neck suggests a calm and relaxed state. Conversely, a raised head with a stiff neck may indicate alertness, tension, or dominance.

Tail: The position and movement of a horse's tail can convey important information. A relaxed, loosely hanging tail typically indicates contentment. A raised tail can signal excitement or aggression, while a tucked or clamped tail can indicate fear or pain.

Body posture: A relaxed horse will have a slightly arched back and evenly distributed weight on all four legs. Conversely, a tense or rigid posture with weight shifted to the hindquarters may indicate discomfort or readiness for action.

Movement: The way a horse moves can also reveal its emotional state. A relaxed horse moves with smooth, fluid strides and swinging motion. On the other hand, stiff, choppy movements or sudden changes in gait can suggest nervousness, pain, or anticipation.

Vocalizations: In addition to facial expressions and body language, horses use vocalizations to communicate. Whinnies, neighs, snorts, and squeals can convey different messages, such as greetings, alarm, or territoriality.

GLOSSARY

A

Accumulator Bet:

A bet involving more than one horse/race. Each winning selection then goes on to the next horse chosen or bet placed. All selections must be successful to win any money back.

Age:

All thoroughbreds have their official birthday on 1 January. In the Southern Hemisphere it is on 1 August.

Allowance

Inexperienced riders (apprentices, conditionals and amateurs) are allowed a weight concession to compensate for their lack of experience against their colleagues. The 'allowance' is usually 3lb, 5lb or 7lb, with it decreasing as the young jockey rides more winners

All Weather (AWT)

An artificial racing surface. There are five all-weather racetracks in Britain (Kempton Park, Lingfield, Southwell, Wolverhampton and Chelmsford City) and one in Ireland (Dundalk), and they stage flat racing all year round. There are three types of surface - Fibresand, Tapeta and Polytrack

Amateur

A non-professional jockey who does not receive a fee for riding in a race, denoted on the racecard by the prefix Mr, Mrs, Miss, Captain etc. Some races are restricted to amateur jockeys.

At the post

When all the horses have arrived at the start before a race, they are said to be 'at the post'.

Abandoned

A race meeting which has been canceled due to bad weather. All bets placed on abandoned races are fully refunded.

B

Backed / Backed-In

A 'backed' horse is one on which lots of bets have been placed. A horse which is backed-in means that the people betting have outlaid a lot of money on that horse and the odds have decreased as a result e.g. "Denman has been backed in to 2/1".

Backstretch / Back Straight

The straight length of the track on the far side of the course from the stands.

Backward

A horse that has not developed fully or not fully fit.

Banker

A horse that is expected to win

Bar

A term used when describing bookmakers' prices. c.g. '4/1 bar two' means that you can obtain at least 4/1 about any horse except for the first two in betting.

Bay (B)

Bay horses range from light brown to the darkest, but always have black manes, tails and legs.

Betting market

A market is the prices offered for each runner by bookmakers on a particular race. The more popular a horse with punters, the shorter its price will be.

Betting Ring

The area at a racecourse where the on course bookmakers operate. Look out for their odds boards and listen out for them shouting the odds.

Bismarck

A betting term used to describe a favorite that bookmakers expect to lose and are therefore happy to take bets on.

Bit

The metal part of the bridle that sits in a horse's mouth. Reins attach to the bit and are used by the jockey to control the horse.

Black (BL)

A horse of the darkest possible color. Pure black thoroughbreds are rare.

Blanket Finish

When a group of horses finish a race in a line. The term comes from the idea that they are so close together you could theoretically put a single blanket across them. The Judge usually calls a photo to decide the official placings.

Blinds

Another name for blinkers.

Blinkers

A form of headgear worn by racehorses, consisting of a hood with cups around the eyes. They are used to limit a horse's vision and reduce distractions, with the aim of making it concentrate. A horse wearing blinkers is denoted on a racecard by a small b next to the horse's weight (b1 indicates that the horse is wearing blinkers in a race for the first time).

Bloodstock sales

The sale of horses at auction

Blowout

A short workout, usually a day or two before a race, designed to clear the horse's airways before the race. Can also be referred to as a pipe-opener.

Board prices

The generally available odds displayed on the boards of on-course bookmakers. It is from these that the starting price (SP) is derived. 'Taking the board price' means taking the last price shown against your selection at the time you strike the bet

Book

A record of the bets made on a particular race or other sporting event.

Bookmaker

A person/company licensed to accept bets. Also known as a bookie.

Bottle

The tic-tac bookmaking term for 2-1

Boxed in

A horse that cannot overtake another horse because it is blocked by other horses.

Boxwalker

A horse that constantly walks around its stable and refuses to settle.

Break (a horse) in

Teaching a young horse to accept riding equipment and carry a rider.

Breather

When the jockey temporarily restrains a horse for a short distance to permit him to fill his lungs during a race.

Breeder

Someone who breeds racehorses. They own the dam (mother) at the time the foal is born.

Breeze

Galloping a horse at a moderate speed. This is slower than racing pace.

Breeze-Up

An auction, usually for unraced two-year-olds, at which the horses for sale run for a short distance to allow prospective buyers to assess them.

Bridle

The leather tack worn by a horse on its head and used to control it.

Bridle, won on the

A horse who won easily, without being hard ridden or challenged by other horses.

Broke down

When a horse sustains an injury during a race.

Broodmare

A mare kept at stud for breeding. Broodmares have either retired from racing or will be unraced.

Brought down

A horse whose fall during a race is caused by another horse.

Brown (BR)

Brown horses can be light brown through to almost black, but will have a matching mane and tail. The most common color among thoroughbreds.

Bumper

A Flat race run under Jump Rules, used to educate young prospective jumps horses before they tackle hurdles or fences. Officially called the National Hunt Flat Race.

Bumping

Interference during a race where one horse collides with another. Often results in a Stewards' Enquiry, particularly when interference takes place in the closing stages of the race.

Burlington Bertie

The tic-tac bookmaking term for 100-30.

C

Carpet

The tic-tac bookmaking term for 3-1. Double carpet is 33-1.

Chaser

A horse that takes part in steeplechase races.

Checked

When a horse's run during a race is momentarily blocked by another horse or horses.

Cheekpieces

Strips of sheepskin that are attached to the side of a horse's bridle. They partially obscure a horse's rear vision, with the aim of getting the horse to concentrate on racing. Horses wearing cheekpieces are denoted on a racecard by a small p next to the horse's weight.

Chestnut (CH)

A reddish or ginger coat color, with a mane and tail to match.

Claimer (jockey)

An apprentice Flat jockey.

Claiming race / Claimer

A race in which each horse's weight is determined by the price placed on them by connections. The lower the claiming price, the lower the weight. Horses can be 'claimed' (bought) by other owners/trainers for the specified price after the race.

Classic

Group of historic major races for three-year-olds in the Flat season. In Britain the five Classics are (in running order) the 2,000 Guineas, the 1,000 Guineas, the Oaks, the Derby and the St Leger - most European countries have their own versions of these Classics. A Classic contender is a horse being aimed at one of these races or is regarded as having the potential to compete at that level.

Clerk of the Course

Racecourse official responsible for the overall racecourse management, including the preparation of the racing surface.

Clerk of the Scales

Racecourse official whose chief duty is to weigh the riders before and after a race to ensure proper weight is carried.

Cockle

The tic-tac bookmaking term for 10-1.

Co-favourite

A horse that shares its position at the head of the betting market with at least two other horses.

Colors

Jacket ('silks') worn by a jockey to identify a horse. A horse runs in its owner's colors which are registered with Weatherbys. The colors to be worn by each jockey are shown on racecards.

Colt

A young male horse up to the age of four.

Combination bet (accumulator)

A bet involving more than one horse with the winnings from each selection going on to the next horse. All selections must be successful to get a return. Combination bets must be placed with the same bookmaker.

Conditional jockey

Jump jockey, under 26, who receives a weight allowance for inexperience until he has ridden a certain number of winners. A conditional jockey is licensed to a specific trainer. Some races are restricted to conditional jockeys only.

Conditions race

A race in which horses are allotted extra weight according to factors including sex, age, whether they are a previous winner etc. This is a better-class race for horses just below Group or Listed level.

Conformation

A horse's build and general physical structure; the way he is put together.

Connections

People associated with a horse, such as the owner and trainer

Course specialist

A horse that is proven at a track by winning or performing well in previous races. Some horses have a racecourse that they perform especially well at.

Covered up

When a jockey keeps a horse behind other runners to prevent it running too freely in the early stages of a race.

Covering

The act of horses mating. A stallion covers a mare.

Cut in the ground

A description of the ground condition where the racing surface has been softened by rain.

D

Dam

The mother of a horse.

Damsire (broodmare)

The sire of a broodmare; in human terms, the maternal grandfather of a horse.

Dark horse

A horse regarded as having potential but whose full capabilities have not been revealed.

Dead-heat

A tie between two or more horses for first place, or for one of the other finishing positions. In the event of a dead-heat for first place, the winnings from a bet are calculated by halfing the money wagered and paying out at full odds. If more than two horses dead-heat, the stake is proportioned accordingly.

Decimal odds

Used on the Tote and betting exchanges, instead of fractional odds. Decimal odds are expressed as a figure (in round or decimal terms) that represents the potential total winning return to the punter. So, 4 (or 4.0) in Tote or decimal odds is the same as the conventional 3-1, as it represents a potential total winning return of

Declared (runner)

A horse confirmed to start in a race at the final declarations stage.

Deductions

When a horse is scratched from a race after the betting market has already opened, deductions are made to the win and place bets placed on other horses in proportion to the odds of the scratched horse.

Disqualification

When a horse is demoted down the finishing order due to an infringement of the Rules following a Stewards' Enquiry.

Distance

The margin by which a horse has won or has been beaten (e.g. a horse might have a winning distance of three lengths). In Jump racing, if a horse is beaten/wins by a long way (more than 30 lengths) it is said to have been beaten/won by a distance.

Dividend

The amount that a winning or placed horse returns for every

Double

Consists of one bet involving two selections in different events. Both selections must be successful to get a return, with the winnings from the first selection going on to the second selection. The return is calculated by multiplying the odds on the two selections: e.g. a

Double carpet

The tic-tac bookmaking term for 33-1.

Draw

A horse's starting position in the stalls allotted in races on the Flat. Stall numbers are drawn at random by Weatherbys (except in a handful of top races that allow each horse's connections, having been randomly selected, to choose the stall number for their horse). A horse with a seemingly advantageous draw is said to be "well drawn". Stalls are used for Flat racing only.

Drifter

A horse whose odds get bigger just before the race due to a lack of support in the market. Often referred to as being "on the drift".

Drop in class/trip

A horse racing in a lower class of race or over a shorter distance (trip) than he has previously run over.

Dual forecast

A bet where the aim is to select both the winner and runner-up in a race in either order.

E

Each-way

A bet where half the total stake is for the selection to win and half is for the selection to be placed (usually in the first three, but in big handicaps the places may extend to fourth or fifth). If the horse wins, the win portion is calculated in the normal way, while the place portion of the bet is settled at a fraction of the win odds.

Enquiry

Review of the race by the Stewards to check into a possible infraction of the Rules of Racing. If the enquiry could affect the result of the race, an announcement will be made on course.

Entire horse

An ungelded horse.

Evens/Even money

A price of 1-1. When your stake brings equal winnings e.g.

Exacta / Straight forecast

A bet picking the first and second in a race in the exact order of finish.

F

Furlong

220 yards or one eighth of a mile. The numbered posts on British racecourses show the amount of furlongs left until the winning post.

Fancied

When a horse is expected to win or at least to be involved in the finish.

Favorite

The horse with the shortest odds in the race.

Field

The number of horses in a race or, in betting, all of the horses in a race except the favorite.

Filly

A young female horse up to the age of four.

First string

Where a trainer and/or owner has more than one runner in a race, the horse considered to be the stable's main chance to win is referred to as the stable's first string. Clues to which horse this is can be whether it carries the owner's first colors, is ridden by the stable jockey and/or is shorter odds in the betting than a stablemate.

Fixed-odds betting

Staking a set amount to win a set amount by multiplying the stake by the odds. As opposed to spread betting, where the amount that can be won or lost on a single bet may vary.

Fixture

A race meeting normally consists of 6, 7 or 8 races.

Flat racing

Racing without jumps. The centerpiece of the Flat racing season is the Turf season, which runs from late March to early November. Races are run over a minimum distance of 5f up to a maximum of 2m6f. However, the birth of All-Weather racing in 1989, has allowed Flat racing to continue year-round, and the official Flat racing season now runs for a calendar year to include those Flat races run on all-weather surfaces.

Foal

Newborn horse up to one year old.

Forecast

A bet where the aim is to select both the winner and runner-up in a race. A straight forecast is the winner and runner-up in the correct order. A dual forecast is the winner and runner-up in either order.

Form

Form is the record of a horse's performance in previous races. In the race card, it normally is arranged as a line of numbers denoting finishing position or abbreviations. Form is runs from left to right, with the oldest races on the left and the most recent on the right.

Front-runner

A horse whose running style is to attempt to get on or near the lead at the start of the race and stay there as long as possible.

G

Gallop

The fastest pace for a horse

Gallops

Training ground where horses are exercised. The major training centers in Britain are Newmarket and Malton (mostly Flat), and Lambourn (mostly Jump) with the Curragh in Ireland. Many trainers have private gallops of their own.

GamCare

The national center for information, advice and practical help with regard to the social impact of gambling.

Gates

The front section of the starting stalls, which open at the start of a

Flat race to release the horses. Used as another term for starting stalls.

Gelding

A male horse that has been castrated.

General Stud Book

Register of all thoroughbred horses, maintained by Weatherbys.

Get the trip

To stay the distance.

Go through the card

To have the winner of every race at a race meeting, either as a trainer, jockey, tipster or punter.

Going

The condition of the racing surface. Ranges from heavy to firm.

Going down

When horses are on their way to the start, they are said to be "'Going down to post".

Green

Used to describe an immature or inexperienced horse.

Grey (GR)

Ranging from bright white to a very dark gray that is almost black.

Group / Graded races

These races form the upper tier of the racing structure, with Group/Grade 1 the most important, followed by Group/Grade 2 and Group/Grade 3. Group races are run on the Flat; Graded races are run over jumps (the most important Flat races in the United States are also Graded).

Group 1 (Flat) / Grade 1 (jumps)

The highest category of race. The Classic Flat races in Britain, as well as other historic races are Group 1. The major championship races over jumps, such as the Cheltenham Gold Cup, are Grade 1.

Guineas (currency)

A guinea was one pound and one shilling (

Guineas (race)

Shorthand for the 1000 Guineasand/or 2000 Guineas. A 'Guineas horse' is one that is considered capable of running in one of these Classic races.

H

Hacked up

Describes a horse winning easily.

Half-brother/sister

When two horses have the same mother (dam), they are half-brothers/sisters. Horses are not referred to as half-brothers/sisters when they share only the same father (sire).

Handicap

A race where each horse is allotted a different weight to carry, according to the official handicap ratings determined by the BHA Handicappers. The theory is that all horses run on a fair and equal basis - the 'perfect' handicap being one where all the runners finish in a dead-heat.

Handicap mark/rating

Each horse, once it has run a few times (usually three), is allocated an official handicap rating by the BHA, which is used to determine its weight if it runs in a handicap. If a horse does well, its handicap rating will go up; if it performs poorly, its rating will go down.

Handicapper

Official responsible for allocating a handicap rating to each horse that has qualified for one, and for allotting the weights to be carried by each horse in a handicap. Employed by the British Horseracing Authority.

Hard ridden

Used to describe a horse whose jockey is expanding full effort on the horse, and using his whip.

Headquarters

Newmarket, traditionally seen as the home of Flat racing, is often called Headquarters.

Home straight

The length of the straight track, from the final bend to the finish line.

Hurdler

A horse that races over hurdles, which are lighter and lower than fences.

Hurdles

The smaller obstacles on a jumps course. Horses usually have a season or two over hurdles before progressing to fences, though some continue to specialize in hurdling and never run over fences, while some horses go straight over fences without trying hurdles first.

I

IBAS

Independent Arbitration Betting Service. An arbitration service that deals with betting disputes between punters and bookmakers.

In running

Refers to events that take place during the course of a race.

In-running betting

Betting on the outcome of a race during the race itself, rather than beforehand. This type of betting is particularly popular on the betting exchanges, though it is also offered by many bookmakers. In-running odds can change rapidly as the race unfolds.

J

Jackpot

The Jackpot is a tote bet that requires the selection of the winners of the first six races at a selected meeting. The minimum bet is 50p.

Jocked off

When one jockey is replaced by another on a horse he usually rides or for which he has already been booked to ride in a particular race.

Joint-favorite

If two horses have the shortest odds in the betting, they are described as joint-favorites; if three or more horses have the shortest odds, they are co-favourites.

Judge

Racecourse official responsible for declaring the finishing order of a race and the distances between the runners.

Juvenile

A two-year-old horse. Every horse officially turns two on January 1, at the start of the second full calendar year following its birth e.g. a horse born in 2010 will turn two on January 1, 2012.

Juvenile hurdler

The youngest category of hurdler - juvenile hurdlers are those that turn four years of age (on January 1) during the season in which they start hurdling.

L

Lay

To take a bet on: a bookmaker's offer quoting the price at which he wishes to trade. 'I'll lay 6-4 this favorite.' May also refer to betting on a horse to lose.

Layer

An alternative term for a bookmaker, someone who lays or accepts a bet.

Left-handed track

Racecourse where horses run anti-clockwise.

Length

A unit of measurement for the distances between each horse at the finish of a race; the measurement of a horse from head to tail.

Level weights

When all horses are carrying the same weight. Major championship races, such as the Derby on the Flat or the Cheltenham Gold Cup over jumps, are run at level weights. There are still some allowances for age and sex (e.g. mares receive a 5lb allowance from male horses in the Cheltenham Gold Cup).

Levy

A surcharge collected from bookmakers, based on their turnover or gross profits, which goes towards prize-money, improvements to racecourses, and other areas such as scientific research. The body responsible for this is the Levy Board.

Listed Race

A class of race just below a Group or Graded quality.

Longshot

A horse that is considered unlikely to win. Outsiders like this will have larger odds because there is less chance of them winning.

M

Maiden

A horse that has yet to win a race; maiden races are restricted to such horses, though sometimes the conditions of the race allow previous winners (e.g. maidens at closing, i.e. those that have not won a race up to the time the entries close), in which case penalties are allotted for later wins.

Maiden handicap

A race for maiden horses aged three or above that have run at least four times and have a maximum official rating of 70.

Mare

A female horse aged five years or older.

Market/betting market

A market is the prices offered for each runner by bookmakers on a particular race. The more popular a horse with punters, the shorter its price will be.

Median auction maiden

A race for two-year-olds sired by stallions that had one or more yearling offspring sold in the previous year with a median price not exceeding a specified figure.

Middle distances

On the Flat, races beyond a mile and up to 1m6f are called middle distance races. A middle-distance horse is one that runs mainly over such distances or is regarded as being suitable for those distances.

Minimum trip

The shortest race distance: five furlongs on the Flat, two miles over jumps.

N

Names

Horse names have to be registered with Weatherbys, racing's administrative body, and are subject to approval. Names cannot be longer than 18 characters (including spaces) and must not be the same, in spelling or pronunciation, as a name already registered. In addition, there is a list of 'protected' horse names that cannot be used - these include past winners of big races such as the Grand National and the Classics on the Flat.

Nap

The best bet of the day from a particular tipster.

National Hunt

Racing over fences and hurdles; officially referred to as Jump racing.

Neck

Unit of measurement in a race finish about the length of a horse's neck.

Non Runner

A horse that was originally meant to run but for some reason has been withdrawn from the race.

Non-trier

A horse that is prevented by the jockey from running to its full ability. Non-trying is a serious offense prohibited by the rules of racing, and jockeys (as well as the horse and owner) can be banned from racing if they are found guilty, while the horse's trainer risks a fine and/or a ban.

Nose

Smallest official distance a horse can win by.

Novice

A horse in the early stages of its career is referred to as a novice after it has won its first race.

Novice auction

A race for novices sold at public auction as yearlings or two-year-olds for a price not exceeding a specified figure.

Novice stakes

A Flat race for two-year-olds or three-year-olds that have not won more than twice.

Nursery

A handicap on the Flat for two-year-old horses.

O

Objection

A complaint by one jockey against another regarding the running of a race.

Odds

The chance offered for a selection to win. Also known as the price.

Odds-against

Betting odds where the potential winnings are higher than the stake. The numerator is larger than the denominator (e.g. 2/1).

Odds-on

Betting odds where the stake is higher than the potential winnings if the bet is successful. The denominator is larger than the numerator (e.g. 1/2).

Off the bridle

Describes a horse that is being pushed along by its jockey.

Off the pace

When a horse is some distance behind the front-runners in a race.

On the bridle

Describes a horse running comfortably, still pulling on the bit. A horse that wins 'on the bridle' is regarded as having won easily.

On the nose (to bet)

Placing a bet on a horse to win.

One-paced

Describes a horse that is unable to raise its pace in the closing stages of a race.

Open ditch

Steeplechase jump with a ditch on the approach side to the fence.

Out of the handicap

In all handicap races, there is a maximum and minimum weight that horses can carry. If a horse's handicap rating means that its allocated weight should be lower than the minimum for that race, it is said to be 'out of the handicap'. e.g. in a Flat handicap where a horse set to carry the minimum weight of 7st 7lb is rated 65, a horse rated 62 should be allocated 7st alb but would have to carry the minimum 7st 7lb in the race - this horse would be described as being '3lb out of the handicap' (ie it will be carrying 3lb more than its 'true' handicap weight).

Out Of The Money

A horse that finishes outside of the place money.

Outsider

Long-priced horses in the betting, regarded as unlikely to win.

Over the top

When a horse is considered to be past its peak due to too much racing/training and needs a rest.

Overnight declarations

Horses entered for a race must be 'declared to run' and this usually happens 48 hours before a race - horses left in a race at this stage are known as '48 hour declarations' and they comprise the final field for that race. At this stage a trainer must also 'declare' the jockey who will ride the horse and any equipment (e.g. blinkers) the horse will carry - this information also appears on racecards in newspapers and at the racecourse.

Overweight

When a horse carries more than its allocated weight, due to the jockey being unable to make that weight. e.g. if a horse is allocated 9st in the handicap but carries 9st 2lb, the jockey is said to have 'put up 2 lb overweight'. This is usually a disadvantage, though sometimes the trainer of a horse may decide to accept overweight in order to have one of the best jockeys on board his horse.

P

Pacemaker

A horse that is entered in a race with the intention that it will set the pace for another horse with the same connections.

Paddock

Area of the racecourse incorporating the parade ring (where horses are paraded prior to the race) and winner's enclosure. Connections of the horses gather in the centre of the paddock before each race and jockeys mount before taking the horses out onto the racecourse.

Parade

Before major races, the horses often lineup in racecard order (numerical order) and lead in front of the grandstands to allow racegoers to see them. At the end of the parade the horses are released to canter down to the start.

Patent

Multiple bet consisting of seven bets involving three selections in different events. A single on each selection, plus three doubles and one treble. One successful selection guarantees a return.

Pattern

The grading system for the most important races, introduced on the Flat in 1971 and later for jumps racing. The top races on the Flat are Group 1, followed by Group 2 and Group 3 (the next highest category is

Listed, which, while not technically part of the Pattern, combines with Group races under the heading of black-type races).

Penalized horses

Horses that have incurred a weight penalty as a result of previous successes.

Penalty

Additional weight carried by a horse on account of previous wins. In a handicap, a penalty is added to a horse's original weight if it has won in between being entered for the race and running in it, as the handicapper has not had the opportunity to re-assess that horse's handicap rating. A penalty (commonly 6lb) is shown after the horse's name on Racing Post racecards - e.g. Horse Name (ex6).

Photo finish

In a close race, where the placings cannot be determined easily, the result is determined by the judge by examination of a photograph taken by a camera on the finishing line.

Placepot

Similar rules to the Jackpot, but your selections have only to be placed.

Pulled up

A horse that drops out of a race and does not finish.

Pulling

When a horse is unsettled during the early part of a race and uses too much energy, fighting the jockey by pulling against the bridle.

Punter

A person who gambles or lays a bet.

Pushed out

When a horse is ridden vigorously, but without full effort by the jockey.

Q

Quarters

The hind parts of a horse, specifically between flank and tail.

R

Racecard

Programme for the day's racing, showing the times, runners and riders for each race.

Rails (racecourse)

White plastic rails are used to mark out the track on a racecourse. The stands rails are those nearest the grandstand and the far rails are those on the opposite side of the track from the grandstand. A horse referred to as being 'on the rails' or 'against the rails' is running close to the rails, which often helps a horse to keep a straight line in a race finish. A horse that has 'grabbed the rail' is one whose rider has maneuvered to a position close to the rail.

Rating

A measure of the ability of a horse on a scale starting at zero and going into three figures. Flat and Jump racing use different scales; the highest-rated Flat horse is usually in the 130s and the top-rated jumper in the 180s.

Return

Total amount received for a winning bet (winnings plus stake) OR the result/final odds for a race e.g. the winner was returned at 4-1.

Right-handed track

Racecourse where horses run clockwise.

Roan (RO)

A Roan horse has an even mixture of white hairs mixed in with another color.

Rule 4

Tattersalls Rule 4 (c): One of the most commonly invoked betting rules, dealing with deductions from winning bets in the event of any withdrawn runner(s) from a race. The rule applies to winning bets struck at prices laid before a withdrawal (other than ante-post bets, which are unaffected by Rule 4 (c)) and to starting-price bets where, after a late withdrawal, there is insufficient time to reform the market. The rate of deductions is in proportion to the odds of the non-runner(s) at the time of the withdrawal.

S

Schooling

Training a horse for jumping.

Second string

The stable's second choice from two or more runners in a race.

Selling plate/selling race

Low-class race in which the winner is offered at auction afterwards; other horses in the race may be claimed for a fixed sum. If the winning stable buys back its own horse it is said to be 'bought in'. The racecourse receives a percentage of the selling price of each horse.

Selling plater

A horse that runs in selling plates. Also known as a seller.

Short Price

Low odds, meaning a punter will get little return for their initial outlay.

Shortening odds

If bookmakers receive a lot of bets on a particular horse, they will shorten or reduce its odds.

Silks

See 'Colors'.

Silver ring

A racecourse enclosure, usually the one with the lowest admission price.

Single

The simplest and most popular bet, normally a win bet on one horse in one race.

Sire

The father of a horse

Soft (going)

Condition of a turf course where rain has left the ground 'soft' (official going description).

SP

Short for starting price.

Spread a plate

When a horse damages or loses a horseshoe before a race, it is said to have 'spread a plate'. The horse has to be re-shod by a farrier, often delaying the start of the race.

Springer

A horse whose price shortens dramatically.

Sprint races

Flat races run over a distance of five or six furlongs.

Sprinter

A horse that specializes in running over the shortest distances (five and six furlongs) on the Flat.

Stallion

A male horse used for breeding

Stalls handler

Member of a team employed to load horses into the stalls for Flat races and to move the stalls to the correct position for the start of each race.

Starter

Racecourse official responsible for starting a horse race.

Starting price

Often abbreviated to SP. The starting prices are the final odds prevailing at the time the race starts and are used to determine the payout to winning punters, unless a punter took a specified price at the time of placing the bet.

T

Tattersalls (racecourse enclosure)

The enclosure next in status to Members. Those choosing this enclosure have access to the main betting area and the paddock.

Thoroughbred

A breed of horse used for racing.

Tic-tac

The sign language used by bookmakers to communicate changes in betting odds on the racecourse. Tic-tacs wear white gloves and signal the odds using their hands and arms.

Tongue tie

Strip of material tied around a horse's tongue and lower jaw to keep it from swallowing its tongue, which can clog its air passage. A horse wearing a tongue tie is denoted on a racecard by a small t next to the horse's weight (t1 indicates that the horse is wearing a tongue tie in a race for the first time).

Tote (betting)

Introduced in Britain in 1929 to offer pool betting on racecourses. All the stakes on a particular bet are pooled, before a deduction is made to cover the Tote's costs and contribution to racing. The remainder of the pool is divided by the number of winning units to give a dividend that is declared inclusive of a

Trainer

The person responsible for looking after a horse and preparing it to race. A trainer must hold a license or permit to be entitled to train.

Treble

A three-leg accumulator. All three selections must be successful to get a return; the winnings from the first selection automatically go on to the second and then on to the third.

Trip

Another term for the distance of a race. When a horse has the stamina for a certain distance, it is said to 'stay/get the trip'.

Triple Crown

In Britain, for colts the Triple Crown comprises the 2,000 Guineas, the Derbya and the St Leger; for fillies, the 1,000 Guineas, the Oaks and the St Leger. Winning all three races is a rare feat, last achieved by a colt (Nijinsky) in 1970 and by a filly (Oh So Sharp) in 1985. The American

Triple Crown comprises the Kentucky Derby, Preakness Stakes and Belmont Stakes.

Trixie

Multiple bet consisting of four bets involving three selections in different events. The bet includes three doubles and one treble. A minimum of two selections must be successful to get a return.

Turn of foot

A horse's ability to accelerate in the closing stages of a race. A horse with a 'good turn of foot' has good finishing speed.

Turned out

1) Racecourses often have a 'best turned out' award for the horse judged to have been best presented in the paddock. 2) A racehorse that is taking a break from racing/training and is out in the fields is said to have been 'turned out'.

Two-year-old

Every horse officially turns two on January 1, at the start of the second full calendar year following its birth e.g. a horse born in 2008 will turn two on January 1,2010. Two-year-old horses are also known as juveniles, and this is the first age at which horses are allowed to compete on the Flat (the youngest racing age over jumps is three years old).

U

Under starters orders/under orders

The moment a race is about to begin. Once the horses are in the stalls for a Flat race, or have lined up at the start for a Jump race, they are said to be 'under starter's orders' as the jockeys are waiting for the starter's signal to begin the race.

Unfancied

Not expected to win.

V

Valet

A person employed to prepare a jockey's equipment in the weighing room.

Visor

Similar to blinkers, but with a slit in each eye cup to allow some lateral vision. A horse wearing a visor is denoted on a racecard by a small v next to the horse's weight (v1 indicates that the horse is wearing a visor in a race for the first time).

W

Walkover

A race involving only one horse. The horse and its jockey must pass the winning post to be declared the winner.

Weighed in

The official declaration ratifying a race result.

Weighing in/out

Each jockey (wearing his racing kit and carrying his saddle) must stand on official weighing scales before and after the race, so that the Clerk of the Scales can check that the jockey is carrying the correct weight allotted to his horse. If a jockey is above the allotted weight before the race, his horse can still compete but must carry overweight. When the weights carried by the winner and placed horses have been verified after the race, there will be an announcement that they have 'weighed in'. This confirms the race result and at this point bookmakers will pay out on successful bets.

Weight cloth

A cloth with pockets for lead weights placed under the saddle to ensure that a horse carries its allotted weight.

Weight for age

A graduated scale that shows how horses of differing ages progress month by month during the racing season, the differences being expressed in terms of weight. This allows horses of differing ages to compete against each other on a fair basis, based on their age and maturity, in what are known as weight-for-age races.

Weights

Lead placed in a weight cloth. When these weights are added to the jockey's weight and other equipment, the total weight should equal the weight allotted to the jockey's horse in a race.

Well in

When a horse is considered to be favored by the weights in a race, it is said to be 'well in'.

Whip

Also known as a stick, it used by jockey as an aid to encourage or steer and balance

White (WH)

This color is very rare among Thoroughbreds. The horse will have pink skin. Most horses that appear to be white will in fact be Grey.

Win bet/only

A single bet on a horse to finish first. Win only markets signify that no each-way betting is available.

Work rider

A stable employee, not necessarily a licensed jockey, who rides horses in training on the gallops.

Y

Yankee

Multiple bet consisting of 11 bets (six doubles, four trebles and one four-fold) on four selections in different events. At least two selections must be successful to get a return.

Yard

A trainer's premises from where racehorses are trained.

Yearling

A one year old horse.

Yielding

Irish term to describe racecourse going that is soft.

ABOUT THE AUTHOR:

 Sultan Zeshan is a talented American creative artist, author, and producer who demonstrates his multifaceted abilities and unwavering commitment to true stories, history, and social justice in his carefully curated works. With a distinguished academic background in medicine and a graduate education encompassing philosophy, religious studies, and African American studies from Louisiana State University, Sultan's expertise shines brilliantly through his storytelling, firmly grounded in meticulous research.

Sultan's creative endeavors not only showcase his depth of knowledge but also reflect his passion for illuminating the lives of forgotten individuals who have played pivotal roles in shaping our world. Serving as a respected board member and advisor for M. Progressive Values (MPV) and a dedicated member of the NAACP, Sultan harnesses the transformative power of nonfiction narratives to breathe life into the stories of these significant figures. His ability to seamlessly weave their narratives into captivating storylines resonates deeply with readers.

Through his writing and storytelling, Sultan inspires and empowers readers, evoking a profound sense of social consciousness and driving positive social change. His works leave an indelible impact on audiences, stimulating thoughtful reflection, nurturing empathy, and inspiring action. Sultan Zeshan's contributions to the literary and artistic landscape stand as a testament to his unwavering dedication to advancing knowledge, advocating for justice, and making a lasting and meaningful difference in the world.

ACKNOWLEDGEMENTS

I would like to express my sincere appreciation to the individuals who have provided invaluable support and assistance throughout the process of assembling this book. I am particularly grateful to Dr. Stephen Finley, my esteemed professor, whose guidance, and expertise have been instrumental in shaping this work. Additionally, I extend my heartfelt thanks to Dr. Lori Martin for her invaluable advice and unwavering support. I would also like to extend my gratitude to Becky from the Keeneland Library and the staff at the International Museum of the Horse for their generous contributions and access to their invaluable resources. Their extensive knowledge and dedication to preserving the history of horses have greatly enriched the content of this book.

Furthermore, I would like to express my deepest appreciation to my mother Talat, Vince Emmett, Keith Neubert, Jay Lilly, Attorney Bernie Lawrence, Attorney Reazalia Allen, Attorney Lela Schmidt, Orell, Patreece, Dominique, Lawrence Law Parker (aka Supreme Street), and my sisters, Hina and Saba, for their significant contributions to this project. Their expertise, insights, and unwavering support have played a pivotal role in enhancing the quality and depth of this book. Moreover, I am deeply grateful to my dear friends who have been unwavering pillars of support throughout this journey: Dr. Lorin Chasar, Woo Ae Yi, and Giovanna Traconis. Their encouragement, feedback, and companionship have been invaluable, and I am truly indebted to them. I am profoundly thankful to these exceptional individuals and institutions, including the Keeneland Library and the International Museum of the Horse, without whom the realization of this book would not have been possible. Their unwavering commitment, generosity, and assistance have been instrumental in bringing this project to fruition.

BIBLIOGRAPHY

"1896 Original Horse Racing Pepsin Gum Pinback Hof Black Jockey Anthony Hamilton." *Cop Block*, https://www.copblock.org/items/1896-Original-Horse-Racing-Pepsin-Gum-Pinback-Hof-Black-Jockey-Anthony-Hamilton_282543436932.html.

"2022 Belmont Stakes Horses, Contenders, Odds, Dates." 2022 Kentucky Derby & Oaks | May 6 and May 7, 2022, https://www.kentuckyderby.com/racing/belmont-stakes.

"2022 Travers Stakes at Saratoga Race Course: August 27, 2022." SaratogaRaceTrack.com, 25 July 2022, https://www.saratogaracetrack.com/travers/.

"Abe Hawkins as a Rider and a Jockey." Facebook, https://www.facebook.com/oldima.md/posts.

"Abe Hawkins." Abe Hawkins | The Chronicle of African Americans in the Horse Industry, https://africanamericanhorsestories.org/research/people/abe-hawkins.

Abe Hawkins, the Antebellum South's Greatest Jockey. https://theauthorscove.com/2020/03/06/abe-hawkins-the-antebellum-souths-greatest-jockey/comment-page-1/.

"Abe Hawkins." Wikipedia, Wikimedia Foundation, 9 Sep. 2021, https://en.wikipedia.org/wiki/Abe_Hawkins.

"Advanced Search." Racing and Sports, https://www.racingandsports.com/search.

"The Afro American." Google News Archive Search, Google, https://news.google.com/newspapers?nid=2211&dat=19241220&id=SjUmAAAAIBAJ&sjid=Ov4FAAAAIBAJ&pg=5174%2C946490&hl=en.

"A Brief History of Civil Rights in the United States: Jim Crow Era." HUSL Library, https://library.law.howard.edu/civilrightshistory/blackrights/jimcrow.

"A Brief History of Horse Racing." America's Best Racing, https://www.americasbestracing.net/the-sport/2021-brief-history-horse-racing.

"A Brief History of Jim Crow." Constitutional Rights Foundation, https://www.crf-usa.org/black-history-month/a-brief-history-of-jim-crow

"A Clever Base-Ballast: The Life and Times of John Montgomery Ward." Internet Archive, New York: Pantheon Books, 1 Jan. 1999, https://archive.org/details/cleverbaseballis00brya

"Abe Hawkins." Abe Hawkins | The Chronicle of African Americans in the Horse Industry, https://africanamericanhorsestories.org/research/people/abe-hawkins

"About Abe Hawkins: African American Jockey (Born: N/A - Died: 1867): Biography Facts, Career, Life." Peoplepill.com, https://peoplepill.com/people/abe-hawkins

Admin. "Moses Fleetwood Walker." Society for American Baseball Research, 17 Dec. 2020, https://sabr.org/bioproj/person/fleet-walker/#sd_endnote_8_anc

"African Americans." Encyclopædia Britannica, Encyclopædia Britannica, Inc., https://www.britannica.com/topic/African-American

"African Americans and Horse Racing." Edited by Encyclopedia Britannica, Encyclopædia Britannica, Encyclopædia Britannica, Inc., https://www.britannica.com/topic/African-Americans-and-Horse-Racing-1984952

"African American Contributions to the Aiken Horse Industry." Aiken, https://www.aikenracinghalloffame.com/Aiken-s_African American_Contributions_to_the_Aiken_Horse_Industry.html

"African Americans in HorseRacing," Black Athlete Sports Network, www.blackathletesportsnetwork.net/artman/publish/article_0581.shtml (January 6, 2006).

"African Americans in the Derby," KentuckyDerby.com, www.kentuckyderby.com/2004/derby_history/african_americans_in_the_derby/jockeys.html (January 6, 2006).

"African Americans in Toledo Sports - Baseball: Moses Fleetwood Walker Part II." HOME - Toledo's

Attic, https://toledosattic.org/exhibits/104-exhibit-themes/toledo-sport-history/174-african-americans-toledosports-essay?start=2

"The African American Odyssey: A Quest for Full Citizenship Acknowledgments." Library of Congress, 9 Feb. 1998, https://www.loc.gov/exhibits/african-american-odyssey/acknowledgments.html

"Abe Hawkins." African American Horse Stories, https://www.africanamericanhorsestories.org/research/people/abe-hawkins

"Ansel Williamson." African American Horse Stories, https://www.africanamericanhorsestories.org/research/people/ansel-williamson

"African-American Sports Greats." Google Books, Google, https://books.google.com.pk/books?id=cLFhNYLJD-sC&newbks=0&hl=en&source=newbks_fb&redir_esc=y

"African Americans Who Were First." Internet Archive, New York : Cobblehill Books, 1 Jan. 1997, https://archive.org/details/africanamericans00pott

"Alonzo Clayton." Wikipedia, Wikimedia Foundation, 23 May 2022, https://en.wikipedia.org/wiki/Alonzo_Clayton

"Alonzo Clayton." Alonzo Clayton | The Chronicle of African Americans in the Horse Industry, https://africanamericanhorsestories.org/research/people/alonzo-clayton

"Alonzo 'Lonnie' Clayton / African American Jockey Historical Marker." Historical Marker, 9 Jan. 2022, https://www.hmdb.org/m.asp?m=162005

"Alonzo 'Lonnie' Clayton, Horse Jockey Born." African American Registry, 20 May 2022, https://aaregistry.org/story/a-kentucky-derby-icon-alonzo-lonnie-clayton/

"Alonzo 'Lonnie' Clayton (1876–1917)." Encyclopedia of Arkansas, 15 Oct. 2019, https://encyclopediaofarkansas.net/entries/alonzo-lonnie-clayton-5300/

Amanda Rogers. Knight Ridder News Service. "Run for Roses Has Long Stem of Tradition / The First Kentucky Derby Was Held in 1875 and the History of the Event Has Grown Richer Ever since." Greensboro News and Record, 24 Jan. 2015.

"American Memory: Remaining Collections." American Memory: Remaining Collections, https://memory.loc.gov/ammem/index.html

Anderson, Ashley. "Top 10 Biggest Horse Races in the World." The TwinSpires Edge, TwinSpires, 2 May 2022, https://edge.twinspires.com/racing/top-10-biggest-horse-races-in-the-world/

Anderson, Ashley. "Triple Crown Records." The TwinSpires Edge, TwinSpires, 27 Apr. 2020, https://edge.twinspires.com/racing/triple-crown-records/

Anderson, Ashley. "10 Top Winning Kentucky Derby Jockeys of All Time." The TwinSpires Edge, TwinSpires, 5 May 2022, https://edge.twinspires.com/racing/10-top-winning-kentucky-derby-jockeys-of-all-time/

"Anna Lee Aldred." Wikipedia, Wikimedia Foundation, 3 May 2022, https://en.wikipedia.org/wiki/Anna_Lee_Aldred

Andrew, Tawana. "Black Jockeys and the Kentucky Derby: A History of Race and Racism." Https://Www.wave3.Com, https://www.wave3.com/2020/09/03/black-jockeys-kentucky-derby-history-race-racism/

"Anthony Hamilton." ANTHONY HAMILTON, https://www.anthonyhamilton.com/

"Anthony Hamilton." Anthony Hamilton | National Museum of Racing and Hall of Fame, https://www.racingmuseum.org/hall-of-fame/jockey/anthony-hamilton

"Ansel Williamson." Ansel Williamson | The Chronicle of African Americans in the Horse Industry, https://africanamericanhorsestories.org/research/people/ansel-williamson

"Ansel Williamson." Ansel Williamson | National Museum of Racing and Hall of Fame, https://www.racingmuseum.org/hall-of-fame/trainer/ansel-williamson

"Ansel Williamson." HRN Menu, https://www.horseracingnation.com/person/Ansel_Williamson

"Ansel Williamson." Wikipedia, Wikimedia Foundation, 28 July 2022, https://en.wikipedia.org/wiki/Ansel_Williamson

"Anthony Hamilton." Anthony Hamilton | National Museum of Racing and Hall of Fame, https://www.racingmuseum.org/hall-of-fame/jockey/anthony-hamilton

"Anthony Hamilton." Anthony Hamilton | The Chronicle of African Americans in the Horse Industry, https://africanamericanhorsestories.org/research/people/anthony-hamilton

"Aristides (Horse)." American Classic Pedigrees, http://www.americanclassicpedigrees.com/aristides.html

"Ascot Racecourse." Wikipedia, Wikimedia Foundation, 18 June 2022, https://en.wikipedia.org/wiki/Ascot_Racecourse

Aulbach, Lucas. "Who Has Won the Most Kentucky Derby Races? Kentucky Derby Trivia Facts You Should Know." Journal, Louisville Courier Journal, 22 Apr. 2022, https://www.courier-journal.com/story/sports/horses/kentucky-derby/2022/02/17/kentucky-derby-trivia-xx-fast-facts-historic-horse-race/6606321001

"Azra (Horse)." American Classic Pedigrees, http://www.americanclassicpedigrees.com/azra.html

"Barnes, Shelby D., 'Pike.'" Omeka RSS, https://nkaa.uky.edu/nkaa/items/show/2701

Bass, Erin Z., et al. "A Legacy of Triumph: The Red Fox of the South & Old Abe of Ashland Plantation." Deep South Magazine, 3 Mar. 2014, https://deepsouthmag.com/2014/03/03/a-legacy-of-triumph-the-red-fox-of-the-south-old-abe-of-ashland-plantation/

Beebout, Christopher, et al. "Explore Ky History." ExploreKYHistory, https://explorekyhistory.ky.gov/

"Beginner's Guide to the Triple Crown." America's Best Racing, https://www.americasbestracing.net/the-sport/2021-beginners-guide-the-triple-crown

"Belmont Oaks." HRN Menu, https://www.horseracingnation.com/stakes/Belmont_Oaks

"Belmont Oaks." Wikipedia, Wikimedia Foundation, 9 July 2022, https://en.wikipedia.org/wiki/Belmont_Oaks

"Belmont Stakes." Home | Belmont Stakes, https://www.belmontstakes.com/.

"Belmont Stakes." Wikipedia, Wikimedia Foundation, 15 June 2022, https://en.wikipedia.org/wiki/Belmont_Stakes

Bfequestrian, and Bfequestrian. "George B. Anderson (Jockey)." Black Male Equestrians, 26 Feb. 2015, https://blackmaleequestrians.wordpress.com/2015/02/25/george-b-anderson-jockey/

"Biggest Horse Races in the World - Reviews, News and Views." British Racecourses, 25 June 2022, https://www.britishracecourses.org/biggest-horse-races-in-the-world/

BlackFacts.com. "Walker, Moses Fleetwood (1857-1924)." Blackfacts.com, https://www.blackfacts.com/fact/walker-moses-fleetwood-1857-1924

Black History. "Isaac Burns Murphy." Black In History, 15 May 2017, https://blackinhistory.tumblr.com/post/160680221718/isaac-burns-murphy

"Black Heritage in Racing: Community Art Contest & Exhibition." Kentucky Derby Museum, https://www.derbymuseum.org/bhir-artcontest.html

"Black Heritage in Racing." Kentucky Derby Museum, https://www.derbymuseum.org/Exhibits/Detail/12/Black-Heritage-in-Racing

"Black History Month: Shining a Spotlight on Notable African American Jockeys." America's Best Racing, https://www.americasbestracing.net/the-sport/2022-black-history-month-shining-spotlight-notable-african-american-jockeys

"Black Horsemen Matter: A Look Back at History." Past The Wire, 13 June 2020, https://pastthewire.com/black-horsemen-matter-a-look-back-at-history/

"Black Jockeys." Soul Of America, 23 Nov. 2020, https://www.soulofamerica.com/us-cities/louisville/black-jockeys/

"Black Maestro: The Epic Life of an American Legend." Harper Collins, 2007. n.p.: n.p., n.d.. 28 July. 2022.

"Black Winning Jockeys in the Kentucky Derby." McFarland & Co., 2002. n.p.: n.p., n.d.. 29 July. 2022.

Bloodhorse. "Jockey Hamilton, Planet Elected to Hof." BloodHorse.com, BloodHorse, 2 June 2016, https://www.bloodhorse.com/horse-racing/articles/129119/jockey-hamilton-planet-elected-to-hof

"Breakout Candidate: Marlins Lefty Fulton." MiLB.com, 22 Feb. 2022, https://www.milb.com/mexican/news/breakout-candidate-miami-marlins-left-hander-dax-fulton

"Brief Biographies - Lewis Oliver." Brief Biographies - JRank Articles, https://biography.jrank.org

Brown, Diane T. "Jimmy Winkfield (1882-1974) ." •, 26 Dec. 2021, https://www.blackpast.org/african-american-history/winkfield-jimmy-1882-1974/

"Brush up on the Your Kentucky Derby Facts Ahead of the 2020 Race." SportsEngine, 25 Aug. 2020, https://www.sportsengine.com/article/equestrian/brush-your-kentucky-derby-facts-ahead-2020-race

Bukowski, John A., and Susan Aiello. "Description and Physical Characteristics of Horses - Horse Owners." MSD Veterinary Manual, MSD Veterinary Manual, 7 July 2022, https://www.msdvetmanual.com/horse-owners/description-and-physical-characteristics-of-horses/description-and-physical-characteristics-of-horses\

Byer, Beverley. "Historical Accomplishments of African American Jockeys in Triple Crown Thoroughbred

Racing." HubPages, HubPages, 6 Aug. 2017, https://hubpages.com/sports/Historical-Accomplishments-of-African-American-Jockeys-in-Triple-Crown-Thoroughbred-Racing

"Calendar of Events." GoToLouisville.com Official Travel Source, https://www.gotolouisville.com/events-calendar/

"Cap Anson." Society for American Baseball Research, Admin /Wp-Content/Uploads/2020/02/sabr_logo.Png, 4 Jan. 2012, https://sabr.org/bioproj/person/cap-anson/

Carey, Mac. "Eliza Carpenter, the Black Jockey Who Made Horse Racing History." Mental Floss, Mental Floss, 29 Mar. 2021, https://www.mentalfloss.com/article/644255/eliza-carpenter-first-black-jockey-horse-racing

"Causes of the Civil War | History Detectives." PBS, Public Broadcasting Service, https://www.pbs.org/opb/historydetectives/feature/causes-of-the-civil-war/

Carter, Aaron. "First Black Preakness Winner All but Erased from History." CNS Maryland, CNS Maryland, 13 Apr. 2012, https://cnsmaryland.org/2012/04/13/first-black-preakness-winner-all-but-erased-from-history/

Chandler, D.L. "Little Known Black History Fact: Alonzo 'Lonnie' Clayton." Black America Web, 27 Mar. 2019, https://blackamericaweb.com/2019/03/27/little-known-black-history-fact-alonzo-lonnie-clayton/

Chandler, D.L. "Little Known Black History Fact: Oliver Lewis." Black America Web, 17 May 2018, https://blackamericaweb.com/2018/05/17/little-known-black-history-fact-oliver-lewis/

"Cheltenham Festival." Wikipedia, Wikimedia Foundation, 15 June 2022, https://en.wikipedia.org/wiki/Cheltenham_Festival

Chilton, Charlotte, and Meg Donohue. "What Do You Know about the Kentucky Derby's History?" Town & Country, Town & Country, 10 Feb. 2022, https://www.townandcountrymag.com/leisure/sporting/a27255219/kentucky-derby-history/

Clark, Kenneth, et al. "The African American Odyssey: A Quest for Full Citizenship in the Civil Rights Era." Library of Congress, 9 Feb. 1998, https://www.loc.gov/exhibits/african-american-odyssey/civil-rights-era.html

"Colin's Ghost: Thoroughbred Horse Racing History" the Futurity, 1888 , http://colinsghost.org/2010/09/the-futurity-1888-to.html

"Colored Troop Regiments from Kentucky, U.S. Civil War." Omeka RSS, https://nkaa.uky.edu/nkaa/items/show/3129

Contributor, Tops in Lex. "Lexington, KY." Tops in Lex, https://www.topsinlex.com/Read/8433/Bridge+lighting+ceremony+set+for+sculptures+on+Oliver+Lewis+Cox , Melvin. "Best of HN: No Room for Bigotry in Equestrian Sport." Eventing Nation, 3 Mar. 2017, https://eventingnation.com/best-of-hn-no-room-for-bigotry-in-equestrian-sport/

Crump, Steve. "Remembering the Last Black Jockey to Win the Kentucky Derby." Wave3.com, https://www.wave3.com/2021/05/01/remembering-last-black-jockey-win-kentucky-derby/

C., Omri. "The Walker Brothers – the First Openly Black Professional Baseball Players." Black Research Central, 13 Sept. 2017, https://blackresearchcentralblog.wordpress.com/2017/09/04/blackbaseballhistory/.

"A Country Built by Horse Power." Horse Journals, 5 Nov. 2021, https://www.horsejournals.com/popular/history-heritage/country-built-horse-power

Dan. "10 First African American Players in Major League Baseball." Sports Management Degree Guide, 25 June 2020, https://www.sports-management-degrees.com/10-first-african-american-players-in-major-league-baseball/

Daniels, Author: CJ. "Churchill Downs Re-Names Derby Week Race after Legendary Black Jockey Isaac Murphy." whas11.Com, 9 Mar. 2021, https://www.whas11.com/article/sports/churchill-downs-isaac-murphy/417-18a2779b-8849-438c-b275-7084c42062ce

Dempsey, Michael. "Why a Triple Crown Winner Has Been so Elusive." Bleacher Report, Bleacher Report, 21 Aug. 2017, https://bleacherreport.com/articles/1644250-why-a-triple-crown-winner-has-been-so-elusive

"Derby (Horse Race)." Wikipedia, Wikimedia Foundation, 7 Feb. 2021, https://en.wikipedia.org/wiki/Derby_(horse_race)

"Diversity on the Track: History of Black Jockeys." WLEX, WLEX, 3 Sept. 2020, https://www.lex18.com/sports/race-to-the-derby/diversity-on-the-track-history-of-black-jockeys

Doherty, Patricia. "This Kentucky Distillery Is Honoring the Black Jockeys Who Changed the Derby Forever." Travel + Leisure, Travel + Leisure, 29 Apr. 2021, https://www.travelandleisure.com/food-drink/cocktails-spirits/woodford-reserve-honoring-kentucky-derby-black-jockeys

Donato, Matthew. "Cracking the Horse Racing Code." Bleacher Report, Bleacher Report, 3 Oct. 2017, https://bleacherreport.com/articles/27781-cracking-the-horse-racing-code

Drager, Marvin. "Belmont Stakes." Encyclopædia Britannica, Encyclopædia Britannica, Inc., https://www.britannica.com/sports/Belmont-Stakes

Drager, Marvin. "Triple Crown." Encyclopædia Britannica, Encyclopædia Britannica, Inc., https://www.britannica.com/sports/Triple-Crown-American-thoroughbred-horse-racing

Drape, J. ``Black maestro: the epic life of an American legend (1st ed.)." Morrow. n.p.: n.p., 29 . 29 July. 2022.

Drape, Joe. Black Maestro: The Epic Life of an American Legend. Harper Collins, 2007.

Drobnicki, John A. "A Day at the Races in Black and White: How an 1898 Horse Race Led to a Whipping, a Lawsuit, and a 1901 Arrest." Taylor & Francis, https://www.tandfonline.com/doi/abs/10.1080/17460263.2020.1778074

"Dubai Racing Club." Home | Dubai Racing Club, https://www.dubairacingclub.com/

"Dubai World Cup: A History of Dubai's Horse Racing Glory - Mybayut." A Blog about Homes, Trends, Tips & Life in the UAE | MyBayut, https://www.bayut.com/mybayut/dubai-world-cup-history/

"Dubai World Cup." Wikipedia, Wikimedia Foundation, 3 May 2022, https://en.wikipedia.org/wiki/Dubai_World_Cup

DuBois, W. E. B. Black Reconstruction in America. Oxford University Press, 2014.

DuBois, W. "E." B. n.p.: n.p., n.d.. 28 July. 2022.

"Early Women Jockeys." Raceday 360, 2 Mar. 2016, https://raceday360.com/2016/03/02/early-women-jockeys/

Eby, Dean. "A Guide to Understanding Horse Sounds & Body Language." Pet Keen, 7 Jan. 2022, https://petkeen.com/understanding-horse-sounds-body-language/

Editor. "A Legacy of Triumph: More Stories of Duncan F. Kenner and Abe Hawkins at Ashland Plantation." Turf History Times, 12 Jan. 2021, https://www.turfhistorytimes.com/a-legacy-of-triumph-more-stories-of-duncan-f-kenner-and-abe-hawkins-at-ashland-plantation/

"Edward D. Brown." Edward D. Brown | National Museum of Racing and Hall of Fame, https://www.racingmuseum.org/hall-of-fame/trainer/edward-d-brown

Ellis, Laura. "Curious Derby: What Happened to Black Jockeys?" 89.3 WFPL News Louisville, 9 Oct. 2018, https://wfpl.org/curious-derby-what-happened-to-black-jockeys/

"Eliza Carpenter." Eliza Carpenter | The Chronicle of African Americans in the Horse Industry, https://africanamericanhorsestories.org/research/people/eliza-carpenter

"Eliza Carpenter." Wikipedia, Wikimedia Foundation, 29 Jan. 2022, https://en.wikipedia.org/wiki/Eliza_Carpenter

Eliza Carpenter Marshall Register in Her Wedding Dress - Florida Memory. https://www.floridamemory.com/items/show/155414#!

"Eliza Carpenter, the Black Jockey Who Made Horse Racing History." National Museum of American History, https://americanhistory.si.edu/collections/search/object/nmah_684275

Essington, contributed by: Amy. "Moses Fleetwood Walker (1857-1924)." 5 Mar. 2019, https://www.blackpast.org/african-american-history/walker-moses-fleetwood-1857-1924/

"Essential Quality Wins 152nd Running of Travers Stakes." USA Today, Gannett Satellite Information Network, 28 Aug. 2021, https://www.usatoday.com/story/sports/horseracing/2021/08/28/essential-quality-wins-152nd-running-of-travers-stakes/48770567/

Equidia. "Prix De L'ATLANTIQUE - Enghien - 24/04/2021 : Partants, Pronostics Et Résultats En Vidéos." Courses Hippiques En Direct, Pronostics Du Quinté+ Et Résultats Du PMU, https://www.equidia.fr/courses/2021-04-24/R1/C7

"Equine Industry in Kentucky." Wikipedia, Wikimedia Foundation, 17 Apr. 2022, https://en.wikipedia.org/wiki/Equine_industry_in_Kentucky

Evans, Jamie. "The Filson Historical Society Preserving Our Region's History since 1884." The Filson Historical Society, Jamie Evans Https://Filsonhistorical.org/Wp-Content/Uploads/Filson-Logo.png, 9 Mar. 2022, https://filsonhistorical.org/

"Exploited Expertise: Enslaved People and Their Equine Skills." Exploited Expertise: Enslaved People and Their Equine Skills | The Chronicle of African Americans in the Horse Industry, https://africanamericanhorsestories.org/explore/stories/exploited-expertise-enslaved-people-and-their-equine-skills

"Fleet Walker's Divided Heart." Google Books, Google, https://www.google.co.in/books/edition/Fleet_Walker_s_Divided_Heart/WmOBGhsItGAC?hl=en&gbpv=1&printsec=frontcover

"Fleet Walker's Divided Heart: The Life of Baseball's First Black Major Leaguer." University of Nebraska Press, 1995. n.p.: n.p., n.d.. 29 July. 2022.

"Fleet Walker Stats." Baseball, https://www.baseball-reference.com/players/w/walkefl01.shtml

"For Fans of Ontario Horse Racing." For Fans of Ontario Horse Racing, 31 May 2021, https://fansofhorseracing.com/5968/

"Formula 1 Grand Prix Le Castellet." Jet and More, https://jetandmore.com/experiences/formula-1-grand-prix-de-france-private-flight-le-castellet?gclid=Cj0KCQjw6J-SBhCrARIsAH0yMZgG-JABLd85ATElzbnSTawqx2FPeLaPnzvIlHa09fXY4FPxOntjeEwaAjUAEALw_wcB

Gaultstats, https://www.gaultstats.com/

Gemma Redrup 14 January, and Gemma Redrup. "29 Fascinating Facts about Horses (That You Might Struggle to Believe Are True...)." Horse & Hound, 12 May 2022, https://www.horseandhound.co.uk/features/horse-facts-653825

"George B. Anderson." American Battlefield Trust, https://www.battlefields.org/learn/biographies/george-b-anderson

"George B. Anderson." Wikipedia, Wikimedia Foundation, 28 July 2022, https://en.wikipedia.org/wiki/George_B._Anderson

"George B." Black Then, 14 Nov. 2018, https://blackthen.com/new-draftgeorge-b-spider-anderson-first-african-american-jockey-win-preakness-stakes/

Genaro, Teresa. "Shelby 'Pike' Barnes to Join the Racing Hall of Fame on August 12." Saratogian, Saratogian, 22 July 2021, https://www.saratogian.com/2011/08/05/shelby-pike-barnes-to-join-the-racing-hall-of-fame-on-august-12/

"George B. 'Spider' Anderson." George B. "Spider" Anderson | The Chronicle of African Americans in the Horse Industry, https://africanamericanhorsestories.org/research/people/george-b-spider-anderson

"Grand National." Wikipedia, Wikimedia Foundation, 27 Apr. 2022, https://en.wikipedia.org/wiki/Grand_National

"Grand Prix Motor Racing." Buuks, https://buuks.co.uk/shop/grand-prix-motor-414580p.html?gclid=Cj0KCQjw6J-SBhCrARIsAH0yMZj-aRdsC1O7sItxqZLHnv0ZgNEN7HMKmkilpn6k4_PAqEnu5w8JHz8aAmG8EALw_wcB

"Grand Prix De Deauville." Wikiwand, https://www.wikiwand.com/en/Grand_Prix_de_Deauville

Goldstein, Richard. "Moses Fleetwood Walker." The New York Times, The New York Times, 1 Feb. 2019, https://www.nytimes.com/interactive/2019/obituaries/moses-fleetwood-walker-overlooked.html

Hall, Gene. "Black Jockeys Dominated Early Days of Horse Racing: Gene Hall." Tallahassee Democrat, Tallahassee Democrat, 6 Oct. 2020, https://www.tallahassee.com/story/life/2020/10/06/black-jockeys-dominated-early-days-horse-racing/5895410002/

"Hall of Fame Picks Jockey Anthony Hamilton and the Horse Planet for Induction." Daily Racing Form, https://www.drf.com/news/hall-fame-picks-jockey-anthony-hamilton-and-horse-planet-induction

Harris, John. "Moses Fleetwood Walker Was the First African American to Play Pro Baseball, Six Decades before Jackie Robinson." - Andscape, Andscape, 22 Feb. 2017, https://theundefeated.com/features/moses-fleetwood-walker-was-the-first-african-american-to-play-pro-baseball-six-decades-before-jackie-robinson/

Hawes, Britt, et al. "Women's Style, Recipes, Relationship Advice and More." The List, https://www.thelist.com/394729/h ow-the-kentucky-derby-got started/

Hays, Jeffrey. "Horses: Characteristics, Behavior and Breeds." Facts and Details, https://factsanddetails.com/asian/cat65/sub422/item2704.html

Heimbuch, Jaymi. "12 Astonishing Facts about Horses." Treehugger, Treehugger, 27 July 2022, https://www.treehugger.com/astonishing-facts-about-horses-4869310

"Heritage, History, Horse Racing." 11, https://www.legacyequineacademy.com/heritage-history-horse-racing/

"Hidden History of Horse Racing in Kentucky." The History Press, 2019. n.p.: n.p., n.d ... 29 July. 2022.

History.com Editors. "Kentucky Derby." History.com, A&E Television Networks, 27 Mar. 2018, https://www.history.com/topics/sports/kentucky-derby

"History of Churchill Downs." History of Churchill Downs | Churchill Downs Racetrack | Home of the Kentucky Derby, https://www.churchilldowns.com/visit/about/churchill-downs/history/?fact2&device=mobileApp&webSyncID=ced268bc-ad49-a285-31ab-0d3a6b03c97c&sessionGUID=009b6bcd-746b-80d8-e8ab-eeaed6ae05c1&page=7

"History of the Triple Crown." ESPN, ESPN Internet Ventures, https://www.espn.com/horse/triplecrown04/s/history.html

"Holding the Purse Strings: East End Wealth and Property." Holding The Purse Strings: East End Wealth and Property | The Chronicle of African Americans in the Horse Industry, https://africanamericanhorsestories.org/explore/stories/holding-purse-strings-east-end-wealth-and-property

Horse Handicapping. "Horse Racing History." History of Horse Racing, https://www.winningponies.com/horse-racing-history.html

"Horse Racing." Bloodhorse.com, https://www.bloodhorse.com/horse-racing/

"Horse Racing Nation – the Fan-Powered Horse Racing Community." HRN Menu, https://www.horseracingnation.com/

"Home." Home | 2022 Kentucky Derby & Oaks | May 6 and May 7, 2022, https://www.kentuckyderby.com/

"Home." TDN | Thoroughbred Daily News | Horse Racing News, Results and Video | Thoroughbred Breeding and Auctions, 15 July 2022, https://www.thoroughbreddailynews.com/

"Honoring Black Jockeys." Woodford Reserve, https://www.woodfordreserve.com/blackjockeys/

Horseman, The Accidental. "Women and Horses: Roots of a Special Relationship." More Discussions of Horse and Man, https://hglanham.tripod.com/Horses/horses11.html

"Horse: National Geographic." Animals, https://www.nationalgeographic.com/animals/mammals/facts/horse

"Horse Racing." Edited by Encyclopedia Britannica, Encyclopædia Britannica, Encyclopædia Britannica, Inc., https://www.britannica.com/sports/horse-racing

"Horse Racing." Visit the Main Page, https://www.newworldencyclopedia.org/entry/Horse_Racing

"Horse Racing." Wikipedia, Wikimedia Foundation, 25 June 2022, https://en.wikipedia.org/wiki/Horse_racing

"Horse Racing by Country." Wikipedia, Wikimedia Foundation, 13 Dec. 2021, https://en.wikipedia.org/wiki/Category:Horse_racing_by_country

"Horse Race Grand Prix De Deauville--Outtakes." University of South Carolina - University Librarian, https://digital.tcl.sc.edu/digital/collection/MVTN/id/4439

Hotaling, E. ``They're off! : horse racing at Saratoga (1st ed.)." Syracuse University Press. n.p.: n.p., 18 . 29 July. 2022.

Hotaling, Edward. The Great Black Jockeys: The Lives and Times of the Men Who Dominated America's First National Sport. Three Rivers Press, 1999.

Hotaling, E. ``The Great Black Jockeys: The Lives and Times of the Men Who Dominated America's First National Sport." Forum. n.p.: n.p., 22 . 29 July. 2022.

Hotaling, Edward. "When Racing Colors Included Black." The New York Times, The New York Times, 2 June 1996, https://www.nytimes.com/1996/06/02/sports/backtalkwhen-racing-colors-included-black.html

Hotaling, E. "Wink: the incredible life and epic journey of Jimmy Winkfield." McGraw-Hill. n.p.: n.p., 28. 29 Jul. 2022.

Hotaling, Edward. Wink: The Incredible Life and Epic Journey of Jimmy Winkfield. Ragged Mountain Press, 2006.

"Hot Seat." IMDb, IMDb.com, 7 July 2022, https://www.imdb.com/title/tt15690300/

"Isaac Murphy." Arthur Ashe Legacy, https://arthurashe.ucla.edu/isaac-murphy/

"Isaac B. Murphy." Isaac B. Murphy | National Museum of Racing and Hall of Fame, https://www.racingmuseum.org/hall-of-fame/jockey/isaac-b-murphy

"Isaac Burns Murphy." Encyclopædia Britannica, Encyclopædia Britannica, Inc., https://www.britannica.com/biography/Isaac-Burns-Murphy

"Isaac Burns Murphy." Isaac Burns Murphy | The Chronicle of African Americans in the Horse Industry, https://africanamericanhorsestories.org/research/people/isaac-burns-murphy

"Isaac Burns Murphy." Kentucky Horse Park, https://kyhorsepark.com/equine-theme-park/park-memorials-statues/isaac-burns-murphy/

"Isaac Burns Murphy: One of the Greatest American Jockeys of All Time." Kentake Page, 8 Apr. 2021, https://kentakepage.com/isaac-burns-murphy-one-of-the-greatest-american-jockeys-of-all-time/

"Isaac Burns Murphy: The Great Black Horse Jockey from Kentucky." Black History Heroes, http://www.blackhistoryheroes.com/2017/08/isaac-burns-murphy-great-black-horse.html

"Isaac Burns Murphy." Wikipedia, Wikimedia Foundation, 16 Apr. 2022, https://en.wikipedia.org/wiki/Isaac_Burns_Murphy

"Isaac Murphy: The King of 19th Century Jockeys." America's Best Racing, https://www.americasbestracing.net/the-sport/2022-isaac-murphy-the-king-19th-century-jockeys

"Ip Bloquée." LeTROT, https://www.letrot.com/fr/grand-prix-detail

"Jackie Robinson." Society for American Baseball Research, Admin /Wp-Content/Uploads/2020/02/sabr_logo.Png, 17 Sept. 2021, https://sabr.org/bioproj/person/jackie-robinson/

"Jackie Robinson." Wikipedia, Wikimedia Foundation, 9 July 2022, https://en.wikipedia.org/wiki/Jackie_Robinson

Jakub, Kristen. "10 Fun Facts about Horses." BC SPCA, 14 Mar. 2022, https://spca.bc.ca/news/fun-facts-about-horses/

"James." Black Then, 30 Aug. 2021, https://blackthen.com/james-soup-perkins-one-youngest-prominent-jockeys-west/

"James Perkins." James Perkins | The Chronicle of African Americans in the Horse Industry, https://africanamericanhorsestories.org/research/people/james-perkins

"James Winkfield." James Winkfield | National Museum of Racing and Hall of Fame, https://www.racingmuseum.org/hall-of-fame/jockey/james-winkfield

Jan Somma-Hammel | jsomma@siadvance.comJoe D'Amodio | damodio@siadvance.com, et al. "Staten Island & New York Sports: News, Blogs, Photos, Scores & More." Silive, https://www.silive.com/sports/

Javorsky, Nicole. "The Woman Who Fought Transit Segregation in 19th-Century New York." Bloomberg.com, Bloomberg, https://www.bloomberg.com/news/articles/2018-10-03/the-forgotten-new-york-story-of-an-1800s-civil-rights-hero

Jennifer Williams, PhD. "How to Read Your Horse's Body Language." Equus Magazine, 21 Mar. 2022, https://equusmagazine.com/behavior/horse-body-language/

Jiang, Fereility. "The Differences Between the Chinese Zodiac and Western Astrology." China Highlights, https://www.chinahighlights.com/travelguide/chinese-zodiac/chinese-vs-western-astrology.htm

"Jim Crow Era." Ferris State University, https://www.ferris.edu/HTMLS/news/jimcrow/timeline/jimcrow.htm

"Jimmy Lee." The Keeneland Library, https://keenelandlibrary.omeka.net/items/show/251

Jockey Records Kentucky Derby (1875-2017). https://www.kentuckyderby.com/uploads/wysiwyg/assets/uploads/Jockey_Records_Kentucky_Derby__1875-2017_.pdf

Jordan, Alan. "Home." The Chicago Crusader, 17 May 2022, https://chicagocrusader.com/

Kelly, Kate. "Black Jockey Hall of Famer Isaac Burns Murphy." America Comes Alive, 24 Apr. 2021, https://americacomesalive.com/black-jockey-hall-of-famer-isaac-burns-murphy/

"Kentucky Derby." Encyclopædia Britannica, Encyclopædia Britannica, Inc., https://www.britannica.com/sports/Kentucky-Derby

"Kentucky Derby." Wikipedia, Wikimedia Foundation, 22 June 2022, https://en.wikipedia.org/wiki/Kentucky_Derby

"The Kentucky Derby and Its Traditions." ASIST Translations, 19 Apr. 2013, https://asisttranslations.com/the-kentucky-derby-and-its-traditions/

"Kentucky Derby History." 2022 Kentucky Derby & Oaks | May 6 and May 7, 2022, https://www.kentuckyderby.com/history/kentucky-derby-history

"Kentucky Derby in the United States." Time and Date, https://www.timeanddate.com/holidays/us/kentucky-derby

"Kentucky Derby Museum Launches Major Expanded Exhibit Giving Black Jockeys Their Due as Founders of the Sport." Yahoo! News, Yahoo!, https://news.yahoo.com/kentucky-derby-museum-launches-major-150600424.html

"Kentucky Derby Week: Kentucky Oaks Presented by Longines." Kentucky Derby Week: Kentucky Oaks Presented by Longines | 2022 Kentucky Derby & Oaks | May 6 and May 7, 2022, https://www.kentuckyderby.com/visit/derby-week/oaks

"Kentucky Oaks." Wikipedia, Wikimedia Foundation, 15 May 2022, https://en.wikipedia.org/wiki/Kentucky_Oaks

Keyser, Tom. "Forgotten Black Jockeys Take Their Place in History." Baltimore Sun, 28 Sept. 2021, https://www.baltimoresun.com/news/bs-xpm-1999-03-14-9903130131-story.html

Kiekhefer, Bob. "Third Running of Saudi Cup Set for Feb. 26." Bloodhorse.com, https://www.bloodhorse.com/horse-racing/articles/254410/third-running-of-saudi-cup-set-for-feb-26

Kirby, Bill. "Augusta Jockey Simms Was an Innovator and 2-Time Kentucky Derby Champion." Savannah Morning News, Savannah Morning News, 3 Sept. 2020, https://www.savannahnow.com/story/sports/2020/09/03/augusta-jockey-simms-was-innovator-and-2-time-kentucky-derby-champion/43074673/

Klein, contributed by: Alexander. "Oliver Lewis (1856-1924) ." African American History, 7 Feb. 2020, https://www.blackpast.org/african-american-history/lewis-oliver-1856-1924/

"Las Vegas Grand Prix: Everything You Need To Know about F1's Newest Race: Formula 1®." Formula 1, https://www.formula1.com/en/latest/article.las-vegas-grand-prix-everything-you-need-to-know-about-f1s-newest-race.7HD0mpbF6pjSFsNatKZTwH.html

Leach, Charles A. Shelby D. "Pike" Barnes, 1 Jan. 1970, http://ohiocountykentuckyhistory.blogspot.com/2014/04/shelby-d-pike-barnes.html

Learn the History of the Kentucky Derby - Raising Edmonton. https://www.raisingedmonton.com/learn-the-history-of-the-kentucky-derby/

"Lee, James (Jockey)." Omeka RSS, https://nkaa.uky.edu/nkaa/items/show/2000

"Legacy of Black Jockeys." 2022 Kentucky Derby & Oaks | May 6 and May 7, 2022, https://www.kentuckyderby.com/history/legacy-of-black-jockeys

"Lexington (KY)." Lexington (KY) | National Museum of Racing and Hall of Fame, https://www.racingmuseum.org/hall-of-fame/horse/lexington-ky

Liebman, Bennett. "Origins of Triple Crown." The New York Times, The New York Times, 24 Apr. 2008, https://therail.blogs.nytimes.com/2008/04/24/origins-of-triple-crown/?mtrref=undefined&gwh=F418357C5F2CB6F492013F27BAC7737B&gwt=pay&assetType=PAYWALL

Louis, Billy Jean. "Despite Once Dominating the Sport of Horse Racing, There Will Be No Black Jockeys at Saturday's Preakness." Baltimore Sun, 14 May 2021, https://www.baltimoresun.com/sports/horse-racing/bs-sp-black-jockeys-20210514-xo452dmptfdy3h5szt65itp3sa-story.html

Louisiana State University LSU Digital Commons. https://digitalcommons.lsu.edu/cgi/viewcontent.cgi?article=1216&context=gradschool_theses

Madden, Compiled by Shirley. "Honoring Black History Month: Isaac Burns Murphy." Manistee News Advocate, Manistee News Advocate, 22 Feb. 2021, https://www.manisteenews.com/local-news/article/HONORING-BLACK-HISTORY-MONTH-Isaac-Burns-Murphy-15962829.php\

Magazine, Smithsonian. "How African-Americans Disappeared from the Kentucky Derby." Smithsonian.com, Smithsonian Institution, 5 May 2017, https://www.smithsonianmag.com/history/how-african-americans-disappeared-kentucky-derby-180963159/

Magazine, Smithsonian. "The Kentucky Derby's Forgotten Jockeys." Smithsonian.com, Smithsonian Institution, 23 Apr. 2009, https://www.smithsonianmag.com/history/the-kentucky-derbys-forgotten-jockeys-128781428/

Malesky, Kee. "Lawn Jockeys: The Kentucky Derby's Earliest Stars." NPR, NPR, 7 May 2011, https://www.npr.org/2011/05/07/136066218/lawn-jockeys-the-kentucky-derbys-earliest-stars

Mancuso, Peter, "The Color Line Is Drawn," in Bill Felber, ed., Inventing Baseball (Phoenix: Society for American Baseball Research, 2013).

Martin, L. "Pay to play: race and the perils of the college sports industrial complex." Praeger, an imprint of ABC-CLIO. n.p.: n.p., 10. 29 Jul. 2022.

Martin, L. "Racial Realism and the History of Black People in America" (2022b). n.p.: n.p., n.d.. 29 Jul. 2022.

Martin, L. "White sports, black sports: racial disparities in athletic programs." Praeger. n.p.: n.p., 8 . 29 Jul. 2022.

Martin, Lori Latrice. The Ex-Slave Jockey and Myth-Making in America: From Abe Hawkins to Present-Day Plantations. Lulu, 2020.

Mehie, Benjamin. "Oliver Lewis, Horse Jockey Born." African American Registry, 8 July 2021, https://aaregistry.org/story/oliver-lewis-horse-jockey-born/

McDaniels, Pellom. Prince of Jockeys: The Life of Isaac Burns Murphy. University Press of Kentucky, 2018.

McDaniels, P. "The prince of jockeys: the life of Isaac Burns Murphy." University Press of Kentucky. n.p.: n.p., 6. 29 Jul. 2022.

McKee, Sandra. "Rich History in Recovery Black Jockeys: After More than 100 Years of Being Written out of Horse Racing's Past, African-American Riders Are Finally Being Recognized for Their Contributions." Baltimore Sun, 29 Sept. 2021, https://www.baltimoresun.com/news/bs-xpm-1997-05-14-1997134123-story.html

Menderski, Maggie. "Wild, Weird and Historic: The Kentucky Derby Infield Has Served as a Sign of the Times." Journal, Louisville Courier Journal, 3 May 2021, https://www.courier-journal.com/story/entertainment/events/kentucky-derby/2021/04/27/kentucky-derby-infield-has-played-historic-role-in-the-past/4594937001/

"Meriwether Lewis." Wikipedia, Wikimedia Foundation, 26 July 2022, https://en.wikipedia.org/wiki/Meriwether_Lewis

Mint Julep Experiences. "The History of Horse Racing in Kentucky." Mint Julep Experiences, 30 July 2021, https://mintjuleptours.com/2021/07/30/the-history-of-horse-racing-in-kentucky/

"Mixed Race Studies." Mixed Race Studies " William Edward White, https://www.mixedracestudies.org/?tag=william-edward-white

Mooney, K. "Racehorse men: How slavery and freedom were made at the racetrack." Harvard University Press. n.p.: n.p., 7. 29 Jul. 2022.

Mooney, Katherine C. Race Horse Men: How Slavery and Freedom Were Made at the Racetrack. Harvard University Press, 2014.

"Moses Fleetwood Walker." Lemelson, https://lemelson.mit.edu/resources/moses-fleetwood-walker.

"Moses Fleetwood Walker, Baseball Player Born." African American Registry, 12 Apr. 2020, https://aaregistry.org/story/moses-fleetwood-walker-born/

"Moses Fleetwood Walker." Omeka RSS, http://michganintheworld.history.lsa.umich.edu/michiganathletics/exhibits/show/key-players/fleetwood-walker

"Moses Fleetwood Walker." Wikipedia, Wikimedia Foundation, 11 June 2022, https://en.wikipedia.org/wiki/Moses_Fleetwood_Walker

"Nakayama Grand Jump." Academic Dictionaries and Encyclopedias, https://en-academic.com/dic.nsf/enwiki/4029149

"Nakayama Grand Jump." Wikipedia, Wikimedia Foundation, 16 Apr. 2022, https://en.wikipedia.org/wiki/Nakayama_Grand_Jump

"National Museum of Racing and Hall of Fame." Wikipedia, Wikimedia Foundation, 23 June 2022, https://en.wikipedia.org/wiki/National_Museum_of_Racing_and_Hall_of_Fame

"News & Results | Nakayama Grand Jump | Horse Racing in Japan." Horse Racing in Japan, https://japanracing.jp/en/horsemen/itn_jump_races/nakayama_grand_jump/

Nicholson, Jamie. "Kentucky Derby." Encyclopædia Britannica, Encyclopædia Britannica, Inc., https://www.britannica.com/sports/Kentucky-Derby

"Notable Kentucky African Americans Database." Omeka RSS, https://nkaa.uky.edu/nkaa/

"Nofable Partnerships: Winning Teams despite Discrimination." Notable Partnerships: Winning Teams Despite Discrimination | The Chronicle of African Americans in the Horse Industry, https://africanamericanhorsestories.org/explore/stories/notable-partnerships-winning-teams-despite-discrimination.

Ockerman, F. "Hidden history of horse racing in Kentucky." The History Press. n.p.: n.p., 12. 29 Jul. 2022.

"Oliver Lewis." Completely Kentucky Wiki, https://completely-kentucky.fandom.com/wiki/Oliver_Lewis

"Oliver Lewis: First African-American Jockey to Win the Kentucky Derby." Black Then, 5 Dec. 2019, https://blackthen.com/oliver-lewis-first-african-american-jockey-win-kentucky-derby/

Oliver Lewis Inner City Thoroughbred Jockey Club - North Little Rock ... http://www.oliverlewisinnercity.org/index.html

"Oliver Lewis." Oliver Lewis | The Chronicle of African Americans in the Horse Industry, https://africanamericanhorsestories.org/research/people/oliver-lewis

"Oliver Lewis." Oliver Lewis - Kentucky Commission on Human Rights, https://kchr.ky.gov/Hall-of-Fame/Pages/Oliver-Lewis.aspx

"Oliver Lewis Biography." Race, Aristides, Kentucky, and Derby - JRank Articles, https://biography.jrank.org/pages/2969/Lewis-Oliver.html

"Oliver Lewis (1856-1924) - Find a Grave Memorial." Find a Grave, https://www.findagrave.com/memorial/94017953/oliver-lewis

"Oliver Lewis (1856-1924) •." Welcome to Blackpast •, https://www.facebook.com/BlackPast, 30 Nov. 2010, https://www.blackpast.org/african-american-history/lewis-oliver-1856-1924/

"Oliver Lewis." Wikipedia, Wikimedia Foundation, 16 Apr. 2022, https://en.wikipedia.org/wiki/Oliver_Lewis

Peoplepill.com. "About Abe Hawkins: African American Jockey (Born: N/A - Died: 1867): Biography,

Facts, Career, Life." Peoplepill.com, https://peoplepill.com/people/abe-hawkins

Perreault, M. "Jockeying for Position: Horse Racing in New Orleans, 1865-1920: Semantic Scholar." Undefined, 1 Jan. 1970, https://www.semanticscholar.org/paper/Jockeying-for-Position%3A-Horse-Racing-in-New-Perreault/df12cb57083b363fd5e45d4c3255f2bb89644f5c

"Preakness 147 - Preakness Stakes - May 21, 2022." Preakness Stakes, https://www.preakness.com/

"Preakness Stakes in the United States." Time and Date, https://www.timeanddate.com/holidays/us/preakness-stakes

"Preakness Stakes." Wikipedia, Wikimedia Foundation, 12 June 2022, https://en.wikipedia.org/wiki/Preakness_Stakes

Press, Associated. "Emblem Road Sprints to 99-1 Upset at Saudi Cup." ESPN, ESPN, 26 Feb. 2022, https://www.espn.in/horse-racing/story/_/id/33377665/emblem-road-scores-99-1-upset-saudi-cup-bob-baffert-country-grammar-finishes-2nd

"Prince of Jockeys: The Life of Isaac Burns Murphy." UNIV PR OF KENTUCKY, 2018. n.p.: n.p., n.d.. 28 Jul. 2022.

"Prix De L'Arc De Triomphe." Edited by Encyclopedia Britannica, Encyclopædia Britannica, Encyclopædia Britannica, Inc., https://www.britannica.com/sports/Prix-de-lArc-de-Triomphe

"Prix De L'Arc De Triomphe Packages 2022." Horse Racing Holidays, https://www.horseracingholidays.com/collections/prix-de-l-ark-de-triomphe

"Prix De L'étoile." Wikipedia, Wikimedia Foundation, 20 Feb. 2022, https://fr.wikipedia.org/wiki/Prix_de_l%27%C3%89toile

"Prix De L'Atlantique." Wikipedia, Wikimedia Foundation, 10 May 2022, https://fr.wikipedia.org/wiki/Prix_de_l%27Atlantique

"Qatar Prix De L'ARC De Triomphe. ." QATAR PRIX DE L'ARC TRIOMPHE -EN, https://www.parislongchamp.com/en/qatar-prix-de-larc-triomphe

"Race Horse Men: How Slavery and Freedom Were Made at the Racetrack." Harvard University Press, 2014. n.p.: n.p., n.d.. 29 Jul. 2022.

Racing, America's Best. "Black History Month: Spotlight on Black Jockeys in Horse Racing History." NBC Sports, 13 Feb. 2021, https://sports.nbcsports.com/2021/02/13/shining-a-spotlight-on-notable-black-jockeys/

"Racing around Kentucky." L.S. n.p.: n.p., n.d.. 29 Jul. 2022.

"Racing Statistics." Statistics | Emirates Racing Authority, https://emiratesracing.com/racing-information/statistics

"Randox Grand National Festival." TJC-Tagline-White.png, https://www.thejockeyclub.co.uk/aintree/events-tickets/grand-national/

Rebecca, / Baseball. "The Walker Brothers." The Baseball Sociologist, 7 Oct. 2020, https://baseballsociologist.wordpress.com/2020/10/07/the-walker-brothers/

Record, Troy. "A Time When Black Jockeys Thrived." Troyrecord, Troyrecord, 22 July 2021, https://www.troyrecord.com/2008/08/24/a-time-when-black-jockeys-thrived/

Renau, L. "Racing around Kentucky." L.S. n.p.: n.p., 18 . 29 Jul. 2022.

Renau, Lynn S. Racing around Kentucky. L. S. Renau, 1995.

Reed, Tom. "Edward D. Brown, the Former Slave Who Won the Belmont Stakes." PlanetSport, PlanetSport, 3 Feb. 2021, https://www.planetsport.com/horse-racing/features/edward-d-brown-slave-belmont-stakes-jerome-park-new-york

Regan, Barry, and skipjen2865. Moses Fleetwood Walker, Black Pioneer of Major League Baseball, 16 Apr. 2012, http://jenkinspanafricanbios.blogspot.com/2015/03/moses-fleetwood-walker-black-pioneer-of.html

Release, Press, et al. "People Archives - Horse Racing News: Paulick Report." Horse Racing News | Paulick Report, 8 Apr. 2022, https://paulickreport.com/news/people/

Republic, Phil Connelly, For the Ravalli. "Meriwether Clark's Run for the Roses." Ravalli Republic, 23 Oct. 2017, https://ravallirepublic.com/news/local/meriwether-clarks-run-for-the-roses/article_dd755704-4d2f-5117-a4cd-340bf1464120.html

Riddle, Becky. "Aristides." ExploreKYHistory, https://explorekyhistory.ky.gov/items/show/157?tour=42&index=23

Riess, Steven A. "The American Jockey, 1865-1910." Transatlantica. Revue D'études Américaines. American Studies Journal, Association Française D'études Américaines (AFEA), 21 Dec. 2011, https://journals.openedition.org/transatlantica/5480

Riess, Steven A. "The Cyclical History of Horse Racing: The USA's Oldest and (Sometimes) Most Popular Spectator Sport." Taylor & Francis, https://www.tandfonline.com/doi/abs/10.1080/09523367.2013.862520

Reilly, Kellie. "Lecomte: The Short Life but Long Legacy of a Louisiana Racing Hero." Brisnet, 16 Jan. 2019, http://www.brisnet.com/content/2019/01/lecomte-short-life-long-legacy-louisiana-racing-hero/

Release, Press. "Historic Review Elects Jockey Anthony Hamilton, Horse Planet to Hall of Fame - Horse Racing News: Paulick Report." Horse Racing News | Paulick Report, 31 May 2012, https://paulickreport.com/news/the-biz/historic-review-elects-jockey-anthony-hamilton-horse-planet-to-hall-of-fame/

"Rex Nelson: Arkansas' Forgotten Legend - Alonzo 'Lonnie' Clayton." Sporting Life Arkansas, 10 May 2013, http://www.sportinglifearkansas.com/rex-nelson-arkansas-forgotten-legend-alonzo-lonnie-clayton/

Riders Up! With Marie D. Jones. "Oliver Lewis: An African-American Horse Racing Legend." Sports As Told By A Girl, Sports As Told By A Girl, 9 Feb. 2021, https://www.sportsastoldbyagirl.com/oliver-lewis-an-african-american-horse-racing-legend/

Riess, Steven A. "The American Jockey, 1865-1910." Transatlantica. Revue D'études Américaines. American Studies Journal, Association Française D'études Américaines (AFEA), 21 Dec. 2011, https://journals.openedition.org/transatlantica/5480

River, Charles. Moses Fleetwood Walker: The Life and Legacy of the Last Black Man to Play Major League Baseball before Jackie Robinson. Independently Published, 2019.

Rothman, Lily. "First American Woman to Be Licensed Jockey: Anna Lee Aldred." Time, Time, 19 Apr. 2016, https://time.com/4290869/anna-lee-aldred-2/

"Royal Ascot 2021 - Race Preview - Day Four." Ascot Racecourse, https://www.ascot.com/news/royal-ascot-2021-racing-preview-day-four

"Royal Ascot Day Four: Novemba Is One to Remember in Coronation Stakes." The Guardian, Guardian News and Media, 17 June 2021, https://www.theguardian.com/sport/2021/jun/17/royal-ascot-day-four-novemba-is-one-to-remember-in-coronation-stakes

"Runhappy Travers." NYRA, https://www.nyra.com/saratoga/racing/stakes-schedule/travers-stakes/.

"Salvator-Tenny Match Race." Horse Racing Free Tips, 23 Apr. 2021, https://horseracingfreetips.com/tag/salvator-tenny-match-race/

"San Francisco Call, Volume 97, Number 125, 24 May 1915." San Francisco Call 24 May 1915 - California Digital Newspaper Collection, https://cdnc.ucr.edu/?a=d&d=SFC19150524.2.168&e=-------en--20--1--txt-txIN--------1

"Saudi Cup." Wikipedia, Wikimedia Foundation, 13 Apr. 2022, https://en.wikipedia.org/wiki/Saudi_Cup

Saunders, James Robert, and Monica Renae Saunders. Black Winning Jockeys in the Kentucky Derby. McFarland & Co., 2002.

Scribner Encyclopedia of American Lives, Thematic Series: Sports Figures. . Encyclopedia.com. 22 Jun. 2022 ." Encyclopedia.com, Encyclopedia.com, 9 July 2022, https://www.encyclopedia.com/humanities/encyclopedias-almanacs-transcripts-and-maps/walker-moses-fleetwood-fleet

"Search." Historical Newspapers from 1700s-2000s - Newspapers.com, https://www.newspapers.com/search/#query=Edward+Dudley+Brown

Sherwin, Collin. "The History of Triple Crown Horses, and Will We Have One in 2021?" DraftKings Nation, DraftKings Nation, 14 May 2021, https://dknation.draftkings.com/2021/5/14/22436483/triple-crown-winners-history-horse-racing-last-time-medina-spirit-mandaloun-justify-bob-baffert

"Shelby Barnes." Shelby Barnes | The Chronicle of African Americans in the Horse Industry, https://africanamericanhorsestories.org/research/people/shelby-barnes

"Shelby 'Pike' Barnes." Shelby "Pike" Barnes, i-5 Publishing, 1 Aug. 2011, https://mydigitalpublication.com/publication/?i=77213&article_id=798960&view=articleBrowser&ver=html5

"Shelby 'Pike' Barnes." Shelby "Pike" Barnes | National Museum of Racing and Hall of Fame, https://www.racingmuseum.org/hall-of-fame/jockey/shelby-pike-barnes

Shields, Aaron. "Top 10 Biggest Horse Races in the World." Casino.org Blog, 18 Jan. 2022, https://www.casino.org/blog/the-10-biggest-horse-races-in-the-world/

"Sign the Petition." Change.org, https://www.change.org/p/churchill-downs-recognize-abe-hawkins-and-other-black-jockeys-historical-contribution-to-horse-racing

Simon, Terri, et al. "First Draft: Stories from New Orleans History." The Historic New Orleans Collection, 15 July 2022, https://www.hnoc.org/publications/first-draft

Smith, G. "The Kentucky African American encyclopedia." University Press of Kentucky. n.p.: n.p., 8 . 29

Jul. 2022.

Smith, Gerald L., et al. The Kentucky African American Encyclopedia. University Press of Kentucky, 2015.

"Sports Legend African-American Jockey Anthony Hamilton Dominated World Racing in the Late 1800s." Delaware Way, http://delawareway.blogspot.com/2019/01/sports-legend-african-american-jockey.html

Sports, Racing &. "Grand Prix De Deauville: Past Winners: Results: France." Past Winners | Results | France | Racing and Sports, Racing and Sports, 14 July 2022, https://www.racingandsports.com/thoroughbred/feature-race/france/grand-prix-de-deauville/1856

"Stakes Entries." Equibase.com, https://www.equibase.com/premium/eqbstakesentries.cfm?SAP=TN.

Staff, Bloodhorse. "Jockey Hamilton, Planet Elected to HOF." Bloodhorse.com, https://www.bloodhorse.com/horse-racing/articles/129119/jockey-hamilton-planet-elected-to-hof

Stanek, Anna. "10 Most Famous Horse Races in the World." Horsey Hooves, 18 Oct. 2021, https://horseyhooves.com/famous-horse-races/

"Stars of Yesterday: Looking Back at Best Rebel Stakes Winners." America's Best Racing, https://www.americasbestracing.net/the-sport/2022-stars-yesterday-looking-back-best-rebel-stakes-winners

"Stars of Yesterday: Looking Back at Some of Best Recent Withers Stakes Winners." America's Best Racing, https://www.americasbestracing.net/the-sport/2022-stars-yesterday-looking-back-some-best-recent-withers-stakes-winners

"Successful Trainers in Kentucky's Foremost Race, Daily Racing Form, 1911-04-30." Search Icon, 30 Apr. 1911, https://drf.uky.edu/catalog/1910s/drf1911043001/drf1911043001_1_4

Taylor, Rupert. "A Brief History of Black Champion Jockey Isaac Murphy." HowTheyPlay, HowTheyPlay, 1 Oct. 2018, https://howtheyplay.com/animal-sports/Isaac-Murphy-Black-Champion-Jockey

TDN, The. "Real World Targets Saudi Cup." TDN | Thoroughbred Daily News | Horse Racing News, Results and Video | Thoroughbred Breeding and Auctions, 13 Jan. 2022, https://www.thoroughbreddailynews.com/real-world-targets-saudi-cup/

Team, Konnect HQ. "Horse Facts for Kids (All You Need to Know!)." KonnectHQ, 23 Feb. 2021, https://www.konnecthq.com/horse-facts/

Teresa. "Remembering Shelby 'Pike' Barnes, Hall of Fame Winner of the 1889 Travers." Brooklyn Backstretch, 28 Aug. 2015, https://brooklynbackstretch.com/2015/08/28/remembering-shelby-pike-barnes-hall-of-fame-winner-of-the-1889-travers/

"The Authentic Kentucky Derby Mint Julep Recipe." 2022 Kentucky Derby & Oaks | May 6 and May 7, 2022, https://www.kentuckyderby.com/horses/news/the-authentic-kentucky-derby-mint-julep-recipe

The Book of Postfix. https://mobt3ath.com/uplode/books/book-27297.pdf

"The Cameo of William Edward White." Society for American Baseball Research, Admin /Wp-Content/Uploads/2020/02/sabr_logo.Png, 3 Dec. 2021, https://sabr.org/gamesproj/game/june-21-1879-the-cameo-of-william-edward-white/

"The Continuing Saga of the Lapierre Family: Mint Julep (Day Two) as Told to Gracie Buckhalter." Google Books, Google, https://www.google.co.in/books/edition/The_Continuing_Saga_of_the_LaPierre_Fami/O5ThCgAAQBAJ?hl=en&gbpv=1&dq=%221889%22%2B%22alonzo%2Bclayton%22%2Blonnie&pg=PT140&printsec=frontcover

"The Day George 'Spider' Anderson Became the First Black Jockey to Win Preakness." Andscape, Andscape, 10 May 2017, https://andscape.com/features/george-spider-anderson-first-black-jockey-to-win-preakness/

The Equine Report, et al. "Abe Hawkins - A Louisiana Racing Hall of Fame Jockey ." The Equine Report, 8 Mar. 2016, https://theequinereport.com/2016/03/abe-hawkins-a-louisiana-racing-hall-of-fame-jockey/

"The Evolution of the Sport of Kings." Chicago Tribune, https://www.chicagotribune.com/news/ct-xpm-1988-05-04-8803140377-story.html

"The Ex-Slave Jockey and Myth-Making in America: From Abe Hawkins to Present-Day Plantations." Lulu, 2020. n.p.: n.p., n.d.. 28 Jul. 2022.

"The Festival™ 2022: Cheltenham Racecourse." TJC-Tagline-White.png, https://www.thejockeyclub.co.uk/cheltenham/events-tickets/the-festival/

"The Grand National 2023." www.grandnational.org.uk , 30 June 2022, https://www.grandnational.org.uk/

"The Great Black Jockeys: The Lives and Times of the Men Who Dominated America's First National Sport." Three Rivers Press, 1999. n.p.: n.p., n.d.. 28 Jul. 2022.

The Hidden Black History of Horse Racing OTSOG. https://www.ontheshoulders1.com/the-giants/the-hidden-black-history-of-horse-racing

"The History of the Kentucky Derby." Arcadia Publishing, https://www.arcadiapublishing.com/Navigation/Community/Arcadia-and-THP-Blog/May-2019/The-History-of-the-Kentucky-Derby

"The Jockey Club." Factbook, http://www.jockeyclub.com/factbook.asp

"The Kentucky African American Encyclopedia." University Press of Kentucky, 2015. n.p.: n.p., n.d.. 29 Jul. 2022.

"The Kentucky African American Encyclopedia." Google Books, Google, https://www.google.co.in/books/edition/The_Kentucky_African_American_Encycloped/-0AoCgAAQBAJ?hl=en&gbpv=1&dq=James%2B%E2%80%9CJimmy%E2%80%9D%2BLee%2BJockey&pg=PA7&printsec=frontcover

"The Kentucky Derby - Then and Now ." Derby Experiences Blog, https://derbyexperiences.com/blog/the-kentucky-derby-then-and-now

"The Man Who Broke Baseball's Color Line before Jackie Robinson." Big Think, 19 Apr. 2022, https://bigthink.com/culture-religion/the-man-who-broke-baseballs-color-line-before-jackie-robinson/

"The Mysterious Life of a Slave Who Became the Most Celebrated Jockey in North America." Thoroughbred Racing Commentary, https://www.thoroughbredracing.com/articles/mysterious-life-slave-who-became-most-celebrated-jockey-north-america/

"The Origin of Horse Racing." Inspiration Unlimited EMagazine, https://www.iuemag.com/j20/sa/the-origin-of-horse-racing

"The Road Less Traveled: Trailblazing Horsewomen." The Road Less Traveled: Trailblazing Horsewomen | The Chronicle of African Americans in the Horse Industry, https://africanamericanhorsestories.org/explore/stories/road-less-traveled-trailblazing-horsewomen

"The Sad History of Racism in American Racing; Topics: Kentucky Derby, Saratoga." Thoroughbred Racing Commentary, https://www.thoroughbredracing.com/articles/shocking-history-racism-american-racing/

"The Saudi Cup." The SAUDI CUP, https://thesaudicup.com.sa/

The Tour of the Historic Bluegrass team. "Shotgun Houses." Tour the Historic Bluegrass, https://tourthehistoricbluegrass.com/items/show/31?tour=1&index=27

The Village Voice, 29 July 2022, https://www.villagevoice.com/

"The World-Traveling Career of Jockey Anthony Hamilton." America's Best Racing, https://www.americasbestracing.net/the-sport/2020-the-world-traveling-career-jockey-anthony-hamilton

"The World's Platform for Change." Change.org, https://www.change.org/?petition_not_found=true&redirect_reason=unknown-petition-id

Teresa. "Remembering Shelby 'Pike' Barnes, Hall of Fame Winner of the 1889 Travers." Brooklyn Backstretch, 28 Aug. 2015, https://brooklynbackstretch.com/2015/08/28/remembering-shelby-pike-barnes-hall-of-fame-winner-of-the-1889-travers/

"Thoroughbred Champions." THE VAULT: Horse Racing Past and Present, https://thevaulthorseracing.wordpress.com/tag/thoroughbred-champions/

"Tod Sloan." Encyclopædia Britannica, Encyclopædia Britannica, Inc., https://www.britannica.com/biographies

"Travers Stakes." Wikipedia, Wikimedia Foundation, 8 July 2022, https://en.wikipedia.org/wiki/Travers_Stakes

"Triple Crown." Encyclopædia Britannica, Encyclopædia Britannica, Inc., https://www.britannica.com/sports/Triple-Crown-American-thoroughbred-horse-racing

Undefeated, The. "The Undefeated 44 Most Influential Black Americans in History." - Andscape, Andscape, 20 Apr. 2022, https://theundefeated.com/features/the-undefeated-44-most-influential-black-americans-in-history/#introduction

"Understanding Your Horse's Body Language." RSPCA, https://www.rspca.org.uk/adviceandwelfare/pets/horses/behaviour/bodylanguage

"Unforgettable Ohioans : Thirteen Mavericks Who Made History on Their Own Terms : McNutt, Randy : Free Download, Borrow, and Streaming." Internet Archive, Kent, Ohio: Kent State University Press, 1 Jan. 1970, https://archive.org/details/unforgettableohi0000mcnu

Urofsky, Melvin I. "Jim Crow Law." Encyclopædia Britannica, Encyclopædia Britannica, Inc., https://www.britannica.com/event/Jim-Crow-law.

User, Guest. "Horse Facts: 15 Fun Facts about Horses." Saluti, Saluti, 16 July 2019, https://www.salutiranch.com/blog-1/horse-facts-15-fun-facts-about-horses

VanHouten, Matt. "Alonzo Clayton (1876-1917) .", 11 May 2021, https://www.blackpast.org/african-american-history/clayton-alonzo-1876-1917/

VanHouten, Matt. "George B. Anderson .", 8 Jan. 2021, https://www.blackpast.org/african-american-history/anderson-george-b/

VisitLEX. "Lexington's African-American Jockeys." VisitLEX, VisitLEX, 15 Oct. 2021, https://www.visitlex.com/guides/post/lexingtons-african-american-jockeys/

Voss, Natalie. "Derby History: Ansel Williamson, the Former Slave Who Trained the First Kentucky Derby Winner - Horse Racing News: Paulick Report." Horse Racing News | Paulick Report, 4 Sept. 2020, https://paulickreport.com/news/ray-s-paddock/derby-history-ansel-williamson-the-former-slave-who-trained-the-first-kentucky-derby-winner/

Voss, Natalie. "Preakness Lore: Simms Made History and Changed the Way Jockeys Ride - Horse Racing News: Paulick Report." Horse Racing News | Paulick Report, 17 May 2022, https://paulickreport.com/news/ray-s-paddock/preakness-history-simms-made-history-and-changed-the-way-jockeys-ride/

Waggoner, Cassandra. "Isaac Burns Murphy (1861-1896) ." •, 3 Dec. 2020, https://www.blackpast.org/african-american-history/murphy-isaac-burns-1861-1896/

"Walker's Interests Were Far and Wide." MiLB.com, 18 Feb. 2008, https://www.milb.com/news/moses-fleetwood-walker-was-baseball-renaissance-man-303457114

Walker, Rhiannon, et al. "George 'Spider' Anderson." Andscape, https://andscape.com/tag/george-spider-anderson/

Walker, Rhiannon. "The Day Edward D. Brown Became the First African-American to Win the Belmont Stakes." - Andscape, Andscape, 7 June 2017, https://theundefeated.com/features/edward-d-brown-first-african-american-to-win-belmont-stakes/

"Wantha Davis." Wikipedia, Wikimedia Foundation, 6 Dec. 2021, https://en.wikipedia.org/wiki/Wantha_Davis

Weir, Tom. "Why We've Waited so Long for Another Triple Crown Winner." Bleacher Report, Bleacher Report, 20 Sept. 2017, https://bleacherreport.com/articles/2086324-why-weve-waited-so-long-for-another-triple-crown-winner

Weldon, Nick. "From Slavery to Sports Stardom: Abe Hawkins's Rise from a Louisiana." The Historic New Orleans Collection, 11 Jan. 2019, https://www.hnoc.org/publications/first-draft/slavery-sports-stardom-abe-hawkins%E2%80%99s-rise-louisiana-plantation-horse-racing

"Weldy Walker." Society for American Baseball Research, Admin /Wp-Content/Uploads/2020/02/sabr_logo.Png, 10 Apr. 2014, https://sabr.org/bioproj/person/weldy-walker/

"Weldy Walker: Honored at Last." The Negro Leagues Up Close, 4 Oct. 2016, https://homeplatedontmove.wordpress.com/2016/10/03/3191/

"Weldy Walker." Wikipedia, Wikimedia Foundation, 28 May 2022, https://en.wikipedia.org/wiki/Weldy_Walker

"We Believe in a World Where Everyone Can Explore and Create Culture." Homepage | Cheltenham Festivals, https://www.cheltenhamfestivals.com/

"Which Country Has the Best Thoroughbred Horse Racing?" Quora, https://www.quora.com/Which-country-has-the-best-thoroughbred-horse-racing

"Who Are the Greatest African-American Baseball Players of All Time?" Yardbarker, 23 Feb. 2022, https://www.yardbarker.com/mlb/articles/who_are_the_greatest_african_american_baseball_players_of_all_time/s1__28469222#slide_4

"William Edward White." Wikipedia, Wikimedia Foundation, 1 May 2022, https://en.wikipedia.org/wiki/William_Edward_White

"Willie Simms." HRN Menu, https://www.horseracingnation.com/person/Willie_Simms#.

"William Walker: A Jockey of Many Talents." America's Best Racing, https://www.americasbestracing.net/the-sport/2022-william-walker-jockey-many-talents

"Wink: The Incredible Life and Epic Journey of Jimmy Winkfield." Ragged Mountain Pr, 2006. n.p.: n.p., n.d.. 28 Jul. 2022.

Wolsey, C, et al. "Biggest Horse Races around the World." Kettle Mag, 4 May 2021, https://kettlemag.co.uk/biggest-horse-races-around-the-world/

Wuky. "And the Winner Is: Oliver Lewis Way." WUKY, 8 Mar. 2019, https://www.wuky.org/local-regional-news/2010-08-31/and-the-winner-is-oliver-lewis-way

Zang, David W. Fleet Walker's Divided Heart: The Life of Baseball's First Black Major Leaguer. University of Nebraska Press, 1995.

"Veterinary Arts in 19th Century America." History Hoydens, 2007, https://www.blogger.com/blogin.g?blogspotURL=http://historyhoydens.blogspot.com/2007/01/veterinary-arts-in-19th-century.html&type=blog&bpli=1&pli=1

"History of the Kentucky Derby." Horse Racing Radio Network, horseracingradio.net/post/history-kentucky-derby.

"Aristides." American Classic Pedigrees, www.americanclassicpedigrees.com/aristides.html

"King Alfonso." American Classic Pedigrees, www.americanclassicpedigrees.com/king-alfonso.html

"Isaac Burns Murphy: Great Black Horse Jockey." Black History Heroes, www.blackhistoryheroes.com/2017/08/isaac-burns-murphy-great-black-horse.html

"Lexington: The Godolphin Arabian of America." Thoroughbred Heritage, www.tbheritage.com/Portraits/Lexington.html#Asteroid

"Grave Matters at Elmendorf Farm." Thoroughbred Heritage, https://www.tbheritage.com/TurfHallmarks/Graves/cem/GraveMattersElmendorf.html

"Horse Racing." Virginia Places, www.virginiaplaces.org/agriculture/horseracing.html

"Edward Dudley Brown." African American Horse Stories, https://africanamericanhorsestories.org/research/people/edward-dudley-brown

"Garrett Davis Lewis." African American Horse Stories, https://africanamericanhorsestories.org/research/people/garrett-davis-lewis

"James Perkins." African American Horse Stories, africanamericanhorsestories.org/research/people/james-perkins.

"Black Jockey Hall of Famer: Isaac Burns Murphy." America Comes Alive, https://americacomesalive.com/black-jockey-hall-of-famer-isaac-burns-murphy?__cf_chl_tk=YymktHl9B1a2ZoEvytNZsiLU62mnhDeL_82G_sov4ko-1694985463-0-gaNycGzNDKU

Moore, John Trotwood. "History of Woodford County, Kentucky." Internet Archive, 1910, https://archive.org/stream/historyofwoodfor00inmoor/historyofwoodfor00inmoor_djvu.txt

Marshall, Lewis Collins. "In Old Kentucky: A Story of the Bluegrass and the Mountains." Internet Archive, 1900, archive.org/stream/inoldkentuckysto00marsiala/inoldkentuckysto00marsiala_djvu.txt.

"Jimmy Winkfield." Arthur Ashe Learning Center, arthurashe.ucla.edu/jimmy-winkfield

"Lewis, Oliver." Biography JRank, biography.jrank.org/pages/2969/Lewis-Oliver.html

"James 'Soup' Perkins." Black Then, blackthen.com/james-soup-perkins-one-youngest-prominent-jockeys-west.

"Remembering Shelby Pike Barnes, Hall of Fame Winner of the 1889 Travers." Brooklyn Backstretch, brooklynbackstretch.com/2015/08/28/remembering-shelby-pike-barnes-hall-of-fame-winner-of-the-1889-travers.

"History of Aristides." Coldstream Research Park, coldstream.uky.edu/history-aristides.

"Ansel Williamson." Completely Kentucky, completely-kentucky.fandom.com/wiki/Ansel_Williamson.

"Edward D. Brown." Completely Kentucky, completely-kentucky.fandom.com/wiki/Edward_D._Brown.

"Robert A. Alexander." Completely Kentucky, completely-kentucky.fandom.com/wiki/Robert_A._Alexander.

"Daniel Swigert." Cross Gate Gallery, crossgategallery.com/product/daniel-swigert.

"May 2, 1942 - Kentucky Derby." Daily Racing Form, drf.uky.edu/catalog/1940s/drf1942050201/drf1942050201_3_1.

"Edward D. Brown." Academic Dictionaries and Encyclopedias, en-academic.com/dic.nsf/enwiki/1212132.

"Woodburn Stud." Academic Dictionaries and Encyclopedias, en-academic.com/dic.nsf/enwiki/3828607.

"1875 Kentucky Derby." Wikipedia, en.wikipedia.org/wiki/1875_Kentucky_Derby

"Ansel Williamson." Wikipedia, en.wikipedia.org/wiki/Ansel_Williamson

"Edward D. Brown." Wikipedia, en.wikipedia.org/wiki/Edward_D._Brown.

"Isaac Burns Murphy." Wikipedia, en.wikipedia.org/wiki/Isaac_Burns_Murphy.

"James 'Soup' Perkins." Wikipedia, en.wikipedia.org/wiki/James_%22Soup%22_Perkins

"James 'Soup' Perkins: His Career Devolves." Wikipedia, en.wikipedia.org/wiki/James_%22Soup%22_Perkins#His_career_devolves.

"Jimmy Winkfield." Wikipedia, en.wikipedia.org/wiki/Jimmy_Winkfield.

"John Hunt Morgan." Wikipedia, en.wikipedia.org/wiki/John_Hunt_Morgan

"Kentucky Derby." Wikipedia, en.wikipedia.org/wiki/Kentucky_Derby.

"Marcellus Jerome Clarke." Wikipedia, en.wikipedia.org/wiki/Marcellus_Jerome_Clarke.

"Meriwether Lewis Clark Jr." Wikipedia, en.wikipedia.org/wiki/Meriwether_Lewis_Clark_Jr.

"Oliver Lewis." Wikipedia, en.wikipedia.org/wiki/Oliver_Lewis.

"Woodburn Stud." Wikipedia, en.wikipedia.org/wiki/Woodburn_Stud.

"Woodford County, Kentucky." Wikipedia, en.wikipedia.org/wiki/Woodford_County,_Kentucky.

"African American Jockey Abe Hawkins." ExploreKYHistory, explorekyhistory.ky.gov/items/show/28.

"African American Jockey Ansel Williamson." ExploreKYHistory, explorekyhistory.ky.gov/items/show/271.

"African American Jockey Edward Dudley Brown." ExploreKYHistory, explorekyhistory.ky.gov/items/show/324?tour=26&index=30.

"African American Jockey Garrett Davis Lewis." ExploreKYHistory, explorekyhistory.ky.gov/items/show/754.

"Kentucky Thoroughbred Breeding Farm Tour." ExploreKYHistory, explorekyhistory.ky.gov/tours/show/9.

"Meriwether Lewis Clark Jr. and the Founding of Churchill Downs." Frances Hunter, franceshunter.wordpress.com/2010/04/13/meriwether-lewis-clark-jr-and-the-founding-of-churchill-downs.

"Isaac Burns Murphy." Kentucky Horse Park, kyhorsepark.com/equine-theme-park/park-memorials-statues/isaac-burns-murphy.

"Abe Hawkins." Notable Kentucky African Americans Database, nkaa.uky.edu/nkaa/items/show/661.

"Ansel Williamson." Notable Kentucky African Americans Database, nkaa.uky.edu/nkaa/items/show/669.

"Edward D. Brown." Notable Kentucky African Americans Database, nkaa.uky.edu/nkaa/items/show/676.

"Robert A. Alexander." Notable Kentucky African Americans Database, nkaa.uky.edu/nkaa/items/show/1904.

"Edward Dudley Brown." Notable Kentucky African Americans Database, nkaa.uky.edu/nkaa/items/show/1906.

"John A. Scott." Notable Kentucky African Americans Database, nkaa.uky.edu/nkaa/items/show/2701.

"Belmont History: Edward Brown Went from Slave to Jockey to Trainer to Owner in a Lifetime." Paulick Report, paulickreport.com/news/ray-s-paddock/belmont-history-edward-brown-went-from-slave-to-jockey-to-trainer-to-owner-in-a-lifetime.

"Belmont History: Edward Brown Went from Slave to Jockey to Trainer to Owner in a Lifetime." Paulick Report, paulickreport.com/news/ray-s-paddock/belmont-history-edward-brown-went-from-slave-to-jockey-to-trainer-to-owner-in-a-lifetime.

"Derby History: Ansel Williamson, the Former Slave Who Trained the First Kentucky Derby Winner." Paulick Report, paulickreport.com/news/ray-s-paddock/derby-history-ansel-williamson-the-former-slave-who-trained-the-first-kentucky-derby-winner.

"Kentucky Farm Time Capsule: Maine Chance Farm." Paulick Report, paulickreport.com/news/ray-s-paddock/kentucky-farm-time-capsule-maine-chance-farm.

Burant, Jim. "Hamilton Horse Racing History: Then and Now." Fall-Winter Hamilton Arts, samizdatpress.typepad.com/fall_winter_hamilton_arts/hamilton-horse-racing-history-then-and-now-by-jim-burant-16.html.

Sanfordsky, Michael. "American Racehorses in England." Stanford University, searchworks.stanford.edu/view/7196808.

"Shelby Pike Barnes." Horse Racing Hall of Fame, www.racingmuseum.org/hall-of-fame/jockey/shelby-pike-barnes

"Edward D. Brown." Horse Racing Hall of Fame, www.racingmuseum.org/hall-of-fame/trainer/edward-d-brown

Veitch, Tom. "An Accidental Historian in Antebellum America: Edward Troye, Thoroughbred Horses, and Representations of African American Manhood and Masculinity." ResearchGate, www.researchgate.net/publication/290445421_An_Accidental_Historian_in_Antebellum_America_Edward_Troye_Thoroughbred_Horses_and_Representations_of_African_American_Manhood_and_Masculinity

Clarke, John. "Lexington, One of the Greatest Racehorses of All Time, Comes Roaring Back to Life." Smithsonian Magazine, www.smithsonianmag.com/smithsonian-institution/lexington-one-of-the-greatest-race-horses-of-all-time-comes-roaring-back-to-life-180980132

"Norfolk." Thoroughbred Heritage, www.tbheritage.com/Portraits/Norfolk.html

"Great Britain." Thoroughbred Heritage,

www.tbheritage.com/TurfHallmarks/racecharts/Steeplechase/SteepleGB.html

"An Accidental Historian in Antebellum America: Edward Troye, Thoroughbred Horses, and Representations of African American Manhood and Masculinity." Smithsonian Institution Libraries, www.sil.si.edu/DigitalCollections/Art-Design/artandartists.htm

"Derby Jockey Walker Influenced Breeders." BloodHorse, www.bloodhorse.com/horse-racing/articles/107867/derby-jockey-walker-influenced-breeders

"Early American Race Charts." Thoroughbred Bloodlines, www.bloodlines.net/TB/Studbook/EarlyA.htm

"Isaac Burns Murphy." Britannica, www.britannica.com/biography/Isaac-Burns-Murphy

"James Winkfield." Britannica, www.britannica.com/biography/James-Winkfield

"John Hunt Morgan." Britannica, www.britannica.com/biography/John-Hunt-Morgan

"Meriwether Lewis Clark Jr." Britannica, www.britannica.com/biography/Meriwether-Lewis-Clark-Jr

"William C. Quantrill." Britannica, www.britannica.com/biography/William-C-Quantrill

"Kentucky Derby." Britannica, www.britannica.com/sports/Kentucky-Derby

"Ku Klux Klan." Britannica, www.britannica.com/topic/Ku-Klux-Klan

"Jimmy Winkfield." Kentucky Derby Museum, www.derbymuseum.org/Blog/Article/327/Jimmy-Winkfield

"First Kentucky Derby, 1875." America's Best Racing, www.americasbestracing.net/lifestyle/2019-visit-horse-country-airdrie-studs-encompassing-industry-influence

"The Epic Journey of James 'Wink' Winkfield." America's Best Racing, www.americasbestracing.net/the-sport/2020-the-epic-journey-james-wink-winkfield

"William Walker: Jockey of Many Talents." America's Best Racing, www.americasbestracing.net/the-sport/2022-william-walker-jockey-many-talents

"The Kentucky Derby: Run for the Roses." America's Library, www.americaslibrary.gov/jb/recon/jb_recon_derby_1

"First Kentucky Derby." Ancestry, www.ancestry.com/contextux/historicalinsights/first-kentucky-derby-1875

"The Punkah: A Project for Fans in the Antebellum South." Atlas Obscura, www.atlasobscura.com/articles/punkah-project-fans-antebellum-south

"John Hunt Morgan (1825-1864)." Civil War Trust, www.battlefields.org/learn/biographies/john-hunt-morgan

"Murphy, Isaac Burns (1861-1896)." BlackPast, www.blackpast.org/african-american-history/murphy-isaac-burns-1861-1896

"Derby Jockey Walker Influenced Breeders." BloodHorse, www.bloodhorse.com/horse-racing/articles/107867/derby-jockey-walker-influenced-breeders

"Derby Jockey Walker Influenced Breeders." Bloodlines, www.bloodlines.net/TB/Studbook/EarlyA.htm

"10 Signs of Internal Illness in Horses." The Horse, www.thehorse.com/177335/inside-information-10-signs-of-internal-illness-in-horses

"Tour the Historic Bluegrass." Tour the Historic Bluegrass, tourthehistoricbluegrass.com/items/show/6.

"Edward Brown (Racehorse Owner)." UK Horse Racing, www.hmdb.org/m.asp?m=58282

"Horse Racing in the 1800s." Alamy, www.alamy.com/stock-photo-horse-racing-1800s.html

"Kentucky Derby." Alamy, www.alamy.com/stock-photo-kentucky-derby.html?imgt=0

"Visit Horse Country: Airdrie Studs – Encompassing Industry Influence." America's Best Racing, www.americasbestracing.net/lifestyle/2019-visit-horse-country-airdrie-studs-encompassing-industry-influence

"Lexington, One of the Greatest Race Horses of All Time, Comes Roaring Back to Life." Smithsonian Magazine, www.smithsonianmag.com/smithsonian-institution/lexington-one-of-the-greatest-race-horses-of-all-time-comes-roaring-back-to-life-180980132

"Norfolk." Thoroughbred Heritage, www.tbheritage.com/Portraits/Norfolk.html

"Steeplechase Racing in Great Britain." Thoroughbred Heritage, www.tbheritage.com/TurfHallmarks/racecharts/SteepleGB.html

"The Mysterious Life of a Slave Who Became the Most Celebrated Jockey in North America." Thoroughbred Racing, www.thoroughbredracing.com/articles/4517/mysterious-life-slave-who-became-most-celebrated-jockey-north-america

"The Shocking History of Racism in American Racing." Thoroughbred Racing, www.thoroughbredracing.com/articles/4735/shocking-history-racism-american-racing

"12 Lost American Slangisms from the 1800s." NPR, www.npr.org/sections/npr-history-dept/2015/07/21/423297371/12-lost-american-slangisms-from-the-1800s

"The 1800s Pain Relief Plant That Doctors Used." Off The Grid News, www.offthegridnews.com/alternative-health/the-1800s-pain-relief-plant-that-doctors-used

"Abe Hawkins: A Louisiana Racing Hall of Fame Jockey." The Equine Report, theequinereport.com/2016/03/abe-hawkins-a-louisiana-racing-hall-of-fame-jockey.

"How to Spot Signs of Illness in Your Horse." WikiHow, www.wikihow.com/Know-if-Your-Horse-Is-Sick.

"Daniel Swigert." WikiTree, www.wikitree.com/wiki/Alexander-21104

"Edward D. Brown." WikiTree, www.wikitree.com/wiki/Brown-118184

"Edward D. Brown." WikiTree, www.wikitree.com/wiki/Brown-137562

"Ansel Williamson." WikiTree, www.wikitree.com/wiki/Williamson-56

"Who Was the Boy Named Sue?" WNKY, https://www.wnky.com/throwback-thursday-who-was-the-boy-named-sue/

Martin, Kevin. "Thoroughbred Horse Racing History - The Futurity, 1888 to ????" Colinsghost.org, 22 Sept. 2010, http://colinsghost.org/2010/09/the-futurity-1888-to.html

Delaware Way. "Sports Legend African-American Jockey Anthony Hamilton Dominated World Racing In The Late 1800s." Delaware Way, 22 Jan. 2019, http://delawareway.blogspot.com/2019/01/sports-legend-african-american-jockey.html

"Wikipedia. "Moses Fleetwood Walker, Black Pioneer of Major League Baseball." Jenkinspanafricanbios.blogspot.com, 15 Mar. 2015, http://jenkinspanafricanbios.blogspot.com/2015/03/moses-fleetwood-walker-black-pioneer-of.html

Editorial. "Moses Fleetwood Walker · Key Players · Go Blue: Competition, Controversy, and Community in Michigan Athletics." University of Michigan - Michigan in the World, http://michiganintheworld.history.lsa.umich.edu/michiganathletics/exhibits/show/key-players/fleetwood-walker

Leach, Charles A. "Ohio County, Kentucky History: Shelby D. 'Pike' Barnes." Ohio County Kentucky History, 9 Apr. 2014, http://ohiocountykentuckyhistory.blogspot.com/2014/04/shelby-d-pike-barnes.html

Hunter, Avalyn. "Aristides (horse)." American Classic Pedigrees, 24 Mar. 2022, http://www.americanclassicpedigrees.com/aristides.html

Hunter, Avalyn. "Azra (horse)." American Classic Pedigrees, 26 Apr. 2020, http://www.americanclassicpedigrees.com/azra.html

Editorial. "Black History Heroes: Isaac Burns Murphy: The Great Black Horse Jockey from Kentucky." Black History Heroes, 11 Feb. 2018, http://www.blackhistoryheroes.com/2017/08/isaac-burns-murphy-great-black-horse.html

Nelson, Rex. "Rex Nelson: Arkansas' Forgotten Legend - Alonzo 'Lonnie' Clayton - Sporting Life Arkansas." Sporting Life Arkansas, 10 May 2013, http://www.sportinglifearkansas.com/rex-nelson-arkansas-forgotten-legend-alonzo-lonnie-clayton/

Editorial. "Alonzo - Lonnie - Clayton, Horse Jockey born - African American Registry." African American Registry, 1 Jan. 1970, https://aaregistry.org/story/a-kentucky-derby-icon-alonzo-lonnie-clayton/

Editorial. "Abe Hawkins - The Chronicle of African Americans in the Horse Industry." African American Horse Stories, https://africanamericanhorsestories.org/research/people/abe-hawkins

Editorial. "Alonzo Clayton - The Chronicle of African Americans in the Horse Industry." African American Horse Stories, https://africanamericanhorsestories.org/research/people/alonzo-clayton

Editorial. "Anthony Hamilton - The Chronicle of African Americans in the Horse Industry." African American Horse Stories, https://africanamericanhorsestories.org/research/people/anthony-hamilton

Editorial. "Eliza Carpenter - The Chronicle of African Americans in the Horse Industry." African American Horse Stories, https://africanamericanhorsestories.org/research/people/eliza-carpenter

Editorial. "George B. - Spider - Anderson - The Chronicle of African Americans in the Horse Industry." African American Horse Stories, https://africanamericanhorsestories.org/research/people/george-b-spider-anderson

Editorial. "Isaac Burns Murphy - The Chronicle of African Americans in the Horse Industry." African American Horse Stories, https://africanamericanhorsestories.org/research/people/isaac-burns-murphy

Editorial. "James Perkins - The Chronicle of African Americans in the Horse Industry." African American Horse Stories, https://africanamericanhorsestories.org/research/people/james-perkins

Editorial. "Shelby Barnes - The Chronicle of African Americans in the Horse Industry." African American Horse Stories, https://africanamericanhorsestories.org/research/people/shelby-barnes

Kelly, Kate. "Black Jockey Hall of Famer Isaac Burns Murphy." America Comes Alive, https://americacomesalive.com/black-jockey-hall-of-famer-isaac-burns-murphy/

Editorial. "The Futurity Race at Sheepshead Bay - National Museum of American History." National Museum of American History, https://americanhistory.si.edu/collections/search/object/nmah_684275

Walker, Rhiannon. "The day George 'Spider' Anderson became the first black jockey to win Preakness." Andscape, 10 May 2017, https://andscape.com/features/george-spider-anderson-first-black-jockey-to-win-preakness-stakes/

Potter, Joan; Claytor, Constance. "African Americans who were first: illustrated with photographs." Internet Archive, https://archive.org/details/africanamericans00pott

Di Salvatore, Bryan. "A clever base-ballist: the life and times of John Montgomery Ward." Internet Archive, https://archive.org/details/cleverbaseballis00brya

McNutt, Randy. "Unforgettable Ohioans: thirteen mavericks who made history on their own terms." Internet Archive, https://archive.org/details/unforgettableohi0000mcnu

Baseball Rebecca. "The Walker Brothers - The Baseball Sociologist." Baseball Sociologist, 7 Oct. 2020, https://baseballsociologist.wordpress.com/2020/10/07/the-walker-brothers/

Baseball Rebecca. "The Walker Brothers' Legacy - The Baseball Sociologist." Baseball Sociologist, 8 Oct. 2020, https://baseballsociologist.wordpress.com/2020/10/08/the-walker-brothers-legacy/

Duggan, Bob. "The Man Who Broke Baseball's Color Line Before Jackie Robinson." Big Think, 28 Apr. 2016, https://bigthink.com/culture-religion/the-man-who-broke-baseballs-color-line-before-jackie-robinson/

Editorial. "Oliver Lewis Biography - Race, Aristides, Kentucky, and Derby - JRank Articles." JRank Articles, https://biography.jrank.org/pages/2969/Lewis-Oliver.html

D.L. Chandler. "Little Known Black History Fact: Alonzo 'Lonnie' Clayton." Black America Web, https://blackamericaweb.com/2019/03/27/little-known-black-history-fact-alonzo-lonnie-clayton/

Editorial. "Isaac Burns Murphy - Black In History." Black In History, https://blackinhistory.tumblr.com/post/160680221718/isaac-burns-murphy

Editorial. "George B. Anderson (Jockey) - Black Male Equestrians." Black Male Equestrians, 25 Feb. 2015, https://blackmaleequestrians.wordpress.com/2015/02/25/george-b-anderson-jockey/

Editorial. "The Walker Brothers – The First Openly Black Professional Baseball Players – Black Research Central." Black Research Central, 4 Sep. 2017, https://blackresearchcentralblog.wordpress.com/2017/09/04/blackbaseballhistory/

Jones, Jae. "James - Soup - Perkins: One of the Youngest & Prominent Jockeys in the West." Black Then, 30 Aug. 2021, https://blackthen.com/james-soup-perkins-one-youngest-prominent-jockeys-west/

Jones, Jae. "George B. - Spider - Anderson: First African American Jockey to Win the Preakness Stakes." Black Then, 14 Nov. 2018, https://blackthen.com/new-draftgeorge-b-spider-anderson-first-african-american-jockey-win-preakness-stakes/

Dempsey, Michael. "Why a Triple Crown Winner Has Been So Elusive." Bleacher Report, 19 May 2013, https://bleacherreport.com/articles/1644250-why-a-triple-crown-winner-has-been-so-elusive

Weir, Tom. "Why We've Waited So Long for Another Triple Crown Winner." Bleacher Report, 7 Jun. 2014, https://bleacherreport.com/articles/2086324-why-weve-waited-so-long-for-another-triple-crown-winner

Donato, Matthew. "Cracking The Horse Racing Code." Bleacher Report, 6 Jun. 2008, https://bleacherreport.com/articles/27781-cracking-the-horse-racing-code

Teresa. "Remembering Shelby 'Pike' Barnes, Hall of Fame Winner of the 1889 Travers." Brooklyn Backstretch, 28 Aug. 2015, https://brooklynbackstretch.com/2015/08/28/remembering-shelby-pike-barnes-hall-of-fame-winner-of-the-1889-travers/

www.ingramcontent.com/pod-product-compliance
Lightning Source LLC
Chambersburg PA
CBHW071635260626
47170CB00001B/109